Anger bor_____n
contrast to Mast_____, Cole straightened
to his full heigh_____ stared into the man's face. "Let
me guess, more 14K cowards?"

Another man stepped forward and cocked his
pistol's hammer. "I show you coward."

As at the Crowne Plaza earlier, Cole refused to
back off, even in the face of impending conflict. "The
coward is the man who needs a gun."

The other with the shotgun pointing at Cole's chest
stood only some seven or eight feet away. "You will
come with us now!"

"Please. Violence is forbidden here," Master Li
spoke again. "The Temple is sacred. We cannot have
this type of behavior."

"Maybe you don't hear so good," the leader
sneered. "He comes with us whether you approve or
not."

"He is a famous American! If you take him, the
government will arrest anyone involved. They will have
no choice but to hold immediate trials and executions."
Master Li cupped his hands together and held them
against his chest.

"Famous American," the man chuckled. "If you are
so famous, what are you doing here then, huh?"

Cole stared straight into the man's eyes. He took
several steps toward the shotgun-wielding thug. "How
about I show you?"

Praise for Michael Houtz

2017 Zebulon Award Winning Manuscript

~*~

"If you're in the market for a fast paced, action filled, page-turning thriller, Mike Houtz delivers a must-read novel. I highly recommend this emotional rollercoaster of a book for every die-hard thriller reader...Get it ASAP!"

~Lima Charlie Review

~*~

"...this work proves that author Houtz is undoubtedly a rising star in the publishing world."

~Andrea Brunais, Author

~*~

"Mike Houtz takes us on fast-pace adventure in *Dark Spiral Down,* a thrilling ride along the border between China and North Korea, where Cole Haufner is in pursuit of his Delta Force brother and a device that has the potential to change the world forever or destroy it."

~Dan Grant, Author

~*~

"*Dark Spiral Down* is a phenomenal debut novel by Mike Houtz. This book has everything readers of the genre love: a great plot, memorable characters, and a powerful voice. It's a must-read!"

~Ammar Habib, Bestselling & Award-Winning Author, Editor-in-Chief of Thriller Magazine

Dark Spiral Down

by

Michael Houtz

This is a work of fiction. Names, characters, places, and incidents are either the product of the author's imagination or are used fictitiously, and any resemblance to actual persons living or dead, business establishments, events, or locales, is entirely coincidental.

Dark Spiral Down

COPYRIGHT © 2019 by Mike Houtz

All rights reserved. No part of this book may be used or reproduced in any manner whatsoever without written permission of the author or The Wild Rose Press, Inc. except in the case of brief quotations embodied in critical articles or reviews.
Contact Information: info@thewildrosepress.com

Cover Art by *Debbie Taylor*

The Wild Rose Press, Inc.
PO Box 708
Adams Basin, NY 14410-0708
Visit us at www.thewildrosepress.com

Publishing History
First Mainstream Thriller Edition, 2019
Print ISBN 978-1-5092-2587-3
Digital ISBN 978-1-5092-2588-0

Published in the United States of America

Dedication

For Jackson and Mitchell—
I would not see my sons stand idle
in the face of those that would do evil.

Prologue

Seven miles from North Korean territorial waters, western shore.
0130 hours (+8 hours GMT) April 21ˢᵗ

Commander Park Chul-Moo watched from the safety of the special operations speedboat as the damaged Sang-O II class submarine carrying his team for the past six hours slipped under the surface of the Yellow Sea toward a watery grave. The nighttime emergency transfer of his five-man squad, along with the device they'd stolen from a secret science conference in *Nagasaki*, Japan, was unscheduled. Since escaping just outside the harbor of *Nagasaki*, the eight naval crewmen, part of North Korea's Maritime Unit submarine squadron, and the five Second Bureau Reconnaissance Special Forces operatives played a deadly game of cat-and-mouse with Japanese and South Korean naval vessels. American air power joined the chase, all in an effort to recover what Commander Park now possessed.

The electric motors on the clandestine submarine ran silent but with limited range. On several occasions, the vessel was forced to surface to regenerate the batteries by switching to its diesel engine. Twice, the commandos approached within only a few nautical miles of North Korean territorial waters along the country's western shores, but both times forced northwest to avoid detection.

During the last resurface under a partial moon, catastrophic engine failure doomed the craft. Park risked a radio Mayday to the west coast maritime headquarters based in *Nampo*, North Korea, and a high-speed boat, disguised as a fishing trawler, was dispatched. Five highly trained men, and the stolen device, conducted a risky ship transfer with ocean swells causing the two vessels to collide several times. On one of the particularly rough bumps, Park's communications specialist lost his grip and fell between the steel hulls. He lay crushed under the weight. The team leader stared at the blood and gore on the dying vessel's metal skin as it tipped backward and dropped lower in the water.

"Commander, what of the submarine crew?" the rescue ship's captain asked.

Hearing grave concern in the captain's voice, Park looked away from the sinking vessel. He narrowed his eyes squarely on the man. "Not your concern. You will get me to the coastal waters immediately or assume the same fate." *Imbecile.* His jaw muscles flexed under skin stretched to its limit across his face.

The shorter, older captain turned ashen and swallowed.

Though both men existed under the same command structure, Park was not to be questioned further. His legend was such that when men did not perform their duties, no matter the circumstances, they were rarely seen again.

"S-sir," the captain stuttered. "When the *Sang-O* hit us, it took out our ability to steer to starboard."

Park's stare did not waver. "Bring your men on deck, now."

"Ye...yes, sir," the man stammered. He turned and bolted for the wheelhouse.

Park pressed the communication button attached to his battle harness. "Everyone on me," he barked.

The other three commandos arrived and formed a line in front of him. The four special operators rose a full-head taller than the average North Korean, chosen both for their physical prowess and for the intimidation they projected.

I will not be denied the glory I deserve.

Within thirty seconds, all hands stood on the top deck, an eerie glow from the moon casting a bouncing shimmer off objects as the boat bobbed in the open ocean. The sailors stood in a tightly packed group, those in front with their eyes cast downward. No one spoke, nor did they dare. Word shot through the ship the submarine crew had not been seen since the rescue boat's arrival, and no attempt to bring them aboard had been undertaken.

With Park's team standing behind him in a loose line, he asked each sailor what his function on the ship was for this mission.

"I load and unload cargo, sir," the fourth man answered.

"I see." Park nodded at the quivering sailor. He then looked to the special operator at his left shoulder.

Wordlessly, his subordinate stepped forward.

Park thought the camouflage face paint gave the warrior a demonic appearance in the moon glow. He tilted his head toward the young sailor.

In the blink of an eye, the Special Forces soldier

3

leapt forward and delivered a devastating punch to the unsuspecting sailor's chest. Before the naval specialist could recover, the commando grabbed him by the shirt and belt then lifted him off his feet and tossed him overboard.

The assault was over before any of the ship's personnel could take a second breath. No cries rose from the young man in the water.

Park's heavy weapons specialist didn't take a second look over the wire railing as he walked back to his post behind his team leader.

No one moved.

Turning attention back to the crew, Park forced strength into his voice. "You will get me to North Korean waters now. Every second delayed brings our enemy closer, as well as the failure to deliver to our Great Leader."

The remaining six crewmen, along with their shaking captain, nearly fell over each other while scrambling back to their posts. The four operatives watched expressionless as the sailors dispersed.

After a few seconds, Park turned to his men who all stepped closer.

"Though regrettable, we have lost our communications specialist. The mission moves forward with the thoughts of his bravery and sacrifice for our country."

The three others nodded, their faces rigid.

"Two men guarding our package and one man rests. Rotate each hour." Park continued, "Stay off the open deck as I fear America's spy satellites and planes look for us.

Without a word, the operators took the four steps

leading down into the hull of the special purpose ship.

Park remained in his position, looking into the easterly darkness and willing himself to catch a glimpse of light from the mainland. The tremble of the craft's internal twin engines barking to life vibrated the soles of his boots. Moments later, the vessel moved forward. The last time he'd checked the nose of the forty-two-foot infiltration boat, his rescue craft pointed north in the direction of the intersection of China and North Korea at their borders.

I will not fail. The world will fear my name.

At thirty-four years of age, Park was already a legendary operative. He could not, would not, accept that a broken rudder or ocean currents could stop him from delivering a twenty-five-pound device to his Supreme Leader—a device deadlier than any atomic bomb.

Chapter 1

Thomas and Mack Center, Las Vegas, Nevada
Saturday night Main Event, April 21st

"Ten seconds!"

From his corner, Cole Haufner heard the cry all the way across the blood-smeared octagon. He held his opponent immobile, letting the clock run out on the second of three periods. He was well ahead in the fight, but a nasty gash over his left eye, one that opened in the late first round from a flying elbow, threatened the outcome due to the amount of blood pouring from the wound. The win was not his primary goal. A six-figure purse for a victory ensured his son's life-saving surgery.

The referee separated both fighters while directing them to their respective corners.

Cole jumped up from the mat, fist-pumped the air for the crowd, and made his way to his corner where two men stood ready to attend to him. As he approached his team, Cole saw the fight doctor walk through the cage door opening with a look of concern. A sense of dread attacked Cole.

"Lemme take a look at that," the physician ordered as he stepped forward to scan Cole's injury.

"I'm good, Doc, I'm good." Blood poured down his face, spreading across Cole's sweat-covered chest and pooling onto the canvas mat.

The fighter's corner coach, Barry Liggit, and cut-man, Scott "Stitch" Bell, leaned in close to see the wound.

"I'm fine. Just get me ready," Cole snarled. He needed the fight doctor to give him a break on the injury.

Beyond the blinding lights shining on the fight ring, more than thirteen thousand fans chanted, "Gentleman, gentleman, gentleman…"

The spectacle of the crowd embarrassed Cole. This unwanted praise railed against everything he'd been taught at the Chinese Buddhist monastery where he lived and studied as a young boy.

"You hear that?" Barry shouted over the noise of the crowd. "They want *you*, Cole. They know you're the next middle-weight champion."

The doctor repeatedly held pressure over the cut and released to see how quickly the wound bled. Each time he let go, a fountain of red erupted.

Cole saw the concern in the physician's eyes. "Doc, you know I need this one," he pleaded. "You know my family story. I swear I'll finish this quick."

"I'm giving you one minute." the doctor shouted to Barry. "I'm not losing my medical license because of his injury." The ER physician turned and nodded to the fight officials outside the cage that Round 3 would start.

The crowd erupted in a roar.

Stitch jumped in front of Cole with packing cream and the frozen steel plate to stem the bleeding long enough to ready the fighter.

Barry leaned close to Cole's face. "You've never had a fight last more than a minute. What's the deal?

You don't have a lot of time! You got me?"

Cole looked to his right. An empty seat remained at ringside. His older brother, Butch, promised to attend. Cole started the headline match with some concern, but now, he worried over his brother's absence. They hadn't spoken in the last twenty-four hours, even though Butch was supposed to have received a special furlough from his military unit to be here. For Butch to break a promise wasn't unusual—it came with his job. Amid one of the most important moments of his life, Cole couldn't help but worry.

A hand jerked his head. "Are you even hearing me?" Barry yelled.

Cole shifted his gaze back to the ring, catching Stitch looking in the same direction.

"Holy shit. Are you dragging out this fight waiting for Butch?" Stitch shouted.

Busted. Cole looked away from Barry, unable to hold his coach's gaze.

Barry put his hands on his hips, lips smashed into a line. "You gotta be kidding me! Well, that would explain why we're in round three. You're one lucky punch away from losing this fight. Don't you think your son needs this win?"

You know he's off limits. For the first time in the match, rage filled his body. The immediate image of his son's physical struggles with a failing heart sent a powerful surge through his nervous system. He glared at his trainer, blood running down his face as the cold plate slipped from the gash. "Shut your mouth," Cole hissed.

Barry swallowed. The corner man quickly recovered "This is it, brother. The crowd wants 'the

Gentleman,' but give them the 'Beast'. Let's see some of that monk shit and finish this fight."

Sorry, Butch, I can't wait any longer. I know you'll understand. Cole opened his mouth so Barry could slide the mouthpiece into place. "Don't blink or you two are gonna miss an old move of mine."

Barry and Stitch grinned.

Dragging out the fight was a stupid move. Even though he'd never met his match, not even close in the ring, Cole faced a professional fighter. Barry was right. Another lucky punch like the one that cut him in round one could lose him the one hundred-thousand-dollar bonus offered for a win. His son needed him.

Focus. Breathe. For Max.

The referee made his way to the center of the octagon and motioned for the fight corners to clear the ring.

Stitch held the cold plate to Cole's forehead cut for three more seconds then followed everyone else out with the door clanging shut.

Vision in Cole's left eye blurred—the blood was already seeping from around the edges of the packing cream.

The ref signaled to the ringside table he was ready then waved with both hands for the fighters to approach the center.

Cole stepped forward in his usual calm manner—the source of the nickname "the Gentleman."

The other fighter bounced on the balls of his feet, just out of reach.

"Ready." The referee continued with a slight pause in between. "Let's bring it!" With that, he jumped back out of the way of the combatants.

Cole ducked as his opponent unleashed a flurry of combinations, trying to finish the fight almost as quickly as it had resumed. He parried the punches and kicks, toying with the other man, aware he had less than a minute before the doctor returned to the ring. Cole only needed a fraction of a second. He searched for an opening.

The onslaught carried on for a full ten seconds before the fighter dropped back, his nostrils flaring like a bull's.

Blood flowed freely again, saturating Cole's chest and shorts while clouding his vision.

The opposing corner yelled to their fighter to go to a defensive position.

"I'm sorry," Cole shouted to his opponent.

The sweating mass of muscle furrowed his forehead. "The hell you say?"

"Sorry about this." Cole stood from his crouch and lowered his fists.

"What are you doing?" Barry screamed from just outside of the cage. "Hands up. Hands up!"

In the blink of an eye, the other man slid forward and threw a powerful right hand.

This moment was Cole's. Rather than defend, he leaped from the canvas, performed a front somersault in mid-air, and extended his right leg, bringing his heel crashing down on top of the man's head. A sickening thud sounded upon contact, and the other fighter collapsed to the mat, unmoving.

Cole rolled forward after the strike, coming to rest in a crouch some five feet away. Though he suspected the instant he'd made contact he'd finished off his opponent, Cole took nothing for granted. He spun in case of a counterattack.

The ref, initially stunned, dove onto the unmoving man. The crowd's collective gasp morphed into a deafening roar when the signal was given the fight was over.

Panting from the effort, Cole watched as the cage door opened, and medical personnel raced inside.

Barry and Stitch rushed through the portal and drew him into crushing hugs amid incredible noise. Literally lifted off his feet, Cole only felt relief in accomplishing what he'd set out to do; he'd likely saved his son's life.

Chapter 2

One hour after the fight

A plastic surgeon sewed the huge gash inside Cole's left eyebrow. The cut exposed bone and two layers of sutures were necessary. Showered and wearing a navy-blue suit with matching red silk tie and pocket square, Cole walked in the midst of three burly bodyguards to a private room behind a temporary stage erected to conduct the live, post-fight broadcast. Seeing the throngs of press jockeying for position with their cameras and microphones, Cole felt perspiration flash on his forehead.

Bile rose in the back of his throat. *I hate this part.*

A young brunette wearing headphones with attached microphone opened the door to his suite with her right hand, a clipboard in her left. Cole recognized her as part of the production crew.

The bodyguards took up positions near the door, blocking anyone unauthorized to enter.

"About ten minutes, Mister Haufner," she said.

Cole smiled and thanked her as he stepped into the room. A reception table was to the right with various finger foods and more bottles of water than seemed appropriate. A leather couch sat straight ahead, and a round table with six chairs stood on the left. A large, flat-screen television mounted on the wall over the sofa flashed brightly with highlights of the fight.

"Da!" a little boy shouted. He pointed a tiny index finger at Cole.

Cole broke into a huge smile. "There's my buddy."

Claire Haufner, holding their son in her arms, walked over and planted a kiss on her husband's lips.

Her long legs, toned to perfection from years as a professional ballerina, made her appear as if she glided across the floor on skates. Claire's blonde hair swept back into a loose ponytail. She wore his favorite outfit, a simple linen summer dress. It clung to her slender body, inviting his mind to visualize what lay underneath. *My God, you are so beautiful.*

Cole reached out to hold his son. The transfer of the sixteen-month-old toddler between parents was cumbersome with oxygen tubing in the way. The G-tube Max used to take in nutrition through his abdomen had been accidentally pulled out on more than one occasion. But, they'd figured out the process, and passing Max was not much of a problem.

"Owie." Max groaned.

Cole jumped back. thinking he'd done something to cause his son to complain.

A chubby hand rose and pointed at Cole's sutured eyebrow.

"Daddy's okay," Cole responded in a soothing tone. He kissed Max's extended finger and then let him touch the area.

Afterward, the youngster leaned forward and gently placed a healing kiss on his dad's injury.

Claire pursed her lips.

Cole could see she came almost to tears at the sweet display of love. He leaned closer and gazed into his son's eyes. "All better?"

Max threw his chubby arms around Cole's neck and squeezed.

A loud noise at the door caused everyone to turn in that direction.

Cole shook his head, seeing his best friend and business manager, Kip Hartman, burst in as if chased by lions. His thinning, short-cropped hair showed signs of aging with flecks of gray, a contrast against the remaining black. Though athletic in build, Kip was a few years past prime fighting age showing early signs of a bulge around his gut. Despite being in his mid-forties, the ex-fighter turned sports agent was the biggest kid Cole ever met.

"Mini-me!" Kip roared.

Max pointed at Kip. "Da."

"Say what? I want child support." Cole said in good-natured complaint.

The two men wrapped their arms around each other in a bear hug while sharing a healthy laugh.

Max reached for Kip.

Cole let the boy fall into his godfather's arms.

The little one smacked Kip in the face with flailing, drool-drenched hands.

Cole got a kick out of watching the beating.

"Let me interject a few feminine hormones into this man-fest." Claire reached for a hug from Kip.

"Congratulations, sweetie," Kip said during the embrace. He pulled back then turned to Cole. "Hey, we have meetings with a few magazines and two new possible sponsors tomorrow. Get ice on that eye of yours."

Cole's German-Chinese heritage afforded him an

exotic look perfect for a diversity-hungry sports media—TV, Internet, and print. Almond-shaped, piercing blue eyes captivated men and women alike. He wore his black hair short with an ever-present spiked cut and style. Both ears were devoid of any sign of disfigurement so common with other fighters. The rest of his six-foot, one hundred-eighty-five-pound frame appeared pure German. Broad shouldered and narrow in the hips, he could have claimed any professional sport, and the observer would have no choice but to believe him based on physique. From the onset, Kip predicted Cole could make millions outside of fighting, if he could just get himself in front of the public. Now that he'd earned a shot at the middleweight title, that prediction was about to be tested.

"As if enough women aren't hitting on *my* husband already," Claire complained.

Cole noticed the subtle turn at the right corner of Claire's mouth. He'd seen *that* look before. She wasn't a jealous woman, and her complaint wasn't about any potential affairs. No, this discussion was one the two had battled for nearly a month.

"Babe, I..." Cole started before she grabbed his chin and tilted his forehead closer to her eyes. Past experience warned him not to finish his sentence. He saw Kip moving over to the couch, tickling Max as he went.

"What did the doctors say about your cut?" Claire asked. "I could barely watch with all that blood."

Aware of her concern, Cole gazed into her dark green eyes. "It's nothing."

Claire leaned close. "I know you promised me just one more and you'd quit. But I don't know if I can watch any more of those fights, and I don't want our son seeing them, either," she whispered.

You know how much I don't like fighting. Despite worldwide opinion Cole was proving to be the best pound-for-pound fighter in the history of the sport, he tried his best to live the quiet life of father and husband. Claire finally admitted three weeks ago she was worried he would fall in love with the fame and money. Cole feared tonight's stunning win, and the crowd's reaction, only heightened her angst. "One more and I'm done. Just like we talked about. I promise."

Her expression never wavered.

Can't we just talk about this later? Cole knew she was worried sick and little would change her mind. His family meant everything to him. Now he'd met his goal of earning enough money for Max's medical bills, perhaps she was right. Maybe walking away was best before even more vultures sank in their claws. Loud enough for Kip to hear, Cole said, "I'll retire tonight. I'll announce it during the conference."

"Say what?" Kip gasped from the couch. His eyes shot wide, unblinking.

Cole turned toward his friend and manager. "The fight bonus money is enough for Max. I did what I set out to do. The time is right." He felt Claire's hands cup his face and looked back.

"No," she whispered. Her gaze softened. "The idea of losing you to that monster on the other side of the door is making me crazy. I trust you. One more."

Cole's shoulders relaxed. He was grateful for the break in the building tension. "I need you to know I'd do anything for you and Max. Anything."

"What? Chopped liver here?" Kip complained.

Cole jerked a thumb at his friend. "Still deciding on that tub of lard over there."

Claire let out a giggle.

He could tell she was relieved—at least for now. He wrapped his strong arms around her and kissed her soft lips.

The fighting will be over soon. I promise.

Kip's phone rang, buried somewhere deep in his pants pocket.

Cole scooped up Max, so his buddy could answer the call. *Please be you, Butch!*

"Your brother?" Claire whispered.

"I hope so," Cole murmured and squeezed her hand. His hopes were dashed when Kip started talking business. "Dammit."

Claire put her hand on his chest. "Probably not a lot of cell service where he's at saving the world."

Again, experiencing a gnawing feeling something wasn't right, Cole nodded. His brother, First Sergeant Butch Haufner, survived more deployments than Cole could count. So, why did this absence feel different? Was hoping Butch witnessed the fight as promised unrealistic, or did this worry involve something more?

In Cole's arms, Max fussed.

"We need to get home. It's way past someone's bed time," Claire said.

Cole looked at the time displayed on the upper right corner of the television. Max was on a specific feeding schedule, and he knew Claire wouldn't deviate from the routine if she could help it. He passed back their son. Cole nodded toward the door. "The interview could take a while."

Kip appeared next to them. "I got it. I have Max's

car seat in the truck."

Cole furled his eyebrows. "Shouldn't you be with *me* on stage?"

"And have millions of people watch me die when you announce your retirement? *F* that," he joked.

"Just think of the ratings," Cole deadpanned.

Kip rolled his eyes. "By the time production gets their act together, I'll be home and back."

The door opened, and loud noise from outside spilled into the room.

"Mister Haufner?" the assistant announced. "About two minutes."

The door shut, once again enveloping them in semi-solitude.

Cole lifted his eyebrows. "You were saying?"

"We'll wait until you start and then make our way out. I'll be back as soon as I get them home," Kip said.

"Sure someone else can't take them?" Cole pleaded. His palms sweated at the thought of doing the press conference by himself.

"I don't trust anyone else," Kip said.

Neither do I. Cole leaned in for a hug from Claire while planting a kiss on Max's chubby cheek.

"Wake me when you get home," she whispered into his ear.

"Why?"

"Don't want to miss my chance with a magazine cover model. Number two on my freebie list." She squeezed his butt with her free hand.

What's number one? Cole laughed then gave her a lingering kiss. He threw out his arms and delivered another strong hug to Kip. Hands clapped on both men's backs.

The door swung open, the noise from outside at a fevered pitch. "It's time," the assistant called out.

Calming his nerves, Cole forced out a lung full of air. He backed toward the door while waving and blowing kisses to his son.

Max fanned his fat little arm back and forth, fingers scrunching in reply.

Only thing missing is you, Butch. Wish you could be here. Cole stopped at the doorway, looking at Kip. "Take care of my babies."

"With my life," his friend replied.

Chapter 3

East China Sea 0230 hours

The Mark 8 MOD 3 SDV—Swimmer Delivery Vehicle—glided north ten meters under the ocean's surface with lithium-ion batteries providing silent propulsion. An hour earlier, the vehicle sat in the cargo hold of a C-130 military transport plane, thirty-six-thousand feet above the earth.

At a designated point, in the thin atmosphere, the aircraft's rear ramp lowered, and the Mark 8 and a five-man American Delta Force team performed a HAHO—high altitude high opening—jump fifty-five miles from their intended landing zone. Opening parachutes at more than twenty-eight-thousand feet, each special operator stacked above the next. The lowest man on the rung used his satellite GPS unit to lead the team the full distance to their intended target. The Mark 8 fell separately, and multiple directional rocket propellant devices strapped to the glass-fiber-reinforced plastic hull helped the stealth vehicle follow satellite directions to its planned landing.

Typically, a SEAL team, not a Delta Force squad, would receive such a mission, but the objective called for this particular unit. These five men extensively trained for current circumstances. Their orders came directly from the Oval Office, as had all of the team's previous missions since the unit's inception two years earlier. A well-earned, three-day break was cut short due to a situation that started in Japan.

Delta team leader, Butch "Dragon" Haufner, sat in the co-pilot position of the submerged underwater vehicle, managing the navigation system in total darkness. Fluorescent green monitors displayed the directional waypoints toward their intended objective.

Piloting the craft and seated to Butch's left, was second team leader, Ron "Hammer" Thompson, manning the steering mechanism.

The three remaining teammates, strapped to Kevlar seats, rode in the rear of the vessel.

The five men wore diving gear as the craft was flooded with saltwater. Every member of the unit connected to the onboard PRC104 UHF ultra-high frequency radio. Transmissions were relayed to and from the USS *California*, a Virginia-class, nuclear-powered fast attack submarine, joining in the chase for the device stolen from a top-secret meeting between Japanese and South Korean scientists. The fact the United States Department of Energy had not been made aware of the conference was not Butch's concern.

Eight hours after the device disappeared off the Japanese coast, a coded message from American Signal Intelligence indicated a fishing vessel departed a North Korean seaport known for naval clandestine work. For the next fifty minutes, the boat loitered off the west coast in an area not noted for abundant seafood. Satellite imagery showed no fishing activity with the ship's long outrigger poles mounted on both the port and starboard sides. When a partially submerged second vessel appeared next to the fishing trawler, the circling

American C130 aircraft unloaded men and machine to interdict the meeting.

Butch's heart rate increased as an update to their target location flashed on the navigation screen. The once-static vessel made a sudden acceleration. He confirmed the new information then gave Hammer a thumbs-up for the new steerage coordinates.

The fishing boat traveled in an erratic fashion, racing north for a short distance before turning two-hundred-seventy degrees to port and making a run at the North Korean mainland. Before the ship reached internationally recognized territorial waters, the nose of the ship drifted due north then repeated the same looping pattern. The craft's speed was highly unusual, setting itself apart from the hundreds of other ships tracked by the United States and its involved allies.

Hammer held out his hand in front of the monitor as if to ask, "What are they doing?"

Butch was about to guess when the boat straightened, heading north again. But this time, the ship made no attempt to loop back. Butch's waypoint stretched farther ahead as the target's speed overtook the Mark 8's ability to keep pace. He silently cursed when the vessel disappeared off the edge of the screen. "Nest, this is One. How read, over?" he spoke into the lip mic inside his diving helmet.

"One" was his call sign for this particular mission. The encrypted signal was received by the USS *California* and relayed to a secure situation room inside the bowels of the Pentagon. Twenty, highly classified computer specialists, part of the command's Intelligence Support Activity Unit, guided the Delta team with signal intelligence and communications.

After a two-second delay, Butch heard through his earpiece. "This is Nest. Good copy. Go."

"Target is outrunning on new vector. Need estimate for their anticipated exfil point."

"Understood. We see it," Nest responded. "Continue and wait one for new data."

Butch opened the map display as far as he could, but the waypoint extended beyond the reach of the topography displayed on the monitor. After a full minute, an icon blinked at the edge of the screen. He tapped the update button, and a new map overlaid the smaller one. A red line extended from his current position toward the top of the screen. A green blinking dot showed the projected intercept of the vessel. His heart pounded. He didn't need to zoom in to know where the new marker was on the world map, but he did anyway. Tapping the screen twice dropped down the satellite image to where the boat headed.

Butch Haufner was going home.

Chapter 4

Mouth of the Yalu River, disputed National territory, 0425 hours

Several hours passed since the American team raced at top speed in pursuit of the suspected boat. The highly-classified, extended-range batteries, developed by a DARPA—Defense Advanced Research Projects Agency—research team, were nearly depleted. In the Delta squad's favor, the target ship slowed to a crawl thirty minutes earlier, and the Mark 8 closed most of the distance to the team's target. Butch's greatest worry was the enemy vessel now straddled the territorial water between China and North Korea near one of the tiny islands that dotted the mouth of the *Yalu* River.

The *Yalu* separates eastern China and the western edge of the Democratic People's Republic of Korea— DPRK. Known to few, the bank on the Chinese side of the river contained several slivers of land belonging to North Korea. On these spots, all that separated the two countries was chain-link fencing. A handful of tiny islands also dotted the river and many of these were sovereign to North Korea.

A key reason Butch made selection for this particular unit in the U.S. Army's Delta Force was his firsthand knowledge of this part of the world. Not only was he one of America's best spec-ops warriors, but he also spent the majority of his youth growing up on the Chinese side of the river.

"Heads up. We're getting close to the target," Butch informed his teammates on the Mark 8's intercom.

"Where they heading, boss?" Master Sergeant Rex "Turbo" Thiery asked from the back of the craft.

Butch keyed his mic. "They should have been in *Pyongyang* by now. Either something went wrong with that boat, or our blocking forces pushed them here. They might try to make landfall at *Sindo*, a small island right next to China, at the mouth of the river where it empties into the sea. That patch of dirt belongs to North Korea. They've been drifting left for the last thirty minutes. Unless they're working with the Chinese, which I doubt, I'd say their plan isn't going so well."

Options ran through Butch's mind while he stared at the map on the monitor. None of them were good. His unit opted for equipment geared toward a water-borne incursion. If his men were forced to fight on land, they'd be at a disadvantage. The weapons they carried were optimized for hallways and ship decks, not open-land warfare. That fact did not sway him from where he thought the fight would likely take place. "With that boat still drifting, money is on them landing on the southern tip of the Port of *Dandong*. That's Chinese soil, just to the left of the North Korean island. If they sneak north along the river's edge, once they get far enough upstream, it's a thirty-foot swim across the canal."

"And they'll be on home turf?" Thompson asked.

"Yep. And, we'll be really screwed then. The handful of farmers and military monitors on the island

25

will fight us to the death. Our families will see us on TV killing North Korean civilians from the cameras China has pointed in their direction. The island's ground is flat and open. No place to operate."

"Not that being on the Chinese side is any better," Thiery said.

"Nope. They'll just torture us to death," Butch responded.

The silence among the men was palpable. Taking down the ship in open water was nothing compared with fighting an unknown enemy on either bank of the Yalu.

Butch didn't want to risk a transmission so close to the Chinese mainland but felt one was absolutely necessary. He switched to the command net. "Nest, how copy?"

"You have twenty seconds," command responded.

"We are in sovereign territory," Butch reminded them. "What is confidence level of target?"

"No transmissions have come from the vessel since satellite intercept except for one thirty-second call to a burner phone in downtown *Dandong*, China. No further tracking of the cell's location is available. We are at eighty-five percent confidence of target ship."

Butch took a deep breath. He'd been briefed by the president himself on the danger to the world if the stolen package remained with the North Koreans. The situation didn't look any better if the item ended up with the Chinese. "Roger that. Hoping for a water intercept in twenty minutes, but we're dangerously low on battery. Water or land, we'll be close to Chinese turf."

"Understood, One. ISA has good tracking, so far.

Recommend go to full black comms. Exfiltration needs to be opportunistic but recommend water. Over."

Butch knew the expectation of his team—they were to recover the device by any means necessary and make their escape via friendly naval forces. The president made it crystal clear this mission could not fail. "Roger, comms going black. See you on the other side." With a single push of a button, he disconnected all communication with the outside world. The five men could speak only to each other.

"How we doing this?" Thompson asked.

"We need to take them on that boat. If they hit land before we reach them, the fight will get ugly. And, we only have a couple of hours before daylight," Butch responded.

Thompson pointed at the controls. "Oh, shit."

Butch leaned over and scanned the monitor. *This detail is not good.* "Change of plan, boys."

****

Thompson scanned his zone of responsibility through GPNVG night-vision goggles. His position next to a rusty shipping container fifty feet from the water's edge offered him a clear field of fire. He saw the target fishing vessel bobbing in the river's current as a man secured the ship with a heavy rope looped around a large metal anchor sunk in the canal's cement wall. The scrawny-looking male was the only person visible, but Thompson knew others were on board. Thirty feet to Thompson's left, Thiery settled on an elevated position atop a small-gauge train engine used for moving materials from inland to the dock.

The Mark 8 closed within eighty yards of the target before the batteries completely drained. The underwater

27

transporter rendered useless, Butch ordered the men to abandon ship. The *Yalu's* current pushed the suspect vessel close to the Chinese shoreline. If the target ship docked before the Delta team could swim to the objective, the device would be as good as gone. Haufner concluded their best chance of recovering the device would be to beat the North Korean men to land and, having arrived first, fight from a position of strength. With so few forces on each side of the impending battle, whoever neutralized the first enemy combatant would have a significant numerical advantage.

The Americans stashed their scuba gear inside the container where Thompson lay then scattered to ambush points on the dock. All five Delta operators wore black coveralls, gloves, and balaclava hoods. Located in the pockets of the men's combat vests were their closed-circuit radios, ammunition magazines, and an assortment of war-making tools.

"In position," Thompson whispered into his lip mic. "I have eyes on one male. Not armed."

"One plus two, ready," Haufner transmitted over the digitally encrypted radio. The team leader, with teammates Cutter and Snake, were farther up the canal in a blocking position fifty yards away.

Thompson looked through his night-vision-compatible targeting scope mounted atop his short-barreled .300 blackout assault rifle. A suppressor and subsonic ammunition in thirty-round magazines were key to keeping firing noise to a minimum. Mounted forward of the scope on the barrel's railing, a laser-aiming unit sat ready.

"Movement in the wheelhouse," Thiery advised.

"About fifty minutes of dark left," Haufner warned. "When we get the box, haul ass to me. I see a boat we can snatch."

Thompson scanned the target ship. Two more men appeared on the top deck. They each grabbed an additional coil of rope and secured the fore and aft end of the boat to the dock. "Total of three personnel, now. No visible weapons."

"Confirmed," Thiery agreed.

After several minutes, Thompson noted a fourth male exiting the bridge, waving his arms toward the three deckhands. A verbal exchange grew heated before another figure rose from lower hull steps. This individual looked well fed, larger than the others. He wore a battle vest stuffed with weapon magazines, and he carried a rifle.

Bingo. That's gotta be one of the bad guys. "Eyes on one, armed, standing on the hull steps," Thompson reported. "The navy guys shit their pants when he showed up."

In a matter of seconds, the four unarmed men ran to the ship's wire railing and climbed onto the stone retaining wall. North Korea, like the Americans, technically invaded China.

The gunman waved his rifle at them, barked an unintelligible phrase, and the four men turned and headed in separate directions along the dock.

Thompson guessed they were guinea pigs sent to scan the area for activity. "Scouts in the wire."

As the North Korean sailors spread out on the landing, Thompson saw two more scrawny men appear on the ship's deck before they too scampered off the boat to join the others. None were armed, and even in the dark, he could see the stumbling of malnourished sailors. Thompson almost felt sorry for them.

"Eyes on objective," Cutter whispered over the radio. "Three armed plus the box."

Butch's voice came through Thompson's earpiece. "Confirmed. Let them get off the boat. We don't know how many more are still on board."

Thompson's vision focused on the three, armed individuals. The assumed North Korean commandos wore dark, military-style clothing and carried what appeared to be AK-47 rifles. One of the individuals held a medium-size box by its handle in his right hand. Intelligence reported the stolen device was roughly the size of a suitcase and weighed approximately twenty-five pounds. Standing on the ship's open deck, the three men stared into the darkness. After ten seconds, the trio walked to the ship's rail.

Thompson's right thumb brushed against the safety switch of his rifle to ensure he was ready to throw lead downrange. Now was not the time to have the trigger locked out by accident.

A commando waved the other two over the railing. The container was lifted onto the dock by the man carrying it. Once all three were off the boat, Thompson heard one of the armed men calling out to the sailors scattered around the area. The boat crew sprinted back to their moored ship.

When he noticed one of the commandos looking in his direction, Thompson held his breath. He was sure the enemy soldier couldn't see him but was concerned a highly-trained North Korean operator, chosen for such a daring raid, might sense his presence.

The sudden sound of a vehicle engine filtered in

from farther inland. The North Koreans didn't react to the noise, which told Thompson the car was expected as part of a preplanned rendezvous. An older, four-door sedan appeared on the landing, its headlights bounced off scattered equipment and men along the dock. The emaciated sailors cowered in the glow. When the car came to a stop, the lamps winked out, and two men exited from the rear, both armed with rifles.

The driver left the vehicle and walked to the armed North Koreans.

Thompson didn't see any handshakes or other signs of greeting. The new arrival appeared robust in size, his demeanor relaxed.

One of the armed men waved a hand at the car, and the driver turned and headed for the rear of the vehicle. He opened the trunk.

"The car doesn't leave. On my mark, eliminate the armed men. Hammer, you have the case," Butch's command came over the radio.

"Roger all," Thompson whispered.

The faintest hint of light glowed at the eastern horizon as the earth's rotation ushered in dawn. Little time was left before China became fully awake.

The North Korean carrying the case headed for the vehicle.

"In three, two—" Butch counted down.

A loud *boom* erupted. An unsuppressed rifle barked from somewhere inside the North Korean boat. Thompson's peripheral vision caught Thiery's rifle cartwheeling off the top of the small train engine. Two things became evident: a sniper inside the boat had night vision, and a teammate was hit.

With the initiative lost, four Delta men squeezed

their triggers, and two armed security men from the car and two commandos dropped to the ground. The third North Korean operator dove behind the sedan as the sailors ran for the water. Chaos unfolded in the darkness as both sides exchanged gunfire.

Thompson saw the case—his objective rested on the ground next to the car's trunk—but a sniper and the remaining North Korean commando still defended the stolen item. "I need cover to get the objective!" he shouted over the noise of continued shooting.

"Hose the boat." Haufner ordered.

All four Americans targeted the floating craft, pieces of wood and equipment flew as round after round penetrated the enemy ship.

Thompson reloaded. "I'm moving!" He silently counted to three then sprinted for the four-door. He vectored to the back end of the car and dropped to his knees behind the rear axle for cover. Enemy bullets flew underneath the vehicle as the defending North Korean commando on the other side sprayed a full magazine. The Delta operator rose and let loose a ten-round burst, keeping the enemy fighter pinned and dropping two sailors as they ran from the carnage.

"Reloading," Cutter announced over comms.

Boom! Another shot erupted from the boat.

"Shit! Cutter's hit!" Snake shouted.

"Moving." Haufner yelled.

Thompson glanced left and saw Snake and Haufner leap off a ten-foot platform. The two teammates disappeared behind additional cover. Sensing his team was losing the initiative, Thompson reached in a side pouch on his vest and produced a device the size and shape of a baseball. The outer shell was clear Plexiglas, and the visible internals consisted of a dozen reflective strips and a light bulb. He thumbed a tiny switch, starting a five-second timer.

"We're back on target." Haufner announced he and Snake were in position to engage the enemy.

"Tossing 'disco'," Thompson warned his teammates. He threw the ball over the car and onto the open deck of the boat. A powerful strobe light split the darkened sky, its five-thousand-lumen light pulsing every second.

As a burst of fire erupted from the opposite side of the vehicle, Thompson recoiled. He considered rushing the commando, but the case was only five feet to his left. "Going for objective. Cover me." Two seconds later, he heard rounds connecting with the car.

The former University of Texas linebacker sucked in two short breaths then darted to the rear of the sedan and grabbed the top handle of the Kevlar case. The weight barely registered as he scrambled back to his original position behind the rear axle. Another *boom* echoed from the boat followed by the staccato of an enemy rifle only feet away. "Moving to the rear and then to you." Thompson notified his teammates.

"Cover fire." Haufner answered over the radio.

With sound-suppressed automatic fire erupting from his two remaining teammates, Thompson ran with all speed back to the cargo container holding the team's diving gear. No time remained to collect himself. "Coming to you." He raced north past a series of cargo boxes lined up in a neat row. Ten seconds later, he'd reunited with his teammates. Out of breath, Thompson forced a question from his burning throat. "What...do we do with Turbo...and Cutter?"

Haufner popped off several rounds. "I don't like it. Finding the bodies will cause a shit storm. I'm sure the police are already on the way."

Snake snapped a series of single shots. "The guy behind the car just dove into the river."

Thompson reloaded. "How about Snake grabs Cutter, and I'll get Turbo? Boss, hold here with the case and cover us. We'll make our way to that transporter tied up over there." He pointed to a forty-foot boat moored along the dock.

Haufner nodded. "Let's get it done."

Thompson turned and sprinted back to where he last saw Turbo. He was careful not to look in the direction of the enemy boat. The strobe light threatened to overload his goggles. He found his unmoving teammate lying on top of the small-scale engine. With no incoming enemy fire, he climbed the three rungs on the side ladder and found no pulse at his teammate's carotid artery. *Shit*. Thompson stepped down to the middle rung, grabbed the back of his teammate's vest, and pulled with all his strength. The lifeless body crashed to the ground, eliciting a loud thud. Turbo's brain was partially exposed by the sniper's bullet. *Sorry, buddy. Let's get you home.*

Thompson's significant muscles flexed as he rolled his teammate's body over his left shoulder for carrying. The effort was immense. "Moving."

"Clear right," Haufner's voice answered over the radio.

Thompson could hear the strain in Snake's voice as he announced he was on the move with Cutter's body. Thompson grunted and cursed under the two-hundred-and-eighty-plus pounds of man and equipment draped over his frame. As he reached Haufner, his team leader turned and initiated a withdrawal, objective in hand, toward the ship the men intended to steal. Farther ahead, he saw Snake lowering the limp body of Cutter to the concrete deck.

Gasping for air, Thompson willed his legs to move faster. The years of training his body to a fine edge took over as he closed within twenty yards of the big boat. Surely, the noise of the battle, and powerful strobe light flashing in the darkness, had authorities on the way to the docks. Worse, somewhere nearby, two North Korean commandos were still in the fight.

Hunched down next to Cutter's body, Snake swung his rifle in wide arcs, providing security to the north.

Thompson sensed his muscles slowing. *Move, you piece of shit.*

Haufner, ahead of Thompson, reached a narrow gangway that would, once unfolded, span the ten-foot gap between boat and dock. He set down the case and grabbed at the metal bridge.

Boom! A single shot thundered from Snake's direction.

Thompson saw his teammate pitch forward then collapse, face first, to the ground. On instinct, he dropped to one knee and rolled Turbo's body off his shoulders. He let loose a barrage of fire to suppress the hidden shooter.

"Get cover left side." Haufner ordered.

Thompson abandoned his dead teammate and sprinted for the nearest containers away from the water's edge. More enemy fire erupted, and he dove the last four feet to safety. "Move," he yelled into his mic.

"Coming to you!" Haufner said.

With breathing coming in sharp pants, Thompson searched for targets as Haufner grabbed the case and dashed toward his position. At the moment Haufner reached cover, a second gun erupted near the original battle site, and a spark flew off a metal post next to the team leader's head.

Haufner dropped to the ground next to Thompson. He looked in the direction of Snake. "Fuck!"

"We're out of time. We gotta exfil," Thompson said.

Haufner reloaded. "We'll get pinned down if we stay any longer. Head inland. Mix with the terrain."

"Fuck me. I can't believe we're leaving our guys here," Thompson swore.

Haufner gritted his teeth. "I hate it as much as you. This case *has* to make it home. We can't let them die for nothing. This situation is a shit sandwich."

Thompson nodded. Leaving his brothers behind went against everything he believed. He also understood, in this situation, if they intended to accomplish the mission, they had no other choice.

"If I go down, you leave my ass, and get this case back to our forces. That's a direct order," Haufner growled.

Thompson readied his feet to move. "When have you *ever* said, 'direct order'?"

"Sounded kinda' cool though, right?" Haufner huffed.

Another shot rang out. A huge hole punched through the metal box right next to Haufner. The enemy sniper was zeroing in on their position.

"Go. Go." Thompson leapt from his crouched position and sprinted away from the firing. He weaved in and out of the rows of transport containers and warehouse buildings to the west. The Delta man ran deeper into Chinese territory. When the sounds of gunfire ebbed, he no longer heard footsteps behind him.

****

Snake couldn't move his legs. With his night vision goggles wrenched away from his field of vision, he laid flat, his right cheek resting on the cool surface of the dock. The familiar smell of blood filled his nostrils. Footsteps crunched on cement as they approached. His weakened left hand struggled to draw the pistol from the drop-down holster strapped to his unmoving lower limb.

Something or someone flipped him onto his back. The dawn cast enough light for Snake to catch a glimpse of a man standing over him. He saw a fleshy, older male with gray chin-stubble on pale white skin. The shape of the stranger's eyes was his most troubling feature. They were round. A foreigner.

"You're a long way from home," the man said in perfect English.

The last thing Snake saw was a pistol raised then a flash of light.

Chapter 5

University Medical Center Trauma Unit
Las Vegas, Nevada

Cole snapped his head upright. The sensation of falling jerked his body. His eyes opened, and the living hell came back into focus. He noticed several monitors, tracing Kip's vital signs as his best friend slept off the anesthesia from his surgery. Five milligrams of anxiety medication gave Cole four hours of sleep in the chair next to the hospital bed. Upon waking, the unwelcome memories of the past ten hours flooded back. His status had changed. He was now a grieving husband and father.

Cole drifted his gaze to the nurse's station outside the room. The wall clock above the desk read six-fifteen a.m. Two policemen stood nearby, both appeared alert.

Rounding the corner, a young female in hospital scrubs entered the room. Her attention turned toward Cole. "Can I get you anything?"

He shook his head and watched as she examined the computer screens and wrote in a medical chart. Cole finally found his voice. "Is he okay?"

"Everything looks good right now. The surgeon should be by in a little while to check his condition.

Cole shifted in his chair. He dropped his head to

avoid her gaze. "Where're my wife and son?" The quiver in his voice was unavoidable.

"I...I don't know. Maybe the officers outside can answer that."

Cole raised his chin to look at her but couldn't find the energy to organize a reply.

Her eyes watered. "Sorry."

He didn't dare gaze at her any longer and turned his head to avoid the pain welling inside. He heard her footsteps retreat from the room. The sudden void of the nurse's absence intensified his distress. The disintegration of his life birthed irrational ideas. Cole fantasized about swallowing an entire bottle of pills.

A shuffling noise stirred him from his thoughts. His gaze set at floor level, Cole saw two pairs of black boots enter the room. They stopped at the foot of Kip's bed. He glanced up at the two muscular police officers he'd noticed moments earlier.

"Mr. Haufner, I'm Officer Tate with Metro PD," the tall, dark-haired cop said. He motioned toward the stockier man to his left. "This is my partner, Officer Jenkins. We're here to ensure things stay quiet and provide any assistance you might need."

Jenkins crossed his massive arms over a barrel chest. "We'll make sure the press vultures keep their distance."

Tate cast a narrowed glare at his partner.

On reflection, Cole had to agree with Jenkins. News reporters, invading his personal space, looking for a quote from the bereaved posed a recipe for physical altercation. He feared if someone said the wrong words, he might do something regrettable. At this point, just about anything someone might say would qualify. Cole nodded. "The only help I want is to kill the animal who ran the red light." He tilted his head and stared at the officers. He thought he mumbled, but their facial reactions to his confession indicated they'd heard.

"I understand," Tate said. "The investigation is ongoing."

"Five minutes in a room. All I ask." A newfound energy took over Cole's body. He didn't even care he insinuated premeditated murder in the presence of police officers.

"Enough."

Everyone froze.

Kip's voice was both weary and high volume. Cole closed his eyes and let his chin drop to his chest. Guilt for waking Kip washed over him.

The officers backed out of the room, leaving the two, grieving men alone.

Tongue-tied, Cole couldn't say anything. Minutes ticked by without a word. "Sorry about that," he whispered.

"It's okay," Kip rasped.

Fifteen minutes passed before a pair of physicians entered the room with nurses in tow. With all the new arrivals taking up most of the limited space around the bed, Cole struggled to draw in enough air. He imagined his constricting chest was what claustrophobia must feel like.

A distinguished, older man stepped closer to the side of the bed. The embroidered left breast region of his white lab coat read, Dr. Wazney, Trauma Surgery Dept. Chair. "Hello, Mr. Hillman. How does the arm feel?"

"It's fine," Kip's gravelly voice responded.

"Let's take a peek." The surgeon sat on the edge of the bed and unwrapped the bandages.

Cole couldn't look. He turned his head to stare at a blank spot on the wall. He listened as Dr. Wazney and the second physician exchanged muted comments during their examination. Knowing his friend lay in a hospital bed because of what happened to Claire and Max hurt like hell.

"Excellent," Dr. Wazney announced.

Cole stole a glance over his left shoulder and, seeing the poking and prodding finished, turned back toward the medical staff.

Dr. Wazney flipped through the patient chart, scribbling on several pages. He closed the binder then looked at Kip. "The surgery was successful and, based on your exam, I'm not expecting any long-term issues. Probably six weeks before you'll start physical therapy. Stitches should come out in seven to ten days."

"When can I get out of here?" Kip growled.

"They'll transfer you out of trauma in a few hours and get you upstairs into a private room. Home in a couple of days."

"No, you misunderstand. What time can I expect to be released *today*?" Kip said through clenched teeth.

"Mr. Hillman, with open fractures, we have to monitor for infection and bleeding. You're also neurologically intact now, but loss of sensation or motor function is a medical emergency all by itself."

"If it does, I know the address," Kip said.

Cole knew any further comment by the doctor was useless. No amount of reasoning would change his friend's mind. *Let's get out of here.*

****

Cole's blank stare caught the blur of evenly spaced palm trees zipping past the dark-tinted windows of the customized SUV transporting him. The vehicle cruised the meandering roads inside the gated Red Rock Country Club neighborhood located on the west side of town. The driver and front seat passenger were private security staff from the promoter of Cole's fight. Two, unmarked police cruisers provided escort. To his left, Kip slouched in the plush, second-row leather seats.

Thirty minutes earlier, Cole watched his best friend sign a document absolving the institute and doctors of any responsibility for his health, as Kip left against medical advice. Cole knew raising his own concern regarding the choice was a fool's errand. He'd stayed quiet through the contentious exchange between patient and physician.

After a twenty-minute drive from the hospital, Cole arrived at Kip's sprawling French-Colonial-style home. The security detail followed the pair to the front entrance before heading back to the luxury SUV. Striding through the huge double doors, he witnessed Kip greeting Zeus, his buddy's German shepherd. Normally displaying boundless energy, the four-year-old male, as if he sensed something amiss, approached with his ears drooped and his tail low between his muscular hind legs.

Kip dropped to a knee and put his left arm around the highly-trained purebred. "Hi, boy. I'm okay."

Zeus then looked to Cole.

Cole gave the familiar dog a comforting pat. He knew how much the shepherd meant to Kip, and he could see why—Zeus's ability to read moods and his owner's wishes were special. Cole spent much of his youth learning Buddhism from his uncle, who instilled the value of respecting all life, not just human.

With Zeus at a heel, Cole followed Kip through the round-shaped foyer and into a huge, two-story, great room. On the left rose a massive stone fireplace big enough to stand inside and to the right was an equally impressive gourmet kitchen. At the sink stood Kip's housekeeper, Lolita.

The sixty-year-old Mexican grandmother saw Kip and rushed toward him with tears in her eyes. Her black hair was pulled back in a tight bun, and she wore a large Catholic cross around her neck. "Oh my, Mister Kip!" she called out.

Cole watched as she struggled to hug him without touching his injured arm.

"Hi, Lolita," Kip wrapped his left arm around her.

Tears streamed down her cheeks. "Oh, Mr. Kip, I pray for you when I hear. My family go to hospital, but they say we no see you. We pray all night outside, and I come fast when I hear you coming home so soon."

Kip kissed her on the forehead. "Thank your family for me. I'm a lucky man to have you."

Lolita made the sign of the cross several times then kissed both his cheeks. She shuffled to Cole with mascara running under both eyes and gave him a big hug. "Mister Cole, I love your family. I can't say words when I find out. My family pray for you. Your family now angels watching over you. God will protect them."

Emotion tightened Cole's throat. Though he felt suspended in some out-of-body void, Cole sucked in a breath, her words and gestures breaking through the shell. A warm feeling overtook him—the first emotion he'd experienced beside anger and despair. He believed she was the most genuine and loving person he'd ever met. "Thank you, Lolita. Your words give me comfort."

She kissed his cheek, crossed herself, and then hurried from the room.

Kip nodded for him to come into the kitchen. The old fighter went to the refrigerator and snatched two cans of beer.

Cole noticed a dozen or more trays of homemade food covering every square inch of counter space. The effects of another dose of anti-anxiety medication dulled Cole's appreciation for the wonderful smells. He grabbed the cold aluminum from Kip's grasp and popped the tabs. He fished the pill bottle from his pants pocket and planted the medication on the island counter.

Likewise, Kip tossed his pain prescription container onto the marble slab.

Against doctor's orders, Cole chugged his can nearly dry before following Kip into the great room. They stood next to each other, staring out the two-story window overlooking the fourteenth fairway running along the back property line.

Kip cleared his throat. "Think you can stay awhile?"

Cole hadn't thought of what to do next. He had a strange feeling that, at any minute, Claire and Max would walk through the front door. The shock and pharmaceutical drugs dulled all but the most basic of his senses. He was, however, sure of one thing. "If I don't, I'm afraid of what I might do."

Chapter 6

Red Rocks Country Club, Hillman Residence

The warm desert breeze ruffled Cole's hair while he lay on a king-sized bed in an upstairs guest bedroom. He'd stood on the small balcony off the back of the house, watching golfers shuttle past, and hadn't bothered to close the door when he returned. The medication was kicking his ass, and that's just what he wanted the pills to do.

With guests in mind, toothbrushes were available in all six *ensuite* bathrooms, but Cole wanted his own.

Lolita drove over to his house, with one of the security men, and stuffed a suitcase full of clothing and toiletries. The bag now sat at the foot of the bed.

While lying on the mattress, Cole leaned over the end and unzipped the suitcase. Some of the contents spilled out: T-shirts, underwear, a framed photo, and a smooth rock. The photograph laid face-down, and Cole hesitated over picking up the frame, afraid of what he might feel. If the picture was the one next to the rock in his bedroom, he already knew who was in it and the location of the camera shoot. He swallowed the rising bile in his throat and shoved the picture under the pile of clothes.

He shifted his attention to the palm-sized rock. The granite felt smooth to the touch, worn down by hundreds of years of Shaolin monks practicing their craft. He picked up the stone and examined the tiny nuances along the surface. For the first time today, he thought of something else other than his wife and son. Instead, he recalled the world of his childhood.

Born to a German father—a renowned nuclear chemist and former semi-professional soccer player—and a Chinese mother—a volleyball star for her native country before coming to the U.S. to study—Cole was raised in Massachusetts along with his older brother, Butch. Tragedy struck when he was six when his mother died of a previously undiagnosed brain aneurysm. His father wished her interment to be where she lived as a child, and the family accompanied her remains to *Dandong*, China.

Cole and his eleven-year-old brother suffered a second tragedy when, hours after the funeral, their father disappeared. Their mother's brother assumed the boys' care while a search ensued. U.S. and German authorities were kept apprised of the investigation that stretched into months with no evidence of foul play discovered. With no other family identified, the boys were allowed to stay with their biological uncle. What ensured the arrangement unique was the fact he was a fifty-year-old Buddhist monk and *Shaolin* Kung Fu master.

Master Li Bingwen served as the head of a lay Buddhist sect located approximately twelve miles west of Dandong. The Temple sat at the base of *Wulong* Mountain. Identified as a *Shaolin* prodigy at the tender age of five, Bingwen entered into the prestigious Martial Monk program and dedicated his life to studying the teachings of Buddha and the *Shaolin* martial arts. The family's sacrifice of their young son to the elite institution did not go unnoticed, and the parents received a very rare opportunity to have a second child. Eventually, a daughter, Eu-meh—meaning "especially beautiful"—was born. The name proved prophetic as she grew to become a most desirable woman.

Because of his mother's teaching, Cole's Chinese language skill was functional, and he found living at the Temple both intriguing and somewhat difficult. The discipline demanded of the boys gave the pair structure and kept them busy. They learned of Buddha and the lessons of the great masters, but the physical *Shaolin* studies allowed ample opportunity to release pain and anger over the loss of their parents.

Butch, approaching his teen years, threw himself into the martial art with an intensity that surprised not only the other students but Master Li, as well. Frequently, he was admonished after particularly brutal sparring sessions. Although he tempered his emotions over those early years, Butch appeared as if a volcano simmered just under the surface.

For Cole, the transition was easier. For all of Butch's every-waking-hour, self-induced physical regiment, Cole found the peacefulness of Buddhism to his liking. The solitude of meditation, even for his young self, helped him deal with the losses. Because of this learned calmness, the monks were very eager to continue his non-martial training. Before long, the boys fully integrated with Temple life.

Not all was introspective study for the younger Haufner. He, too, learned *Shaolin* Kung Fu. Whether by his abundant *qi gong*—his spiritual inner life energy—

or simply raw physical talent, Cole quickly developed into a true phenomenon in the ancient martial art. As the years progressed, whispers at the Temple surfaced he would surpass even the great Master Li in ability. The rumors created jealousy among a few students. Master Li was Cole's uncle, but his leadership position didn't stop a few verbal barbs to the effect Cole didn't "look" Chinese enough to become a full-fledged member. Between meditation and speaking with trusted friends, he always moved past the taunts.

For the protective older brother, however, forgiving wasn't so easy.

In one instance, a jealous rival to a then-thirteen-year-old Cole referred to him as "*Gweizai*," a derogatory word for a non-Chinese boy.

The eighteen-year-old Butch erupted in a rage, and blood and curses flew. Stopping the fight required several instructors. Butch was demoted and instructed to perform countless hours of meditation while the offender was expelled from the Temple for not following the Buddhist teachings of inner harmony and respect.

Shortly after the episode, Master Li approached a frustrated Cole. "*Wai sheng*-nephew," Li greeted him. "You appear troubled."

Master Li's approach, employing a rare, familiar address, caught Cole off guard. He could not remember the last time they spoke as family members. "*Sifu*," he answered in the proper manner. "It is true. My mind plays tricks on me. My focus is not what it should be."

Master Li motioned for Cole to sit with him on a stone bench. "Just the two of us are here. For you to speak of me as *jiu jiu*—uncle—is okay."

Cole smiled. He loved the great Master Li as much as his own parents, and this private moment filled him with joy. "Thank you, uncle."

"I have seen that same frustrated expression on many boys' faces as they approached early manhood," Master Li said. "Share your feelings with me."

Cole looked down at his feet. "I find my thoughts going back to when I still lived in America. I don't remember having problems with friends then. Now, here at the Temple, I find it not so."

His uncle pondered then gave a nod and a slight grunt. "You have accomplished much in a short time. I would expect nothing less. You see, I believed I had the same problems when I was your age."

"You did?" Cole's mouth hung open. *How is that possible?*

Li sported a huge grin. "Of course! You see how jealousy poisons the body? It is a terrible human trait, one not easily let go."

"Why would someone be jealous of me? I am only half-Chinese and look even less so."

Master Li gazed off into the distance. "The way you *look* is very much like your father, yes. But inside, where we matter most, you are very much like your mother. For that, you are most definitely Chinese."

A tremendous emotional weight lifted from Cole's shoulders. He suddenly had a greater appreciation for the Buddhist teachings. What he experienced on the outside wasn't what possessed great meaning, the inside mattered most. His young mind finally grasped what he'd learned over the past seven years. Cole turned up his face to his uncle and smiled for the first time in a long while.

Master Li nodded. "What is that expression? 'I see the light bulb'?"

Cole giggled. His uncle had a terrible memory for American slang, but the Master possessed wisdom far beyond anyone he'd ever known. "*Jiu jiu*, do I have a purpose beyond the Temple? What do you see for me?"

Master Li bent over and picked up a smooth rock from the ground. "This small stone, would it make a splash in a bucket of water?"

"Of course, Uncle."

"Would it not make a visible splash in the river?"

"Yes, Uncle. But I remember being high in the air when Butch and I came to China." Cole extended his arm as tall as he could reach while simulating an airplane using his hand. "The world was covered with a great ocean."

"That is true. But, one day, this rock will make such a splash in the ocean that everyone will see."

Cole furrowed his brow, not quite understanding but trusting that, like today's epiphany, he would someday understand Master Li's words. His uncle then placed the rock into his hand and gave the young teenager a gentle squeeze. Love filled Cole's heart, and he felt less like a troubled child and more like a young man.

The vivid memory of that day faded as Cole's mind came back to the present. He rolled onto his back, the breeze outside scraping palm leaves together. He wondered if last night's events were what his uncle meant when he gave him that rock all those years ago. Or was some other event in store?

Chapter 7

Hillman Residence, twenty-one hours post-fight

Cole woke with a startle. He recalled dreaming about last night's fight but nothing more. The digital clock on the nightstand showed he'd slept for two hours. The twilight sun glowed behind the Red Rock Mountain peaks to the west. Were it not for his full bladder, he would have rolled over and covered his head with a pillow.

At the bathroom sink, Cole glanced at the mirror. The cut over his eye was moderately swollen, but the stitches did their job connecting flesh to flesh. A few other scrapes scattered over the rest of his face. Little else indicated what he'd endured in the octagon. *Take that, magazine covers*.

Looking for his cell phone, he wandered the bedroom. Not finding it, he headed downstairs. Hearing Kip's voice in the kitchen, Cole dragged himself in that direction.

"Make this happen or, I swear to God, I'll rain down an epic shit storm. I better not hear 'I don't know' from you again." Kip hissed and slammed down the receiver on the kitchen counter.

Cole pulled a chair from beneath the kitchen island, the scrape of metal on tile causing his friend to turn. "Making new friends?"

"You know me." Kip snatched his pain meds off the counter, popped the cap, and fished out two tablets.

The bags under Kip's eyes made him appear as if he hadn't slept in a week. Cole nodded at his bandaged arm. "How's it feeling?"

"Eh." Kip shrugged. With the help of a beer, he downed the pills. He waved the summer pilsner at Cole.

Cole held up his hand, declining the silent offer to join in a drink. *Probably should slow down, buddy.*

Kip still wiggled the bottle when Lolita stormed into the room.

"Mister Kip, why you no go to bed and rest like doctor says? And you no more drink with your medicine. That is bad for you!"

Damn. Cole hadn't seen her this upset in the years he'd known her. "You been down here the whole day?" he asked. He barely possessed enough humanity to think of his best friend's well being.

Kip rolled his eyes as she swept past him, confiscating the bottle and dropping it with a *clang* amid the others at the bottom of the trash bin. "Just a couple of things that can't wait," he said.

"You go to bed." She shook her index finger at Kip. "Everything can wait."

Kip grumbled a few unintelligible words as he skulked around the island to exit the kitchen. He gave Cole a tap on the arm on his way to the stairs.

Cole thought his friend might not have the strength to climb. "Have you seen my cell phone?" he whispered.

Lolita watched Kip ascend to the second story then turned to Cole. With lips pinched, she pulled the phone out of her pocket and handed it to him. "Mr. Kip, he say to keep it turned off. He went through the messages so you no have to listen to everyone. He love you. He think this his fault."

"Damn you, Kip," Cole muttered. "You didn't do anything wrong." *Their deaths are on me. If I didn't do the press release, they'd still be here. I should have taken them home. This tragedy is all my fault.*

She put a hand up to his cheek. "You rest, too. For me, please."

Cole closed his eyes and gave a nod. *Never gonna happen.*

Lolita patted his chest then charged upstairs.

Cole watched her disappear at a no-nonsense clip. *Heads up, buddy.* He sat on a stool then powered on his phone. He saw dozens of new text and voicemail messages from the past hour populate the device. He assumed Kip cleared everything prior to that time.

He hovered his finger over the photo album button. His irrational thoughts gave false hope that gazing at the pictures would somehow bring back his family. He swallowed hard then tapped the screen. He missed and, instead of choosing the photo icon, he hit the call button. The misstep redialed his last attempted number. The screen showed a picture of Butch. The last time he'd tried to reach his older brother was minutes before the big fight last evening.

Two rings echoed out of Cole's earpiece before Butch's recorded greeting answered. "It's me, do your thing." The terse command ended with a beep.

"Hey." The word sounded choked. Cole cleared his throat. "I really need to talk to you. I don't know if you've heard anything yet, but please call me. It's Claire and Max." He lowered the phone to the counter.

His shoulders shook violently with no noise escaping his lips. Consciously suppressing his voice, he cried silently. Tears dropped into his lap. He hoped no one would see him like this. His emotional suffering felt unbearable. *They can't be gone. Am I dreaming?*

The phone vibrated, startling him. An incoming call from a blocked caller ID woke his cell phone. Resisting the temptation to throw the device across the room, Cole swiped the screen to accept then immediately disconnected the line. Ten seconds later, a second blocked call rang. "Quit calling!" He hung up.

When the phone vibrated a third time, Cole felt ready to burst. "Listen, you prick. Call me again, and I'll hunt you down."

"Don't call your brother's phone anymore," a male voice said.

Adrenaline shot through Cole's veins. "Wa...wait. Who is this?"

"He wanted you to know that he is going home. Don't call his number anymore."

Cole jumped to his feet. "I have to talk to him. Where is he?"

"We've lost contact. He wanted me to tell you that he headed home."

Panic enveloped his body. His chest tightened. Cole couldn't think. "Is he alive? What do you mean you lost contact? Does that happen a lot? I need to get a message—"

"Listen very carefully. I'm calling you from a burner phone that cannot be traced. He wanted you to know he *went home*. I have to go. Good luck."

The line went dead. Cole hit redial, but his call ended in a rapid beeping tone. He frantically repeated the effort several more times with the same result. Shaking, and despite the mysterious man's warning, he dialed his brother. An automated voice stated the number was no longer in service.

His mind at work, Cole paced. He knew his brother's missions remained highly classified, and he shouldn't expect more details surrounding Butch's disappearance. His brother didn't have a home. He either crashed at Cole's house or with one of his military buddies.

"He *went* home," Cole spoke out loud. *Where are you, brother? What am I missing?*

Chapter 8

Binhai Highway, Dandong, China

Traveling north along Binhai highway, the bouncing of the solid-axle transport truck sent constant shockwaves through Butch Haufner's injured ribs. The canvas-sided fish hauler reeked of rotting seafood. The poorly paved road ran along the edge of the *Yalu* River, separated from North Korea at times by a mere ten feet and chain-link fencing. Hidden amid the fifty-gallon barrels of fish, Butch calculated his next move. He sucked in air through clenched teeth every time the careless driver swerved or drove into a rut.

The sniper's bullet that struck him in the back in the predawn hours nearly ended the mission, not to mention his life. The 7.62-caliber round destroyed the satellite radio attached to the rear of his assault vest before the tumbling lead crashed into the steel plate of his ballistic armor. The force knocked him to the ground and possibly cracked ribs. Whether bruised or fractured, he didn't yet know. When he recovered, he couldn't find Hammer anywhere. Odd his teammate disappeared without a word. With the destruction of the radio, he couldn't verify if his second-in-command escaped.

Fearing the North Korean commandos were closing in, Butch had no choice but to abandon a search for his teammate and, objective in hand, make his escape. As the sun poked over the horizon, the North Koreans spotted him, and a twenty-minute, running gun battle unfolded. Ducking in and out of cargo containers and warehouse buildings, he headed north through the harbor.

With daylight came the dock workers, filtering in for their daily grind.

Butch dodged the noncombatants and lost sight of the enemy. And, yet, the cat-and-mouse game continued. He needed a way out of the harbor, and that's when he noticed a dirty, soft-side delivery truck parked near his hide site. After workers loaded a dozen, large barrels of fish into the back of the vehicle, Butch knew he found the perfect getaway vehicle— particularly if search dogs were on the loose. At the moment the truck rolled out, he hopped into the cargo hold with the hope of clearing the docks. Butch was anxious to retreat from the battle zone. Despite this newfound opportunity to escape, his problems were far from over.

He scanned the case and found a tiny device, possibly used for tracking purposes. The ladybug-sized item adhered to the case using a magnetic property, and he popped it off before dumping the metal object in the dirt outside the truck. Not knowing if the jarring from the road trip would cause damage to the internal mechanical parts, he maintained a firm grasp on the handle. He shuddered to think about the Chinese government's response when, at dockside, they found the bodies and shattered boat. Having lived in the region as a child, he knew the authorities spared no one in their investigations.

The truck traversed the second of two bridges in the small farming area of *Beidajian*. Leaving the hamlet, Butch knew he'd passed the first of many obstacles to his escape. He didn't dare poke his head outside the rear flaps rustling in the wind, because the vehicle was minutes away from the larger agricultural community of *Guawanggou*. He recalled two bridges marking the opposite edges of town, one on the northeast end and one on the southwest. He willed the truck to be on the northeastern section, signaling an exit from the tightly congregated housing of the small town. Suffering from the constant jarring of his rib injury, he eventually heard the change in pitch of tire noise on bridge pavement for a fourth time. The highway led into the farming fields, away from concentrated civilization. He breathed a sigh of relief.

Standing six-foot-one-inch, Butch towered over the local population. His Mandarin expressed the regional dialect, and his facial features seamlessly blended with the community. He felt confident most people would only remember him as the "tall guy."

The smart plan called for disposal of his weaponry. Chinese farmers were not unlike those from the American Midwest—alert and observant to anything out of the ordinary. He required clothes to blend in with the population. The next critical step involved discovering a method to communicate with JSOC command. He needed to work fast since the longer he stayed in China, the worse were the odds of mission success. Knowledge of the area remained his greatest asset. Only one small canal bridge stood between him and the city of *Dandong*—his target location.

A sudden deceleration caused too-thin brake pads

to grind against drum rotors.

Suffering the piercing, high-pitched squeal, Butch grabbed one of the fish containers lest he slam into the back of the cab, giving away his position to the driver. His heart raced, and he imagined what caused the vehicle to drop speed. He sensed little road traffic and didn't remember any road signals this far out in the farmland. He prayed the slowdown was only temporary.

The truck screeched to a halt.

He strained to hear signs of trouble.

The driver's window rolled down. A male voice outside the vehicle came within earshot. Approaching footsteps scraped against pavement. The loud idle of the engine drowned out the conversation between the driver and outside man.

Then, one word rose above the din causing Butch to flinch—*xianfan*. The authorities were mobilized, looking for a suspected criminal.

Chapter 9

Binhai Highway, four miles south of Dandong

Butch's heart pounded against his chest. To his right, North Korea butted up against the road. To his left, wide-open Chinese farmland stretched as far as the horizon. He knew of at least two North Korean-controlled military gates along the road to *Dandong*. He hovered his right hand between the silenced pistol holstered against his thigh and the combat knife strapped to the front of his black harness. If the truck idled next to a North Korean gate, even if he successfully avoided capture, soldiers would report the incident.

Crouched on the balls of his feet, Butch was ready to move if necessary. He heard the man outside say "*Zhu,*" ordering the driver not to move. Something about the way he pronounced the word caught Butch's attention. The accent didn't sound natural. Footsteps grew louder as they approached the rear of the truck. He ducked low behind a barrel.

Hearing the tarp flutter, he held his breath. He grasped the hilt of his combat knife. A soft grunt gave way to someone coming to stand in the cargo hold. The shuffling of feet grew louder.

The intruder coughed. "*Heom-aghan.*"

Shit. Butch wasn't completely fluent in Korean but,

growing up in *Dandong*, he had a functional understanding of the language. The man commented on the nasty fish smell. This guy wasn't Chinese. Because North Korea was mindful not to unnecessarily upset its bigger neighbor, this inspector would not have casually stepped outside the border gates onto Chinese soil. He would not only be a member of their military apparatus but also likely under strict orders from his superiors to inspect vehicles traveling this route.

Butch heard boots scraping on the thin metal bed. He assumed the man carried, at minimum, a pistol.

The intruder stopped for a couple of seconds then took one more step.

He couldn't risk being spotted nor being put on the defensive. Surprise was his ally. In one swift move, Butch leaped from behind the barrel, drew his knife with his right hand, and clamped his left over the man's mouth.

The inspector wore a dark green uniform jacket, no insignia or other identifiers visible. He stood no more than five-foot-six with a slender build, typical for men from the other side of the fence. The North Korean's eyes were wide and unblinking.

Pulling the suspected soldier in tight with his left arm, Butch jammed his right knee low against the back of the man's legs.

Completely off balance, the terrified soldier could not respond to the assault.

"Shh." Butch hissed. He pressed his blade hard against the other's throat and chose to speak in Mandarin. "I am PLA here to search for defectors. I should take you to my headquarters now."

The much-smaller man waved his arms, mumbling

under Butch's clamped left hand.

The acronym PLA stood for the People's Liberation Army—China's military. Butch imagined the terror endured by this North Korean soldier captured outside the gate by a Chinese Special Forces commando. He counted on his battle dress and obvious skill in subduing the man to pull off the part of a soldier enlisted in China's covert operations group. He drew the frantic male in closer with a yank. "Who are you looking for?"

"*Meiguoren*," the little man croaked in clumsy Mandarin.

Butch choked off any more verbal response. *Dammit*. Word spread of an American loose on the border. Did he also know about the case? Worse yet, did the Chinese know? He pushed the knife even harder against the man's throat. "Tell your superiors the PLA is watching them. If I see another North Korean on Chinese land, they die. Do you understand?"

The soldier nodded, gasping for air.

Without easing his grip, knife still held against neck, Butch led him to the rear gate of the cargo hold. He sheathed his blade then drew his pistol, allowing the long, black cylinder protruding from the barrel to hover before the frightened man's eyes. "Wave away the driver and get your ass off my country's soil. You do anything else, and I'll put a bullet through your face. Got it?"

A rapid nod from the North Korean indicated understanding.

Butch shoved the soldier from the truck, making him fall roughly to the ground. He aimed his pistol.

The man was already making tracks toward the

gate. The North Korean waved the driver on before retreating toward safety inside the guard shack.

Butch heard the grinding of the manual transmission gears then felt the lurch of the truck as it picked up speed. He secured the flap of tarp then gingerly made his way to the back of the bed. He didn't know how fast word would shoot up the North Korean chain of command regarding the encounter, but he was more worried than ever the Chinese would soon be on his tail.

He sat next to the case, wincing from the stabbing pain in his ribs. *Does that asshole have to hit every pothole?* Checking his diving watch, he estimated ten to fifteen minutes before the truck breached the city limits of *Dandong*. So many things needed to go perfectly, which allowed a moment of self-doubt. The fear of dying didn't worry Butch—the fear of failing remained his overriding concern. If success didn't appear, one or more nations could find themselves on the brink of extinction.

Chapter 10

City of Dandong

Wearing dirty, black pants and a light brown overcoat, Butch pedaled a rust-colored bicycle with a creaking chain in desperate need of oil. A dingy, *Mao*-style hat topped him off, and he rode with a slight limp, his body leaning left during each down-stroke to that side. As twilight engulfed the border city, Butch acted the part of a simple peasant laborer riding the streets of *Dandong*.

The homemade, wooden flatbed extending off the rear of the bike carried an assortment of junk, whose appearance wouldn't give anyone a second thought. Or so Butch hoped and calculated because, beneath the scrap metal and filthy burlap covering, enough evidence to implicate the U.S. in an invasion with the intent to destroy an entire nation lay waiting to be discovered.

The daylight escape from the fish truck had carried great risk. At one point, the vehicle turned left off the highway and stopped.

The driver hopped out of the cab and chatted with someone on the left.

Sneaking a peek out of the rear flaps, Butch spotted a row of old metal workshops on the opposite side of the two individuals. Grabbing the case, he slowly lowered himself to the ground and escaped amid the structures. For several hours, Butch hid in a closet inside one of the shops. By late afternoon, with no workers in sight, he scoured the place for anything useful. He found a pair of old, musty pants and a stained jacket on top of a work bench. The clothing was small, but a few strategic cuts from his knife made the garments useable. Though the temperature hovered near eighty degrees Fahrenheit, the sack-like coat worked well to hide his muscular frame.

Escape and evasion training included instructions on ways to blend with local populations. Butch's biggest concern was his considerable size and military bearing. A true alpha male stood out in a crowd. Humans, no matter their culture or ethnicity, were hardwired from the dawn of humankind to discern threats. Extensive training taught him methods of minimizing that impact by using body position, downward eye gaze, and a variety of passive behaviors to reduce his signature from revealing himself as a predator.

Dressed like a local, Butch left his weapons and the case hidden in the shack and cautiously ventured from his hiding spot. He walked to the edge of a small village, called *Dong'anmin*, a quarter of a mile away. Near a cluster of ramshackle homes, he found transportation. The bike leaned against a tiny home with no lock or chain securing it. Crime was almost nonexistent in this part of the country. The single-geared transport sported a large trailer to carry his weapons and, more importantly, the case. Astride the bike, he hurried to collect his belongings. Once the weapons and case were secure, he rode at a leisurely pace.

Though Butch *had* lived near *Dandong* for some ten years, he resided nearly twenty miles northwest of the city at the mountain Temple. Rarely had he ventured this far south. To avoid detection, he needed to ride west of the downtown proper area, away from the thousands of city cameras posted along every major road and avenue of travel. Adding to electronic snooping of the population, North Korean agents and sympathizers infiltrated nearly every facet of the workforce. China allowed the exchange for the cheap labor and as a show of good faith to their neighbor. North Korea took care not to abuse the offering, but Butch saw firsthand the lengths the foreign government went to recapture the case. The gate guard stopping the fish truck on Chinese soil was a not-so-subtle hint.

Butch pedaled for several miles north on *Shanshang* Street. The road ran along the western edge of the dense city eight blocks from the *Yalu* River. With the setting sun, colorful neon lights from the businesses bathed the sidewalks in shades of red, green, and blue. Dehydration caused a wicked leg cramp. Though painful, his discomfort served a useful purpose in hiding his true identity. The road remained busy in the late rush hour, but no one paid him any attention.

He couldn't help but notice the city's vast growth during his ten-year absence. Newly erected high-rise apartments and office buildings replaced smaller structures, and the heavy auto traffic displayed expensive foreign imports. A glance in every direction provided evidence of China's economic boom in this eastern border port town of just under a million residents.

Butch sought a specific location north of

downtown. He'd visited there many times as a young man. If any historically significant addresses survived the developers' cranes, surely the residence remained standing. As he passed the Resist America Aid Korea Memorial Hall on the left, he became more familiar with the surroundings. His destination was close.

A half-mile farther, his body tensed. On the right stood the *Dandong* People's Hospital. He thought of his dead and missing teammates. Though he couldn't properly mourn them, not yet, he wondered if the authorities found their bodies and brought the Americans here for medical exams. Fighting the instinct to stare at the entrance as he passed, Butch snuck a peek to his right, searching for a police or military presence. Seeing no unusual activity at the front of the building, he exhaled, relief shooting through his body.

With renewed energy, he rode on, passing various schools, karaoke joints, and the *Quidao* police station, which appeared to be operating business as usual. The constant smell of food from sidewalk vendors reminded him he hadn't eaten in almost thirty-six hours, but water was a more urgent need.

Finally, up ahead, the street sign for *Yujia* Road entered Butch's vision. He turned left off *Shanshang* then an immediate left at the first street, avoiding the *Yujia* Police Station on the right side of the crossroad. He pedaled approximately fifty feet and turned right. Though far from his ultimate goal of returning the case to U.S. forces, he allowed a grin for reaching this far in his escape. The short side street dumped him squarely onto the grounds of the *Mituo* Temple—a *Shaolin* Monastery he'd visited many times as a youngster.

The Temple's serene atmosphere contrasted with

the bustle of the city. The tranquility of the well-groomed surroundings encouraged contemplation, and a large, white statue of Buddha greeted everyone walking along the center path. An immediate false sense of comfort and safety crept over him. He dismounted onto shaking, cramped legs. After a minute, he regained his balance then pushed the bike toward the Temple residence on his right. He didn't see any visitors but hoped the Temple caretaker was home.

He left the case and his gear under the tarp and approached a simple wooden door. A small, round doorknob hung loosely from the left edge of the oaken portal. Butch paused to take a deep cleansing breath then raised his hand and gently knocked. A moment later, the door opened and a portly man with a shaved head wearing a traditional, yellow monk's robe stood in the glowing light of a dozen or so candles.

"*Ninhao*," the monk greeted him. "How may I help you?"

Hearing the polite *hello*. Butch bowed respectfully. "*Ninhao*. May I ask if brother Li Shen is at the Temple today?"

"You may. And you have also found him. Do I know you?"

The familiar ring of the monk's vocal tone sagged Butch's shoulders. He removed his cap and raised his head to gaze upon the holy man. Though the Buddhist was a bit heavier than he remembered, the small mole at the religious man's left lower eyelid provided positive identification. As Butch allowed his back to straighten, he rose to his full height. He witnessed the monk's eyes grow wide. "Hello, cousin."

Chapter 11

Bunkers Memory Garden Cemetery, Las Vegas, Nevada

The musky smell of freshly dug earth hung in the air. Not even the strong spring winds could wash away the reminder of why more than one hundred people gathered on the manicured lawn. Those in attendance, wearing black, experienced the ninety-five-degree temperature under a searing sun. But no amount of suffocating heat compared to the suffering Cole experienced on the inside.

The coroner's office expedited the post-mortem review of Claire and Max, thus allowing for speedy burials. Claire's family, Irish Catholic to the core, wanted a Christian burial for their daughter and grandson. Cole's upbringing and beliefs favored cremation, but he acceded without a word. He was too numb to voice his view.

On Claire's four-foot-tall headstone, a ballerina carved into the marble struck a pose from a picture provided to the stonemason. Under Claire McGinnis-Haufner, the inscription read: *Beloved daughter, loving wife, ferocious mother, and mother-to-be*. Max shared the monument with Claire—the word "Da" placed under his name. Mother and child lay together inside the velvet-lined coffin, together for eternity.

The autopsy reported the certainty Claire was between six and seven weeks pregnant. Earlier this morning, her sister, Tisha, pulled aside Cole and relayed what Claire told her days before the tragic accident. Not wanting to distract him before his big event, Claire chose to wait until after the fight before sharing the good fortune of the pregnancy. Unable to cope with any more bad news, he merely nodded when his sister-in-law relayed the conversation.

While a priest invoked a passage from the Bible, the white, brass-trimmed casket slowly lowered into the ground.

Cole closed his eyes and turned his face toward the searing overhead sun. Thank God for friends. Two men who were especially close to both Kip and Cole stood next to the grieving godfather, physically holding him back lest the old fighter throw himself into the hole. If he hadn't taken an extra dose of antianxiety medicine, Cole might have dived in, too.

Seated to Cole's left, Claire's mother sobbed while her husband did his best to comfort her. His face projected pain and anger.

The priest blessed the crowd, and the funeral concluded.

Cole sat slumped in his chair as people streamed by expressing condolences. He simply nodded, going through the motion of repeated handshakes with no effort. *You should have been here. Where are you, Butch?*

Sobbing, Kip knelt at graveside, repeatedly punching the ground with a balled left fist.

Cole walked over to his friend and placed a hand on his right shoulder. He had no words of comfort. "It's not your fault."

Kip nodded an acknowledgment but remained silent.

Cole stared at the top of the gleaming coffin. His throat spasmed in an effort to suppress a scream. *I didn't take care of you. This funeral is all my fault.*

A full minute passed before Kip regained some level of composure and stood, unclenching his fist. Cole watched the dirt leave his grip and fall to the ground. The two embraced, rocking back and forth.

Through tears, Cole glanced over Kip's shoulder and saw a muscular man in a blue T-shirt standing fifty feet away. Next to him stood a tall, imposing male in a dark sport jacket. Both wore black, wrap-around sunglasses. Cole's heart pounded against his chest. "Butch?" he whispered. Cole let go of his friend and sprinted toward the men. When neither appeared to be his brother, an altogether different feeling of dread overcame him. He stopped ten feet from the pair.

The man in the sport coat fished an envelope from an inside pocket.

Cole flew into a rage and waved his arms. "No, you can't give me that. That letter isn't for me. Stay back! You hear me?"

The man in the jacket held out both hands. "Cole, it's not what you think."

With his heart pounded against his chest, he pointed a finger at the stranger. "You can't be here. You have to go!"

Kip arrived beside him. "Where's Butch?"

Neither answered. The taller man held out the envelope.

Kip looked at Cole, then at the paper, before

reaching with his good hand to take the parchment.

"We were never here," the man said.

As the strangers turned to walk away, Cole trotted to catch up with the mysterious individuals. Despite his earlier protests, he wanted to know more. "Wait. What's in the letter? Is my brother alive?"

Both men stopped. The taller man removed his sunglasses. "I don't know. What I *do* know is he is the toughest, meanest asshole on the face of this earth I've *ever* had the privilege of knowing. I have zero proof, but I can't help but think he's still with us."

The admission caused Cole to shake his head, as if recovering from a body blow. He couldn't form more words.

The stranger replaced his shades. "You might find your answer from what's in your hand."

He watched the two men walk toward a black SUV. They hopped inside and drove off, leaving him with more questions and no answers. Over the past few years, Cole met some of Butch's military colleagues. Their presence amazed—they embodied the antidote to self-doubt and fear.

The two grieving friends shared a look.

Cole snatched the envelope from Kip's grasp and opened the flap. *The hell? Nothing's inside*.

"Why did he say to look at it?" Kip asked.

Cole reexamined the front. Affixed to the upper-right corner was an imprint. Something in his mind clicked. *He went home*. He handed the envelope to Kip. "I know where you use those stamps."

Kip's eyebrows furled. "So?"

"So..." Cole started with a newfound coldness to his voice. "I know where my brother is."

Chapter 12

Cole Haufner's residence

Cole's modest three-bedroom home stood testament to his and Claire's desire to live a simple life and not get caught up in the money and fame of the sport that glamorized his unique skill. In an attempt to keep news trucks and gawkers at bay, police cruisers sat at either end of the street running through the mature neighborhood. To a point. Nearby homeowners suddenly had many "friends and family" over to visit.

Claire's family arrived at his house after the funeral, where catered food sat uneaten on the kitchen counter. His wife's possessions needed sorting and decisions on what to do with them had to be made. Muted conversations remained short and to the point. Periodic episodes of weeping filtered from outlying rooms. Sadness permeated every inch of the home.

Still dressed in his dark suit and tie, Cole stood in the backyard, staring at the spare tire turned sandbox he'd built for his son. A tiny shovel and plastic dump truck sat idle, ready to be pressed into use for the boy's next project. He blinked back tears, aching to brush the rocky grit from his son's hair one more time. Standing outside allowed him to avoid being in the same room as Claire's sister and her cousins, while they talked about his wife's jewelry and clothes. Thankfully, Tisha had short, brown hair and stood several inches shorter than Claire. Any physical reminder of his wife would have made his sister-in-law's presence too difficult to endure.

The sliding glass door to the kitchen opened. Someone approached from behind. Cole glanced back to see his father-in-law, Peter. "Hey," he whispered.

The sixty-year-old chief executive of a large computer company held out a glass of iced tea. The two men stood the same height, Peter with side-parted, graying hair. He looked every bit the part of a business leader.

Cole nodded then grabbed the drink. He turned back to the sandbox. He feared his father-in-law could somehow see the guilt in his eyes.

Peter cleared his throat. "Mind if I ask who those two men were at the ceremony?"

"Honestly, I don't know." Cole sighed. "Sounded like the guy in the jacket knows my brother." His head dropped. "He didn't say much other than he thinks Butch is still alive."

"Sorry to hear. I didn't realize his absence was that serious."

Cole stared at his hands. "For him to miss today, something must be really wrong." The envelope held the key to his brother's location, but he didn't feel compelled to share his guess work with Peter.

The conversation stalled.

Bending over, he picked up the tiny, plastic shovel. He brushed off grains of sand clinging to the toy.

"We're all lucky, you know?" Peter said. "We all know how much you love Claire and Max. You're a great dad and husband. Not everyone can say that about a son-in-law."

Cole's throat tightened. That Peter thought highly of him only inspired more guilt. He remained convinced he failed, somehow, in protecting his family. The feeling of loss and pain intensified, and he began to cry, tears dropping onto Max's tool. "They call me the greatest fighter ever... I didn't keep them safe."

Peter grabbed him by the shoulders. "No, wait, Cole. I can't have you saying things like that. You weren't even there."

The words bounced off of him. "I should have taken them home." Cole blinked away the tears. "Maybe they'd still be with us. I should have been in the truck with them."

Peter's eyebrows furled. "Cole, you will *always* be a part of this family. I don't think you realize how devastated everyone would be if we lost all three of you in that crash."

"I died, too." Cole wiped the mucus from his nostrils. "I died with them."

Peter shook him. "I won't have that. You hear me? I won't have that kind of talk."

As his father-in-law released his strong grip, a calm took over Cole's body. The mental anguish faded, replaced by another sensation. Clarity filled his thoughts, and for the first time in twenty-six years, he truly understood his brother. Like Butch, he needed a mission.

Peter leaned close to connect gazes. "You'll always be my son, Cole. We will always be a family."

"Yeah." Cole nodded. "We will." Walking into the house, he placed the tiny shovel on the kitchen counter. He heard Tisha upstairs in a side bedroom, talking in a hushed tone. He took the stairs and headed for the master bedroom. On the bed, items lay scattered on top of the quilt: pictures, dresses, and jewelry.

Cole lifted a photo showing Claire holding up her shirt, exposing her toned stomach with Cole kneeling before her. He kissed her tummy with her hand on top of his short, spiked hair. A friend had taken the picture the day the two discovered she was pregnant with Max. A smile crossed his lips. He didn't bother to gaze in the direction of the approaching footsteps from the hallway.

Tisha, accompanied by one of her female cousins, stopped short in the doorway. "Oh, sorry. I didn't know you were in here. We'll come back."

Still grinning, Cole waved the framed picture. "I'm keeping this."

The two young women looked at each other and then back at him. "Oh, sure, Cole," Tisha said. "I hope you don't think I was taking all of this."

He kept his gaze on the photo. "I don't need anything else. Take the rest." An uncomfortable ten-second silence fell across the room.

"We can talk later." Tisha grabbed her cousin's arm and left.

Cole hardly noticed their departure. He scanned the room, but nothing else caught his eye. He walked into the closet and pulled a big duffel bag from the top shelf. Without further thought, he grabbed clothes from dresser drawers and tossed them inside. He didn't pause to see if anything matched or whether any underwear made it into the mix. When the duffel reached near capacity, he remembered an important item necessary for overseas travel.

In the guest bedroom that doubled as an office,

Cole reached into the filing cabinet's bottom drawer for a small, fireproof box. He plopped it on the desk. Lifting the lid, he found birth certificates, a few legal documents, and what he hoped to find—his passport.

"What are you doing?" Kip's voice boomed from the doorway.

Cole waved the government-issued booklet, bumping past his friend back to the master bedroom, leaving Kip to follow.

"I'm asking you a serious question. What the hell is going on?"

"Packing." He stuffed the travel document into the duffel bag before heading to the bathroom for toiletries.

Kip pulled at his arm. "Peter and Tisha are worried about you and, frankly, so am I."

Cole escaped his friend's grasp then yanked open cabinet drawers. "When did you get here?"

"Where do you think you're going?"

"Dammit. Man, my good toothbrush is back at your house," he groused.

Kip leaned against the doorframe. "Ya' can't leave now."

Cole stopped what he was doing and looked at his friend. Kip finally had his attention. "Why not?"

"We have to settle a ton of crap."

Cole shrugged. "Like what?"

"She's named in most of the business legal documents. Your home mortgage needs to be changed. The insurance policy and bank accounts have to be settled, too."

Straightening, Cole rolled his eyes. "You're my lawyer. You do it."

"You have to be here to sign a lot of paperwork."

Cole put a hand on Kip's shoulder. "I. Don't. Care." He pushed past with a handful of toiletries to add to the duffel. After zipping shut the bag, he exchanged his funeral clothes for sweatpants and a T-shirt.

Kip rubbed his forehead with his functioning left hand. "Can I ask where you're going?"

Though Cole cared deeply for Kip, he couldn't spare any more emotion for his best friend. "I know where Butch is. He's somewhere in *Dandong*. I have to go."

"What? *You're* traveling to China to find him? Not the CIA, not military intelligence, but, somehow, a guy with zero experience in this sort of operation can find a missing Delta operator. Don't you think the best of the best are already working the problem?"

He's my flesh and blood. I have to find him. "No one knows that area like I do."

Kip shook his head. "You think Butch would want this?"

Cole chuckled. "We both know the answer to that." He sat on the edge of the bed and tied his sneakers.

"Please, Cole. We're all hurting and losing you would make the situation so much worse. Can't you give me at least forty-eight hours?"

Cole stood then grabbed the handle of the suitcase. He locked gazes with Kip. "Take the money from the fight and pay off the house. Use the rest of the cash for whatever Claire's family needs. Peter won't take the offer. Check with Tisha."

Kip placed a firm hand against Cole's chest. "What about the accident? That asshole who hit us deserves to fry. What if a trial is scheduled?"

Cole imagined facing the driver who killed his family. His throat tightened, and his hands trembled. "A trial will never happen," he sneered.

"What do you mean?" Kip whispered.

"If I return, the case will *never* reach the court."

Chapter 13

Dandong, China

Despite the delicious smells of fresh-cooked noodles wafting into the upstairs apartment from the restaurant on the first floor, Park Chul-Moo, North Korea's Fifth Reconnaissance Special Forces unit commander, could not think of eating. His safe house—a sparsely furnished, one-bedroom apartment—exuded comfort unattainable by most of his countrymen. As one of North Korea's most successful operators, he lived a life of luxury offered only to those held most dear by the Great Leader—as long as he produced results.

The second-floor dwelling occupied a corner position inside a five-story building on a small side road just off *Jinshan* Street, a six-lane thoroughfare running parallel to the *Yalu* River. Less than one mile away, the Sino-Korean Friendship Bridge created a direct physical link between two countries by running a daily train from *Dandong*, China, to *Sinuiji*, North Korea. A simple matter of acquiring forged travel papers and buying a ticket to cross back over to home soil existed for Park. Without the case stolen from him at the dock, he would likely face a firing squad for failing the mission.

He glanced at the only other remaining member of

his five-man elite squad, Park Soon. The shorter, thirty-year-old team sniper appeared unfazed by the events leading up to the pair's escape from the harbor, his grit and determination never in question. Though not related, both men shared the same surname, giving them a sense of additional loyalty to one another.

Commander Park knew an American now possessed the device—he'd seen one of their number escape from the dock. He marveled at how the soldiers aggressively engaged his team and their cleverness displayed during battle. Though Park was a highly intelligent man, his life-long indoctrination included the image of American fighters in the evil, mythical terms defined by North Korea's government. In essence, the North Korean soldier was far superior to any other military man in the world. The Americans had simply been lucky. Surely, his unit was a more skilled fighting force. Even his Dear Leader, a living god, had told him so, and that fact was all Park needed to know.

At a creaking noise from the hallway, both men readied for confrontation. The North Korean sniper drew his service knife and crept off to one side of the doorjamb. Park hoisted the American rifle he'd taken from a dead U.S. soldier. Should he need to shoot an intruder, the weapon's long suppressor afforded him a greater sense of security. He slid to flank his subordinate then nodded. The sniper tapped the blade against the door twice. In response to the challenge, two raps followed by a slight pause then a third.

Park took over the lead position and cracked open the door just enough to identify his contact, an ex-CIA agent named Barrett Jennings. After visual conformation, he stuck his head out into the hallway to ensure the man was alone. With no visible threats seen, the North Korean agent grabbed the man's shirt and whisked him inside.

The pudgy American with graying, thinning hair dropped two plastic bags on the simple wooden table in the middle of the room. The man in his fifties withdrew bottles of water and small food containers. "I can get more if you need," he said in accented Korean.

Park waved Jennings toward a wooden stool. After the American sat, he gazed at his subordinate then tilted his head toward the supplies.

The sniper stepped to the table and dove into the containers of food.

Park leveled the rifle on Jennings, who sat off to one side in an old wooden chair. He knew better than to trust the traitorous ex-CIA man, and he planned to wait a full ten minutes after the sniper ate to determine if the rations were poisoned. The American had plenty of reasons to kill him and his partner—his earlier assistance notwithstanding.

Jennings chuckled. "After years of working together, why would I assassinate you now? I believed you when you said this was the last time I was required to assist your government."

"I haven't lived this long by being careless," Park replied.

Jennings shrugged. "No doubt." He cleared his throat. "My men swept the area and cleared the evidence of the struggle. The dead are hidden in a derelict storage container. Your boat took on too much water and could not be moved. We scuttled your ship in place. I'm certain the dock workers will eventually discover sufficient reason to alert the authorities."

Park narrowed his gaze. He loathed this toad of a man, but the loss of the device necessitated reliance on him to continue the mission. The North Korean despised anyone who was so easily and willingly corrupted into betraying his own country. "What of the case?"

Jennings threw up his hands. "I don't recall stealing anything and trying to escape back to North Korean waters. Whatever is in that box is *your* headache."

Park raised the rifle in his hands. "Well, I suppose I have no further use for you."

The ex-CIA man's jaw dropped. "You still have need of me. I'm confident of my team's ability to locate the soldier and the package."

"I would like to meet this *team* of yours." Park spat.

"Any contact with people outside this room could jeopardize your mission. The Chinese still do not know you are here," Jennings blurted.

Sensing he'd put the American back in his place, Park switched gears. "How does your *team* propose to solve my problem?"

Barrett leaned forward in his chair. "As you may or may not know, China's military has a very sophisticated cyber-warfare team called PLA Unit 61398. Several other groups exist, such as Unit 61486, but the first is crucial to your mission. I am told 61398 numbers over one hundred officers, many of them educated in the West at the most technical universities. This department also uses proxy hackers—patriotic individuals who can be held at arm's length—to perform very specific, and sometimes dangerous, electronic work. Chinese officials retain deniability but reap the benefits of what these lone-wolf agents accomplish. I have a source, one of these hackers, who I trust completely. They have extensive access to nearly all of the PLA's technological arsenal."

For a brief moment, Park mulled over this information. "How is this access leveraged to my favor?"

Barrett sat straighter in his chair. "For instance, the PLA has sophisticated facial-recognition software that can be matched with nearly every security camera posted in and around *Dandong*. This program can be used to filter for Caucasian males. Purchases of computers and cell phones can be traced through electronic cash registers. Information gleaned using this method is vital because the Americans will need to establish communication back to their headquarters. We can examine cash withdrawals from banks, wire transfers, and monitor inbound electronic traffic from nearly every other country. A whole group monitors known message boards, self-destructing text messaging sites, and obscure email servers. They can do much more, things far beyond my knowledge."

Park grunted, impressed with China's reach but hesitant to acknowledge Barret's claims.

"With your permission, I would also like to use some of our human intelligence capabilities. Many North Korean sympathizers live in this city such as waitresses, taxi drivers, hospital workers, and many others who can be on the lookout for Americans. Of course, I wouldn't speak of you or your mission."

Deep in thought, Park rubbed his chin. His mission success required both human and electronic surveillance. Once the foreign device was in the hands of the Great Leader, North Korea no longer needed nuclear weapons. The Americans would bend over backward in concessions for denuclearization. Then, while his country enjoyed the fruits of a negotiated peace, the United States and her allies would meet their final doom without a single shot fired.

Park turned his gaze directly at Barrett. "Deploy your assets. But I do not have to warn you what will happen if my mission or presence is leaked to anyone. If I think for a moment you have betrayed me, I guarantee you will wish I had only killed you."

Chapter 14

Barrett understood Park's threat. His stomach churned. A twenty-year-old blunder haunted him. Over the past two decades, the former CIA field agent learned to twist his memories into justified resentment toward his former employer and erase his personal involvement in what was considered one of the agency's biggest failures no one ever heard of.

Not far from this barren apartment, years before, he was on his first field assignment in China tasked with babysitting a prominent scientist. He chafed with superiors when ordered to chaperone an egghead from America. His wealthy, East-Coast upbringing, replete with expensive boarding schools and chauffeured limousines, instilled the sense of entitlement to pick and choose his work duties. The sad truth was his father, a recipient of a family-owned railroad company, had bought the post for his son by employing connections and political donations.

Soon after a thirty-year-old Barrett completed training and embarked on his first overseas posting, he lost his mother and father due to a plane crash. What looked to be an enormous financial transfer of wealth to their only son blossomed into a scandal that splashed headlines. Ongoing investigations into Barrett's father, and his company, showed massive fraud. The financials revealed multiple attempts to cover up the details. He watched with horror as his family legacy was publicly dragged through the mud. Worse still, the money disappeared. Marooned, Barrett could no longer count on his father or family name for protection. He was ill prepared for the China mission.

Park handed the American rifle to his subordinate. "If he does anything foolish, kill him."

Cradling the weapon, the sniper showed a tiny smile at the corner of his lips.

As Park ate, Barrett hoped the agent's mood would improve. The commander's hate-filled eyes reminded him of another North Korean agent who'd saved his life from a CIA assassin's bullet. He'd never been allowed to forget the favor, one brought on by his failure to protect the American scientist and his former employer looking to eliminate the man responsible. He lived like a caged animal in China under the watchful eye and protection of the Hermit State—all because he'd allowed one of the greatest scientific minds of the twentieth century to be kidnapped twenty years ago by the North Korean regime.

Despite personal shortcomings, Barrett displayed extraordinary survival instincts. He still lived because the North Korean commander found him useful and discreet. He lacked knowledge of the details of Park's mission but sensed the stakes were high. Hundreds of shell casings, three dead Americans, and the shot-up boat were evidence. If he played his cards right, he could crawl from under the thumb of North Korea and escape to the Virgin Islands. The money promised for this mission was enough to establish a quiet setup where he could live his life in obscurity. America's short memory and multiple changes in administrations played to his favor where the possibility existed in creating a new life without further fear of dying at the hand of another hired killer. That is, of course, if he somehow rid himself of these two, filthy mongrels and their stolen device.

In an effort to bleed the nervous energy pulsing inside him, Barrett rubbed his hands together. He stole glances at the man wielding the American rifle. He dared not make any sudden moves. Barrett was confident the commando needed little reason to shoot him. His rising anxiety craved some indication he would be allowed to walk out of the tiny apartment. "Are we still in agreement with the terms?"

Park's eyes narrowed. He drained the last of his water bottle then tossed aside the plastic. "The money will be in the account when you locate the American and the case. Where you go after my mission is completed is not my superior's concern. You will not be followed."

Barrett didn't believe him but had little choice but to play the part of the fool. He smiled. "Wonderful. I will get to work immediately."

"See that you do. Or, I will make sure your little secret is exposed. The Jennings name will again sit at the top of your propaganda news channels. I'm sure the CIA would *not* fail a second time."

"Right," Barrett mumbled. He needed no additional reminder this situation was do-or-die.

Chapter 15

Barrett parked his rented car outside a mid-rise apartment building and made his way through the rear entrance. His own car, riddled with bullet holes and leaking various fluids, sat in a scrap yard, awaiting complete destruction by a crushing machine. He didn't know if the Chinese were aware of the battle at the docks. Swift action by the authorities was surely imminent. The moment his name escaped the lips of someone under enhanced interrogation by internal security, his life was forfeit.

Climbing the five flights of steps to his apartment, he swallowed the bile rising in his throat. He cracked open the stairwell door then inspected the narrow hallway for a police presence. Seeing the corridor empty, he crept past the first two apartments before coming to his own. Inserting a key, he turned the lock tumblers. He fought the desire to run then swung open the door. Seeing only the living room furniture, he let out a deep sigh and quickly entered.

The modest, two-bedroom unit sat on the top floor of the five-year-old building. The monthly electric bill was significantly higher than any normal family's usage, but the Chinese authorities already knew the truth. Situated in the second bedroom, a powerful computer server hummed inside a water-cooled rack. The PLA's computer warfare division gifted the system to an extraordinarily talented hacker who was a proxy to the government's own team.

Barrett walked directly toward the back bedroom. The door was open, and he saw a familiar figure sitting at the sprawling operations desk. Four, large monitors displayed all types of data. He entered the cramped room and patted the hacker's shoulder.

The nineteen-year-old woman spun in her chair to regard him.

Her bobbed, black hair did little to accent her soft, feminine features. She wore a pair of thick, black eyeglasses that almost swallowed her face. Despite initial impressions of her looks, she wasn't completely unattractive. A little sunlight, a different haircut, and some makeup would do wonders for her appearance. But, she rarely ventured out. Her line of work created a security issue requiring discretion in public. She was also Barrett's primary means of income. He could ill-afford young suitors drawing her away from the computer. "Anything I need to be aware of, Lilly?"

"Nothing yet." She pushed up the oversized glasses on her nose.

Lilly was known to fiddle with them whenever she was nervous.

"I created a loop of clean security footage from the harbor and erased the original. But, I can do nothing about the sunken boat."

Barrett knew no one could do a damned thing about a North Korean vessel resting at the bottom of the river. "Any cell traffic?"

"All normal. I've adjusted for full filtering of anything outbound to the U.S., as well as their foreign military bases. I also have access to one of their key satellites and haven't seen anything unusual."

"Facial recognition?" he asked.

"A few partials pinged but turned out negative."

Lilly's short, cold responses concerned him. "What's wrong? You seem worried."

Lilly adjusted her glasses. "Do you think they will leave us alone? I mean, if we can find the American."

Barrett patted her hands. "Yes, I have complete confidence they will. Whatever Park is looking for is worth risking North Korea's relationship with China. He offered a great deal of money to find the case."

Her eyes bulged. "What did they steal? Is nuclear material inside?"

He pulled at his lip. "I don't know. Park wouldn't tell me. I'm certainly not asking him."

Lilly trembled. Her shoulders slumped.

Don't freak out. Not now. He dropped to one knee and put his hands on her arms. "We *will* find what Park needs. Then we will leave, together. I promise."

She nodded, her reddened eyes blinking back tears.

Barrett had been promising to take her away from this wretched place since she was seven years old.

Lilly's mother suffered a sexual assault by a gang of criminals, resulting in the birth of a daughter. Despite the circumstances surrounding the pregnancy, the stigma of living as an unwed mother made her a societal outcast.

He met her mom a year after Lilly was born, and he found a kinship in their shared experience of loneliness and feelings of abandonment.

In ill health since the attack, Lilly's mother died three years later.

He took on the task of raising the little girl, but his

efforts did not follow the traditional life of a normal child. He kept her hidden from society, and he taught her English and other useful tradecraft. By her eighth birthday, Lilly mastered multiple programming languages and navigated past all but the most robust security firewalls with ease. She experienced the world from the safety of a keyboard. Barrett quickly determined he could earn a living from her talent in financial markets and providing useful research espionage pulled from American companies. He'd discovered a way out of his dismal existence.

The two developed a symbiotic relationship—Lilly seeing him as a parental figure, and Barrett relying on her for income. But, for the first time, he found himself caring for someone besides himself. Now, under the threat of death from the North Korean agents, they clung tighter to one another in the hope of escaping to a better life.

Barrett gazed into her watering eyes. "Can you find out what they stole?"

She dabbed at tears and sniffed. "I'll try."

He smiled. "That's my girl." If Lilly couldn't locate the American soldier, then Barrett needed leverage to keep them alive. What was in the case? Did the contents pose an immediate proximity risk? With North Korea negotiating denuclearization with the U.S., a weapon of mass destruction appeared less likely. If not a bomb, then what? Barrett required more information than he currently possessed. His life might very well rest in the hands of a scared teenager.

Chapter 16

Daban Bridge underpass, Shendan Line
2010 Hour

Ron "Hammer" Thompson watched the last rays of sunlight fade along the western horizon. He'd lost sight of his team leader sixteen hours earlier. Unable to raise Butch on the radio, he escaped inland. Still in contact with Joint Special Operations Command back at the Pentagon, Thompson received information from real-time satellite feeds showing Butch moving north with the package toward the city of *Dandong*.

His team leader eluded a North Korean checkpoint and headed into the city limits on a bicycle. The overhead feed lost visual of the Delta man in the clutter of rush-hour traffic. His satellite-fed, encrypted navigation unit downloaded Butch's last known location. Thompson thanked God his teammate still lived, but he remained dubious. He was an east Texas boy in a foreign country with no significant language skills appropriate to his current location. He was also armed to the teeth and, if captured, would make an exciting feature story on the state-run news.

After a desperate attempt to locate his teammate, Thompson expertly managed his escape and evasion. He found a train with its engine running. Just as morning light appeared, he'd found a spot beneath a coal car and wedged himself just above the greasy wheels. Eventually, the long line of cargo haulers crawled forward. As the train crossed a bridge on the southwestern side of *Dandong*, he jumped into the water below—a highly risky move.

The battery-level indicator showed thirty percent remaining on his satellite radio. At regular intervals, he activated the device for a quick update and comms check before powering off. The Intel staff back in the States scrambled to determine the team leader's next course of action. They calculated a seventy percent chance he'd make contact with the Buddhists who raised him. Tucked underneath the trusses of the railroad bridge since noon, Thompson spent the daylight hours considering his next course of action.

With darkness now upon him, he opened a topographical area map on his hand-held GPS unit. Satellite imagery showed a distance of three miles between his position and the *Dandong* Airport. The airplanes didn't interest him but rather something commonly found in the remote parking lots. Still wearing his combat gear and night vision, Thompson left his hide spot and traveled west, on foot, through the farmland in total darkness. The crops and oppressive humidity slowed his progress, but he eventually arrived at the outskirts of the airport without incident.

Hunkered in a ditch, Thompson observed a trickle of cars coming and going along the airport feeder road. Late in the evening, operations centered mainly around maintenance and security crews. Without any knowledge regarding the shift change hours, he avoided the employee lot. The long-term parking for travelers posed the best opportunity to secure transportation.

Staying outside the ring of lights, he circled to the back corner. He didn't identify any security cameras or other signs of electronic surveillance.

His gaze settled on an aged sedan parked in the last row of the lot. He crept to the edge of light glowing from a tall lamppost. One last scan through his night vision revealed no human activity. After two quick breaths, he broke cover and scampered to the driver's side of the car. A peek through the window revealed a cheap interior with no navigation system and no telltale signs of an alarm.

Thompson dropped to one knee and, sliding his hand into his leg pocket, removed a lock-pick gun. After one last look around, he inserted the metallic arm deep into the door mechanism and sprung the tumbler. Staying low, he opened the door and crawled into the driver's seat. After wrestling his rifle and backpack into the passenger foot well, he defeated the ignition system. Likely a symptom of the car's advanced age, the sedan proved difficult to start. A nerve-wracking sixty seconds passed before the engine coughed to life. When the gas-level indicator showed the tank half full, he breathed a sigh of relief. He estimated total elapsed time at two minutes to secure the ride. *Not my record, but it'll do.*

Thompson pushed his seat as far back as the rail allowed. Stuffing a six-foot two-inch athlete with a bodybuilder physique into an economy car invited additional scrutiny from anyone gazing at the spectacle. Thompson flipped on his communication unit and established a secure line back to JSOC. "This is Two. I have personal transport and need best method to reach objective." Several seconds passed.

"Understood. Wait one for details."

An excruciating ten seconds elapsed before the digitized voice came through his earpiece. "Waypoints downloaded. Still no word on our friend. Check in upon arrival."

Thompson acknowledged and closed down his comms. He fired up the GPS unit and saw a red line tracing north. The crooked line ended with a small blinking indicator near the *Wulong* Mountains. No one knew for sure Butch's ultimate destination, but the odds favored Haufner reconnecting with his childhood home. Thompson's arrival at the Temple was a long shot in reuniting with his Delta teammate. No other viable options existed. He adjusted the rearview mirror then stepped on the gas pedal.

Chapter 17

Mituo Temple

Butch Haufner woke with a startle. Instinctively, he reached for his pistol in a drop-down holster on his right leg. His hand slapped against his empty thigh. The missing weapon caused him to fully wake, an adrenaline surge coursing through his veins. An immediate search for his assault-vest knife proved fruitless. Then he remembered where he was and how he'd arrived here.

Noise from the basement door opening preceded Butch's view of a robed monk walking down the five steps from the upper level of the living quarters.

"*Biao di*—cousin," Shen said.

Butch sat at the edge of the bed, taking in slow breaths to calm his pounding heart. "What time is it? Where's my equipment?"

Shen motioned with a hand toward one side of the small room.

Butch slanted his gaze to his combat gear lying in the corner. His rifle rested against the case. He tilted back his head then let out an audible sigh.

"The clock reads five a.m.," Shen answered the first question.

Collecting his thoughts, Butch shook his head. "Morning meditation?"

"As I recall, you were not keen to perform your waking duties at the Temple."

He pushed his hands toward the ceiling and slowly arched his back. "On that, you and I are in full agreement."

"Tea and food are upstairs."

Butch regarded his cousin, sorry to have placed him in jeopardy because of his mission needs. "Thank you for accepting me into your home. I know my presence places you in danger. I hope you will forgive me."

"You know all too well my beliefs do not allow me to turn away anyone in need." Shen stepped closer. "For your own safety, you cannot stay for much longer. I assume your journey does not end here?"

"No, *biao di*, my mission is far from over, and my visit to the Temple is an unexpected occurrence. Though, I do not regret the opportunity to see you."

Shen gave a slight nod. "Life is full of surprises. I am happy you are here."

Butch grunted. *You have no idea the surprises.* "Forgive me for not asking sooner. How is Master Li?"

"He is as well as to be expected."

What's wrong? Is he okay? "What do you mean?"

"Much has happened since you left. 14K members caused trouble for one of our younger monks." Shen's gaze drifted toward the floor. "Master Li intervened but was injured when one of the ruffians fired a gun."

"14K? Is *Sifu* well?" He knew of the criminal organization. They operated mainly in southern China and Hong Kong. Extortion, bribery, gambling, and prostitution were their primary sources of income. Their presence this far north appeared odd.

Shen's demeanor remained calm and no wrinkles marked his forehead. "He has recovered, yes, but still experiences daily pain in his leg where the bullet struck."

Admittedly, Butch's rocky relationship with his uncle stemmed from his own anger issues. Despite their often strained relationship, he owed Master Li a great debt for shaping him into the man he'd become. For now, knowledge of the attack provided fuel to the fire that constantly burned under the surface. "I wish I could have been there to help."

"Your path followed another course. Now, you have other pressing needs."

Butch nodded. Establishing communications with JSOC remained his top priority. Only then could he make his escape from China, case in hand. With his radio shot to pieces, he possessed no means of reaching command. In addition, the longer he stayed, the greater the risk for unwanted attention toward his cousin from both Chinese investigators and the North Korean agents. The contents of the case were worth killing anyone in close proximity to the device, and a few Buddhist monks didn't change that reality. The question remained how to move about the city without being identified. Looking at Shen's clothing, Butch experienced a flash of brilliance. He was sure of his next move. "Do you have an extra set of robes I may wear?"

"You wish to rejoin with your childhood brothers?"

Butch looked over at the case then back at his cousin. "Friends of mine have died to protect that object and, if it is not returned to a safe place, millions more might perish."

Shen's eyebrows rose. "I am indeed sorry for your loss. Are we in immediate danger?"

He'd drawn his cousin into a deadly association. The enormous implications of mission failure provided temporary comfort over his regret of placing family in peril. "The original purpose of the device is to help mankind. As long as I maintain possession, no harm will follow. But, as with all human inventions, some would employ the contents for evil intent."

"You wish to remain hidden from these men?"

Butch straightened his spine. "Many innocent lives depend on my success."

Shen grunted. "Then, yes, I have an extra set of robes." He placed a hand on Butch's shoulder and smiled. "And, a razor or two."

Chapter 18

Dandong, China

With a freshly shaved pate and wearing the traditional yellow robes of a Buddhist monk, the Delta operator strode alongside his similar-appearing cousin. Having lived the life of a holy man for over a decade, Butch required no additional thought to maintain the disguise. He hunched his shoulders and kept his chin low to minimize exposure to overhead security cameras. Thumbing through a strand of prayer beads, he avoided gazing too long at any one person. The eyes were always the first to betray a man's true identity.

The morning commuters crowded the city sidewalks. Men and women acknowledged the pair with a slight bow of their heads. Shen's weekly pilgrimage along this same route provided familiarity to the daily pedestrians and shop keepers.

His cousin explained he often met with one of the females at the *Yuanbao* Library who frequented the Temple. Shen's growing friendship with the woman, a widow in her early sixties, required no additional reason to visit her. He made a point to check on her once a week at her part-time job and believed she would welcome meeting another monk who practiced with him.

For Butch, the ultimate goal was gaining access to

the library's public computers. He needed to contact JSOC. If his communication became compromised, any trace would lead authorities to the library—a dead-end for investigators. Butch thought the plan's simplicity and high probability of success warranted the attempt to reach command. An uneventful, twenty-minute stroll ended in the lobby of the two-story building. The library looked empty.

A woman, with short, gray hair, and glasses appearing too small for her weathered face, occupied a long desk. Upon seeing Shen, she broke into a wide smile. She hurried around the furniture and bowed respectfully before taking Shen's hands in hers. "Good morning, brother Li. I have looked forward to seeing you today."

Butch guessed she couldn't be five feet tall.

"Good morning to you, sister Cheng," Shen replied. "How have you been?"

"Thanks to your guidance, my meditation continues to provide for me."

"Your improved internal harmony is wonderful to hear." He turned to Butch. "Let me introduce brother Yao. He is visiting from the *Wulong* Temple."

The older woman turned to Butch and bowed. "A profound honor to meet you, brother Yao."

Butch tilted his head. "And you, sister. Brother Li has spoken many kind things of you. I have been looking forward to meeting such a devout follower." His gaze flicked to his cousin. He understood the conflict Shao faced regarding his spoken lie to the woman.

She gazed at Shen, a warm smile spreading across her face.

Butch found the transition to Buddhist monk much easier than he'd expected. The mannerisms of conversation, and the respect shown by the older Chinese, were both familiar and welcome. The tableau suited his needs. Her happiness was the emotion he hoped to exploit.

Shen explained brother Yao required the use of a computer to communicate with fellow monks and hoped she would allow him access to expedite electronic messaging. She was more than happy to assist her new guest and escorted Butch to an older computer deep in the library.

He suffered through a painfully long description on how to use the Internet. He counted silently to distract himself and soothe his frayed nerves. She frequently backtracked through instructions while remembering useless tidbits of information. Mercifully, she finally relinquished control.

Shen escorted her to the front desk.

Making sure he was alone, Butch navigated through a series of dead-drop servers before reaching his final destination at a small university in Greenland. From that location, he connected to a bulletin board used by men seeking other men for casual sex. The electronic address was an effective means for emergency communication. Due to the nature of the discussion topics, government agents in the Muslim and Asian communities eschewed monitoring this type of forum.

Butch created a new thread then typed his coded message. He wrote that he was happily married but sought something more than just the events of his humdrum life. He was an "inexperienced submissive" and wanted someone to guide him. Although eager to get started, he required extreme discretion. He ended the discussion stating, due to his job, he required more time than usual to answer anyone who might show interest. He used the signature appellation "lonely but anxious." "Happily married" meant he was uninjured and the mission still in progress. "Lonely" signified he was on his own.

He sent the message then logged off. He scrubbed his entire history chain then opened a generic email site. After entering a user address he knew from memory, he wrote an innocuous message to a fellow *Shaolin* Buddhist. JSOC's ISA intelligence staff maintained the account through an Internet café in St. Louis. All traffic sent to this particular recipient signaled the Pentagon Black Hats to check all of the predetermined forum sites for a coded message.

Satisfied with his encoded communication, Butch signed off but left the email history intact in case anyone reviewed his activity. He was well aware just how deeply the Chinese government kept track of the population's cyber adventures. He couldn't risk waiting here for a reply. If the message triggered scrutiny from the cyber teams, the data trail signaled the library as ground zero for the PLA. *Time to move.*

Chapter 19

Mituo Temple

Butch and his cousin returned to the Temple just before noon. The Delta operator remained on guard, but the journey concluded without incident. Along the way, they spoke little, as would any Buddhist monks out for a stroll. He mulled another plan to enlist friendly forces, but this time he focused inside the borders of China. Two hours west of his position, a CIA Special Activities Division team remained on alert to assist him.

Over a light lunch of rice and fish, Butch delivered his request. "*Biao di*—cousin. I have asked so much of you, but I desire one more favor."

"Yes?"

Butch cleared his throat then set his fork on the table. "In *Shenyang* is a U.S. consulate building. I need a message delivered there. Do you know someone who could perform the task?"

The bald man sat back in his chair. "What about buying one of those throw-away phones?"

He picked up the fork and waved the utensil side to side. "Despite wide opinion, those devices are easily tracked. The consulate is likely heavily monitored, and any electronic message to or from the facility is watched by the PLA's computer teams. That's why I didn't send them a message today from the library."

Shen's eyes widened. "Then whom did you contact?"

"Better that you don't know."

"I suppose that statement is true," Shen conceded then paused. "The distance is greater than two-hundred kilometers from here. Someone from the Temple traveling as far as *Shenyang* and visiting an American facility might raise suspicions."

"Then the message *could* be passed to the Americans?" Butch allowed excitement to creep into his tone.

"We would first need permission."

"Who would—" Butch stopped mid-sentence.

Shen stared at him without saying more.

Ten years had passed since Butch left the *Wulong* Temple. The manner in which he and his brother, Cole, departed was both cruel and heartbreaking. In the middle of one hot summer night, Master Li shook awake the Haufner boys. They were told the Temple was no longer safe for them to remain, and they must immediately return to the United States. Butch approached his twentieth birthday, and Cole was only fifteen. Though the younger rapidly matured physically, he was still a boy. He cried and grasped at Master Li's robes, wailing that he didn't want to leave.

Butch saw something in his uncle's eyes he never witnessed before—fear. The great Master Li was so frightened by something he couldn't hide his concern. Butch employed every ounce of his considerable strength and tore Cole from their uncle. With barely a word, he dragged his younger brother into a waiting car, and the two had been whisked away without a good-bye to their only remaining parental figure. Cruel abandonment now repeated itself. He met his cousin's gaze. "Does another way exist?"

"I'm afraid not, *Biao di.* Only Master Li grants permission to travel that great a distance."

Butch lowered his head. A part of him still loved his uncle, but he never made peace with his anger over the psychological damage Cole suffered. He remained haunted by the cries of his brother from that evening a decade ago.

"Do you want me to talk to Master Li?" Shen offered.

For several seconds, Butch thought. "No. I must risk a meeting with *Sifu.* Only then will he realize how serious the situation is."

Shen nodded. "I understand. If you must leave behind your possessions, I need your assurance the contents of your case will not harm the people visiting the Temple."

He placed both hands on the table. "As I said before, in current form, the device cannot harm anyone. Only a handful of scientists in the world know the invention's true potential. Fewer still possess the knowledge necessary to convert the contents into an object of devastation."

"Who would benefit from such evil?" Shen's eyebrows scrunched together.

"A close neighbor."

Shen gasped. "North Korea? You are running from their agents?"

Butch's stomach clenched. He instantly regretted divulging the information to his cousin. If questioned or interrogated, the less he knew, the safer he remained.

On the other hand, Shen needed to understand the potential danger if the case landed in the hands of the wrong people. He carefully chose his next words. "I fear if the man who created the device is still alive, he might very well be in North Korea. He could be forced to engineer the case into a weapon capable of wiping out an entire continent. The history of Chinese Buddhism would be lost forever."

"Our two paths are now one. If Master Li will not listen to you, he will consider my opinion." Shen stood. "You and I must proceed to the *Wulong* Temple."

Butch nodded. "Immediately."

Chapter 20

Laowu Line Road, Wulong Mountain

A gentle rain subsided, leaving behind oppressive humidity and the dank smell of decaying wood. Water droplets streaked the side windows of the sparsely occupied bus traveling from the *Dandong* city terminal toward its final destination, the *Wulong* Mountain Ticket Office. Seated in the second to last row, Cole Haufner swiped away a drop of sweat on his forehead. The rough edge of the stitches in his left eyebrow reminded him of home.

He'd flown to *Beijing* and taken an eleven-hour bus ride to the southeast port city of *Dandong*. Rather than find a hotel room in the city he once called home, Cole purchased a one-way pass from a tourism outfit running daily shuttles to the public areas of the *Wulong* Mountains eighteen miles northwest of the city.

Before finding his seat, Cole whispered to the driver he wished to exit the bus at the last turnoff prior to the *Wulong* ticket office. A twenty-dollar U.S. bill allayed any of the man's potential misgivings. A handful of people occupied the vehicle including a British couple and a small group Cole supposed were Hong Kong residents on holiday.

Many hours of travel he spent considering what he would say to his uncle, Master Li, when he arrived at the Temple. He practiced his internal monologue, but now as the road turned upward at the base of the mountain, all of his planning went out the proverbial window. Much of his fear and angst that overtook him ten years before, when he was turned out with his brother in the middle of the night, crept back into his jet-lagged mind. His anti-anxiety supply exhausted, Cole wished he brought more of the numbing agent.

Nearing the last turnoff, the bus dropped speed.

His heart pounded against his chest. He caught the gaze of the driver seeking him in the large, internal rearview mirror. He grabbed his travel duffel then lurched down the swaying aisle. Arriving next to the driver, Cole questioned whether his travel was worth the effort. He feared any more disappointment. Then, he remembered why he'd come to China. Now was the time to leave childhood fears behind.

The bus screeched to a halt.

Cole leaned toward the driver. "*Xièxiè*—thank you."

The old man nodded then opened the door.

He stepped off the transporter and onto the last paved section of ground he would see for the next mile.

The bus drove off toward the visitor's section of the mountain.

The final trek to the Temple was his own. With the canvas bag slung over his shoulder, he walked around the sharp right bend in the road for approximately seventy-five feet before coming to a dirt road. He turned and began the uphill, one-mile journey to the *Wulong* Temple. He'd traveled this path, carved through the dense forest, hundreds of times as a child. The smell of rich soil and tallow trees filled his nostrils.

The sun peeked from behind the passing rain clouds. He turned up his face and met the warm rays. Memories flooded his mind as each step brought him closer to his old home.

As he approached the final two-hundred yards of the dirt path, Cole trembled with anticipation. He expected, at any time now, someone from the Temple would show himself. *Will anyone remember me? Will I be turned away?* No matter the reception, he remained certain of his own intent—locating Butch was his only concern.

The trail emptied into a grassy clearing. He walked toward the crest of the hill. When he saw the roofline of a two-story structure, he couldn't stop his hands from shaking. Reaching the elevated position, Cole absorbed the full view of his childhood home. Like many things from youth, building structures didn't retain the same large dimensions preserved in memory. The main Temple appeared smaller than he recalled, but the greens and yellows of the wooden structure remained just as vivid. In a strange way, Cole felt as though he'd come home from a long trip.

Movement caught his attention. He saw a group of young men performing the Monk Pillar Stance—standing on a single, large pole in an almost seated position. An instructor had placed teacups on their heads and watched to make sure the china did not fall off and shatter on the ground. Cole recalled the grueling training with a knowing grin at its difficulty. He pressed forward to within fifty feet of the Temple.

The lead instructor left his trembling students and jogged forward. "*Huānyíng*—welcome."

The yellow-robed monk greeted him in traditional

Chinese language. Cole reverently bowed. "*Zhè shì wǒ de róngxìng*—The honor is mine," he responded in perfect Mandarin. "I come from America to pay my respects to Master Li. I was once a student here."

"Your language is local, that I can hear. May I ask your name?"

"Of course, brother. My name is Cole Haufner. I lived here at the Temple some ten years ago."

The monk's eyes bulged. "Please wait here. I will see if Master Li is available." The young instructor turned and hurried toward one of the attached buildings.

Cole stood, admiring the students as they grimaced and struggled to maintain their positions atop the poles. He, too, had been toughened by this exercise in his youth. He wished the young men strength and fortitude in their enduring quest toward completing their training.

Melancholy gave way to anxiety when the instructor reemerged with a small group of monks in tow. Two, shirtless men wearing yellow, baggy pants projected strength and confidence as they strode toward him. Based on their appearance and bearing, both monks were the senior Kung Fu practitioners. Behind the men, an older male in full yellow robes strode with poise. Cole swallowed the rising lump in his throat. At the proper moment, he dropped to the ground with head bowed.

When the footsteps halted, a single voice spoke, "I am Master Li. Who is this man visiting sacred ground?"

He recognized the familiar voice of the man standing over him, and his throat seized from the flood of childhood memories. He turned up his face, tears streaming from his eyes. "*Jiu jiu…*" The choked word ended in a sob.

Chapter 21

Wulong Temple

Dating back over three hundred years, the main hall represented the oldest of the building components. The cracked, tiled floor showed its scars from the centuries of daily practice of the same Kung Fu movements. Evenly displaced divots served as a guide to proper foot placement when training or displaying one's knowledge during performance. Thick wooden beams supported the clay roof overhead.

At the head of the large, barren room, an ancient chair, older than the Temple itself, sat upon a raised dais. The hand-carved throne displayed its occupant, Master Li Bingwen.

The heavily-robed holy man appeared much older than Cole remembered, the Master's face creased and dotted with wisps of completely grey facial hair. Was *Sifu* already in his mid-sixties? Despite the obvious signs of aging, Master Li's gaze remained as it appeared in his youth—a steely calm.

Cole recovered from his earlier display of emotion, and he followed the group's retreat back into the main hall. The digital age was not foreign to the resident monks, and they knew of his exploits. The Temple buzzed with the return of such a talented man. Tea was served. Master Li presided over an impromptu meeting of the heads of the Temple. Cole, the honored guest, sat closest to the dais, anxious to disclose why he'd come all this way.

Whispering among themselves, six monks sat on velvet rugs.

Master Li held up a hand, and the room fell silent. "*Wai sheng*—nephew—you have returned, no longer a boy. I am aware of your fortunes as a martial artist back in your home country. You appear quite famous."

"Yes, *jiu jiu*. But, I do not desire the attention. I performed only so I might provide for my wife and sick child. I planned on retiring from the sport after one more competition." Cole lowered his head, hiding his tears. Just the mere mention of his family brought the emotional pain to the surface. *Dammit. Get ahold of yourself.*

Master Li reached down and touched Cole's head. "I felt devastated when I learn of what happened. The meaning of such tragedies escapes my knowledge."

Hearing the sadness in his uncle's voice only deepened his grief. Cole nodded, wiping away tears.

The old man took an audible breath. "You have traveled a great distance and returned to your *Wulong* brothers. What do you seek from the Temple?"

Cole took a moment and collected his thoughts. Just as he opened his mouth, he was uncharacteristically interrupted by the lead Kung Fu teacher seated to his right.

"Come live with us again. Your presence honors our home—your home. We would all learn much from you, Cole. I relinquish my role as the head instructor."

The other monks chimed in with a chorus of excited agreement.

Once more, Master Li silenced the room with a raised hand. "Our brother's return has brought great pleasure to the Temple. Upon seeing my nephew, my heart filled with joy. But, let us not think of our own wants. He seeks our counsel. *Wai sheng*, please tell us why you have come so far."

Cole cleared his throat and sought eye contact with the other men before speaking. "As you know, my brother, Butch, was also a member of the Temple." To their nods, he continued, "He is a member of a secret organization in my country's military. He is missing. I believe he is somewhere here in China. Possibly even in *Dandong*."

The monks gave a collective gasp.

Master Li stood. "You are all dismissed to your duties. Go!"

None lingered. The elders moved fast, exiting the great room almost at a run.

Cole—shocked, confused, even angry at his uncle's outburst—could not help but question the holy man. "Why?"

"Your brother's secret will not remain so if you continue talking openly. You might have put him at increased danger."

"He's already in danger." His uncle remained silent, which further infuriated Cole. "He's all that I have left."

Master Li placed his hands behind his back. "You have me. You have this Temple. Have you forgotten?"

As Cole assessed the mild rebuke, he glanced down, an unhealed wound opening. "I've forgotten nothing! You who woke me in the night and cast me off like an unwanted child. I didn't leave of my own will."

He stabbed a finger toward his uncle's chest. "My parents were gone and then *you* abandoned *me*. I loved you like my own father."

At the accusation, Li's lips trembled.

Though he'd nursed the thought for ten years, Cole immediately regretted the words. He couldn't have hurt him any worse. Easing the blow, he softened his voice. "Why, *jiu jiu*? You never told me."

Master Li laid a hand on Cole's arm. "The Temple was no longer safe for you and Butch. I loved you both. You were as my own children. I feared the same evil behavior that took your father reached out for you, too."

The explanation confused Cole. The Chinese authority's investigation into his father's disappearance never bore fruit. The U.S. and German consulates uncovered no additional leads. "But no one knew anything. What evidence pointed toward unseen danger? Did somebody say something to you?"

"More rumors than facts, but I feared powerful influences just the same."

Cole stifled his growing array of questions surrounding his father's disappearance. His main focus involved finding Butch. To help his brother, he knew Master Li could be invaluable if enlisted. But his uncle made his position clear he wanted no part in Cole's risky tactic. He believed the monks were his best chance in determining if his brother was in China and, if true, help pinpoint Butch's location. Such was the reach of the *Shaolin* Buddhists.

Anxious to return to the reason why he'd come to the Temple, and distance himself from his earlier outburst toward Master Li, Cole explained what little he knew about Butch's disappearance. The mysterious caller the day after Claire and Max were killed, the two men appearing at the funeral, and the envelope were his only clues. He sought his uncle's agreement the stamp contained a message regarding Butch's whereabouts.

"If what you say is true, perhaps your CIA and others are looking for him? Professional people?"

Cole cleared his throat. "Maybe. But China lends my government much of the money necessary for our country's economy. The U.S. treads lightly when the situation involves finances. Perhaps forgetting one man is easier than jeopardizing a key global relationship."

Li shook his head. "I'm afraid I don't know anything, *wai sheng*. In a way, our times are even more dangerous than before."

Something was not right. Cole believed in his uncle's love for him, his love for Butch, but instinct told him he would not like Master Li's next words.

"I have enjoyed seeing you again, but I must insist you do not meddle in affairs that involve nation states. You would only hurt your brother's chances of survival."

A robed monk entered from a side door. The portly Buddhist with a small mole at his left eyelid approached Cole.

He ignored the newcomer and glared at his uncle. His face flushed. "You would abandon us? Again?"

"I would protect you. As family."

The newcomer bowed to both men.

Master Li stretched out his arm toward the other monk. "This is brother Shen. He will escort you back to town. Perhaps when the affair concludes, you and I can discuss things further."

Flabbergasted, Cole could not keep the words from

tumbling out, in English this time. "Why did I even think you'd help?"

Master Li bowed his head. "Until we meet again."

Cole swelled with rage, and he switched back to Mandarin. "You won't *ever* see me again."

Chapter 22

Dandong, China

Cole spent the trip toward the city in silence. He and Shen set out on foot, but the driver of an old van stopped along *Wulong* Mountain Road and offered a ride.

The monk thanked the stranger for his generosity before climbing inside.

Despairing and exhausted, he stared out the passenger window, unwilling to meet anyone's gaze, as the clunker banged along the poorly maintained road.

Brother Shen offered no conversation.

Cole was grateful. He feared lashing out at someone, anyone, for all the pained emotions. He recalled Kip's request to not leave so soon after the funeral, and he wished he'd possessed the strength to heed his friend's words. The weight of all the misery settled on his shoulders. The sky grew darker, and the worn shocks and suspension rattle couldn't keep his eyelids from shutting.

When the van came to a stop, Cole bolted upright in his seat.

The driver announced they'd arrived at the city Temple.

He rubbed the sleep from his eyes then glanced out the dirty window to get his bearings. Across the quiet street, a modest, well-groomed garden greeted his vision. To the right side, two, single-story buildings were tucked neatly away from the central grounds. Several graveled paths led to the central feature of the Temple—a large, seated Buddha statue. Cole recalled visiting only once or twice the entire time he lived in the region. *Looks smaller*.

Brother Shen pointed toward the retreat. "This is where I live."

Both men climbed out of the vehicle. Cole slowly arched his back to loosen the kinks. Both jet lag and the time change made their presence felt. The nap provided a short reprieve from his disappointment and pain. He wondered if consciousness was worth the price.

The driver waved to the two men then urged his van back out onto the city street.

Shen held out his hand toward the nearest cottage. "May I offer you tea?"

Cole didn't immediately respond. With his hasty plan crushed, he was unsure of his next move. Eager to rid himself of the Shaolin monks, he knew he couldn't stay. He needed a clean slate—one that included zero reminders of his failure at the Temple. "No thanks. I'm heading into town."

The monk nodded. "Do you need help finding a room?"

Cole shook his head. He then recalled, from youth, a favorite hotel among foreigners. "Is the Crowne Plaza nearby?"

"Very close. Recently remodeled. Appears popular with travelers."

"This way?" Cole pointed east, deeper toward the city center.

"Yes," Shen replied. "May I show you?"

Cole hoisted his bag over his shoulder. "No, thanks. I'll find it." Without further acknowledgement, he turned to leave.

"He loves you like his own son. Please take some measure of comfort from this fact."

Stopping, Cole looked over his shoulder. "How would you know? I don't know you. You know nothing of me!" No sooner had the words left his mouth when a strange look came over Shen's face. Sadness or something else? Cole couldn't decide.

"I have known him my whole life," the monk responded. "True, you and I never met. But I know his heart aches for you."

Cole turned and jabbed a finger at the monk, his exhaustion allowing bitterness into his voice. "After our father disappeared, Butch and I had no choice but to live at the Temple. Then, because of some tingling sensation in the universal life force, he abandoned me, *and* my brother, when we were still kids. Now he turns me away for a second time. I have no more need of this place. *Sifu* and the Temple can kiss my ass." Without waiting for a response, Cole spun and stalked away, grateful the robed man could not see the fresh tears.

Chapter 23

Outskirts of Dandong

Thompson woke with a start. Unwilling to give away his position due to unnecessary movement, he lay motionless. He waited a full minute, straining with all of his senses for signs of a threat, his right hand on the combat knife strapped to his chest rig. Eventually, with no sign of imminent danger, he relaxed. At that moment, he realized his current situation and glanced at his diving watch. *Dammit*. He'd missed his communication check with JSOC. Local time read 1600 hours—two hours past due. Curled up inside a large cement ground pipe, Thompson mentally inventoried the hours after stealing the car at the airport.

After traveling six miles, the old sedan broke down with a final gasp from its aged engine. He placed the transmission into neutral and pushed the vehicle off the road and, covering his tracks, made his way into a field. He continued east. Miles from the *Shaolin* monastery, he grimaced at the rising sun threatening his exposure to a hostile world. The water pipe provided cover, and sleep proved irresistible.

Thompson slowly stretched his legs. Mobilizing cramped muscles caused his joints to ache. He flipped on his satellite comms. As the unit powered up, he noticed what little battery life remained. After the green light flashed, he peered out both ends of the pipe. His surroundings looked like an abandoned construction site. Seeing no human activity, he pressed Send. "Nest, this is Two, how copy?"

In seconds, the digital reply came from Operations Command. "Clear comm, Two. We're dodging strong countermeasures. What's your sitrep?"

"I'm at one-hundred percent. A long way from objective. Can't move for another three hours. No sight of One."

"Understood. The Temple is no longer your objective. A new player entered the equation, and an updated rendezvous package is ready for your download. Can confirm One is operational east of your position, but his exact location is unknown. He hasn't made contact since exfil. An extraction team is mobilized and heading toward the city. SAD unit arriving at 2200 hours. Initiate contact with new player and recovery team. How copy?"

Thompson knew better than asking any questions. The Chinese had few peers when hacking voice transmissions. He'd wait for the data on his GPS unit. "Clear. Standing by for update. Battery low on my device."

"Roger. We'll monitor open-source radio, cell, and data traffic. Water extraction is currently no-go. If compromised, navigate to nearest friendly facility."

Thompson understood if the mission completely fell apart, his best chance for survival meant ditching all his gear and heading to the embassy in *Shenyang*. "Good copy, Nest. Will contact you at 2100 hours."

"Roger. Data coming now. God speed."

With that, Thompson shut down the radio and

waited for the info dump to his GPS monitor. After ten seconds, an icon appeared at the upper-right of the three-inch-square screen. He tapped the blinking cursor and immediately recognized the materializing topographical map of *Dandong*. A red line extended from his current position to a location deep in the city. The destination coordinates marked the rescue team's rendezvous site. Six miles separated him from the anticipated meeting point.

He hit the right arrow on the monitor, and a photo appeared. After a moment, he recognized the face of the man identified as the 'new player' and his grip tightened. The male figure was Butch's brother, Cole— the celebrity, mixed martial arts fighter. *Holy shit.* Thompson traced the dotted line from the picture to a blinking dot on the map marking the fighter's location. He drilled down, looking for landmarks. The cursor landed squarely on a downtown hotel. *What the hell are you doing here?*

Questions swirled in Thompson's mind. Was Cole sent here? Had he come on his own? Did the fighter know his brother was MIA, or, worse, had Butch broken strict rules and confided in Cole regarding the mission? Potential answers to the mystery of the younger Haufner's presence in *Dandong* were many. All represented degrees of further complications at best and new dangers at worst. Butch's little brother created significant new risk factors.

He read the additional data JSOC supplied including a comprehensive background of the American fighter. Cole's knowledge of the area and local language rivaled Butch's. Command believed the younger brother possessed the ability to provide key support, at least until the CIA SAD team arrived. Thompson's instinct told him the fighter's arrival wasn't coincidence, and he remained dubious of Cole's ability to help.

He drank the last of the water from his pack bladder then grabbed the only food he carried, a protein bar. He ate while studying the map of *Dandong*. A bold attempt to enter the heavily populated Chinese city undetected required no small amount of luck. He'd survived some extraordinary situations in past missions but wondered if his new order set was beyond his abilities. He was certain of one thing—a well-known American, located in the vicinity of one of the world's deadliest devices, added a whole other level of complexity.

Chapter 24

Barrett Jennings' Residence

With a bag of groceries in each hand, Barrett climbed the last of the steps leading to his apartment. When under stress or time pressures, Lilly often skipped eating. The terrified young woman needed every advantage toward finding the missing American. But her frayed nerves threatened a positive outcome. He planned a nice dinner with the intention of improving her stamina and mental well-being. Even more important, she remained their only hope to stay alive.

He approached his apartment door, fishing out keys, and unmastered all three locks before heading inside. After shutting the door and relocking the tumblers, Barrett called out his arrival and dropped the bags on the tiny kitchen counter. Eager for news about any progress, he hurried toward the second bedroom. Turning the corner, he stopped dead.

Next to a sobbing Lilly, who sat in her chair, stood the North Korean sniper. He stroked her hair and whispered something in her ear.

"Take your hands—" Hard metal pressed to the back of his head interrupted further complaint.

"Now you've gone and broken her concentration."

A familiar Korean voice chastised from behind.

Barrett swallowed the acidic bile rising in his throat then raised his hands and turned. His gaze fell upon the cold stare of Park Chul-Moo. The North Korean aimed a pistol at his forehead. "How did you get inside?" Barrett croaked.

"Why does the search take so long? I grow impatient with the delay."

A bead of sweat rolled down Barrett's cheek. Park's scowl scared Barrett almost as much as the gun. "More than a million people live within the city limits. The American is a professional. We've only had hours to work. These things take time."

Park pressed the barrel against his head. "Time is something you *don't* have." The agent then held up a family photo, plucked from the wall. "Neither does your precious daughter, Lilly."

Seeing the picture, Barrett swiveled his head and looked at her. Inside the computer room, Lilly continued stifling her crying.

The sniper leered, stroking her hair.

The painful rap of the barrel against the back of his head forced Barrett to turn his attention to the more immediate threat. "Please don't hurt her. She's innocent."

Park scoffed. "After witnessing what she does on that computer, I know that's not true." With a wave of his pistol, the North Korean agent urged him toward the bedroom.

A flush rose in his face. He turned to the hallway, his tunnel vision focused on Lilly. As if on wooden legs, he shuffled forward. The walls closed in on him. *Will he kill us?*

All four crammed into the monitor-filled room.

Park closed the door and took a position next to his teammate.

Barrett stood next to Lilly, placing a paternal arm around her shoulders.

She burrowed her face into his stomach.

Moisture from her tears soaked through his thin shirt. *Please don't hurt us.*

Park leveled his gun on the pair. "Tell us, dear Lilly, what you have discovered. My patience demands results."

"It's okay, honey." Barrett patted her back. "Answer his questions, and no harm will come."

Nearly a full minute passed while she struggled with her emotions. Sniffling, she eventually turned to her computer station. She typed on the keyboard, her fingers swift. In an instant, several windows popped open, displaying video footage and scrolling computer code.

Barrett's attention turned to the monitors. He hoped Lilly, back in her element, would regain some semblance of control. He remained hypervigilant of Park's demeanor and wanted nothing more than the man's appeasement.

She pointed to the top left screen. "None of the city video feeds have located the American. I ran several facial recognition programs, including the PRC protocols, and nothing came up positive. I've been tracking all of the known foreign agents but found no unusual activity."

Park pointed at a second video. "What's this?"

Lilly expanded a window showing a CCTV live stream positioned at the front of a large building. "I assumed the American requires help getting out of the city with a package. I've been monitoring all of the American Embassies in China, as well as border countries. If he gets the object within the walls of an embassy, what you seek is considered on their sovereign soil and will be lost." She glanced up at Park. "Perhaps if I knew what the—"

"That is not your concern! You find the man only. I will worry about the rest," the North Korean barked.

Lilly flinched then looked back at the computer. "I've noted an increase in activity at this particular American facility in *Shenyang*. I hacked into the flight manifest of a U.S. government plane landing in that city early this morning. I tracked the occupants' locations of origin and traced the names of four males to an airbase in Afghanistan. Two of the men are linked to the American CIA."

Park nodded. "Why is the activity unusual at this embassy? Foreign agents come and go all the time."

Barrett noted a distinct change in Park's calmer tone. He assumed the detail of her investigation satisfied the North Korean agent—for now.

Lilly opened another screen containing line after line of computer-code. "I penetrated one of the U.S. spy satellites and found a surge of coded messages transmitted to that facility just hours before the men from Afghanistan boarded the aircraft. I can't read the communications, but I've worked with burst electronic traffic in other cases. The PLA unit I primarily work for use this type of information to excellent results in determining foreign agent movement and intent."

Barrett watched Park kneel next to Lilly. He immediately knew the commando's reason. Recognizing the pattern, he gritted his teeth. First, the agent scares the mark into fearing for his or her life. Once useful information flowed, the agent slowly changed behavior, transforming from an adversarial to friendly posture—almost collegial.

Lilly, like any terrified person in her circumstance, grasped the newfound feelings of safety and acceptance with great relief. Her shoulders relaxed. "I'm monitoring all foot and vehicle traffic in and out of the embassy. I'm unsure if the plane occupants will risk their cover by traveling to their embassy, but I anticipate the new arrivals helping the missing American soldier in some fashion."

That's my girl. Though Barrett chafed at the manipulation of his daughter, he welcomed Park's approval of her investigation. The tactic was a simple, effective technique, working on experienced field agents as well as frightened teenaged girls.

Park studied the monitor for several seconds. "Have you seen many people leave this place today?"

Lilly nodded, her black hair bounced up and down. "Yes. Slaving city security cameras, a special computer algorithm tracks all foot traffic and vehicles entering and exiting this location and several other suspected buildings. The footage also includes feeds taken from private businesses. Currently, the computer is tracking eight individuals and four cars."

Park placed a hand on her shoulder. "Excellent, Lilly. What of the men on foot? How do you know if they are conducting a meeting with others?"

She smiled. "My unit works with top scientists in kinesiology, medicine, and biomechanics. The software interprets human movement and discerns unusual behavior such as brushing against other individuals, head rotations, speed, and many other parameters. I upgraded the code to evaluate a suspect entering a crowded area such as a bus or train."

Park's eyes shot wide. "Truly?"

Lilly sheepishly grinned.

Seeing his daughter succumb to Park's spell, Barrett fought the urge to strike out at the North Korean. He knew his emotion was a foolish reaction. He'd likely die before landing a single punch. The positive aspect to the interaction was Park appeared pleased with her capabilities and plan. He applauded anything capable of buying more time until he determined a way out of the situation.

"As soon as you find the American, you will let me know. We can then leave you in peace. Does that please you?" Park cooed.

She lowered her gaze and nodded.

Park patted her arm then stood and motioned for his subordinate to follow.

The sniper opened the door for his superior.

Barrett caught Park's signal, no more than an incline of the head, that he was to join them. He gave his daughter a light kiss to the top of her head. "I'll be right back. Let us know when you have something." Back in the living room, he witnessed the return of Park's cold, dispassionate facial expression. "Lilly is an exceptional computer specialist. One of the best in China. I swear I will contact you as soon as we find your man."

Park made an exaggerated display of sitting on the small couch. He consulted his wristwatch then addressed Barrett. "No need. We will stay right here." The North Korean paused for five seconds before adding, "She will find the American in the next four hours. If not, my friend will go into that room and do whatever he pleases."

Barrett darted his gaze to the sniper who showed the tiniest upper curl at the corners of his thin lips. He feared Lilly falling to the same horrific fate as her mother. *Please, no.*

Chapter 25

Crowne Plaza Hotel, Dandong

Nestled in the heart of the commercially resurgent downtown center, the Crowne Plaza Hotel stood like a beacon of progress. The steel structure was an emblem of China's booming economy. The building's recent overhaul launched the facility to international four-star status. The hotel catered to well-heeled foreign businessmen and women who traveled to this region in greater numbers. Tens of thousands of entrepreneurs stood poised for the moment North Korea dropped the security charade and opened their borders. The anticipation of a regional, if not global, economic boom proved too valuable a new market to miss.

Cole, after checking in at the front desk, received a personal escort to a junior suite—the only room available without a reservation. The accommodations reminded him of those along the Las Vegas Strip back home. Liberal use of marble and polished brass accentuated the oversized quarters. The bathroom rivaled the size of his home's master bedroom. He imagined Claire's smile at the extravagance—the visual stabbed at his heart. She scoffed at spending too much for a hotel room but would have enjoyed the luxury. *Don't be mad when you see the bill, sweetheart.*

After thanking and tipping his escort, Cole walked

straight to the king-sized bed. Without unpacking a single item from his duffel bag, he collapsed onto the pillow-top mattress. For the next five hours, he lay unmoving, blissfully unaware in slumber.

A noise interrupted his sleep. Consciousness pulled him to the present. The telephone on the nightstand rang in the background of his jet-lagged mind. The caller appeared motivated to remain on the line indefinitely. He cracked open an eye and saw a red light flashing on the cordless phone's base. Clumsily, he snatched up the receiver. "Hello?"

"Terribly sorry for disturbing you, Mr. Haufner."

A young woman's voice spoke with a British accent. Cole dragged himself upright and glanced out the huge window facing the North Korean border across the *Yalu* River. Bright evening lights on the Chinese side contrasted with the total darkness engulfing the Hermit State. Cole rubbed his head. "What time is it?"

"The time is nine o'clock in the evening, sir," the woman responded. "The reason for my call is my records indicate you have not checked in with the local police. The authority's expectation is all foreign travelers report their arrival within twenty-four hours."

Shit. I forgot. "Thanks for the reminder."

"I have another reason for the call," she added. "Your presence has not gone unnoticed. You may be aware high-profile Americans, especially the sporting kind, are quite popular here. I'm afraid the staff is abuzz over your arrival. To be certain, this type of information will soon cause a stir."

"Terrific," he grumped. His hope in finding his brother might fall victim to a fan's Internet search. Still unfamiliar with the pitfalls of fame, Cole wished he'd used a pseudonym.

"Can I help with other accommodations? Somewhere else in *Dandong*, perhaps?"

He stood, staring out into the blackness across the water. The bleak view drew him in, and dark thoughts crept to the edge of his mind. Cole turned from the window. "No, that's okay. I might head out for a while."

"Very good, Mr. Haufner. Should you need any further assistance, please don't hesitate to call me. My name is Melody. I'm available for the remainder of the evening."

After thanking her, Cole hung up. A trip to the bathroom revealed an unshaven face, mussed hair, and bleary eyes. On a positive note, the swelling resolved around his sutured eyebrow. If the district police required registration, perhaps not looking like a drug addict was best.

With a razor in his hand, he stared into the giant sink mirror. Should he hop on a plane bound for the States and avoid the local authorities altogether? Clearly, he wasn't receiving the help he'd hoped from the monks. What's more, after discovering the city's recent growth, Cole realized his odds of finding Butch remained grim—even if Butch *was* in *Dandong*. The longer he stood at the sink, the more he wavered in his resolve. Either sensible doubts settled in, or he was second-guessing himself. No matter the reason, a quick exit might be the smartest course of action.

Cole showered and brushed his teeth. Refreshed, he dressed in a pair of khaki pants and the least wrinkled of his collarless shirts. Absently, he noticed the usual tightness missing from the blended cotton over his muscular upper body. Given the stress and skipped meals, he dropped below his fighting weight. The desire for food had disappeared.

With indecisiveness ruing the day, Cole sat on the bed contemplating his next move. He replayed the interactions with Master Li and Kip. Those closest to him expressed deep concern toward his plan seeking Butch. Were they right? Was his search a fool's errand? Perhaps, but he couldn't shake the feeling his brother was somewhere nearby. Needing to clear his head, Cole grabbed his room key and wallet with no particular destination in mind.

After exiting the elevator on the ground level, he turned right and stepped into the main lobby. Several people entered through the front entrance, all carrying dripping umbrellas. He stopped, not exactly in the mood for a stroll in the rain. Looking farther down the corridor, past the front desk, he glimpsed signs advertising several of the hotel's restaurants and coffee shops. Farther still, neon signs flashed over the bustling entrance to a nightclub. He noticed furtive glances from the staff manning their posts. *Damn celebrity.* Not an A-list film star, Cole wouldn't attract throngs, but he wasn't in the mood for unwanted attention of any kind. He turned in retreat to his room before bumping into someone.

"Oh, my goodness." A young woman's voice called out.

He recognized the accent, as much a giveaway as the hotel's signature uniform and her nametag, which, of course, read *Melody*. She was petite, twentysomething, with long black hair pulled back in a ponytail, large green eyes and pale-colored skin giving away her heritage as anything but Chinese. She was beautiful—model beautiful.

She glanced up at him. "Oh! I'm so sorry, Mr. Haufner. I should mind my walk. My deepest apology."

Cole grinned. Few nationalities apologized better than the British. "Now I have a face to put to my police-reminder service. Are you okay?"

She ran a hand over her jacket then pushed at her ponytail. "Why, yes. Just clumsy of me. Terribly sorry."

A moment passed where neither moved or said anything. He caught the stares of the front desk staff. In near unison, five workers looked away. The comedy of the group action escaped him. He turned his attention back to her. "Mr. Haufner was my dad. Please, call me Cole."

"Okay," she responded before repeating, "Cole."

"One more thing." He pointed toward the opposite hallway. "What's down that way?"

She cleared her throat. "Two very nice restaurants, a few shops looking to scalp unsuspecting tourists, and a bar with dancing. It's popular with the locals."

From his peripheral vision, Cole noticed the front desk workers repeating their earlier surveillance of the meeting. His annoyance grew. "Could you do me a favor and show me?"

She cast a quick glance toward her coworkers. "Gladly."

After he escaped visual contact with the lobby, Cole noticed Melody's shoulders relax. He recalled from his youth the level of gossip enjoyed by the native population. A foreigner living in the city, especially a young, attractive female, often found herself a target of increased scrutiny.

When Melody neared the door to the first restaurant, she pointed at the menu posted outside. "This establishment serves—"

Cole held up his hand for her to stop. "I'm not hungry."

Her proper employee façade never wavered. "I'm sorry. I keep blundering."

"Not at all!" He looked to place her at ease. "How long have you worked here?"

"Two years…" Her words faltered.

"What's wrong?" He heard the concern in his voice. For the first time since the funeral, he worried about someone else.

She laid her fingers over her lips. The beginnings of tears formed at the corners of her eyes.

"Have I upset you?" *What did I say*?

She grabbed at his arm. "No, no. It's not you. Not directly."

"I don't know what you mean." *What the hell?*

Melody fished a business card and pen from her jacket pocket. She wrote something then handed him the paper stock.

He read the newly scribed international phone number under her printed name and work title. He swallowed his rising nervousness. "Hey, look. If this was another time, but…"

Melody let out a quick laugh, tears still in her eyes. "You're such a guy." She smiled. "My confession is I saw the others researching your name on the Internet. I read of your personal tragedy. I'm so, so sorry. I truly am. Something similar happened to me almost three years ago." She choked up again and waved off any more words with her hand.

"Oh, boy." He let out a long sigh. "Sorry you had to relive that. I guess we understand each other's pain."

Nodding, she wiped at the tears on her cheeks.

Cole sensed his growing discomfort of possibly talking about Claire and Max. *Anything but my family. I can't.* Instead, he choked out a question. "Does the pain ever go away?"

Melody grabbed his hand and shook her head. "The gut-wrenching part doesn't hit quite as often now, but the thought makes my heart ache when an image arrives in my mind's eye. The episodes come at weird, unpredictable times." She paused a moment. "My daughter dreamed of becoming a ballerina. She said they were so beautiful."

Cole's throat tightened, tears streaming now like salty rivulets. "She was right."

Melody's flawless pale skin flushed. Her gaze turned to the floor. "My daughter kept a picture of your wife from her last performance in London on the nightstand."

Cole's pent-up emotions came to the surface, and he allowed himself to submit to both the agony and the comfort Melody offered. She tugged at his hand. He reflexively leaned down and wrapped his arms around her. They embraced for an indeterminate amount of time. He remained unaware of the comings and goings of other hotel guests. He shook while stifling the sobs threatening to burst from his throat.

Their bodies lingered long enough. Melody pulled back.

"Thank you," he choked out. He gave a weak smile. "I guess I needed a hug."

Her green eyes sparkled from the overhead lights. "I know I did." She glanced back toward the main entrance. "I must return to work. I hope you will call me sometime."

Cole opened his mouth to respond but stopped short when he witnessed the color drain from her face.

She stood motionless, her eyes staring past Cole down the hallway.

He recognized the fear response, his hands balled into fists. "What's wrong?"

"A…a group of men…they're coming," she stammered. "When they get close, I'll give a slight bow. Just copy what I do."

"What men?" He made to turn in the direction of her gaze, but he felt her tug at his arm to stop.

She leaned closer. "This group—they're gangsters. They're 14K Triad. Bow and look down." A moment later, Melody slowly and gracefully lowered her head.

Ignoring the advice, Cole spun to face the cause of her worry.

Chapter 26

Four males wearing open-collared silk shirts and baggy pants walked abreast, taking up nearly the entire width of the hallway. Of average height for Chinese men, they stood in the five-foot-seven range, but their demeanor didn't match that of the citizens living in the city. They exuded confidence, glaring at anyone who dared share the walkway.

Cole instantly realized the reason for Melody's fear—they were trouble. Having stared down many of the toughest men in the world in the octagon, he reacted very differently than the innocent people around him.

"Please, Cole," Melody whispered.

He scowled. Bullies were the scum of the earth. Those that preyed on others deserved a fate worse than they projected. Cold emptiness filled his heart. *Fuck with me. I dare you.*

As the group neared, the young man closest to Cole pointed a finger.

"I'm begging you. Please don't," Melody rasped.

He knew their attention landed squarely on him. A surge of adrenaline heightened his senses. His breathing rate increased. With his left hand pushing on her arm, Cole urged Melody to step behind him. *All right, you pricks, come to Papa.*

The four men created a loose semi-circle around the pair. "You! You bow now. You show respect, now." The shortest thug demanded in broken English.

Cole towered over the punk, but his larger physique didn't intimidate the gangster. "If I did," he said in perfect Mandarin, "I'd still be taller than your puny ass."

Melody gasped and cowered behind him.

To a man, the menacing group froze.

He assumed few people spoke to them in such a manner and lived. "Go hump someone else's leg before I teach you about real pain."

One of the men took a couple of steps forward. "You're from here." The man was in his mid-twenties—older than the others—and postured as the leader of the pack. He pointed at Cole. "Your language is from here."

"Sounds like you're from here, too. A little too far from Hong Kong for your own good, 14K," Cole spat.

The leader smiled, showing a gold front tooth. "We are far and wide, but I guess you're too stupid to know that. Are you a big man that wants to die?"

The other men snickered.

Cole took one step forward. He pushed his chin toward the boss. "I am. Are you?"

"You are making a deadly mistake," the leader hissed.

"Let's test that theory. Though I doubt you have the balls to try."

One of the gang members nodded toward the leader. "He will take you apart. He is a great martial artist."

"Is that so?" Cole chuckled.

The leader grinned. "I am a champion."

"I guess you didn't see my fight last week on

television?" He noted two of the men's mouths drop open. The group's demeanor changed from aggression to apprehension.

"What's your name?" The nearest man demanded.

He stared at the punk. "How bad do you want to find out?"

"Maybe your woman will tell us." The gang member reached for Melody.

Cole caught the man's right hand, flexing the wrist, palm up, placing the joint in extreme hyperextension.

The punk gasped. He rose on his tip-toes in a futile attempt to relieve the pain. He groaned while dancing on the ends of his feet.

The three others had no chance to respond to the lightning-fast strike. They stood frozen, unable or unwilling to rescue their own.

"Now, now. Such bad manners," Cole chided. Adding even more insult, he slapped the face of his victim.

"You are a dead man," Gold Tooth announced.

"Apologize to the lady," Cole said to the man in his clutch.

"I'll kill you," the dancing punk gasped through clenched teeth.

"I have all night. Unfortunately, you don't. I'll count to five," Cole warned in a steely voice. "One, two…"

"No, Cole, please," Melody begged.

He caught movement from the second punk to his right. The kid's hand went toward the back of his waistband. Cole recognized the action as a reach for a weapon. Rage filled him. He lashed out with his right foot and connected with the gang member's left knee.

The impact collapsed the joint.

Howling, the kid dropped to the floor grasping at the grotesque injury.

"Three." Cole shouted.

"Stop." A new voice called out from beyond the circle. Brother Shen, from the Temple, stood with his hands held outward. "Do not bother with them. Please, Cole," the monk begged.

"Cole?" The gang leader repeated the name then his eyes went wide. "I know you."

"You're about to know me a whole lot better," Cole snarled. His first victim still squirmed in his grasp.

Gold Tooth jabbed a finger forward. "You. You're the one that had me kicked out of the Temple."

Holy shit. Is that you? Cole recalled this so-called gang leader was the same boy Butch pummeled in punishment for his having bullied Cole. The penultimate fight occurred when they were boys. Irrationally, he burned with desire to exact revenge for all the hurt this punk placed on him as a youngster at the Temple.

"He has no worth," Shen spoke. "We must leave."

Hearing the monk's words, Cole held fast against his desire for revenge. He glared at the leader. "You're a coward who preys on others. You always have been."

Though Gold Tooth held his position, he displayed none of the earlier bluster. His gaze jumped between the man standing to his right and the two incapacitated to his left.

Deep down, Cole knew heeding the warnings from Melody and Shen was the correct move. The recent loss and pain, now heightened by the memories of wrongs suffered during his youth, blocked his reasoning. He slapped the man in his grasp across the face a second time. "Four."

"Cole, please leave with me. I know of what you seek," Shen interjected.

A shockwave raced through his body. He glanced at the monk. "Is this truth?"

"Of course."

Cole glanced down at the man in his paralyzing hold. "I'll miss our little chat."

The diminutive gangster turned up a sweaty face toward him. "I'll kill you," he announced again through stained, clenched teeth.

"Well, until then." With a lightning-fast motion, he flexed the wrist farther, causing several bones to break with sickening snaps.

An anguished cry erupted from the man.

Cole witnessed Gold Tooth leaping toward him, and he thrust the punk in his grasp forward into the group leader.

The two men collided and tumbled to the floor, the one holding his wrist giving an agonized scream.

Without waiting for further repercussions, Cole snatched Melody's hand and pulled her through the growing crowd toward the lobby.

Shen spun lightly on his feet and followed.

Just as the trio reached the main area, Cole grabbed Shen's arm. "I'll meet you outside. Give me one minute."

The monk nodded and made for the front doors.

Three security men appeared from the other end of the atrium and jogged in their direction.

Melody pointed. "Those men, down the hall, tried to attack me. Hold them for questioning!" She issued rapid-fire orders.

At her command, the men took off at a run toward the gang members.

Cole briefly watched them go before turning to Melody. "I might need your help."

"I don't know what I can do." She wrung her hands. "I'm probably in a lot of trouble with my boss."

"The fight is my fault. I lost my cool. Dammit! I should not have put you in that situation." The lobby area filled with gawkers. He glanced in all directions then pulled her around the corner. The small alcove provided respite from the noise and prying eyes.

"Do you have anyone special in this city? A boyfriend, husband, family, anyone?"

She shook her head, her eyebrows furrowed. "No, no one, I…why?"

"Do you have your passport?"

"Why are you asking—"

We're out of time for twenty questions. He took hold of her shoulders. "Do you?"

"At my apartment. You're scaring me!"

Cole sucked in a deep breath. He forced himself to calm down so she wouldn't think better of associating with him. "I'm sorry. Listen, these people won't stop until they have their vengeance. You're in danger here." He reached into his back pocket and offered her his door key. "I'm in room 535. Inside my duffel bag is a leather pouch with American dollars. I want you to take the money, go get your passport and a few things, and leave the city. Once you're away, call this number." He pulled out his phone and Melody's business card then quickly tapped out Kip's cell phone number, texting her. "I sent you the contact information for my best friend, Kip. He's my business manager, and he's also a lawyer. Tell him everything that's happened."

Her mouth hung open. "You want me to just take off with your money, and then call a stranger and leave everything I have behind? Your suggestion sounds insane!"

Cole slid his hands down her arms. He took both of her hands in his. "When you left London, you had no plan and nothing left to lose. Am I right?"

"Yes," she whispered.

"Then please trust me this situation is similar with different circumstances."

"But, I have nowhere to go." Melody covered her face with her hands.

"You do, but you just don't know it yet," he rasped. "My friend will take care of everything. Please, Melody, I can't bear to see another innocent person lost."

A surge in noise from the lobby interrupted their conversation.

The growing crowd edged into Cole's field of view. He suspected only a matter of minutes remained before the police showed, if they hadn't already.

"Why do I trust you?" Her lips quivered.

"Because I would never see you bow to any man ever again."

She put a soft hand to his cheek. "I didn't think men like you existed anymore."

Her eyes, even tearing, had a captivating sparkle. Cole smiled, hoping he saved at least one worthy person from this hellhole of a city. "I have to go. So, do you."

"Wait." She held up an index finger. "I'll put your

bag in the luggage storage. Tell my friend, Xiu, at the counter you need my help in gathering your things. The information should buy us both some time."

"Okay."

Melody gripped his hands. "Cole. Will I see you again?"

"Of course, you will," he responded quickly.

She threw her arms around him and squeezed tight. "Please come back," she cried, her face buried in his chest.

He couldn't say another word. He didn't have the energy to lie.

Chapter 27

Outside the Crowne Plaza Hotel

After he bid Melody farewell, Cole skirted the lobby crowd and exited the building from a side door. The night air felt heavy with humidity from the recent rain. Expecting to find a massive police presence, he saw only a smiling doorman forty feet to his left. People on the sidewalk went about their business as usual—no flashing lights or swarms of officers visible. Seeing no new threats, he second-guessed his persuading Melody to abandon the city. Had he overreacted? *Don't tell me I screwed up again."*

Head on a swivel, Cole searched for Shen. If he couldn't find the man, he might never know the reason for the monk's arrival at the hotel. Stewing, he wrestled with the notion of calling Melody but dropped that idea when he caught a glimpse of the robed man standing at the other end of the block. Cole hustled toward the monk. They met on the wet sidewalk at the southwest corner of the hotel.

"Is the girl safe?" Shen asked in a hushed tone.

"Yes. For now." *No thanks to me.*

"Is the gang leader the same person Butch fought at the Temple? The one Master Li removed from training?"

Cole blinked away several errant raindrops that

landed on his face. "Yes, he is the same person. He was never worthy of the Temple."

Shen grimaced then shook his head. "Much has changed in Dandong since you left. Some for the better and, as you now know, some worse."

I don't recognize this city anymore. He glanced in all directions before returning his gaze to Shen. "Where are the authorities? I can't believe the police are not here."

"This hotel is very important to the politicians. Bad reviews drive away foreign visitors and investors. The altercation will remain an internal issue. People have learned to not question such activities."

"A blessing, I suppose." Cole shrugged.

Shen stepped off the curb and headed west. "You came seeking your brother, yet your actions only draw bad attention. You make things difficult."

Following the monk, Cole crossed the street. Neon signs in small store fronts faded to black as shopkeepers closed for the night.

"I'm not looking for trouble. I'm searching for my brother."

"Yet, you find difficulties like a flame for the moth."

"You remind me of Master Li." Cole recalled similar pronouncements from his uncle when the Haufner boys made trouble at the Temple. "Why did you come looking for me?"

"You said you were walking to the hotel."

Cole studied Shen's face. "*Why* did you come looking for me?"

Shen glanced in multiple directions. "I conveyed your frustrations to Master Li."

His heart raced. "And?" Though Cole professed not to care what Master Li said or did, he grew anxious.

"I believe he regrets the manner in which he spoke."

Cole's eyebrows furrowed. He stopped and grabbed Shen's arm. "That's all? You came to the hotel to tell me *that*?"

Remaining silent, Shen shrugged off his grasp and walked westward.

"Bullshit." Cole jogged to catch up. "Why aren't you telling me the *real* reason you came? If you know something, you better tell me now."

The monk ignored him and crossed yet another street.

Cole trotted after him but, once across the road, stopped. *I'm too tired to deal with him. He's screwing with me.* "I've had enough. I'm done with this place, *and* I'm finished with you."

Shen glanced over his left shoulder. "Then you will not find that which you seek." The monk kept walking.

"Wait—what did you say?" He raced ahead of the robed man. Shuffling backward, he faced the monk. "You said I would find something. Is it Butch?"

Never breaking stride, Shen gave a simple nod.

What felt like a bolt of electricity raced through him. *I'm right.* He finally received confirmation of the unwavering sense his brother hid somewhere in the city. "Why are you holding back?" Cole's hands shook. "Where is he?"

"We cannot speak here," Shen replied in a lowered voice.

"Where then? I can't keep walking backward."

The monk skidded to a stop and focused on

something over Cole's shoulder.

He spun and then scanned for what caught Shen's eye. Across the city street sat the gardens of the Temple he saw earlier today. In the distance, situated deep in the center of the grounds, a large statue of Buddha glowed from artificial light.

"There is where we may speak," Shen said.

The stranger's phone call and message suddenly came to mind. *Is this Temple what the caller meant when he said you 'went' home?*

****

Butch Haufner headed southwest, away from the library, as quickly as he dared, having waited for the less-congested evening hours to risk another venture in public. Miss Cheng appeared surprised but pleased to learn the guest monk from the *Wulong* Temple required additional access to the library computer. For as long as he deemed necessary, Butch visited with and exchanged pleasantries with the widow. Finally—and only after he pointed out the late hour—she allowed him use of the computer.

The message received from his query for male companionship made clear JSOC's plan. A three-man, CIA Special Activities Department team, composed of former Navy SEALs, was inbound from the *Shenyang* embassy and planned to rendezvous with him at the Crowne Plaza Hotel at eleven p.m. Despite any inter-service rivalry between Delta and SEALs, Butch knew the men brought significant experience to his desperate mission. If anyone missed the time cutoff, all parties would rally at the *Mituo* Temple at midnight. A grin rose to his lips when he read that his teammate, Hammer, survived the earlier battle and received the same orders. His reply detailed his new appearance, including monk's robes and shaved head. He scrubbed the message and left the library just as visiting hours expired.

Willing himself to continue walking at a normal pace, Butch wondered what the remainder of the night would bring. *The world is counting on you, Haufner. Even if they never know how close they are to Armageddon.*

Chapter 28

Outside the Crowne Plaza Hotel, 10:23 p.m.

Thompson performed a masterful job making his way to the primary location under the cover of darkness. He'd secured an old bicycle, and he'd broken down his rifle. He stashed the smaller components of the weapon inside his assault pack. With a four-foot-square piece of worn, brown tarp tied around his carry-all, he pedaled freely along the roads while wearing a mishmash of locally made clothes he claimed along the way. The grease paint camouflaging his face and neck had long ago smeared, disappearing under heat and sweat, giving him the appearance of a hardworking farmer from the outskirts of town. The darkness further camouflaged his American features.

Near the top of his list of worries was the little battery power remaining in his communication device. Even so, he transmitted repeated updates of his position to JSOC, who then relayed the information to the three-man CIA SAD unit coming in from the *Shenyang* Embassy. The unknown, complicating factor was his team leader's brother, Cole.

He arrived early at the rally site, and he considered his options regarding contacting Butch's brother. Whether the younger Haufner knew or not, the MMA star was exfiltrating with the rest of the team. For obvious reasons, Thompson couldn't risk entering the hotel. Three options remained—create a scenario where the building evacuated, call him directly, or wait for Butch's arrival and have his team leader find his brother inside. While he conducted a third, slow pass of the Crowne Plaza Hotel's front entrance. The pros and cons of each option swirled in his mind. Twenty yards ahead on the left side of the street, movement caught his left peripheral vision.

Thompson witnessed a lone male exiting the hotel through a side door, twenty feet from the main entrance. The man's height, build, and hair color matched with the dossier JSOC sent earlier in the day. *No fucking way I'm that lucky.* The Delta operator coasted to a stop and watched his possible target looking up and down the sidewalk on the opposite side of the street. Something caught the guy's attention who then made a beeline toward a yellow-robed monk on the far end of the block. *What the hell are you doing?*

The man he suspected was Cole and the monk met briefly before crossing to his side of the road then disappearing behind the three-story building sitting at the corner of the intersection. Thompson faced a critical decision—stay and rendezvous with the team and Butch, or pursue this individual, confirm his identification, and bring Cole back for the extraction. He desperately needed JSOC on comms, but he couldn't risk attempting contact, exposed as he was on this major road. He decided to follow Cole and the monk around the corner.

The Delta operator pushed off the curb and slowly pedaled to the intersection. Turning right, he caught sight of the pair farther ahead on the sidewalk. Cole's body language gave the appearance of someone angry while the monk offered few visual cues about the tenor of their talk.

At a safe distance, Thompson witnessed the men cross over another intersection heading west. Seeing the street and sidewalk clear of other traffic, he swiftly fished out the earpiece from under his collar and pressed On under his clothes. He brought the bike to a stop. "This is Two, how read?"

"Clear, Two," Command responded.

"I have visual of a male I suspect as New Player. He's speaking with a bald man wearing yellow robes, and both are walking away from the primary site heading west. The second subject is *not* One. How copy?"

"Good copy, Two. Wait one for Papa Bear."

Papa Bear was the mission code word for the JSOC commanding officer, General Scaturro. He was a brilliant, hard-charging Green Beret who oversaw all of U.S. Special Operations and reported directly to the Joint Chiefs. For this mission, though, the general spoke only to the president and his chief of staff.

"Two, this is Papa Bear. How you holding up, son?"

The general's familiar voice energized Thompson. The pair last spoke over video comms on the Delta team's flight just before their jump into the China sea. He loved the old man and his no-bullshit style. "Papa, I'm one hundred percent. I'm in a jam with a situation. Need your guidance. Over."

"Spooks here think they're heading for the Shaolin Temple. What's New Player's status?"

Thompson observed the man he suspected as

Butch's brother walking backward. He appeared agitated with the bald man. "If that's our guy, he's breaking the balls of some monk. I think they know each other. New Player sought him out after exiting the hotel."

"Understood. The recovery unit is ten clicks out. One is making way to primary site. No word on package yet."

Thompson noticed the two men ahead stopped at the edge of a narrow road. No street lights existed on the other side of the pavement. "Roger that. How do I proceed?"

"What's your gut tell you?"

Reports indicated Butch shaved his head and passed himself off as a local monk. Cole talking to someone dressed in a similar manner didn't appear coincidental. The Haufner boys, having grown up in the area, likely maintained strong contacts. Should he follow Cole or head back and rendezvous with Butch? The latter seemed the smart move in terms of the mission. He railed against his own indecision. Thompson opened his mouth in response to the general's question but held his tongue when he sensed movement to his rear.

The noise of a near-idling car engine and the crunch of tires on asphalt broke the still night. Lack of headlights heightened the sinister nature of the situation. The driver obviously avoided detection. Without looking back, he pushed off the sidewalk and pedaled forward. "Stand-by," he murmured into his mic.

Thompson pushed ahead to the intersection, crossing over to the left side at the stop sign. He saw the monk and Cole start across the street to the gardens before turning left onto the boulevard himself. Twenty feet ahead, he spotted a side alley on the left and turned down the access driveway. Clearing the entrance, he dumped the bike and spun to face the road. A moment later, the front clip of a dark gray sedan edged into the intersection. With lights still off, the car gave Thompson a bad feeling. "Papa, I have suspicious vehicle near my position. Someone is tailing New Player. Over."

"Clear copy. SAD team is inbound. Can you identify the occupants?"

"Negative without exposing myself."

"Copy that. Provide over-watch. The team will proceed as planned."

"Copy all. Two Out." Thompson scanned between the car and the two men fading from sight in the darkened garden. The road remained clear of any other vehicles. As seconds ticked by, he grew more convinced these guys were bad news.

A soft *tick* came from the car and then the sound of a foot stepping onto the blacktop. The interior dome light failed to shine. *The driver ain't making a social call.* Speed born from years of training kicked in. He set down the pack and withdrew the pieces of his rifle. He laid out the upper and lower receivers and the suppressor. Keeping an eye on the front of the car, he assembled the weapon by feel alone. His rifle ready, he donned his assault vest and bump helmet. *Game time.*

Two more doors opened. *How many men now?* He peeked through the scope's aperture and saw the familiar red-dot illumination.

The tap of footsteps increased in number. He

ducked deeper into the alley. From his hidden position, he counted four men heading into the garden. They all stood average height for the region—approximately five-foot-seven with thin builds. Their lack of size didn't make them any less lethal. Two wore open-collar shirts and gold chains around their necks. He didn't believe these intruders represented any government agency. "Nest, I have four bad guys inbound on New Player. They look like gang or hired help. Over."

"Clear copy, Two. Team is less than five minutes out and can redirect on your go. A redirect is secondary to primary mission. Over."

Thompson thought he saw one of the men holding a short-barreled weapon close to his side. A quick scan of the others showed unmistakable bulges from under their shirts. They crossed into the garden. "Break, break. Hostiles armed with long gun and pistols. Moving for position. I have secondary. Do *not* redirect."

"Copy, Two. You are cleared hot."

"Stand by, Nest." Thompson poked his head farther out from the alley. The car hadn't moved. Dropping into a low crouch, he crept out of his hide spot, hugging the wall while shuffling toward the vehicle. Stealth was paramount, and he didn't risk the noise of feeding a round into the weapon's chamber. With his rifle secured tight across his chest by a single-point harness, he drew his battle knife and stopped short of the car interior's field of view. If the driver still sat behind the wheel, he could alert his crew if the Delta operator lost the initiative.

Almost on hands and knees, Thompson peered around the next corner. The driver's head barely cleared the ledge of the front door's window sill. Staring across the street, the man showed no indication he sensed movement from the side. The driver's window sat half open. Thompson silently approached his target. In position, he sprang up, snapping back the driver's head with his free hand while plunging the knife deep into the left side of the man's neck. He pushed the blade horizontally to the right side. The strike cut through the carotid and jugular vessels, as well as the trachea and esophagus. Blood dumped everywhere.

He held the man's skull against the headrest, keeping the body from making contact with the car's horn button. Thompson shoved him sideways until his victim slumped toward the passenger side. Seeing no movement from the corpse, he dropped to the pavement, crawled under the car, and pulled his rifle into shooting position. Lying on the rough cement, he barely made out the four intruders pushing ahead into the darkness.

He flipped down his NVGs over his eyes. The four men sprang into clear focus in a green glow. "Nest, I'm in position. Four targets. The driver is neutralized. Bad guys are hunting. How copy?"

"Clear copy. Nest on standby."

Thompson inserted a magazine into his weapon. The killing was far from over.

Chapter 29

Jennings' residence

Sitting on the living room couch, Barrett Jennings bounced the heel of his right foot against the floor. Sweat trickled down the middle of his back.

The sniper stood in the kitchen eating a fourth banana while Park occupied a small wooden chair staring at a wall clock.

The ex-CIA man's gut churned watching the time advance with no word from Lilly. Twice, he offered to check on her progress and both times was told to sit and shut his mouth. Almost one hour passed since his last attempt. Lost in thought, Barrett flinched when Park uncrossed his legs and stood.

Instantly, the sniper dropped the fruit, scooped up his rifle and veered around the kitchen counter.

Panic rose in his chest. *Please don't kill us.*

Without a word spoken, Park headed for the back room.

The sniper blocked the hallway and stared down Barrett, the muscular North Korean's forearm muscles flexing from his grip on the weapon.

He caught a glimpse of Park whispering something to his daughter. His throat tightened.

Lilly's head shook side to side. She directed his attention to something on the main monitor.

Michael Houtz

My God, she hasn't found the American. Barrett's cell phone, lying on a small side table, sprang to life, the silent ring vibration rattling the aluminum body against a wooden surface. He started for the device but was intercepted by the sniper and roughly pushed away.

Park rushed into the living room and snatched up the phone. He shoved the screen to within inches of Barrett's face. "Who is this calling?"

"One of my informants."

"Put him on the speaker," Park ordered.

Barrett tapped the appropriate icon. "What do you have?" he asked in Mandarin.

"We found an American that fits your description," the man on the other end announced.

Yes! Relief swept over him. "Where?"

"Some of our men ran into him at the Crowne Plaza. He injured two of our members then left with a woman and a monk."

Ignoring Park and the sniper, Barrett brushed past them and sprinted to Lilly. He tapped her on the shoulder. "Crowne Plaza Hotel. Inside." He waved for the North Koreans to join him in the computer room.

Lilly's fingers danced across her keyboard. Computer code and new CCTV video feeds populated the multitude of monitors.

Barrett gestured to Park to pass him his cell phone. With the device in his hand, he pushed the microphone close to his lips. "Is the man detained?" he asked the informant.

"Too many witnesses. You told me not to involve the police."

"Yes, yes." Barrett stared at Park. "Where is he now?"

"My men followed the American and the monk to the *Mituo* Temple. They are there now. What do you want me to do?"

Before Barrett answered, a red flashing box popped up on Lilly's screen. A photo grab from a city CCTV camera showed a dark sedan. Two males sat in the front seat and possibly one more in the rear. The driver appeared Caucasian.

Park grabbed the cell phone from Barrett's hand then placed the call on mute. He pointed at the computer monitor. "Who are these men, Lilly?"

She opened a second tab displaying a photo showing the same make and model vehicle leaving the American Embassy earlier in the evening. "That is the same car that left *Shenyang* almost three hours ago. The license plate matches in both pictures. The driver is familiar in both images. They came from the American building."

Park pushed the phone back toward Barrett. "Tell your man you will call him back in one minute with instructions."

"Yes. Of course." Barrett complied and hung up. He watched as the North Korean agent pulled at his lip.

After a moment, Park leaned over Lilly's left shoulder. "Can you see inside the hotel?" he asked.

On the top right monitor, she pulled up the live feed from the lobby.

Barrett spotted a few employees and wandering guests. *Everything looks normal.* Another camera showed a long hallway with the front desk at the right edge of the picture. Again, nothing looked out of the ordinary. If an altercation occurred, why no police presence? Doubt of the caller's veracity crept into his thoughts.

"Do you want me to gain access to the hotel security archives?" she asked.

"Can you accomplish such a thing?" Park replied.

"I believe so."

Park patted her shoulder then whispered something to the sniper.

Barrett couldn't make out what was said, but he hoped this development represented their big break. A bullet to the back of his head delayed, his thoughts drifted to the suitcase fought over at the dock. His witnessing, first hand, the lengths Park and his assassins expended in search of the mystery item delivered the only logical conclusion—the North Korean promises of massive wealth and freedom were a sham. *Park can't afford any loose ends.*

With her usual deftness, Lilly broke through the hotel intranet firewall and accessed a recorded video feed from the facility's computer system. The scene, time-stamped nearly one hour earlier, provided a view of the lobby, and a second camera angled down the main hallway leading to the business wing of the building.

Parked leaned in. "Is this place the hotel?"

"Yes, sir." Lilly clicked on the play button. The scene advanced at two-times normal speed.

Twice, Park ordered her to pause the footage for closer inspection, but nothing came of the images.

When the time stamp showed nine-thirty p.m., Barrett pointed at the monitor. "Right there!" He identified a tall, white male standing in the lobby speaking to a hotel employee. "Lilly, play at normal speed."

She expanded the video window to occupy the entire screen and complied with his order.

Barrett watched the man in the image walk down the hallway with the hotel employee, a dark-haired female. Moments later, the tall male defiantly stood his ground against four gang members—part of the local 14K organized crime syndicate hired by Barrett to assist in this mission. The ex-CIA man gasped when the man injured two of the gangsters with lightning-fast movements. *Incredible.*

"He is *not* an ordinary person! He appears highly trained." Park announced.

Barrett nodded. "Suspicious, yes. Lilly, can you get an I.D. on him?"

She swung the computer cursor to another monitor and opened a window displaying scrolling lines of code. "Obtaining the information will take a few moments. The hotel registration system is on a separate network. If I find he is a guest, I will know his identity right away."

Park scanned the other monitors. "And what of the men in the car?"

Lilly expanded another tab. A grainy, close-up photo of a bearded, white male sitting in the front passenger seat appeared on screen. Underneath the picture, a set of numeric values pulsed red. "My program is ninety-eight percent certain the man shown is the American agent flown in from Afghanistan."

With the news, Park straightened. His eyes narrowed, and his jaw clenched.

Barrett recognized the hunter inside Park come to the surface. He hoped not to see that same glare in his direction in the near future. "What do I tell my informant?"

"Detain the man at the Temple. Warn your people he is a dangerous adversary."

"What about the men in the car?"

"I will handle that personally."

More lambs to the slaughter. Barrett knew, firsthand, Park's methods of conflict resolution. Having lived here for twenty-plus years, he knew more dead bodies would not escape the watchful gaze of Chinese authorities.

Chapter 30

Mituo Temple

Standing at the edge of light surrounding the marble statue of Buddha, Cole remained silent. Since Shen refused to answer any of his questions, he'd given up pleading with the monk for news of Butch. Only his own desperation kept him from leaving the Temple grounds. What the two waited for, only the monk knew. His distress grew with each passing second. "Why are we here? Is Butch coming?"

Shen held out a hand. A shuffling noise rose in the night air.

On reflex, Cole held his breath. He immediately recognized the man approaching from the other side of the statue. "What the—"

"Good evening, *wai sheng*—nephew."

Master Li's greeting was placid and matter-of-fact. Cole felt an avalanche of emotions. Out of habit, he bowed to his uncle. "I…I don't understand."

"My heart is filled with joy that I may speak to you. That which I have withheld from you was for your own good."

Cole's mouth hung open. The shock from seeing Master Li caused his mind to cease reasoning. In an effort to clear his confusion, he shook his head. "Just what is going on? Is Butch here?"

"Please allow me to apologize for the manner in which I spoke at the Temple. Circumstances prior to your arrival caused me great fear for your safety—similar to your childhood. I agreed to a promise that now I find myself breaking."

Cole sensed his uncle's conflict. He found Master Li's pained facial expression too much for his heart to bear. "*Jiu jiu, I* must apologize. I spoke as a child only to hurt you. I'm ashamed."

Master Li grinned and threw open his arms.

Stepping forward, Cole hugged the man who'd raised him as his own child. He held nothing back as the sobs rose from deep in his chest. In the flood of emotions, the greatest was relief—relief that Cole no longer felt compelled to harbor hatred for his uncle.

"Ah, this reunion is wonderful!" Master Li exclaimed. "Here is the young man I remember—so full of love and affection. These attributes are the true path to enlightenment."

Finally, Cole pulled back, brushing away tears and feeling anything but enlightened. He could only hope some of the words Master Li professed during his ten years at the Temple helped form his character.

Brother Shen nodded.

Cole thought he caught a glint in the monk's eye. *Sorry. I understand why you couldn't say anything.* He returned the gesture to Master Li's protégé. Only a moment passed before his mind drifted back to his brother. "Master Li, what could you not tell me at the Temple? Is your promise with Butch?"

The older man glanced at Shen then back to Cole. "My promise to another I cannot keep." Master Li grabbed him by the shoulders. "*Wai sheng*, your brother

168

is here."

"In *Dandong*?" The words barely escaped his throat. The long day took on a dreamlike quality. The admission of Butch's presence confirmed all of his instincts. "How do you know? Have you seen him? Is he okay?" Cole asked each question in rapid succession.

"I have answers to many of your questions. Let us go to Shen's residence and discuss them over tea. Then you may decide what course you take."

The noise of a gun cocking stifled Cole's reply. He and the two monks froze.

A small man wearing gold chains around his neck emerged from the darkness brandishing what looked like a short-barreled shotgun. "You will go nowhere."

Cole's fright turned to horror as three other men carrying handguns emerged from the trees.

As the strangers advanced, Master Li put out his hands in supplication. "Gentlemen, we are simple, religious men. We have nothing of value to you."

The first man aimed the shotgun at the old Master. "Oh, something here is of great value."

Master Li took a short step forward. "This place is a temple of worship. We live a life of self-imposed poverty. You know I speak the truth."

"I'm not here for gold." The man shifted the gun's aim toward Cole.

Anger born of helplessness rose in his chest. In contrast to Master Li's placating tone, Cole straightened to his full height and stared into the man's face. "Let me guess, more 14K cowards?"

Another man stepped forward and cocked his pistol's hammer. "I show you coward."

As at the Crowne Plaza earlier, Cole refused to back off, even in the face of impending conflict. "The coward is the man who needs a gun."

The other with the shotgun pointing at Cole's chest stood only some seven or eight feet away. "You will come with us now!"

"Please. Violence is forbidden here," Master Li spoke again. "The Temple is sacred. We cannot have this type of behavior."

"Maybe you don't hear so good," the leader sneered. "He comes with us whether you approve or not."

"He is a famous American! If you take him, the government will arrest anyone involved. They will have no choice but to hold immediate trials and executions." Master Li cupped his hands together and held them against his chest.

"Famous American," the man chuckled. "If you are so famous, what are you doing here then, huh?"

Cole stared straight into the man's eyes. He took several steps toward the shotgun-wielding thug. "How about I show you?"

Chapter 31

Cole watched the index finger of the man holding the shotgun drop down into the trigger guard and turn white from the pressure placed on the firing mechanism. He braced himself for impact. The coming blast—did he on some level welcome the end to his suffering?

Thwack. Flesh, blood, and soft tissue exploded everywhere. But not Cole's.

The shotgun dropped to the ground, followed by the man brandishing the weapon. Most of his skull simply disappeared in a misty cloud.

Gore coated Cole's face and torso. The robes worn by Master Li and Brother Shen displayed the contrast of bright red against brilliant yellow. None present moved—the shock effecting friend and foe, equally.

In the stalled moment, the head of the pistol-wielding thug just left of the dead body snapped forward with the same bony *crack* filling the still night air. The second man's body collapsed next to his partner.

Cole and the two monks dove to the ground.

The third gang member's chest exploded outward, and he dropped face first, his right arm twitching.

The fourth man ran into the sparse woods, away from the Temple. The limb of a tallow tree exploded, creating a spray of deadly shards. The punk kept running, and when his gun fell out of his hands, he made no effort to retrieve his weapon.

At the sight of a mostly intact human lung inches away from his face, Cole's stomach lurched. Moving on all fours, he scrambled to Master Li, reaching him before Shen. He rolled the older monk onto his back. He saw that his uncle's eyes remained open and moving, and although Li displayed no visible signs of injury, he noted the man was clearly in distress. "*Jiu jiu.* Are you hurt?"

Master Li reached up with his right arm, the left flaccid, and he moved his lips. No sound emerged.

Cole tore open the yellow robes exposing his uncle's torso. No sign of gunshot. *What's wrong?*

"His heart!" Shen exclaimed. "He refuses medicine for a condition."

"*Jiu jiu!*" He turned to Shen. "Where's the closest doctor?" A rough hand grabbed Cole by the shirt and yanked him downward. His nose almost touched his uncle's.

"No. Do not think of such things," Li's voice rasped.

Not another family member. The shock scrambled his thoughts. "*Jiu jiu*, please. We must get you to the hospital."

"Listen to brother Cole." Shen cried.

Tears forming in his eyes, Master Li shook his head. He let go of the shirt and placed his weathered hand on Cole's chest. "You must find your brother. He is here. He is in great danger."

"Where is he, *jiu jiu*? Where's Butch?"

Master Li clutched at his chest, spasms gripped his body, and caused him to jerk.

Suddenly, a huge man charged toward them from the trees.

Cole saw an enormous figure wearing a backpack and black coveralls carrying a military-style rifle. Four tubes, attached to a helmet, protruded forwarded in front of his eyes. Cole looked to the shotgun that lay a few feet away but held his position as the face became clearer.

"Butch?" Cole gasped.

"We're clear," the stranger said in a Texas drawl.

Neither Cole nor Shen moved as the man came to a quick stop before dropping to a knee next to them.

"American Special Forces," the big man announced. The stranger ran his hands over Master Li's upper body. "No entrance wounds."

"Did Butch send you? Did you kill those men?" Cole asked.

"One got away. Cole Haufner?"

"Yes. You?"

"The cavalry. Call me Hammer." The soldier flipped up his NVGs.

He thought the man's facial features matched those of his toughest MMA opponents—strong chin, square jawline, raised cheekbones, and intense eyes. "Is Butch with you?" he asked a second time.

Hammer glanced at Shen then back to Cole. "We can discuss that later. First, let's get your man out of here. Where can we take him?"

Translating the question to Mandarin, Cole queried Shen regarding the nearest safe location.

The monk stabbed a finger at a small, single-story bungalow fifty yards away.

"I'll take care of the bad guys. You two get your

man out of here," Hammer ordered.

Both men struggled to carry Master Li, twice stopping to adjust their grip. Finally, they safely transferred him to Shen's living space.

After laying the old monk on a sleeping cot, Shen used a landline phone and alerted the main Temple to Master Li's condition.

Cole knelt beside his uncle. The image triggered fresh memories he preferred to forget—an impossible task. The thought of his son, Max, popped into his head.

Master Li's eyes rotated toward Cole. "I am so glad to see you," he whispered.

"I want to take you to the hospital." Cole heard the sadness in his own voice. He gently kissed his uncle's hand.

Li shook him off. "No, *wai sheng*, my time has come, like the masters before me."

Hearing the finality in *Sifu's* words, Cole's body trembled as if warding off the cold. "I don't want to lose you. We have each other, again."

"My time of passing is not for you to decide," his uncle croaked. "You must find your brother."

Shen returned and dropped next to the bed. "I have alerted the Temple elders."

Master Li's lips curled into an uneven smile, his eyes took on a far-off stare. "My children," he whispered. "Walk in peace."

In a detail Cole knew he would remember the rest of his life, he heard the slow release of air from his uncle's lungs.

Chapter 32

Mituo Temple

Cole knelt beside his uncle, his hand on Master Li's lifeless right arm. With his head cast down, Cole's memories of Claire and Max replayed in his mind's eye. He felt frozen, unable to move but also to think of anything other than death. He believed his own presence brought a lethal inevitability to those he loved. His thoughts begged him to end the suffering—permanently.

Between sobs, Shen's prayer rose. His eyes clamped shut, the young monk rocked back and forth, his words nearly unintelligible.

Numb to any sensation, Cole thought Shen's show of such emotion odd, even in the face of the loss of the Master of the Temple. Up until this moment, he'd never seen another monk react in such a way.

After a full minute, Shen finished his grieving recital. He kissed Master Li's forehead.

I should have taken him to the hospital. We're in the twenty-first century. He would still live. Cole's detached emotions gave way to anger. His mind railed against the rigid monastic bullshit of tradition, as well as the self-imposed exile from modern society. *How could you be so selfish.* "Why, *jiu jiu*?" Cole asked loud enough for Shen to hear.

"It is our way," the grieving monk replied.

"Should we take him to the hospital?"

Shen gazed at Cole. "For what purpose?"

Cole ran his hands roughly through his hair. "I don't know. Can't they do something?" His body shook. He stood, venting the explosive energy building inside him.

"I wish that were true," Shen replied.

Cole rocked back and forth on his feet. "Can't we just take him to the hospital?"

"We cannot. He wished to live without modern medicine."

Cole's lips quivered. "What about what *I* want? What about what *you* want? Doesn't that count?" his voice rose.

Shen furrowed his eyebrows. "Have you not learned anything from *Sifu*? Life is not about *wants*. Happiness abounds from giving."

"Oh, that's great. Giving." Cole put his fingers in the air with imaginary quotation marks around his last word. "Was he *giving* me another dead family member? Well, that's such an *awesome* gift."

"I understand you have been through—"

"You think?" Cole shrieked. "But, ladies and gentlemen, we have more. Now, we delve into the mystery surrounding his brother, Butch—made all the more interesting because the man who knows his location is now dead!" He paced the small room like a caged tiger.

Shen, still kneeling, dropped his head and whispered another prayer.

Cole halted near the tiny, two-person table. With hands balled into fists, he considered turning the furniture into kindling. Never one to physically lash out in times of despair, he stilled, his instinct entering new territory. He closed his eyes and took in a deep, cleansing breath. In a moment of clarity, Cole caught a few words of Shen's prayer. He froze. As a young monk in training, Cole attended several funeral ceremonies, both at the Temple and at public events. Only direct family members recited this particular intonement.

Cole rushed to Shen at bedside, listening more intently to the chant. Nervous energy caused a tingling in his extremities. When the prayer ended, a single question dominated his thought. "Are your words even possible?"

The monk gazed up at Cole, a river of tears below each eye. "Yes, *biao di*—cousin. *Sifu* is my real father."

****

Maintaining his disguise as a *Shaolin* monk, Butch Haufner calmly strode along the sidewalk, nearing the Crowne Plaza hotel for his scheduled rendezvous with the SAD team. Despite the cool night temperatures, a thin sheen of sweat covered his bald head. Little time existed for an effective SDR—surveillance detection route. At this late hour, doubling back on his direction, using windows as a reflective means of locating tails, and dropping in and out of stores were not options. Staying in character, and arriving on-time, meant he walked directly to the hotel without delay.

His orders were simple—pass the front of the hotel from east to west, turn left at the first road, and circle to the rear of the building. A four-door sedan in the alley awaited his approach. Learning Hammer was part of the greeting party gave him a huge morale boost. His teammate equaled any ten men the opposition brought to the table. Buoyed by these reinforcements, Butch planned on collecting his equipment and the case from the city Temple before driving to the embassy in Shenyang. Once inside the walls of the facility, diplomatic immunity protected the men and device. Two hours and he was home free.

Butch saw the glow of the hotel marquee two blocks ahead. His heart pounded against his chest. He darted his gaze in all directions looking for threats. Mission success depended on what happened in the next five minutes.

While passing the entrance to the hotel, he noticed the doorman nodding reverently toward him. Butch did not notice anything in the man's gaze indicating imminent danger—no dilated pupils, no nervous look over his shoulder. *Slow breaths. One more minute.*

Following the plan, he turned left at the intersection and headed toward the back-alley entrance. Making a show of looking for oncoming cars, he peeked left down the narrow service road. *There.* Farther ahead, near the other end of the block, sat the darkened outline of a sedan. His heart leaped at the view of his recovery team's presence.

Butch darted into the alley and trotted toward the vehicle. Within the seconds, he confirmed the license plate. He slowed, concerned about night workers exiting the rear of the building. With no evidence of any other human activity, he grinned as he approached. After one last scan of the alley, he grabbed the left rear passenger handle and opened the door. He jumped inside and gave a thump to the chest to the man sitting to his right. "Damned good to see you, boys. Let's get the hell out of here." Relief washed over him. *Wait, where's Hammer?*

None of the men in the car responded to his voice. Butch's head snapped to the right. He noticed a dime-sized hole in the bearded American's left temple. He jumped. *Oh shit!* Only a tiny trickle of coagulating blood marked the entrance wound. The dead SEAL's unblinking eyes stared straight ahead. A quick scan of the two men in the front seat revealed similar lethal injuries. An ambush.

Butch scrambled out of the car and shut the door. His heart raced from the adrenaline surging through his bloodstream. Using his yellow robe, he quickly wiped the handle free of his fingerprints. *Think!* He fought his flight instinct. *Finish the mission. You have transportation. Get to the Temple.* He reached for the driver's side door when a loud *bang* echoed down the alley. Butch dove around the front end of the vehicle. Peering out from under the front bumper, he identified a short male wearing a food-stained, white apron carrying empty boxes. Lying on the ground, he worried at being spotted by a passing car or pedestrian from the main road fifty feet to his rear. *C'mon, man, go back inside.*

But the worker didn't leave. The man leaned back against the hotel wall, fished a pack of cigarettes from his shirt pocket, and pulled out a cancer stick with his teeth.

Butch silently cursed as a spiral of smoke rose only twenty feet away. He couldn't risk making his move to the driver's side. Wearing monk's robes or stripped down to a loin cloth—his two options—he couldn't conceal the suspicious nature of commandeering the vehicle. The odds fared even worse when authorities armed themselves with a description of the vehicle from the hotel employee. *Hurry up and finish.*

Butch glanced at the man smoking then the street behind him. A vehicle cruised by along the main road. Little time remained before someone noticed a monk crouched in front of a car this late at night.

Another *bang* rang in the night air. Two male voices bantered.

Swinging his gaze back to the smoker, he saw a second male enter the alley.

A moment later, a third man joined the growing group. The latest arrival nodded toward the sedan.

The smoker shrugged.

Shit. I can't drive all the way to the embassy in that car without getting busted.

"What idiot parked in the alley?" one of the men asked.

"I'll go ask," the smoker responded.

Sorry, guys. I know you'll understand I have no choice. Bidding the American team a silent farewell, Butch hunched low and backed out of the alley, keeping the vehicle between him and the two remaining workers, until he reached the city street. Knowing little time remained before authorities learned of a multiple homicide, he determined his best course of action meant racing to the Temple, collecting the objective, and finding a high-speed method to the embassy. At the T-intersection, he turned left then froze. *They're already here?*

Flashing lights atop a parked police cruiser filled the street.

The doorman to the hotel stood next to two uniformed officers near the entrance. He pointed toward the door then walked inside with the policemen following close.

A handful of pedestrians stood on both sides of the street watching the interaction. Several of the witnesses held up cell phones, as if recording the occurrence.

Those cops aren't here because of the rescue team in the alley. What the hell is going on? The direct path to the Temple blocked, he turned in the opposite direction and mentally plotted a separate course to Shen's residence. With police activity brewing in the streets, Butch feared his disguise worked against him as a monk found walking this late at night, alone, did not fall into the normal pattern of life in *Dandong.*

He covered the next two blocks without incident.

Near the next four-way intersection, another police car crept into view on the western side of the street, blocking the route.

He ducked into a doorway before the cruiser's interior offered the officers a view of his position. The moisture disappeared from Butch's mouth. Few, if any, options remained for the Delta operator. With the SAD team dead, and now his path to Shen's house blocked, he chose the only other open action. *I have to warn JSOC.*

Risking exposure to the cops across the street, Butch stepped out of the doorway and curled around the corner to the right, away from the police car. Familiar with the library, he headed back to the computer used in earlier communications. He doubted the facility remained open—though locked doors did not pose a huge hurdle to entry. He conducted a series of turns heading in a general northern direction. Precious seconds ticked off during his evasion.

As Butch approached the library, his mind swirled with questions. Where was Hammer? Who possessed enough skill to ambush and kill a trio of experienced SEALs? How did the assassins know of the team's existence? He worried Hammer fell into enemy hands and succumbed to enhanced interrogation. This scenario topped his list of likely reasons. Whatever the cause, mission success depended on how quickly the Chinese authorities found the car and dead Americans. Warning command of the impending discovery became his top priority. The city of *Dandong* sat on a powder keg, and the fuse already burned.

Chapter 33

Jennings' Residence, 11:43 p.m.

The two North Koreans left the apartment almost an hour ago. During that time, Barrett Jennings ran the full breadth of emotions. Should he take Lilly and run? Should he—of all things—contact authorities? Or did a way exist to financially profit then disappear in some far-off country? No matter his choice, he assumed North Korea's memory of his betrayal lasting a second longer than his final heartbeat.

At one point, he nearly picked up the phone and summoned help, but his opportunistic tendencies got the better of him. He chose a plan that fed his desire to come out ahead financially. Despite his personality failures, Barrett's natural intelligence recognized the strength of his own ego.

"Father?" Lilly called.

Barrett hurried from the kitchen and entered the back room, anxious for any positive developments. "Did you find something?"

"The man from the hotel is a well-known American."

"Are you kidding me?" The evidence plastered on all six computer monitors suggested otherwise. Video clips, news articles from major sports magazines, and hacked hotel registration data confirmed her claim. The photos certainly looked like the man in the hotel video. "So, who is he?"

"Cole—

"Haufner." He tilted his face toward the ceiling and closed his eyes. *Mother of God. Can this situation get any worse?*

"He is from here!" she exclaimed. "He studied and lived with the monks at the *Wulong* Temple."

Barrett did not share her enthusiasm. In fact, the last name registered viscerally. Two decades ago, the Haufner name turned his life upside down. Because of this family, he found himself in a deadly situation with the North Koreans. He hoped with all his being for a different identification. "You are sure?"

"I'm positive." Lilly beamed.

Barrett now understood why the man in the hotel video proved his superiority to the 14K hired help. Cole trained with the Shaolin monks. And his skill level? The magazine articles Lilly discovered suggested the young Haufner owned the top spot for the best pound-for-pound MMA fighter in the sport's history. *How did I miss hearing about him?*

The memories of his days in the CIA came flooding back. In his last job as a U.S. spy, Barrett held full blame for the kidnapping, by the North Koreans, of American scientist, Markus Haufner, out from under his nose. Desperate to squash the agency's greatest failure, the CIA hired a local assassin for cleanup duty. A North Korean agent, Park's uncle, thwarted the attempt and held this fact over his head for the last twenty years. His mind raced at the implication of Haufner's return.

Barrett wondered if some way existed of turning the knowledge of Cole Haufner's presence in the city to his advantage. His cell phone vibrated with an incoming call. He didn't recognize the number but answered anyway. *At least the caller isn't Park.* "Yes?"

"We encountered a problem," a young man on the other end spoke in rapid Mandarin.

Barrett froze. "I do not know who you are or what you're talking about."

"The man you told us to follow and detain escaped. Everyone is dead except me."

He felt light-headed. "What do you mean 'dead'? Where did the man go?"

"We surrounded him and two monks. All of a sudden, our men started dying. They were shot by a gun that made no noise. I'm the only one that escaped."

Both panic and confusion coursed through Barrett's body. "Who was shooting? The man? The monks?"

"No, no. Someone we did not see."

Knowing the extent of the increased danger Cole's return placed on his mission, Barrett tightened his grip on his phone. "What happened to the man you were to detain?"

"I don't know. I ran before they could kill me. Our men were dropping so fast. I never saw the shooters!"

Barrett immediately thought of Park. *Did those two maniacs kill my men? If so, for what purpose?* He thought the North Korean commandos targeted the American Embassy personnel. A deduction rose from the depths of his confusion, one that frightened him even further. *Did another American survive the fight at the dock?* "Keep out of sight, and do not speak to anyone! I will call you back with instructions." He disconnected the call then turned to Lilly. "Where is this American, Cole Haufner, now?"

"After he walked outside, he headed west with the monk. The cameras no longer tracked him once he walked into the Temple gardens." She pulled up the last video feed showing Cole and the robed man crossing a large road before disappearing from the frame. "No cameras exist on the west side of the street."

"Your computer has not seen him since?" he asked.

"He has not reappeared."

Barrett slumped against the computer desk and ran a hand over his face. His mind raced. A ghost from his past returned as an adult, taking apart the 14K gang he maintained as hired help. Some unknown person or people, perhaps even a surviving American from the initial battle, thwarted the attempt to capture Cole, killing several men in the process. Is this person working with Cole? And, of course, Park posed the most immediate threat to Lilly and him. He expected the two North Korean's return any moment now. They'd want results.

Still something nagged at the back of his mind regarding Cole Haufner and this unknown shooter. Was Cole's arrival a smokescreen for another American military team inserted into *Dandong*? Barrett knew how enamored the Chinese populace became with famous people, particularly American athletes. He wondered if the CIA dangled Cole as a carrot to draw away attention from some hidden truth.

A metallic key inserted into the front door lock interrupted his thoughts. He quickly turned to Lilly. "Get rid of all the information! Do not speak of what you discovered. Act as if you are still looking into the hotel system."

"But Father, commander Park will want to know the American's name." Lilly covered her head with her hands.

"If you want to stay alive, you will do as I say."

She quickly scrubbed the screen of all the individual windows then opened the hotel registration system.

Hearing footsteps enter the apartment, Barrett turned toward the living room.

The two North Koreans rounded the corner and headed for the bedroom.

As they neared, he thought he smelled fresh gunpowder, reminding him just how dangerous these men were.

Park pushed past Barrett. "Lilly, what have you learned?"

"I am going through passport travel to determine the identity of the man from the hotel."

"You have not found the man's name yet?" Park's voice reverberated off the walls. "You are taking too long."

Lilly threw up her hands in front of her face and cowered in her chair.

Barrett noted Park's anger and the change in tone. Whatever happened with the American Embassy team did not sit well with the North Korean. "What is the status of the men in the car?"

Park cast a quick glance at his sniper. "They are no longer a concern. We do not have much time." He jabbed a finger into Barrett's chest. "Tell your men to bring the American here. Also, send someone immediately to the hotel and dispose of the car in the alley."

His throat suddenly dry, Barrett swallowed hard. Had Park displayed a hint of disapproval toward his subordinate? What happened to the Americans in the car? Terror filled him at the thought of Park discovering his withholding information. *What should I do?*

"Another recognition." Lilly proclaimed.

Barrett closed his eyes and silently released the air from his lungs. He turned his attention toward the monitors. A video feed displayed someone in yellow robes walking alone along the city sidewalk. When the individual glanced up, while passing under a bright neon sign, the screen froze. The blurred image refreshed every few seconds, slowly revealing a clearer picture of a bald man. The software scrubbed the feed of digital noise. After a minute, the word "complete" displayed at the bottom of the window.

"The match is eighty-nine percent confident," Lilly excitedly announced.

Park leaned close to the monitor. "Where is this man now?" he growled.

Lilly tagged the image and fed the data into another program. The video feed fast-forwarded until synching with the current time.

The man, dressed as a monk, headed east, now six blocks from the Crowne Plaza Hotel.

Park tapped the monitor with his index finger. "Lilly, find out where he came from."

Barrett shook from the adrenaline coursing through his body. *Is this Cole in disguise?*

Park whispered something to the sniper.

His subordinate nodded curtly.

Lilly pulled up earlier surveillance footage showing the subject coming out of the city library. She hit Play and fast-forwarded the feed a second time.

Shown in ten-second increments, the monk walked directly to the hotel. He tarried in the rear alley for less than two minutes then reappeared, heading in the same direction from which he'd started. The video ended at the subject's current location.

Park turned to Lilly. "Pull up the building plans on that library and get your laptop." He then glanced at Barrett. "You two are coming with us."

"Us?" Barrett stammered. "Where are we going?"

The North Korean pointed at the live video feed of the front of the library. "That building."

He held out his hands. "Why? A mistake must exist within the program. He's just a monk."

"That's no monk," Park grinned. "He's our man."

He hoped the North Korean's assessment held true. Barrett knew Park's focus elsewhere hid his lie regarding the identification of Cole Haufner.

Chapter 34

Mituo Temple, 11:23 p.m.

Cole felt only minimal relief when the American with the Texas accent reported no evidence of police activity. He didn't bother asking the man his method of disposal of the bodies. A large part of him desired full disclosure to the authorities of everything he'd witnessed this evening. Missing the twenty-four-hour window for registering his arrival with the authorities, Cole's failure paled in comparison to the non-reporting of a triple murder. Self-defense mattered little in a country where individual rights existed for only a select few. The shock of events and loss of his uncle masked any awareness to his fugitive status.

Shen covered Master Li's body with a sheet, leaving his face open to viewing. The body's pose would remain so until the brothers from the *Wulong* Temple took their master up the mountain. For hundreds of miles, the faithful would journey to honor a highly respected leader. Shortly after, a new name marked the start to the next generation.

Cole gave a wide berth to the soldier fieldstripping his rifle on the floor. He pulled aside his cousin. "*Biao di*, how long before the others arrive?" he asked in Mandarin.

"Within the hour." Shen's eyes still ringed red.

Cole glanced at Hammer before refocusing on Shen. "I can't remain here any longer. You should stay away from me, as well as the soldier. I fear for your safety."

Shen nodded. "Cole, say good-bye to Father. The brothers will arrive soon. The American must leave before that time."

"Ain't that the truth?" Hammer asked without looking up from his rifle.

Cole dropped his jaw. "You know Mandarin? You understood the entire time?"

"Picked up a few words here and there. I can't speak a lick."

"Bullshit." Cole threw his hands on his hips "By the way, why in hell are American soldiers in China? What is my brother doing here?"

At last, Hammer glanced up from his weapon assembly. "Do me a favor and shut your mouth until we're out of this country."

"How's that?" Anger flashed in his voice.

"You're fucking up the most important mission your brother has ever received in his life." Hammer's eyes narrowed. "When you arrived unannounced, you forced me to split from a rendezvous with Butch to come save your ass."

Standing five feet away, Cole jabbed a finger toward the man sitting on the floor. "I didn't ask you or anyone else to rescue me."

"You had a plan to save your other friend here?"

Cole fell silent. Even through his anger and grief-fogged thinking, he couldn't refute Hammer's point. Now that Cole was truthful with himself, coming to China wasn't the only foolish thing he'd done these past few days. At the Crowne Plaza, Melody urged him to bow to the gang members. If he'd swallowed his pride and done so, perhaps his uncle might still live. *What have I done?* The burden of guilt crushed him. "You're right. How do I fix things?"

The muscled Delta operator dropped his cleaning rag and reassembled the weapon with lightning speed. In under thirty seconds, he finished then slapped a magazine into the assault rifle and chambered a round.

Cole couldn't take his gaze off Hammer's deft movements. He noticed Shen staring at the display of skill.

"You ain't in the octagon, son. You're out of your element."

"Look, maybe I *have* screwed up. But I'm not a complete jerkoff." Cole's shoulders relaxed, and his facial features softened. "I want to help. I'll do whatever you tell me."

"You will sit right here." Hammer nodded toward the floor.

A flush heated Cole's face. "I can't just do nothing."

"You can, and you will." Hammer stood, rifle in-hand. "Your brother will be here any minute."

Cole's body numbed. He closed his eyes. "If I find out you're lying, I'll kill you."

Chapter 35

Butch—coming to the apartment? The possibility created the first sense of joy Cole experienced since before the funeral. But the prospect was bittersweet. Witnessing Shen praying over Master Li's body reminded him of unanswered questions.

Cole knelt beside his cousin, whose prayers seemed never-ending. Despite Shen's outward composure, his eyes expressed the pain of someone struggling with his emotions. Finally, the prayer ended. "*Biao di*, how is Master Li your father?" he whispered.

Shen took in a deep breath then blew out the air. "As you know, the lay Buddhist sect has historical instances of higher ordained monks and nuns marrying."

Cole recalled the practice from teachings at the Temple, though he'd never witnessed the arrangement himself. "I remember, yes."

Shen straightened his back and glanced at Cole. "At an early age, Father became a high-ranking member. Back then, many nuns studied and traveled throughout the area. One such woman visited the Temple many times, and she and Father fell in love. The *Shaolin* Elders allowed them to marry. Mother passed away during a difficult childbirth. The other nuns raised me at the Temple."

I've never heard this story before. "I didn't know I

had a cousin. Why was I never told about you?"

"Back then, *Dandong* faced many difficulties." Shen grimaced before continuing. "The economy struggled. Fewer people donated to the Temple. Father grew desperate to provide enough food for the monks. A wealthy man stepped forward and offered what they needed, but he was very traditional and demanded the monks and nuns live apart."

"Did this benefactor know about the child—about you?"

"For fear of losing the support, Father transferred me to the *Fenghuan* Mountain Temple farther west. My new home sat deeper into the countryside. I was only three years old when I left *Wulong*. *Fenghuan* is where I grew up."

For Cole, losing his parents at six years of age proved almost insurmountable. *I can't imagine how much worse was the pain for someone younger.* He glanced toward Master Li. "I wish I had known, *jiu jiu*."

Shen put his left hand on Cole's right shoulder. "Father faced a difficult decision. Many at the Temple wished for me to live even farther away. As time passed, the secret became easier to accept."

Cole studied Shen's facial features and noted subtle similarities to his uncle's own. "When did Butch and I arrive?"

"You and I are the same age. Three years later, you came to *Dandong*. I did not know of you until I was eleven years old."

Sudden guilt attacked at the idea he'd replaced his cousin as Master Li's son at *Wulong* Mountain. He dropped his chin. "Did you resent me?"

Shen sighed. "Feelings, at first. But the Buddhist teachings helped me deal with the childish anger. I never harbored any ill will toward you, Cole. You filled a void in Father's soul caused by my absence. *Sifu* and I wrote each other and visited periodically. I felt his love. Nothing that's transpired is your fault. I have a good life."

Head still hung low, he nodded while stifling the cry poised at the edge of his lips. More tears streamed down his cheeks. He placed his trembling hands over Master Li's. "I should never have come back, *jiu jiu*. If I'd just stayed home, you would still..."

Shen put an arm around him. "Your presence did not cause his death, *biao di*. His heart did not work properly. He rejected the doctor's recommendations for surgery. Father desired a natural life free of mankind's artificial intervention. He accepted his health issue with a positive spirit."

Cole shook his head and swiped at fresh tears. "No, I am the reason. I'm the reason my family is dying all around me."

"Do not talk of such things," Shen spoke. "Father saw us—all of his children, even Butch—on his last day. Your brother visited the Temple earlier, and he spoke with *Sifu* for some time. Butch made Father swear to never tell anyone of his presence. And yet, he broke his promise because you needed him. I watched Father's face when you embraced him. I do not recall seeing more joy. You gave him peace."

Even Shen's forceful certainty could not overturn Cole's vision of a swirling black cloud rotating like a scythe, with him at the center, cutting down everyone who stood nearby. He feared his presence causing his brother's demise. Straightening, he let out a long sigh. "What happens now? For you?"

"I will do what I must, *biao di*." Shen stood and folded his hands inside the sleeves of his robe. "We will place Father in his rightful position with the other masters then choose another Temple leader. We have done so for over one thousand years."

"Or," Cole rose to his feet. *Is my idea crazy?* "You can come with us. With Butch and me. The American soldiers will keep us safe."

Shen's eyebrows furrowed, and his head shook. "I understand your concern. Your offer, though generous, is not my path. My place is here."

"I'm sorry." Cole realized how desperate and absurd his suggestion must sound to his cousin. "You're right, of course. Too often today, I've spoken without thinking."

Shen's expression softened. "A shame we did not grow up together. Father told me your love for family is your best quality."

Cole took in a deep breath. "I'm afraid I don't share in *jiu jiu's* optimism." *My love is killing what's left of my family. I can't allow this curse near Butch.*

Chapter 36

A disgusted exclamation from across the room interrupted Cole's thoughts. He glanced up and heard Hammer swear under his breath. *What's wrong? Is Butch okay?* He rose to his feet.

The big man shook his head and waved him off. "Nest? Do you copy?" Waiting several seconds, the Texan swung his pack off his back and dug out what looked like a heavy-duty radio. The headset and tiny lip mic he wore synched to the unit by a thin wire. Hammer tested the connection and pressed a couple of buttons.

Dread filled Cole. "What's wrong?"

Hammer closed his eyes, dropped his head, and roughly jammed the device back into the pack. "Everything."

"Butch?"

Frowning, Hammer reslung the pack then grabbed his rifle. "I lost comms with the guys running the show. The rescue team hasn't checked-in. I have no idea where your brother is now. The pickup point was at your hotel."

Cole rolled his shoulders back. "The Crowne Plaza? Why choose a busy part of town?"

"You coming here complicated things. Remember?"

"Dammit," Cole mumbled. *Point taken—again.*

"What do we do now?"

"*We*" Hammer wagged his index finger at Cole—
"get the hell out of China and go home." The big man
then pointed at himself. "*I* get back to the rally point
and find Butch before the bad guys do."

Cole set his jaw. "I'm sure you don't believe me,
but I can help. I know the area and the language, and
I'm not too bad in a fight."

"Listen, boy, real combat doesn't have referees or
rules. I know you're hot shit in the ring." He jabbed a
finger toward the floor. "This situation is way beyond
you. You've done enough *helping.*"

"*Biao di*, I must show you something." Shen
grabbed Cole's elbow.

He continued staring at Hammer. *This asshole
realizes I'm one fight away from the World Champion
title, right?* Cole finally glanced at his cousin. "What
are you talking about?"

Shen turned toward the far side of the room.
"Please come." The monk motioned for both men to
follow him.

Cole watched Shen open a small door before the
monk stepped down into the shadows. Following, Cole
stood at the top of a short set of stairs. He barely made
out his cousin below in the darkness.

The monk toggled a wall switch. A single light
bulb hanging from the low ceiling blinked on, casting
an eerie shadow in the partial basement room. At the
edge of the light, on the far wall, Shen pushed against a
wall sconce. A *click* sounded, and a pop-out door
opened. The monk quickly stepped through.

Cole descended three wooden steps onto a dirt
floor in the cool ten-by-eight-foot room. The four walls

appeared carved out of solid rock. Several dingy tapestries hung from ceiling to floor. The air smelled of moist earth. A rustling noise preceded his cousin's reappearance in the main room holding what looked like the same type of pack Hammer wore.

"What the hell?" the Special Forces soldier exclaimed from the stairs. He joined the men below.

"Butch was here this morning. Since he took on the appearance of one of the brothers from the Temple, he desired leaving his belongings with me," Shen explained.

Hammer snatched the combat pack out of Shen's grip and stepped to one side of the room. He dumped the contents onto the floor.

The monk ducked back inside the enclave and produced Butch's remaining gear, including his coveralls.

"What about a box? A suitcase?" Hammer rattled.

Cole translated and received the reply. "He's says Butch left nothing more."

"He's sure?"

Cole thought Hammer's squint implied a warning against lying. "Are you positive, *biao di*? The soldier seems certain the item is here."

"I am quite certain the room is empty," Shen nodded toward the archway.

Seeing a fresh scowl on Hammer's face, Cole didn't think the Delta man appeared satisfied. "He would tell us if such a case was in his home. The Shaolin monks do not lie."

Hammer pushed aside both men, pawed through the chamber, and exited with a mumbled curse. Rummaging through the scattered pack contents, he grabbed the satellite communicator. He held up the unit closer to the light. A bullet hole the size of a half dollar displayed the catastrophic damage. "That's the reason we became separated," he whispered.

"What do you mean?" Cole's question went unanswered.

"Where did Butch go when he left?" Hammer demanded of Shen.

For clarity, Cole again translated to and from Mandarin. Shen gave details of Butch's trips to the library.

"Where is this library located?" Hammer removed several spare rifle magazines from Butch's vest and stuffed them into the pockets of his own.

A soft rap on the upstairs door filtered down to the chamber. All three froze.

Cole locked gazes with Hammer. "Butch?" He mouthed the words. For the first time since he met him, he saw concern in Hammer's face.

The American slowly shook his head from side to side.

"The brothers might have already arrived," Shen whispered.

"Or the police," Cole feared what a visit from the authorities meant for himself and Shen, not to mention Butch.

The monk grabbed a dirty tapestry hanging on one of the walls and pulled aside the aged rug. A darkened tunnel led out of the room. "The passage leads west into the forest."

Cole glanced up toward the first floor. He hadn't said a proper good-bye to his uncle. "*Jiu jiu.*"

"Your call, Haufner," Hammer said.

Undecided, Cole looked to his cousin.

A second, louder knock sounded.

"Go. Father would wish for your safety."

Hammer jammed the pack contents back into the bag. He collected all of Butch's equipment, including his weapons, and headed toward the escape route.

Cole stared into Shen's eyes. The finality of their meeting caused a churning sensation in his gut. "Goodbye, *baio di*. Say a prayer to *Sifu* for me. I hope to see you again in this lifetime." He delivered a brief, strong hug to his cousin.

"As do I. Go in peace."

As he followed Hammer into the dark tunnel, he thought Shen's phrase absurd.

Chapter 37

West of Mituo Temple, 11:45 p.m.

In the pitch-black darkness, Cole couldn't avoid bruising encounters with the hand-hewn subterranean rock. Their hasty escape offered no time for retrieval of the night-vision goggles from the combat packs. He climbed out of the escape tunnel stretching at least two-hundred feet deeper into the woods, west of the main Temple grounds. Once above ground and out of the tunnel, he took stock of his position. Moonlight filtered through the thin forest, casting moving shadows from the tree limbs swaying in a light breeze.

"You sure you wanna go with me?" the Texan whispered.

Cole stuck out his chin. "I'd rather you kill me than tell me I can't."

"Don't say I didn't warn you." The Delta operator unpacked Butch's gear, laying items on the ground. "I'll explain the hardware."

Cole marveled at the equipment his brother used on his missions. He soaked in Hammer's description of each object's purpose and proper use. He pulled on the battle vest then slung the assault pack straps over his shoulders. His borrowed accoutrement fit well, and he was glad he and Butch shared similar physiques. Next, he donned the Kevlar bump helmet with attached

NVGs. With the lip mic next to his mouth, he synced communications with Hammer.

The final lesson involved Butch's rifle and pistol. Hammer hoisted the short-barreled assault weapon, cleared the chamber of a live round, and only then handed Cole the firearm.

The gun felt solid but not particularly heavy. He looked through the scope and saw the aiming dot in the center of the glass. Even with the attached suppressor, the nine-inch barrel kept the weapon short and maneuverable. Unsure if Hammer entrusted him with the rifle, he offered up the firearm.

The Delta man waved. "All yours, now. Ever shoot before?"

"A couple of times with Butch's pistol when he rotated back home. I never fired anything like the longer one, though."

"All right, then, let me give you the condensed version on this bad boy."

Thompson demonstrated the basics of the safety switch, proper holding, and the trigger on the rifle. He pointed out the magazine release used when ammunition ran out. Time was short, and the training was spare. Somewhat familiar with Butch's pistol, Cole quickly worked the action then slid the handgun into the custom holster attached to the combat vest.

"Welcome to the military," Hammer said.

He narrowed his gaze. "Why do I get the feeling you guys get a little more practice time?"

"Just a little." Hammer's voice lowered. "Listen, this situation isn't some video game, okay? If you get caught with any of this stuff, your life is forfeit. You'll wish you were dead once they start working you over."

Cole swallowed hard. "What's this mission about? Why are you guys here?"

"You're smart enough to know I can't tell you."

You'd think risking your life came with a little detail on this operation. "But, whatever's in play, the U.S. is risking a war with our most lethal enemy, right?"

"World changing. If we don't do our job, nobody has a safe place anywhere on planet earth."

"Is your mission related to the suitcase you asked about earlier at the Temple?"

Hammer scanned the woods. "If the Chinese acquire the objective, we're screwed. But if that thing is taken across the border into North Korea...game over for the world."

"A nuke? Chemical bomb?"

"Neither. Time's up. We gotta get moving."

Asshole. Cole accepted two offered extra magazines and stuffed them into the front pockets of his vest. All of the gear carried some weight, but the load felt well balanced. On numerous prior occasions, he trained with weight vests, and this setup felt very similar. The pair flipped their night-vision goggles into position. Looking through the NVGs, he saw the forest come to life with relatively clear detail.

"You ready?" Hammer asked.

Cole audibly exhaled. "Let's go." He stood and racked the first round of custom-loaded .300 Blackout into the chamber. Leaving on the safety switch, he brushed his thumb over the metal tab, ensuring muscle memory if the situation deteriorated into a gunfight.

The two men weaved through the thin forest and covered the distance back to the Temple garden in under a minute. Hammer signaled for a stop inside the tree line. Both scanned their area of responsibility through rifle scopes.

Cole focused his attention to their left. Nervous energy caused his hands to tremble. The grass surrounding the large Buddha statue looked undisturbed. If he hadn't witnessed the carnage himself, he wouldn't believe men died near that very spot within the past hour. Scanning farther, he picked out Shen's residence. Whoever knocked on the door no longer waited outside. Zero police presence along the street offered him hope the Temple brothers caused the noise. *Please stay safe, baio di.*

"Clear right," Hammer announced.

"Clear left. Shen's house looks quiet," Cole responded.

Hammer flipped up his NVGs and glanced over to Cole. "You good?"

"Scared as shit, actually. I don't want to screw up."

"You're doin' great. Just do what I tell ya' when I tell ya'."

Cole nodded once then raised the night-vision goggles from his line of sight. At the midnight hour, the streets remained empty of car traffic. A couple of seconds passed before his vision returned to normal. Cole recognized the road T-intersection and saw what looked like a dark-colored sedan parked nose forward on a small side alley about twenty feet to the right.

"The car facing us is our ride," Hammer said.

"Understood," Cole responded. "I know these streets. I should drive."

"I go first. Stay here and cover my movement. I'll jump into the backseat and tell you when the coast is clear. Get in behind the wheel and then drop your gear in the passenger foot well. Those damned surveillance cameras cover every inch of this town."

Cole pulled the rifle to his shoulder and nodded. "Ready."

Hammer paused for a moment then sprinted across the fifty-yard clearing. Without stopping, he crossed the narrow street and dashed into the side alley.

When Cole lost sight of the Delta operator, he sucked in a breath, his heart thumping against his chest. He realized how much comfort he drew from Hammer's physical presence. *Why did I volunteer? I don't want the responsibility of getting anyone else hurt or killed.* No longer a simple visitor to China, he assumed the role of a foreign combatant, a participant in a covert mission with no backup and no diplomatic cover.

"I have eyes on you." Hammer's voice in Cole's left ear came low and reassuring. "Clear to move."

I can't believe I'm doing this. Cole rose onto the balls of his feet, scanned quickly in all directions, and leaped into the clearing at full speed. In what felt like the longest ten seconds of his life, he reached the darkened car. He spun and dropped to one knee, facing back toward the clearing. He jammed the buttstock into his right shoulder and swept the area with the muzzle of his suppressed rifle. No threats identified, he pulled open the door and dove inside. As quiet as possible, he wrestled off the gear and jammed everything into the passenger side foot well.

"Where did you learn moves like those?" Hammer asked from the rear seat.

"Just seemed like the smart thing."

"Keep impressing me, Cowboy."

A strong, unpleasant odor assailed Cole's nostrils. "Damn. What's that smell?"

"Your 14K friends are partying in the trunk."

So, that's where you put the bodies. Cole let out a long stream of air, barely absorbing the magnitude of his actions. Fully committed, he had no option of turning back.

Chapter 38

Crowne Plaza Hotel, 0012 Hour

Cole found a darkened section of road one block south of the hotel. A nonfunctioning overhead light offered him a prime spot for parking the car. The streets sat quiet at this hour. Only the odd reveler from a nearby bar staggered about or called for a taxi. Given the number of businesses catering to international travelers, he expected minor activity. The odd neon sign, left on by owners, splashed bright colors on the wet city sidewalks.

The plan the two men discussed in the vehicle was brief and to the point. Step one, Cole entered the hotel and approached Xiu. Step two, check out of his room. Step three, make a point of stating his next moves— take a taxi to the *Dandong* airport for the first flight to *Beijing* then purchase a ticket back to the United States. With his alibi—travel plans—in place, he would exit the hotel and circle the building, allowing either Butch or the embassy team a visual of him. After making a slow pass, he would walk past the car, returning to the sedan only after Hammer, watching for any tail, called the all clear. Hammer hoped any teammates trailing Cole would offer him an opportunity for a rendezvous.

Cole taped the lip mic just below the neckline of his shirt, but he couldn't risk wearing the earpiece. Any conversation ran only one way between Hammer and him. He took cleansing deep breaths, struggling for control of his nerves. "Any last advice?"

"If you get busted, blame the 14K gang for pursuing you from the hotel and your reason for running. The attempted kidnapping will give you plausible denial. Play up your fame."

"Okay." Cole nodded once to himself then exited the car. Standing on the sidewalk, Cole felt completely exposed. All of the weaponry—Hammer's and Butch's—remained inside the vehicle. He turned and headed toward the southeast corner of the hotel. He arrived at the intersection and crossed the street. Farther ahead, a man and woman walked arm-in-arm. He turned west, heading along the hotel's southern edge. As he passed the rear service alley, he saw blue-and-white flashing lights near the other end. The sight of the police car made his heart jump, and he picked up his pace.

"Cops at the back of the building," he mumbled into the lip mic. Without the earpiece, he had no way of knowing if Hammer heard.

Throat suddenly dry, Cole turned right at the corner and headed for the front entrance. Everything appeared normal. The smartly-dressed bellman tipped his cap and welcomed him back to the Crowne Plaza. With some relief, he entered and approached the front desk. Melody's friend, Xiu, stood behind a computer monitor. Maintaining his composure for the benefit of the hotel staff monitoring the security cameras, he smiled while closing the distance.

Turning her attention from the computer screen, Xiu reflexively grinned. When her gaze landed squarely on Cole, her face turned hard.

Seeing the change in her demeanor, he inhaled, his heart pounding at the expectation of an impending disaster. He swallowed the bile in his throat. "Any messages for Cole Haufner?" he asked in a pleasant tone.

"One second, Mr. Haufner," she replied in passable English then tapped the keyboard. "I'm sorry, sir, no messages for you this evening."

"Ah, I see." He hid his disappointment. "Well then, I plan on checking out earlier than expected and heading back to America. Can I complete my bill now?"

Her facial features softened. "A very wise decision, Mr. Haufner. One moment for the printout of your statement."

A wise decision? What does that comment mean?

Xiu took a sheet from the printer and placed the bill on the counter. "Please *carefully* review the charges to your room. I will retrieve your luggage. One more moment, please."

Cole watched her step through an opening in the back wall behind the counter. He scanned the statement and signed at the bottom.

She reappeared almost immediately.

"Here you are, Mr. Haufner." She handed him the duffel. "Do you have any questions regarding the items on your statement?"

"I'm sure everything is fine."

With a finger, she pushed the sheet of paper toward him. "Please check the comments section at the bottom of your bill on your way out. Best of luck."

Confused, Cole turned away. *An odd thing to say.*

While constantly scanning for Butch, he immediately forgot her request. He threw the bag over his shoulder and kept his stride casual while exiting the building. Once on the sidewalk, Cole stuck to the plan. He lingered for a moment, in case the recovery team or Butch maintained watch of the front of the hotel.

The doorman approached. "May I provide assistance?"

Cole shook his head. "No need, thank you."

Moving onto phase two, Cole slowly walked north. Now traveling clockwise around the facility, he recalled the police presence at the rear of the hotel. He hoped the investigation did not involve his brother. A rustling noise caught his attention. His grip tightened, and he realized he still held the now-crumpled hotel statement. He smoothed out the document and glanced down at the printout. When his gaze settled on the comments section, he froze.

Cole jammed the paper into his trouser pocket and turned back. Employing every ounce of his self-control, he forced a normal walking pace. Lengthening his strides, he cleared the front of the building and turned toward the hotel's south side.

"Get ready to move," he growled into the hidden lip mic. His palms sweated, and his heart raced. Rational thought proved an impossible task. Passing the rear alley, he ignored the swirling blue and white lights on his left.

Rounding the southeast corner, Cole saw his car. As he approached the vehicle, he twirled in a three-hundred-sixty-degree turn, scanning in all directions for a threat. Ignoring the necessary steps for Hammer's all clear, he grabbed the door handle and jumped into the driver's seat.

"What the hell? You trying to get us both killed?" The Texan chastised from the rear seat.

Cole yanked the paper from his pocket and dropped the parchment into Hammer's lap.

"What's this?"

Sucking in a quick breath, Cole glanced in the rearview mirror. "Look at the bottom."

"Three Americans dead in alley. Police are asking for you. Run," Hammer read aloud.

"Is Butch one of the three?" Fear and anxiety overtook his voice.

"The rescue team comprised of a trio of men from the embassy. I doubt he's one of them. Dammit!" Hammer cursed. "Who gave you this note?"

"A sympathetic hotel worker." Cole started the car then pulled onto the street heading south.

Hammer let out a lungful of air. "Sounds like the recovery team got ambushed. Now I know why they didn't check in. Someone got to them."

"What about Butch?" Cole couldn't fight the rising panic from his voice. Several uncomfortable seconds passed. His grip tightened on the steering wheel.

"Head for the library," Hammer growled.

As Cole turned the car northeast, he realized the weight of the Chinese authorities now rested on his shoulders. *Hang on, brother. I'm coming for you.*

Chapter 39

Dandong Library, 0047 hours

Few scenarios in *Dandong* appeared more out of place than a yellow-robed monk in front of the main city library after midnight. But standing outside the building was exactly where Butch Haufner found himself. After the discovery of the murdered CIA team, he mulled every conceivable method for alerting JSOC. He even reconsidered risking police capture by weaving through blockades on routes back to the *Mituo* Temple. But he feared whoever ambushed the American squad also knew his identity, and he dared not risk exposing Shen or drawing the unseen enemy closer to the stolen case.

Out of money, he couldn't buy a disposable phone. He considered stealing one, but the risk was too great, including signaling the PLA if that's who killed the CIA team. The Chinese government, drawing much of their strength from the army, possessed virtually unlimited resources. Once they turned attention on him, nothing in the world could stop them.

Standing in the shadows of a clump of trees, Butch studied the library's exterior. The stand-alone, two-story structure displayed smooth-stone walls with open ground on all sides. At this hour, he assumed all doors remained locked. No light escaped the windows and glass door. Wide-angle cameras, mounted high on the upper story, covered all four corners of the building.

Scanning for a weakness in the security, Butch noticed an oddity with the camera at the northwest position. On closer examination, he discovered the device angled upward, more so than the rest. Something caused a more skyward tilt in the lens angle. Using his best judgment, he assumed this section of the wall went uncovered. Seeing no pedestrians, he sprinted at an angle toward the northwest corner of the library.

When he reached the stonework, Butch flattened against the wall. *Scan. Control your breathing. Don't move.* He held still for five seconds. Facing north, he peeked around the corner to the west side of the building—the rear. A camera mounted twelve feet above the ground on a one-foot extension off the wall covered the grassy area of the back of the library. Judging by the CCTV's protruding angle, Butch felt confident of his ability to reach the back door without detection. He plunged forward, hugging the stone siding. Ten feet ahead, a small service door came into view. A warning sign posted at eye level indicated electrical equipment inside. Butch wiggled the exterior handle. *Locked.*

The Delta team leader placed his back to the door and with a powerful kick sent the heel of his right foot into the metal just under the handle. With a booming rattle, the door gave slightly. He spun and pushed with all his strength. In a slow, drawn-out groan, the steel door relented under the applied force. Butch scanned one last time around the dark yard before squeezing through the narrow gap in the doorway. Once inside, he pulled the door shut as far as the bent hinges allowed.

Against the hum of the building's electrical equipment, a few blinking lights provided the total sum of illumination. Feeling along the wall adjacent to the doorjamb, Butch finally located a light switch. Weak overhead bulbs revealed the cramped, narrow utility room. Mounted along the left wall, a large electrical panel displayed a multitude of thin cabling. Farther ahead, telecom equipment sat inside a rack system. On his right stood the heating and cooling unit with large conduits running into the ceiling. Ten feet ahead, a closed door marked the end of the hallway.

Butch searched the electrical panel, seeking the breaker switch controlling the security system. He identified a phone line exiting through the ceiling. Holding his breath, he pinched the terminal clamps and disconnected the white cable. When the removal of the wire didn't cause audible alarms, he tripped the breaker switch for the security system. The building remained silent. Confident he'd bought time, he exited through the door leading into the building's interior. Recognizing the downstairs lobby, he headed upstairs toward the old computer he'd used during his previous visits.

Butch dimmed the computer monitor light until the screen barely displayed icons. Taking a deep breath, he quickly accessed the Internet. The twirling hourglass in the middle of the monitor signaled an impending connection. In the darkened room, he sensed movement. He couldn't explain the sensation other than his instincts suggested a threat present. He'd come to rely on his gut many times, and more than once this reliance saved his life and those of his teammates.

The search engine screen popped up. Knowing he

couldn't risk exposing a link to JSOC through his intended method, he connected to his alternate email address and typed a short sentence. A single red dot danced across the screen. A red dot not generated by the Internet.

"Hello, again." The voice came from behind.

Fuck. Butch went to his safest tactic—he placed both hands flat on the desktop. "Who is here?" he asked in Mandarin.

A man stepped out of the shadows.

He approached close enough that Butch saw his face. The man appeared portly, white-skinned, and sported thinning hair on a bulbous head. The Delta man figured the guy's age around fifty-plus years old. He didn't appear Chinese—the accent being decidedly American. Despite the man's movements, the red dot never left the computer screen, indicating someone else present.

"You've caused a lot of trouble." The older man sniffed.

Butch responded as he knew a monk would in a similar circumstance. "I am ashamed."

"My friends with the guns are quick with a trigger. Hands on top of your head, stand up, and back away from the computer. If you're inclined to remain alive, no sudden movements."

Swallowing the rising bile in his throat, Butch complied with the man's instructions. He stopped at the man's command about eight feet from the desk then dropped to his knees. A pair of rough hands zip-tied his own behind his back. A thin rope looped around his neck, cinched tight against his throat, and ran down his spine before attaching to his wrists. *These guys know what they're doing.*

The man with the American accent read the typed note on the computer then gave a snort. He motioned for someone behind Butch.

He caught sight of a girl, he guessed a teenager, walking to the chair he used moments before his capture. He watched her tap the keyboard with amazing speed.

"My young colleague will determine your purpose for sneaking into the library. Feel free to improve my mood by telling me why you are here."

East Coast accent. Why would an American involve himself with the Chinese? What do you know? With no other viable solutions, he decided his monk role held his only potential for survival. "In the old days, Lay Buddhists once married. But some time ago such unions became forbidden. I have met someone and cannot help my feelings for her. I have dreamed of the time when I can follow the old tradition and marry."

"So, you broke into the building and wrote her a love note."

The man's voice dripped with skepticism. Butch soldiered on. "Again, I am ashamed. Please forgive me." He hoped his contrition sowed a seed of doubt. *I'm just a monk looking to get laid.*

"How twenty-first century. A touching tale of cyber-love." He motioned to someone standing behind Butch.

Footsteps fell.

A stocky man with black eyes stood over him. The male's face displayed no emotion. Butch recognized the weapon the man held in both hands. *Fucking North Korean. I'll kill you for taking Snake's rifle.* Butch held hope he hadn't visibly reacted to the appearance of the man or his teammate's weapon.

An unseen pair of hands yanked down on his monk's robes, exposing his entire upper body. He noticed the North Korean with the rifle studying him.

"My friend is interested in knowing where you received those scars," the American said. "Let's start with the one on your left shoulder. Nine-millimeter?"

"A difficult childhood." Butch held little hope for completing his mission. These men conducted themselves like professionals. The question now remained—how long before he broke?

Chapter 40

Over-watch position southeast of the Dandong Library

Thompson's military operational experience included visiting many hotspots in the world, under extreme conditions, but his current hide location ranked with the all-time worst. Rotted fish mixed with weeks-old cabbage lined the dumpster behind a restaurant where he hid. Peering over the top of the garbage receptacle, in a northwesterly direction, he saw the front of the city library approximately one hundred yards away.

Cole parked the car down a narrow side street running west from the library grounds, and he covered the building on the opposite side of Thompson's vantage point. The library sat in the middle.

His choice in using the dumpster wasn't the most ideal position, but this location provided the best chance for avoiding detection from the ever-present security apparatus.

"How copy?" Thompson whispered into his lip mic.

"Loud and proud," Cole's voice answered in the earpiece.

Good. The MMA fighter's spirits remained high. Cole's attributes—speed, coordination, willingness to listen—were advantageous. He knew Cole's greatest asset was his motivation for finding Butch.

"What do you see?" Thompson asked.

"I can see the rear and most of the north side. I'm not complaining, but I'm having a hard time dealing with the smell from the trunk."

Thompson shifted his weight, and the decompression of the left foot released new odors from the cabbage and fish. "I bet."

"What now?"

"Hang tight. Tell me if you see any movement."

On the drive from the hotel, Thompson insisted he take possession of Cole's cell phone. Thankfully, the device remained off. If and when the police expanded their search for Cole, they always followed a suspect's digital footprint. No matter how careful, the Texan remained convinced the owner's discovery inevitable. The question was how much time existed before Cole's eventual capture. In any event, at this juncture of the mission, he deemed further risk necessary for the operation.

Without Butch, the case containing a long-held secret was certainly lost. *I need you, buddy. Where are you?* Thompson retrieved Cole's phone from a vest pocket and powered on the device. Synching with an encrypted server monitored by JSOC, he transmitted a short, live video feed of his location, including a zoomed shot of the library. He gave a whispered narrative of the twelve-second clip. Any electronic eavesdropping of the transmission led to a dead-end ISP address in Geneva. Unsure when JSOC might response, he made a mental note of checking the server every ten minutes for an update.

As he slipped the cell phone back into his tactical vest pocket, Thompson thought he caught movement behind the glass front door of the library. He quickly drew up his rifle to his shoulder and peered through the scope. His instincts told him he'd seen motion. Scanning, he spotted nothing. He silently cursed the missed opportunity. "Cole, look sharp. Possible movement."

"Did you see Butch?"

This guy is on edge. "Take a deep breath and relax, amigo," Thompson spoke calmly. "Stay cool."

"Sorry," Cole huffed.

Minutes passed without visible activity. He craved news from command—anything to improve his chances of bringing Butch and the case back to safe soil. *Come on, buddy, show me that's you.*

His gaze flicked between the front of the library and his black diving watch. Morning light, now less than seven hours away, brought doom, not only for the mission but for the remaining Americans. Thompson's earpiece came alive.

"Rear door is opening," Cole blurted.

"Feed me the info." Thompson brought his rifle tighter to his shoulder. Looking down the narrow street on the wrong side of the building, his action was little more than muscle memory.

"I see two people. One is younger, maybe a girl, wearing glasses. Now…an older guy, thin, graying hair. He's chubby and glancing around like he's nervous. Wait, he's not Chinese. A white guy. Both of them are walking really fast from the building. What do I do? Do I go after them?"

"Hold tight. Are they carrying anything?"

"The young one has a shoulder bag but nothing else. I don't see Butch."

He toyed with the idea of breaking from his hide spot and making his way toward Cole. He understood the fear and angst Haufner must feel. Hearing the tone of Cole's voice, he feared the fighter doing something irrational.

"Keep watching. See where they go."

"Okay, okay," Cole repeated. "They're walking straight to an older car. I can't tell the make. The old guy opened the driver's door, and the girl walked around to the passenger side. Do I follow them?"

"Can you see plates?" Thompson asked.

"I can't make out the numbers."

Thompson heard a faint ringing noise through his earpiece. "Do you hear something?" Two seconds later, the sound repeated.

"I hear a noise coming from the trunk. Sounds like a cell phone ringing," Cole replied.

He swore he'd checked all the bodies thoroughly after the gunfight at the Temple. A bad feeling came over him. *What else did I miss?*

The ringing continued.

"I...I think they started the car. Should I...should I go after them?" Cole stammered.

"Listen carefully. Mark the direction they travel. Once you no longer see them, come pick me up. Drive calm," Thompson said.

"Okay."

After climbing out of the dumpster, he dropped down behind a stack of cardboard boxes and reached for the cell phone for a quick check-in with JSOC.

"Another car is right behind me!" Cole shouted.

The audio turned garbled, and he heard Cole curse. The situation took an ominous turn. Thompson sprang from his hiding spot. "I'm on my way!"

Chapter 41

Northwest of City Library

The blinding reflection in the rear-view mirror assaulted Cole's vision. For a split second, he saw a car directly behind him then a beam of light shot out from the headlights. In that moment, he lost his sight. Blue dots swirled in every direction. Fumbling for the key in the ignition, Cole called out to Hammer. In the subsequent blindness, his earpiece slipped out and the lip mic dropped to the floorboard. He didn't hear a reply.

Shit. I can't find the key. Instinct kicked in—he dropped low in his seat. He rubbed his eyes. "I can't see," he shouted, hoping the mic picked up his raised voice.

Visually impaired, Cole heard male voices outside. Dark shapes floated into view, and the dancing colors faded. Cole glanced up. A face appeared in the driver's side window. He saw a hand rise and point an object.

"Out." A man's voice barked.

His compromised eyesight caused a dizzying effect. Cole shook his head to clear his vision. "Wait a second."

A hand pounded on the glass. "Get out, now."

Cole's door opened. He saw a man pointing what looked like a billy club. Two other thugs carrying the same blunt object stood behind him, appearing anxious and ready. Cole's vision returned enough to identify their tight pants and partially buttoned silk shirts—the garb of 14K thugs. The vision of Master Li lying on the ground sent waves of rage through his body. "What do you want?"

"You." The thug who'd torn open the door reached for him.

Cole narrowed his eyes. He launched a devastating heel kick straight into the man's solar plexus.

The punk in the purple shirt collapsed to the ground.

The car door flew wide from the attack then bounced back and clicked shut. The two other 14K members were cut off from jumping him. He used the moment, pulled Butch's pistol from under the seat, and brought the weapon into firing position. As soon as the door reopened, Cole squeezed the trigger.

Nothing happened. The trigger didn't budge. By the time he remembered the safety switch, his opportunity passed.

The next thug dove for him.

Cole deflected the club coming straight for his face—the blow missed him by inches and sent the handgun bouncing off the dash. The punk's foul, nicotine-laced breath blew into his face. Cole formed a "knife hand" and struck the 14K member with a lethal attack in the Adam's apple.

The man grasped at his smashed windpipe with both hands. Mortally injured, the man collapsed next to him.

The third attacker piled on top of Cole, swinging his bludgeon.

A fraction of a second before he received the lead-weight club to his head, Cole grabbed his second victim by the shirt and yanked him into the weapon's path. The number-two man's head took the blow with a sickening *crack*. Cole recognized the sound of a skull bone splintering. The 14K gangster shuddered and fell limp.

The third man remained in the fight. Cole grabbed the neck of the unconscious man lying on top of him with his right hand and whipped up the head into the final attacker's face.

Blood sprayed in all directions as nose and teeth violently impacted with the second man's head. His third victim slipped out of the car doorway and crashed to the ground. Cole paused only when he saw the front teeth from the third man buried in the back of the second man's head. With two men lying on the ground outside the car and one likely dead, Cole emerged from the vehicle relatively unscathed.

He grabbed the pistol off the floorboard, stepped over the two squirming bodies, and headed toward the car with the man and girl inside. Standing in front of his own stolen vehicle, he faced the library. The old sedan hadn't moved from the parking spot. He locked gazes with the gray-haired man sitting behind the steering wheel. Something touched his left arm.

His communications headset dangled by the cord attached to the small box under his shirt. While staring at the man behind the distant windshield, he grabbed the lip mic to reposition the headset.

Without warning, his driver's side mirror shattered.

Cole jerked from the explosion of steel and glass then dove to the ground. "Someone is shooting at me!"

he yelled into the lip mic. Hearing no response from Hammer, he repeated himself. He hugged the front bumper for cover. When he brought the pistol to bear in the direction of the shot, the communication cord, wrapped around his left arm, ripped out of his comms device. *I'm fucked.*

Chapter 42

Confident the muffled gunfire originated farther behind his vehicle, Cole scanned the one-way street using the two earlier men writhing on the ground as additional cover. Whoever shot wasn't interested in taking him alive. Past midnight, the darkness offered the unseen assailant maximum advantage. *He's definitely opposite the library.* Complicating matters, the first man Cole kicked recovered and rose to his knees. Cole switched off the pistol's safety and scanned past the rising thug.

The gang member lifted his head level with the car door's handle. A sound erupted—something akin to a baseball bat hitting the side of a slab of beef. The top of the man's head exploded outward—a concavity the size of a plum formed along the wound channel. The gang member collapsed in a heap on top of the man with the crushed face and missing teeth, pinning him underneath.

Unable to locate the sniper nor resist the urge to run, Cole scrambled to his feet and dashed toward a shop's doorway, ten feet to his right. He leaped over a raised threshold, and pieces of mortar exploded, showering him with shards of cement. Cole squeezed himself into the two-foot-deep section, feeling trapped and wondering if Hammer knew he was under attack. Only a brief moment passed before he realized his terrible mistake in changing his location. *Man, I'm a sitting duck here.*

The only sound Cole heard was from the man, minus his front teeth, pinned under a dead body and calling out to someone. He chanced a glance farther down the narrow street but saw no threat. Still, he knew, someone waited—hunting him. Remaining in the doorway meant risking certain death.

I need Butch's rifle. Cole peered toward his car. The weapon lay in the backseat—both rear doors remained closed. The driver's door sat open, but successfully entering the vehicle meant risking significant exposure to the shooter. Without thinking, he popped his head out from his hiding spot and immediately ducked back inside the doorway. More stone from the building snapped past his head. *You asshole.*

The clock was running out on him and his brother. *I can't miss Butch.* If his older brother remained anywhere near the library, Cole knew he would never forgive himself for staying in hiding. A thought surfaced—what would the Special Forces soldier do in a similar situation?

Why didn't I think of this before? The overhead streetlight about fifty feet away cast enough light on his position for his attacker's needs. He then glanced at the car parked directly behind his, its engine still idling and, thankfully, the headlights now turned off. No way existed for safely reaching either his own car or the thugs' unless he first took out the streetlight.

Tucked inside the doorway alcove, Cole knelt and took aim at the street lamp. He broke the trigger resistance, producing a mechanical *clack* from the pistol's top slide cycling another round. The light continued marking his position. Concentrating on his breathing, just as Butch taught him at the shooting range, Cole settled the weapon's front post directly onto the middle of the large bulb. He exhaled slowly as his finger gently pressed on the trigger.

The street lamp exploded from the ruptured vacuum seal. The *pop* echoed down the narrow street.

Cole lost his night vision for a good ten seconds as total darkness replaced the bright light. As soon as he made out shapes, he darted from his spot.

Out in the open, he heard something sounding like an angry hornet zipped past his head. He sprinted then dove for the front of his car. Rolling to a crouch, he caught his breath, thankful his plan worked. He cast a glance back at the library and saw no movement. He caught a glimpse of the parked car from earlier but, with his night vision still compromised, he couldn't make out if the older man still sat inside.

On the right side of the car where he hid, Cole poked out his head twice without hearing another bullet whiz past. *Dammit, Hammer. Where are you?* Counting to three, he darted around the driver's side, grabbed the doorframe, and threw himself over the squirming body of the third man on the ground. Sprawled across the front seat, with the interior dome light casting a dull glow, he witnessed a hole punch through the inner door panel—the damage erupted just above his extended leg, insulation material spilling out like intestines. He crawled over both the unconscious thug splayed out on the front seat and the center console, making his way onto the back seat.

The unknown shooter took another crack at Cole.

The rear window glass shattered and showered him with thick, sharp pieces.

He safely dropped down into the rear foot well. With his right hand, he grasped Butch's rifle from the backseat. Peering into the scope, he saw the bright-red glow of the aiming point. Making sure, this time, the safety was in the Off position, he shifted his body to the far left inside the vehicle with the intent of shielding himself from gunfire. He still hadn't spotted the shooter's hide location. He brought up the barrel to rest at the top of the backseat. *What would Butch do now?*

Check for positions. What perch gave the sniper an improved angle on his location? Cole glanced through the scope but discerned little in the darkness. *Get the night vision, you idiot.* Staying low, he reached for the pack. Groping inside, he removed the helmet with attached NVGs. He powered on the device then swung the black cover onto his head. Flipping the four tubes over his eyes, he saw a dark, night sky turn a brilliant green. He noticed details outside the car with ease, including the upper portions of surrounding buildings.

Shouldering the rifle, he scanned from right to left, looking through the scope, slowly assessing upper and lower portions of the structures lining the narrow street. He couldn't see anyone in the windows or on the rooftops. Adjusting his body, he brought down the barrel to near street level only to see a flash erupt from a doorway to his right about one hundred-fifty feet away.

Instantly, the front-seat headrest exploded in a cascade of white stuffing.

Reflexively, Cole ducked. A preternatural calm settled over him. He pushed open the rear door, brought the barrel into firing position and, recalling the shooter's position, spotted a man looking down a long-barreled rifle.

Thwak. A bullet smacked into the open door.

Cole dropped the red dot onto his attacker's chest. *Your ass is mine.*

Chapter 43

Cole could not anticipate what happened next—he froze. Even with his own life in mortal danger, he hesitated long enough for his target's retreat inside a doorway. The kill had not occurred. Some unseen force held his finger in check. No such second thoughts surfaced about using the handgun a minute earlier. Why didn't he shoot the SOB? Confusion and anger swamped him. He dropped low in the backseat, cursing. *You dumb shit. Get back in the fight.*

His hesitation equaled failure. Rather than eliminate the threat, he allowed his adversary a second opportunity in ending his life. *What now?* He stole a glance at the front seat, where one of his victims lay motionless. An idea hit. He let the rifle slip from his grasp and fall onto the rear cushion. He reached over the center console with both hands and grabbed the man's shirt. With as much strength as he possessed, Cole lifted the dead weight until the man's head rose higher than the front seat. Just when he thought he could no longer hold the body, he saw the top of the dead 14K man's head explode with a sickening sound. Brain and bone sprayed the dash, and the body flew from his grip.

Cole rearmed himself with the rifle and waited. Seconds later, footsteps approached the car, measured and light. Stealthy, even. Cole slunk low and pointed the suppressed barrel toward the rear passenger window on the opposite side. Sensing someone closing within ten feet, he sucked in a breath, his cardiac rate climbing until his heart thumped against his chest wall. He nearly held his breath. He couldn't afford a blown second chance. *Show yourself.*

"Anyone else inside?" a male voice near the rear of the car asked.

"Just the one," the man with the missing teeth, lying at the base of the open driver's door, groaned.

At the proximity and volume of their voices, Cole tightened his grip on the weapon. *Don't let this guy win. Finish the job.* The scrape of a shoe signaled a closer approach—a tiny portion of a male's head showed at the rear window. Cole noticed a massive scope mounted on top of the man's rifle.

The guy snuck toward the driver's side with his weapon pointing toward the front seat.

When the gunman fully appeared in the side window, Cole raised the rifle and leveled the red dot on the man's torso.

The would-be assassin froze. He turned his gaze directly at Cole.

He held no additional thought. His rifle bucked, and he saw the man vanish outside the shattering, rear-door glass. The pungent smell of gunpowder rose into his nostrils. A sudden, terrifying thought entered Cole's mind. *Did I miss?*

He cautiously pushed open the door. The assassin lay crumbled on the ground. He slid across the seat, raking over broken glass but not feeling any pain. Rising slightly, he saw the scoped weapon on the pavement.

The shooter's index finger twitched.

Rifle at the ready, Cole carefully slid out of the car. The rest of the man's body came into view. In the green glow of his night vision, a shimmering hole in the middle of the assassin's chest marked the entrance wound from his .30-caliber bullet.

Staring wide-eyed at his dead comrade, the man with the missing teeth rose to his knees.

Numb, Cole paid little attention to the remaining survivor. He stared at the man he'd just killed. A burp escaped his lips. Then, acidic bile rose up in his throat. In the hope of eradicating the burning sensation, he swallowed. Beads of sweat rose across his forehead. The rifle shook in his trembling hands. Unable to suppress the tidal wave of nausea, Cole leaned over and violently retched.

The kneeling man dove for the sniper's weapon.

Cole witnessed the long barrel swing in his direction. Without thought, he pointed Butch's rifle from his hip and squeezed the trigger. He sensed minimal recoil then watched the man spin to the ground. Now alone, he surveyed the carnage. He felt no emotion.

Several more times, Cole vomited. Spent, he glanced at the bodies sprawled in their death poses. The combined odor of gunpowder and human waste created a sickening stench. How did his big brother deal with killing? Did ending a man's life become routine? Cole struggled with making sense of the scene, but few thoughts came promising comfort or sanity. A fleeting thought snapped him out of his reverie.

Butch! Cole stepped over the bodies and headed toward the library. He started at a jog, distancing himself from the car. He'd told Hammer he would do whatever necessary to rescue his brother. But that pledge didn't mean he was capable of his claim. He found pulling the trigger easy. What happened afterward was the tough part.

He scanned for the old man in the vehicle but found the parking spot empty. Motion at the library's rear door caught his attention—the same door the man and girl exited minutes earlier. With the aid of night vision, Cole counted three individuals. A large figure in the middle caused him to pull up short.

A hulking figure wearing monk's robes, a hood covering his head, frequently stumbled and faltered in keeping pace with the men.

Two, smaller males dragged the individual from the building. The bookends handled the monk roughly, their arms propping up the much larger person.

Cole flipped up the NVGs, and he saw night turn from green to black. The building's rear light flooded the area, and the illumination revealed the robe's brilliant yellow color—the garb of the Shaolin monks. He noted the man's physical build far larger than any other man of the Buddhist sect in Dandong. A surge of adrenaline flooded his system. "Butch?" *Who else but him?*

Cole dropped to his right knee and shouldered the assault rifle. At less than two hundred feet to target, the scope's red dot marked the exact location of the bullet's entry point. He would not hesitate. Not this time. He chose the small man on the far right as his first victim. Following the trio with steady aim, he placed his index finger on the trigger. Dropping the red dot onto the moving target's chest, he exhaled.

Electricity shot through Cole's body, and all of his muscles contracted simultaneously—the sensation so painful his vision narrowed to a tiny speck. His four limbs seized, involuntarily flexing in terrible spasms. He saw the pavement rush up to his face but couldn't buffer the impact. The loud chatter of electrical pulses delivering the surge split the night. His insides erupted in a sea of fire.

Pain and cramping continued but, curiously, the white-hot, searing jabs suddenly halted. Cole's eyes slowly focused. He discovered his rifle off to his right, but his arms flailed ineffectually. He no longer saw the three men outside the library.

An unknown force rolled him onto his back. His vision filled with pitch-black sky. He felt the lug sole of a boot push on his chest.

"Now, you bow to me."

The voice registered immediately, and he stilled. *I'm sorry, Butch. I failed you.*

Chapter 44

Xindong Street metal shop, 0120 hours

Three miles northwest of the library, a metal workshop stood at the end of an unlit, unpaved road. The owner was a sixty-three-year-old North Korean who, ten years earlier, established a one-man business as part of a cultural exchange program between the two nations. Never married, he maintained unwavering support for his birth country.

A few minutes earlier, while sleeping in his tiny living quarters attached to the rear of the small, tin-roofed garage, a knock roused him from his slumber. A serious-looking comrade explained his need for the older man's workspace. The owner offered his assistance without question. The promise of a great reward from the Dear Leader provided the necessary motivation for the aging welder. Smartly, he finished dressing and left.

Barrett shared Park's opinion the monk was anything but a man of religion, if only by the many scars covering the heavily muscled Chinese man. Back at the library, he identified no less than five healed gunshot and knife wounds. But, where did the Chinese man fit in the big picture?

For her part, Lilly found no evidence on the library computer shedding further light on the monk's presence in the building. She announced the website and email address benign. Without her cyberwarfare group's hacking tools, she could not delve deeper into the system.

The appearance of the man, outside the library, caused Barrett great concern. *Who was he?* Even in the darkness, Barrett identified a lone male wielding a pistol. The man stood physically taller than anyone involved with the local 14K group, but lack of light hid additional identifying features. Was the lone gunman part of the American team from the docks? If not, he worried the PLA might already know about the North Koreans and their operation.

The sounds of suppressed gunshots provided the necessary motivation for moving his car to an adjacent street. He anxiously counted the seconds while the North Koreans corralled their suspect. Park never mentioned he heard weapons firing—another critical detail Barrett kept from the commander.

A guttural cry from the prisoner pulled Barrett from his thoughts. Observing the cruel actions of the two men from North Korea's Second Bureau Reconnaissance Battalion, he felt a moment's sympathy for the supposed *Shaolin* monk chained to a small blast furnace against the back wall. The North Koreans worked over the man found inside the library for almost thirty minutes.

The suspect never departed from the love story he provided.

Standing near the only door leading in and out of the workshop, Barrett held Lilly tight. He soothed her with soft-spoken words. With every punch and slap, she recoiled and gasped. He worried the trauma she witnessed might hamper her ability in further assisting Park. Barrett knew worse treatment awaited the victim.

With the monk drifting in and out of consciousness, his head slumped. Groans escaped his bloodied lips.

Park glanced at his wrist watch, and a scowl crossed his face.

"We are getting nowhere," the sniper said in Korean.

The subordinate's comment was the first time Barrett heard him speak. He worried Park's frustration might turn in his direction. He sensed the increasing pressure the North Korean men fell under in finding the missing case.

"I don't believe him," Park said to his comrade. "He knows something. We are running out of time." He turned to Barrett. "What drugs does the CIA use for interrogation?"

Barrett held out his hands. "I've been out of the game for a long time. Toward the end, drugs like scopolamine and sodium amytal obtained a bad reputation. The concoctions provided only mild efficacy, and all of the information received required external verification. The primary use for the drugs was creating amnesia around events leading up to interrogation, much more so than actually extracting information."

Park and his subordinate huddled and whispered back and forth.

The sniper nodded and walked to the other end of the small shop.

Park glanced at his watch then scowled. He moved close to Barrett. "We do not have more time. My comrade will commence with further interrogation. You will assist."

"Me?" Barrett's eyes grew wide. "You haven't told me anything regarding your mission. What am I supposed to ask?"

"You will assist," Park hissed. "My man does not speak Mandarin well enough for conducting an *interview*."

Barrett furrowed his eyebrows. "Why won't you conduct the interrogation?"

"I must work on the next phase of the operation."

"There's more?" *This mission appears never ending.*

"Before any payment release, we must secure our return to the homeland with our objective in hand." Park stuck a thumb toward Lilly. "I am in need of her skills."

Barrett panicked. Tightness attacked his chest. "Where are you taking her?"

"Back to your apartment." Park's eyes narrowed to slits. "Or do you have another idea?"

He swallowed his fear. "Forgive me. Just a father's over-reaction."

Park continued his glare. "Where is the man your agents detained at the Temple? Why is he not here?"

"I have been with you." He pointed at the prisoner, his breathing coming in short gasps. "This man consumed our time."

Park grunted acknowledgement. "See that the detainee is immediately brought here. When I return, I will obtain answers from the new arrival."

"As you wish." Barrett didn't dare reveal the American's escape at the Temple nor the significant number of men killed by an unseen assassin. Revealing the information would only ensure a bullet to the head sooner rather than later, perhaps right here in the shop. Stress and lack of sleep made the North Koreans even more dangerous. He knew the only remaining option was buying more time—at least until he figured out his next move.

The sniper walked back with an old bucket and spoke to Park in hushed tones. The subordinate nodded and stepped over to a large iron sink. He opened the water spigot.

Barrett swallowed hard. He knew what came next. No matter his training, the so-called monk would not withstand the next torture method.

"Lilly, once again, I need your expertise on the computer," Park said in a friendly voice. "Let me take you home."

Lilly stiffened. "What about my father?"

"He will follow shortly. Once you complete this task, you will never again see me. Do you find my offer acceptable?"

She nodded several times.

Barrett saw Park flash a shark's grin. He could not deny—once Lilly helped with the travel, and he helped the sniper locate the case—the two of them were no longer needed by the North Koreans. Worse, they were liabilities. Park would not leave loose ends. Barrett needed a plan—fast.

Chapter 45

Somewhere in Dandong

Cole had been knocked unconscious only once during his short, but meteoric, career as a professional mixed martial artist. During a training session, he caught a sharp elbow to the side of the head. As Cole roused after the incident, thoughts were jumbled, his visual field narrow, and his muscles felt extraordinarily weak. The sensations lasted only a few minutes, and the dozen or so other men in the gym made friendly jokes and showed great compassion as fellow sportsmen often do at such times. Now, as he experienced the familiar confusion and weakness, he woke to his surroundings. But unlike his gym-mates, the men here expressed no empathy or congeniality.

Cole fluttered his eyes, and he caught glimpses of several men. In the dim light, he found his surroundings unfamiliar—his initial impression unfavorable. Ten feet away, on the other side of a dingy, cluttered room, a wooden workbench stood with his travel duffel perched on top.

A man stood close holding a pistol in one hand and a cell phone in the other.

Two other men positioned themselves on either side of the cramped room.

The scent of motor oil and fuel permeated the air.

He tried standing but found the simple task impossible. Unable to move, Cole developed sudden clarity.

"He's awake," someone said in Mandarin.

Cole opened his eyes wider and saw ropes securing his ankles to a metal chair. When he tried bringing his arms forward from behind his back, the unmistakable rattle of handcuffs identified the reason pressure wrapped both wrists. He raised his gaze to the man standing over him. A gold-capped tooth twinkled from the reflection off a ceiling light.

The man with the gun glared at Cole. "Who are you?"

Cole never wavered his stare. "I'm the exterminator. I kill all the little insects."

Gold Tooth cocked the hammer on a large, black pistol and shoved the barrel against his forehead. "Who are you?"

Cole snickered. *Go ahead. Pull the trigger.* "The guy…who keeps killing…all your flunkies."

Without another word, the gang leader pistol-whipped the side of his head.

Intense pain pulsed at his temple. Several seconds passed before his eyesight cleared. Cole glanced at the other two punks in the room then turned his attention back to the leader. "These two assholes all you got left? Not much of a gang."

"Who are you?" Gold Tooth roared.

Cole spat on the floor. "Eat shit."

Gold Tooth reared back and bounced the gun off his head a second time.

The room tumbled in a psychedelic swirl of colors. Voices took on a muffled tone. Several minutes passed before Cole regained his senses. Blood oozed down the left side of his scalp, through his short, black hair, and over the top of his ear. Cole's hatred toward bullies, and his belief he held direct responsibility for his family members' deaths, pushed him beyond reasoning. He grinned at Gold Tooth. "You hit like a girl."

"Why did you come back? You CIA?" Gold Tooth tapped Cole's forehead with the gun's barrel.

He tilted back his head. "Nah. I just couldn't live without seeing you again."

Smack. The gang leader punched him a third time.

The metal connected with his ear, causing a pain so intense he nearly vomited. Gold Tooth's face turned red.

"Explain the fifty-thousand-dollar bounty on your head!"

Cole froze. What? A bounty? This asshole's comment didn't make sense. He arrived in the country less than forty-eight hours ago. Why was someone looking for him? His world turned upside down, and he didn't understand the reason. Cole worried the money somehow linked to Butch. "Is the offer for me dead or alive?"

Gold Tooth crossed his arms. "Tell me about the bodies in the car's trunk."

Cole understood any answer, the truth or a lie, would not change the course of his captivity. He quickly decided he held zero chance of walking out of the small room alive. He remained certain of one thing—he would *never* give up Butch or his teammate, Hammer. That knowledge he'd take to his grave. Period.

"You're the pricks chasing me all over town. If you haven't seen the news lately from America, I'm pretty famous back home. Do yourself a favor and cut me loose. Be the first smart thing you've done all day."

Gold Tooth spun and walked to the workbench. He lifted the rifle Cole used against two of the 14K men. "Where did you get this gun?"

"Found that in the car." Cole shrugged.

Gold Tooth shook his head. "Looks like American military. Just like the night-vision glasses and all the other things you wore."

He grinned. "You can buy the craziest things on the Internet."

Gold Tooth approached and leaned close to Cole's face. "Good to know. Because after I find out why you're here, I'm gonna see who will pay more for you—the PLA or the North Koreans."

As steadfast as Cole felt about not divulging his brother to these punks, he possessed a healthy fear of the Chinese and their troublesome neighbor. He knew agents from either country *could* make him talk. The information he possessed would place his brother in more jeopardy.

A knock sounded to Cole's left.

The nearest man opened a small, wooden door.

A familiar-looking male walked in, pulling a small handcart with his left hand. His heavily bandaged right arm hung in a sling. He recognized the guy whose wrist he'd broken at the hotel, and he noted the man's satisfied grin made a promise of revenge. Cole glanced toward the bottom of the dolly and saw what looked like a car battery. His body tensed. He understood the next phase of his imprisonment.

"Before I turn you over to the highest bidder, my friend here will ask you a few questions. His methods bring out the honesty in men," Gold Tooth said.

Watching the injured man connect jumper cables to the two pole ends of the battery, Cole's heart raced, and his chest heaved. He'd seen torture devices like this only in movies. A large part of him desired death, and he hoped his wish came sooner rather than later. Only one goal remained. *I'll die right here, without regret. I'm not giving you a fucking thing.*

Broken Wrist held the two, unattached ends of the battery cables. He stood over Cole and touched the separate metal clamps together, creating hissing sparks. "Remember me?"

Preparing for the impending physical torture, Cole took a deep breath, willing a separation of mind from body. The Temple elders taught him the skills necessary for placing pain in a different location from his spiritual self. But he'd never experienced a test of this magnitude. He recalled his love for Master Li then his wife and son. He watched their smiling faces pass before his mind's eye. Then, he turned his thought to his unborn child and the beautiful face he'd never meet. Anxious for a reunion with his loved ones in the afterlife, he readied himself.

"You will tell us everything," the punk announced.

Cole fixed his cold gaze upon the gang member. The secret to causing his own death resided in pushing the punk beyond control. "You'll never break me. You don't have the balls."

Chapter 46

Outside the City Library

Thompson ran for all he was worth. After hearing Cole's shouts in his earpiece about a car, and subsequent threatening Chinese voices, the big Texan left his hide spot and sprinted toward the library, hoping to intercept whoever confronted the MMA fighter. A fully armed American running with impunity along Chinese-controlled pavement offered a juicy target for the authorities.

Not far from the dumpster, a car passed close, bouncing headlights across his large frame. Another followed and threw the Delta man in a second flash of light.

He dove into an alley to escape detection.

Moments later, a police cruiser materialized.

Crucial seconds passed. His earpiece came alive with the sounds of a struggle, a warning about a gunshot, and then the connection ended.

When the squad car cleared the road, Thompson dashed toward Cole. The same police vehicle circled back across his path two blocks closer to the library. His inner voice told him the car followed a search grid. He absently touched Cole's cell phone, wondering if the authorities already triangulated on the connection from his last check-in with JSOC. He remembered the note written by the employee at the hotel.

She warned of the cops looking for Cole.

Thompson grew more certain additional assets joined the search for the American hotel guest. With daylight just five hours away, new actors further complicated his mission. How long before the PLA joined the hunt?

After several false starts, Thompson eventually arrived at Cole's last known location. Once on scene, he found no signs of his partner. Panic rose in his chest. He pulled the cell out of his pocket and swiped the Off icon. *Jesus, did the police find Cole?* He couldn't risk contacting JSOC—not until he cleared the area.

Time ran short for the mission. He didn't need a reminder of what failure meant for him—and possibly for millions of innocent people.

****

The sights and smells of the small workshop were all lost on Cole. His world narrowed to a single sensation—unholy pain. He imagined millions of fire ants dancing along his nervous system. His brain flew into a panic so intense his autonomous body functions ceased operation.

A moment's respite.

He barely drew a second breath before the reapplication of two clamps to his skin. His back arched in grotesque hyperextension. A scream lasting a microsecond escaped from his throat before the larynx spasmed and stifled his cries. The assault on his body distracted him from the smell of burning flesh and hair. Striving for mental control, he focused on the faces of his family, reminding himself each jolt of electricity brought him one step closer to them. He deserved death, but his eventual demise took too damned long for his liking.

"Stop." Gold Tooth ordered.

Cole's senses ebbed and flowed as if on a great ocean wave. An unseen force pried open his eyes, but he registered little of the visual images. Then, a hand clamped over his mouth and nose, cutting off his oxygen. His struggle for air triggered immediate focus, and his fight drive kicked in.

"He is not dead," someone said.

Cole's vision sharpened. He glared into the face of Gold Tooth who suffocated him.

The 14K leader removed his hand and stood straight.

Cole drew in a painful but needed breath. He panted heavily, re-oxygenating his brain and body. He noticed the men in the room staring.

"Now, you will answer my questions," Gold Tooth sneered.

His ears buzzed with tinnitus, his arms and legs throbbed from electricity-induced agony, and he sat in his own urine. Last week, he held the title of Featured Athlete during the largest pay-per-view broadcast in television history. Now, he was a grief-stricken foreigner in China with a bounty on his head, tortured by a notorious group of gang members. The absurdity of the transformation brought on a paradoxical response, especially given the situation's excruciating brutality.

He grinned, and a chuckle escaped his lips. A few seconds later, the snicker escalated into full-blown, boisterous laughter. Tears streamed down his cheeks as, finally, Cole roared in delight. When he saw a couple of the thugs cracking smiles, he flew into a near seizure. The room reverberated from his eruption.

The 14K leader crossed his arms. "I'm glad you find amusement in your predicament. I recall a distant memory, many years ago, of you crying like a little girl while hiding behind your brother's skirt at the Temple."

Cole recognized Gold Tooth's attempted provocation. He held no such memories of needing Butch's protection when they lived at the *Wulong* Temple. The reality was Butch kicked this punk's ass, and anyone witnessing the fight knew the truth, including the man standing over him. The leader's claim purely existed for supposed benefit of the other gang members.

Gold Tooth squatted and stared directly into Cole's eyes. "Your precious uncle stopped the fight too soon. How is he? I hear he has a bad heart."

At the mention of Master Li, he swallowed his sudden rage. The emotional pain of his uncle's passing still felt raw. "*Sifu* understood people intent on violence have no honor. You're proof of his wisdom."

"Well, lucky for Butch, *Sifu* stopped the fight." He paused. "Perhaps I should bring your brother here. He can watch me finish you off."

"Best of luck finding him," Cole mocked.

"Oh? Is he here in *Dandong*? Did he come here with you?" His grin grew wider with each question.

Cole imagined bashing in all his teeth. When his arm and back muscles flexed, he heard the handcuffs rattle against the steel spindles of the chair. Cole grew more agitated by this prick. *Don't let him win.*

Broken Wrist tapped together the battery clamps, causing flying sparks.

"Butch will enjoy the show," the leader said.

Cole glared at both men. A new overwhelming thought overtook his mind. He no longer desired his own death. The mention of Master Li and Butch regenerated his craving for long-awaited revenge. He wanted to live—at least, until he killed every bastard in this room.

Chapter 47

0215 hours

With each searing hit of electricity, Cole grew more resolute. *Stay conscious. Stay alive.*

Between each jolt of battery juice, Gold Tooth added his own assault with his fists.

The punishing toll included both eyes nearly swollen shut, likely multiple facial fractures, and loose teeth rattling in their sockets. He neared the edge of darkness. His sensation of physical pain barely registered. Stars danced at the periphery of his remaining vision. When he reached the end of his ability to remain conscious, the torture halted.

The other 14K members smiled and nodded to Gold Tooth.

Cole caught a glimpse of his attacker sweating profusely and panting like a sprinter.

Taking in the adulation, the leader appeared pleased with himself.

Gold Tooth roughly wiped his hands across Cole's torn shirt. "Looks like our special guest is ready to talk."

Cole's head lolled to one side. He witnessed one of the gang members dump the duffel contents onto the floor. Clothing spilled out along with his shaving kit.

The punk stooped and picked up an object then

waved over his buddies to share his discovery.

The men's whispers remained unintelligible. Clear thought and understanding escaped him.

Gold Tooth snatched the find from his subordinate. He approached Cole and waved a small piece of paper in his face. "What does the letter say?"

In an attempt to sharpen his vision, Cole blinked his eyes several times. A scribbled note, written in English, read: "*I owe you 5,000. Please come home safe—Melody.*" A warm feeling washed over his broken body. *She found the money. I hope you escaped before the police found you.* Thinking of her created a small measure of satisfaction at convincing her to leave the city. His current situation confirmed his worry for her. *I wasn't crazy. I was right!* Hopefully, she fled far from *Dandong*. This small victory gave him a psychological boost. "A written verse to a song."

Gold Tooth's eyes narrowed. "Bullshit."

"You don't recognize the ballad?" Scanning the faces of the other men, he noted their looks of confusion.

"I owe you five thousand dollars... " Cole sang the written words slowly in English as if lyrics to a tune.

The gang members exchanged glances. A couple of men shrugged.

"Maybe it's from her," the man who'd found the note spoke.

Her? Who the hell is this guy talking about? From the pile of his belongings, now scattered across the dirty floor, Cole watched Broken Wrist pluck a small-framed picture from the ground and hold up his discovery. *God, no.*

Gold Tooth snatched the family photo from Broken

Wrist. After studying the picture, he wiggled the evidence of Cole's former life in his face. "Now, I understand. The song is a love letter from another woman. A mistress?" A grin creased his ugly face. "The woman in the photo is not the same person from the hotel."

The other gangsters emitted lecherous chuckles.

Cole assumed the men found pleasure at discovering his supposed indiscretion. "You have unlocked my secret. I didn't want my wife knowing about my girlfriend."

"I knew it," Broken Wrist shouted.

Gold Tooth smacked the injured punk in the head with the picture frame. "Stupid." He returned to the workbench and snatched Cole's rifle. He held the weapon in the air. "Who would bring American weapons into China to screw a whore?"

The others glanced at the floor.

"Morons," Gold Tooth mumbled. He dropped the rifle onto the counter in favor of the pistol with the attached long, black suppressor. He walked to Cole and shoved the end of the barrel against his forehead.

Cole never flinched. He stared directly into the man's eyes.

"I have an idea. Some friends will visit your wife. Show her a real man, for once."

Cole fought his instinct for issuing a counter threat and employed every ounce of his waning energy in holding back his desire. He sought to live his life in honor of Claire and Max—not die in a pissing match with this scum over their virtues.

Gold Tooth tossed the framed photo back to Broken Wrist.

With mimicking groans escaping his lips, the injured punk licked the picture while thrusting his pelvis.

Impassive, Cole stared at the twisted display. He pulled on both ends of the handcuffs, and his forearms strained against the metal loops.

Gold Tooth's cell phone chirped, and he reached into his pocket. Producing the device, he stepped back. "Yeah. We've got him." The leader paused. "No…not yet. But, he will."

Cole took in the man's threat as the other punk continued defiling the photograph. Pinioned, he nevertheless pulled harder against the metal restraints around his wrists. He resolved holding his tongue where silence might bolster his chances of survival.

"You're sure?" Gold Tooth asked. He paused again. "Okay. Ten minutes." He stuffed the cell phone back in his pants and turned to the man nearest the door. "Go get the car."

The gangster nodded and left.

Gold Tooth turned his attention to Cole. "I know where those guns came from."

Holy shit. Did something I say endanger Butch? Who called discussing the origins of the weapons? Who the hell else is involved? Panic grabbed his chest. He declined to allow a physical or verbal expression to betray his emotional response to this latest news.

"We're going for a ride. Someone very important waits for you. You'll talk then." Gold Tooth grinned.

Cole shook with fright. *Please God, don't let the person be Butch.*

Chapter 48

The thought of his brother in captivity sent unrestrained panic through Cole's body. He couldn't resist the urge for action. With every bit of strength he possessed, he pulled up with his right arm and pushed down with his left. An intense, immediate pain in his left thumb signaled a dislocation or fracture. His handcuffed right arm flew forward through the gap in the chair's backrest, free of his left extremity.

The gangsters froze with mouths hanging open.

He lashed out with a balled fist, connecting with Gold Tooth's gut.

The leader collapsed, his captured pistol clattering to the floor.

Cole caught sight of Broken Wrist scrambling for the handgun. He sprang to his bound feet, swinging the short connecting chain of the cuffs. The move caught the punk with a sharp blow near the man's injury.

The gangster collapsed to the floor, an agonized scream escaping his lips.

Cole scanned the room. *One more.* He spotted the guy near the workbench. His disabling of Gold Tooth and Broken Wrist gave the last man critical lead time for drawing a black pistol from his waistband. His legs still secured to the chair by rope, he hopped twice and closed the distance. Extending his still-cuffed right hand, he clamped down on the top slide of the gun. He rotated the barrel down and twisted the steel inward toward the gang member. The sweat and grime on Cole's hand allowed slippage with his grip.

When the top slide of the pistol broke free, a shot rang out.

The gunman gasped and dropped to one knee.

Still clutching the weapon, Cole struck the man in the face with the hardened steel. Upon impact, the pistol slipped from his hand and skidded across the room.

Pieces of teeth flew in multiple directions, and the 14K member crashed against the bench then fell to the ground.

Cole spotted a fixed blade on the counter and freed himself from the chair. Hearing a noise behind him, he turned and saw a black suppressor rotating in his direction.

Gold Tooth, kneeling on the ground, held Butch's pistol in his grasp.

Performing a long side-step, Cole snap-kicked with his left foot into the man's outstretched, gun-wielding hand.

The force of the attack dropped the leader but not before he fired. The pistol's muffled bark barely registered.

The bullet connected with Broken Wrist's kneecap, and a new level of screaming erupted.

Cole dropped his full weight, driving his right knee into the back of Gold Tooth's neck, and a sickening *crunch* sounded.

A gasp escaped from the man's throat, and his lower legs quivered.

After he rose, he stomped Gold Tooth's right wrist

twice before the pistol fell from his grasp. His attention turned to Broken Wrist rolling back and forth on the floor a few feet to his left. He approached, grabbed the back of the punk's shirt, and dragged the wounded man to the battery cables used for torture only a few minutes earlier.

Careful of the metal ends, Cole took up each cable terminal. He clamped them to the punk's body, whose screaming stopped as soon as the gangster's body closed the electrical circuit loop. He watched impassively while the blood flowing from the gunshot wound popped and sizzled like frying bacon grease.

A moment later, he moved his attention to Gold Tooth's wheezing noises. He noticed the man lay prone, unmoving. Cole suspected he suffered a cervical spine collapse rendering him immobile.

At the sound of a car engine filtering into the work space, he scrambled and recovered Butch's silenced pistol. He moved to the door and took a hidden post at the right side of the entry. The doorknob rattled.

The last gang member stepped inside. "I got the—"

Cole drove the end of the silencer squarely against the man's trachea.

The driver's hands flew up to his throat, a choking sound escaping his lips.

Employing Butch's weapon, he placed two rounds into the gagging man's forehead.

The body dropped with a loud thud. A spreading pool of blood encircled the gangster.

Examining the carnage spread out over the shop, he stilled, feeling numb. Cole didn't stop and think how each successive kill became easier in execution. The emotional hesitation in taking a man's life no longer existed. *Have I become like you, Butch?*

A groan broke him from his thoughts. He glanced toward Gold Tooth.

The leader's eyes bulged.

Cole stepped close and sat next to the man's head. He set the pistol on the floor.

Throbbing in his left hand drew his attention. He noted a significant bulge at the first joint of his thumb. With his right hand, he pulled on the end of his digit while simultaneously placing downward pressure at the base of the knuckle. Using nearly all his remaining strength, he succeeded in placing the bone back into alignment. Shock and adrenaline dampened the pain of the procedure. Despite the swelling, he felt immediate relief. Though difficult, and with limited movement, his thumb showed functionality. Cole glanced at Gold Tooth and found the thug regarding him with what looked like fear. "Where's my brother?"

"I don't know," he wheezed.

Are you stalling? Cole lifted the pistol and casually pushed the barrel into the man's left eye. "Where is he?"

"Why do you think I know?" he responded between noisy gulps of air.

He jiggled the pistol in his hand. "This gun belongs to my brother. So does the rest of the other stuff. Where is he?"

"What is Butch doing here?"

Instinct told him the gangster didn't know any more information regarding his brother. "Who called you?"

"Jennings," he spat out between wheezes. "An American living here since we were kids."

Why does that name sound familiar? He couldn't put a face to Gold Tooth's answer. "Where is this Jennings?"

"Don't know. I was waiting for a call back with directions." He punctuated the statement with a groan.

"Why did he want me? Is he the man placing a bounty on my head?" Gold Tooth either refused an answer or fell unable to respond. No matter the reason, Cole assumed further questioning was not worth the time and effort. He stood and, with his foot, rolled Gold Tooth onto his back. He fished the cell phone from the man's front pocket and swiped the screen.

A password prompt popped up.

Grabbing the leader's hand, he placed the thumb over the Home button. The fingerprint unlocked the cell phone. At Settings, he eliminated password protection, affording him complete access. He searched the other pocket, found the key to the handcuffs, and freed himself of the bracelet still secured to his right wrist. *What now?*

Enjoying a hint of satisfaction, Cole surveyed the destruction he'd caused without a twinge of conscience. Back at the workbench, he checked all of Butch's weapons and equipment. Other than the team radio, destroyed during the earlier gun battle, everything appeared in working order. After gathering the equipment, including the pistol, he placed the items inside the battle pack.

He then stuffed his personal belongings back into his duffel before picking up the picture of his family. Cole brushed away broken pieces of glass stuck to the glossy photo. He pulled the image from the frame, kissed the visual reminder of his lost loved ones, and slid the paper into his back pocket. Slinging the assault rifle, he pondered his next move.

Deep in thought, Cole rubbed his chin. An idea flashed in his mind, and he removed Gold Tooth's cell phone from his pocket and opened the messaging app. With his finger hovering over the virtual keyboard, he typed a note to the last incoming phone number.

—If you want the American, I need an address—
Verify yourself

Out of ideas, Cole snapped a picture of the grotesque scene and attached a not-so-subtle threat. Unsure if Butch fell into the current situation, he fished for a response from the person on the other end.

—Let him go, or you're next—

He didn't waste time waiting on a reply. Scanning the room, Cole found a gas can under the workbench. He unscrewed the cap and dumped fuel in all directions, covering people as well as objects. Finding a lighter was a simple matter—all of the 14K gang members smoked. He pulled an American-made model from the pocket of the dead driver. In quiet contemplation, Cole repeatedly flipped the metal top open and shut.

He turned his attention to Gold Tooth, who still labored with his breathing. *You've lived twenty years too long.* He walked to the gangster and stood over him. Cole struck the flint and held the flickering flame in front of the paralyzed man's dark eyes.

"You're a monk. You can't do this!" A hoarse voice groaned.

"I'm no monk." He let slip the lighter. "I'm Karma."

Chapter 49

Two hundred yards northwest of the library
0235 hours

After dodging two additional police vehicles, Thompson made his way inside the city library and swept the interior of the building. Despite finding no signs of Butch, he spotted blood splatter on the second floor indicating some type of altercation. He followed red droplets downstairs and into a utility room. Here, he noticed disabled phone lines and security system. Farther ahead, a rear door hung at an awkward angle with a large dent near the handle. He sensed Butch's presence.

Thompson headed back to Cole's last location for a closer examination. Using his NVGs, he saw fresh oil and possibly blood on the ground. A .300 Blackout shell casing hid in a crack in the street. Someone executed a rapid cleanup of the area, but not so deftly Thompson couldn't reconstruct what occurred here. A firefight proceeded Cole's disappearance.

Pocketing the spent brass, he pulled the cell phone from his vest for a sitrep with JSOC—a risky maneuver but one of his few remaining choices. He powered on the device and, once he established a connection, typed an alternate phone number used in extreme emergencies. He waited for the computer software encryption of the open-source call. A simple tone sounded signaling secure comms. "This is Two, how copy?"

"Identity confirmed. Good copy," a computer-altered voice responded.

"No visual of One but suspect his presence at city library. Increasing police patrols suggest this device made their active search list. Also, New Player engaged in short firefight with One's primary weapon against hostiles with unknown final outcome. Over."

"Confirm New Player was in fight with One's weapon?"

Thompson knew his decision to include Cole in the mission spelled massive trouble with command. Now was not the time for explanations nor to worry about the ramifications of an American civilian involved in the recovery of a potentially catastrophic device. "Confirmed New Player fired weapon in defense without One's presence. Over."

"Understood," the voice replied.

Despite the thousands of miles between them, and a computer-altered voice transmission, Thompson heard the man on the other end convey disgust in his single word reply. *Yeah, that's how I feel, too.*

"Sitrep update," Command started, "Last digital comms from One indicates he sensed his situation compromised and is possibly in custody of unknown forces. Our satellite over-flight is interdicted and cannot provide detail. Rescue squad intercepted and combat ineffective. If you have ideas, we need them now. Over."

Shit. He clenched a fist. *Both Haufners taken by an enemy force?* With Butch and Cole MIA, and the satellite taken out by the PLA, few options remained. If the Chinese government held the pair, the mission held zero chance of success. Only his team leader knew the location of the case. If Butch still lived, whoever captured him would torture the information out of him. The device was as good as gone.

Beside letting the case fall into despicable hands, Thompson's other worry involved his own capture—alive. Even in death, his body increased the tally of the already scandalous American body count from this illegal mission. The fallout from either scenario would forever alter the political landscape between the two largest superpowers—a change for countless future generations.

Before Thompson organized a game plan, he heard the chirp of an incoming text. He pulled the cell phone from his ear and gazed at the screen. A photo showed the front of a car centered in the middle of the frame. The Delta operator recognized the plate as a local number. Not knowing the origin of the communique, he gripped the device tighter. Thompson quickly put the phone up to his ear. "Nest, are you receiving this image?"

"Affirmative. Running through the database now."

Wrong number

—*This is Cowboy. Am I still impressing you?*—

The Delta operator stifled a whoop. The news, if confirmed, brought a new opportunity for mission success.

What's your status?

—*I'm good, but not so much for these assholes*—

The attached graphic image showed four bodies sprawled on a floor. The dead men looked Chinese in ethnicity, and their dress resembled the men he killed at the Temple. "Nest, you still receiving?" *What the hell is going on?*

"Copy, Two. Still running the plate. We're mirroring your device and receiving the incoming images and texts. Can you verify their identity?"

Thompson chuckled. "That's New Player. I don't know his status, but I see he's alive and kicking ass."

"We need verification. Over."

"Roger, Nest. Standby." He typed another text message.

Can you go live with video?

The call connection ended and, seconds later, the phone buzzed on silent ring. Thompson swiped the icon and established the connection. A darkened video filled the small screen.

"What's up, Hammer?" Cole's voice came through the tiny speaker.

He couldn't identify the image, but he recognized the voice. "Can't make out the picture too well. Got a light source?"

"Got a really nice one. Let me turn around."

Thompson saw flames jumping on one side of the screen. A face came into focus. He barely recognized Cole with the fighter displaying massive facial trauma. Despite the swelling, crooked nose, and caked blood, he positively identified the man. "Damn, son. You okay?"

"Yeah, but you should see the other guys. Oh, wait, you can't. They're having a barbecue."

"What's with the fire?"

"A little going-away party." Cole pushed his face closer to his phone. "I got the name Jennings. He's supposedly an American living here. I have a strong hunch he's connected to Butch and maybe his disappearance.

"Good work. ISA will check the information," Thompson said. *How in the hell did you come up with that nugget?*

Cole's eyebrows furrowed. "Hey, something else. Besides the older man and younger woman, I saw three other people leave the library. One wore monk's robes."

The new information sent a jolt through Thompson. "What do you mean?"

"Two males hauled out a guy wearing robes. I can't be sure, but my first thought was they weren't Chinese. Maybe North Koreans? I had a hard time deciding because of the night-vision goggles. Their facial bone structure reminded me of the DPRK folks living here. The guy wearing monk robes was a big dude...I'm really worried he was Butch."

I bet you're right. Saving Cole from additional trauma, he tamped down any visible emotion. "Don't have any idea. But I'll check it out. Okay?"

Cole's head nodded on the screen. "Yeah, okay. Listen, we don't have much time before the city wakes. What now?"

Thompson thought for a moment. Unless he received a new thread from the ISA team, he had no other option but reconnect with Cole. "If you have access to the car behind you, can you pick me up?"

Cole fished out a set of keys from his pants pocket and jiggled them. "I can see the city lights nearby. Shouldn't take me long."

Outstanding. "The cops are stepping up their search for you. We need to destroy the cell phones. You okay with that action?"

"I really need my family pics on my phone."

Despite the facial swelling, Thompson noted Cole's pained change in expression. He sympathized with the guy. *I can't imagine what you've been through this past week.* "What if I told you our tech guys have a full set of copies?"

Cole turned down his face, hiding his eyes. He simply nodded on the video.

"Ya' done good so far, Cowboy."

Raising his head, Cole glared into the camera lens. "I'm just getting started."

"Let's finish the mission and get you home." *You Haufners are some badass dudes.*

Chapter 50

The metal shop
0235 hours

Barrett Jennings finished typing a message on his cell phone, demanding verification from his 14K contact before revealing his location. He hadn't lived this long without adhering to his CIA training regarding operational security. He disliked dealing with gang members, nearly all of them being sloppy and lacking most forms of discipline. But they did serve his purposes on occasion—particularly in this case, since they'd captured a dangerous ghost from his past. Cole Haufner remained a thorn and loose end from two decades ago. Barrett planned on closing this open wound within the hour. He waited for the code word to his challenge.

"What is he saying?" the North Korean sniper hissed.

The question pulled Barrett from his cell phone. He heard garbled Mandarin coming from the man undergoing enhanced questioning—waterboarding. The so-called monk endured simulated drowning far longer than expected.

"What does he say?" The sniper barked a second time.

"You...can't have the..." the prisoner choked out

in Mandarin.

Barrett leaned closer to the victim. "Have what?" When five seconds passed with no reply, he nodded toward the sniper.

The North Korean poured a steady flow of water into the sinuses of the prisoner.

Barrett watched the bald man thrash against his chains. After ten seconds, he held up his hand. The water stopped flowing.

"Fusion…fusion," the monk spat.

He knelt next the man's head and pulled back the soaking-wet rag covering the victim's face. "Tell me, or we keep going."

"No. Stop!" the man choked out. "You can't have the fusion unit. The device isn't safe."

Barrett couldn't make sense of the words. The North Koreans hunted some type of fusion device? The suitcase was quite small for a WMD. The idea of a nuclear unit on the loose in China scared him. The thought of the North Koreans in possession of a miniature weapon of that magnitude sent a chill through his body. "Who made this nuclear bomb?" he whispered.

The Chinese man stared. "It's not nuclear. It's fusion."

"What does he say?" the sniper shouted in Korean.

Barrett waved away the commando. Now that he psychologically owned the prisoner, he couldn't afford any interference stifling the flow of information. He leaned within inches of the man's ear. "What do you mean by fusion? It's not nuclear?"

"A different type of fusion…a clean fusion device. Not nuclear. If weaponized, the explosion is many times more powerful than nuclear," the man answered in English. Tears welled in his eyes then flowed down his cheeks.

How is such a discovery even possible? Barrett stood slowly, questions swirling in his mind. The prisoner's pained facial expression reflected terrible internal conflict. The fact this man held out against the torture for so long indicated extensive training. *Did this guy have a hint of Boston accent to his English? Are you CIA or part of the military unit from the docks?* A strong hand jerked him from his thoughts.

The sniper grabbed Barrett's shirt and yanked him close. "He spoke in English. What does he say?"

He couldn't think with this loon shadowing him and gave little thought to his response. "He said his partner has the device."

The North Korean's eyes bulged. "What partner? Where is this person?"

"The, um...." Barrett started. A fleeting thought passed through his mind. "The other man my people have in custody."

"Bring him here now." The sniper shoved him away.

"Yes, yes," Barrett responded halfheartedly. *Why did I say that? I'm a dead man, now.* For the North Korean government, the discovery held the potential of forever changing the world political landscape in their favor. Worse, a new arms race among the super powers raised the risk of a global conflict. Among the potentially disastrous scenarios sat great potential for the man holding the keys.

His mind turned to the other puzzle. *Fusion?* Clean fusion? Cold fusion? Potentially limitless energy...or had scientists weaponized the unit so anyone with extra hydrogen and piping held the knowledge for building a never-ending supply of devastating, undetectable weapons? Either way, he now understood the North Korean mission and the lengths Park went in his pursuit of the device.

Once in possession of the suitcase, North Korea's capitulation to the West over nuclear disarmament masked their true intent—world domination. The prospect of such devastating power in their Supreme Leader's hands frightened Barrett even more than Park's threats to his and Lilly's lives. With his latest betrayal sealing his fate with the commandos, Barrett chose the one path with the greatest personal gain.

"Why do you wait? Call them here," the sniper growled.

Resolute of his choice, Barrett nodded. Before he dialed, he heard the chirp from an incoming call. *Oh shit. Park's calling me.* "I am here," Barrett answered nervously in Korean.

"I am finished with Lilly and ready to proceed," he announced. "What has the prisoner revealed?"

Before completing his betrayal, Barrett cleared his throat. "The captive's partner, the person in the video from the hotel, has custody of the device. My team successfully recovered both the man and your objective."

"The American?"

Please let him believe me. His hands shook. "You are correct. My men await your orders."

"Put my teammate on the phone," Park barked.

As he extended the phone toward the sniper, Barrett masked his concern. "He will speak to you."

"I am here." The commando never broke his gaze upon Barrett. A moment later, the sniper passed back the cell phone.

Had Park ordered his termination? His hands trembled. He brought the device to his ear. "Yes, sir?"

"Have your men bring the American and the case to your location. You will wait for me. I will return within ten minutes. After you make your call, you will relinquish your phone to my man. Are my instructions understood?"

"Yes, sir." *At least he's not killing me, yet.*

"Call them now," Park ordered.

When the line disconnected, he noticed a text message awaited his attention. He tapped on the icon and watched a picture fill the screen. He turned away from the North Korean, drinking in the image of all four of his 14K men, bloodied and dead. An upended metal chair lay centered in the room. As if he needed further proof of Haufner's escape, he read the attached comment.

—Let him go, or you're next—

He swallowed the bile rising in his throat. His heart rate spiked, causing tightness in his chest. He assumed ten minutes remained before he experienced his own death. The only question was the identity of his killer.

Chapter 51

Outside apartment building 41
0310 hours

Navigating the barren city streets, Cole drove to a physical address JSOC gleaned from their investigation of Gold Tooth's cell phone. He remained both excited and worried of what he might find. His imagination ran wild with images of his brother's condition. Only a couple of hours remained before the early risers started their daily grind. Little time remained for a successful rescue.

Cole provided details of the events involving the library, as well as the torture site. He enjoyed a minor satisfaction in conveying vital information to the Delta operator. Hammer interrupted only twice for clarification of descriptions. Talking about his experience helped him cope with the awful memories.

Hammer, in turn, shared the fruits of the ISA team's labor. A run on the car's license plate turned up nothing, but computer specialists, employing highly classified hacking tools, identified a location from Cole's text exchanges with the unknown person. The address belonged to one Barrett Jennings.

Was Butch at the site? Cole asked the question.

Hammer couldn't say.

After JSOC obtained all of the data from Cole's

device, his cell phone needed disposal before the authorities captured him. While driving over a bridge, Hammer crushed the SIM card and tossed the pieces out the window and into the river below.

Cole approached a cluster of modest, high-rise apartment buildings off *Jiuwei* Road. Compared to the surrounding structures, these units appeared newer than the rest.

"Kill the headlights," Hammer ordered.

Cole twisted the left turn signal stalk, and the lamps winked off. Guided by the building's ambient light, he turned onto a rear service entrance marked for use by city utility workers. He rolled the car to a soft stop and cut the engine.

Both men sat in silence, heads on swivels looking for threats. Their target, directly ahead, was a specific apartment—number 304—inside Building 41. A small service light cast a weak glow upon the rear door.

Hammer rummaged inside the glove compartment.

"What are you looking for?" Cole whispered.

"Maybe the clown you capped has a key to Barrett's apartment."

Cole ran his hands under the seat but found only a couple of coins and a few scraps of garbage.

"Guess we do this my way," the Delta man said.

"What's that?"

Hammer pulled a small, black device from the drop-down pocket on his pants leg. "The keys to everything." He held a lock-pick gun.

"Look. Obviously, your mission...." He looked away from Hammer. "I know what you're doing here is bigger than my life. Bigger than Butch's. All I want is my brother home safely."

"I get your meaning," Hammer acknowledged. "You're right. More *is* at stake. For now, focus on your goal."

"Who is this Jennings guy?" Cole gazed at the soldier.

"About twenty years ago, working for the CIA, he screwed up some big mission. Afterward, he dropped off the radar. That is, until your work surfaced his name. Our cyber-team is busting their asses but haven't found much useable intel. This guy's history is locked up tight inside the agency."

"Twenty years ago? That's around the timeframe when Butch and I came to *Dandong* as little kids." Cole scratched his head. "I don't know why that name sounds familiar. When I first heard...something's resonating."

Hammer's fingers coiled around the door handle. "Ready?"

Cole let out a deep sigh. "Let's go."

The two men hid their rifles in the backseat under an old blanket found in the trunk. Armed only with pistols, they stayed in the shadows, making their way to the rear access door. Cole stood guard while the big Texan attacked the lock mechanism. In less than a minute, both men swept through the doorway.

A wall-mounted stairwell light cast a dull, yellow glow. Three feet ahead, Cole saw a ground-level door with a placard displaying Mandarin characters. "Maintenance room," he whispered.

Thompson tilted his head toward the cement stairs to their right. Aiming his silenced pistol upward, he silently ascended the steps.

Cole followed and swept his gaze between the

floors above and their rear. Once at the third level landing, he watched Hammer place his ear against the interior access door.

A moment later, the Delta man tested the handle. "Be ready." Hammer cracked open the door, poked his head through the doorway, and glanced left and right. He pulled back into the stairwell and carefully closed the door. "We're going left. Put your left hand on my shoulder and cover our backside with your pistol. The apartment is a couple of doors down. Keep your finger off the trigger."

Suddenly nauseous, Cole nodded an affirmative. He dreaded the thought of making a mistake. Was Butch on the other side of the apartment door? Would he find Jennings? Horrible visuals of his brother lying in a pool of blood filled his thoughts. Knowing his anxiety raised the risk of screwing up, he shook the images from his mind.

Hammer grasped the door handle and mouthed a countdown. At "One," he swung open the door and crept left.

Holding onto the Delta man, Cole walked backward with his weapon pointed down the hallway. He prayed for an empty corridor. He felt Hammer stop, and he snuck a peek over his right shoulder. His gaze landed on the number 304 stamped next to a doorframe. Still training his weapon to their rear, he caught glimpses of the Texan working all three imbedded locks. *Come on, hurry.* A moment later, the *snick* of the last tumbler indicated the door ready for entry.

Hammer stashed the tool and drew his sidearm from his thigh holster. He leaned close to Cole's ear. "If I see a door chain, I'm gonna bust through."

Cole nodded. He stacked behind the big man and waited for the signal.

The Delta man slowly turned the doorknob. Glancing over his left shoulder, he mouthed a three-second countdown. Then he swung wide the door and pushed ahead.

Both hands on his pistol, Cole followed his partner. Kitchenette on the left. Clear. Three steps later, a small living room showed no signs of his brother. Now, a hallway led away to the right.

Hammer stopped at the edge of the wall.

Stepping close, he placed his left hand on the Texan's shoulder.

The soldier 'cut the pie' by extending his weapon in front of him while simultaneously sweeping right through the opening.

Cole followed with his weapon tucked close to his chest.

Hammer slowed and waved toward a door on the left.

Cole rotated and aimed his gun at the portal. He struggled seeing the front sight clearly through his swollen eyes.

The soldier pointed at his own ear and then toward the wall.

You heard something? Cole nodded his understanding. *Butch?* He fought the rising anxiety in his mind. *Please be you, brother.*

Hammer pushed his firearm at the door and, with a jerk of his head, summoned Cole. Taking the doorknob in his left hand, he mimed the three-two-one countdown before flinging open the door.

When Hammer peeled left, Cole cleared the

doorway and turned right. He spotted a bed against the back wall of a bedroom. At the sight of a human figure, he swiveled and took aim at the target's torso.

"Check fire. Check fire!" Hammer shrieked.

Cole immediately let off the trigger and spotted the reason for the command. Bound and gagged, a young woman lay atop the mattress with terror etched across her face. Her torn shirt exposed a white bra, and her lowered skirt, pulled down to her knees, indicated something worse. Her bulging eyes glistened with tears.

"Stay with her," Hammer ordered then rushed out of the room.

Cole holstered his sidearm. He held up his hands in a gesture of openness. *"Yǒushàn, yǒushàn*—friendly," he repeated in Mandarin.

Despite assurances, the young woman shook her head and curled her legs inward. Her muffled cries filled the room.

While attempting to soothe her, Cole realized he'd seen her before.

Chapter 52

Cole freed her wrists and removed the gag. *What the hell? Who are you?*

Her body shook, and she stayed silent. Remaining in a defensive ball at the head of the bed, she clutched at a pillow and stared at the wall. Her bobbed, black hair swayed from her tremors.

Despite his own torture, Cole couldn't imagine the terror she experienced at the hands of some unknown entity. Her situation disgusted him, and he wanted to lash out at whoever assaulted her.

"Psst." Hammer summoned from the hallway.

Reluctantly, he left the girl and met the Delta man outside the bedroom. "I'm not completely sure, but I think that's the girl I saw at the library."

"Really? Check this out." Hammer led him to a room at the end of the hall.

"What the hell?" A massive amount of computer equipment occupied almost the entire space. Multiple monitors filled his vision. His first thought was he stumbled onto an entire IT department at NASA.

"Yeah," Hammer agreed. "We need answers and *fast*."

"The Chinese government?" Cole asked.

"If you're right about seeing her at the library, something is wrong. *Really* wrong."

Cole motioned toward the first bedroom. "Let me

talk to her, alone. Both of us hanging around might further traumatize her."

"Agreed." Hammer pointed to his own chest. "I'll sweep the place. See what you can find out."

Cole headed back and knocked on the open door. "Okay if I come in the room?" he asked in Mandarin.

The young woman nodded but said nothing. With her clothes back in order, she kept her defensive posture.

"It's okay, it's okay. I'm not here to hurt you." Cole maintained a soothing tone. "Can I get you anything?"

The girl shook her head.

"Are you sure? Some water?"

"My...my glasses, please," she murmured.

"Oh, sure. Okay." Cole entered and scanned the small bedroom. He spotted the black frames lying on the floor. Retrieving them, he noted the significant thickness of the lenses, suggesting extreme myopia. Careful of encroaching in her personal space, he passed the glasses at the end of his reach.

"Thank you." She slipped them onto her face.

In a continued effort to place her at ease, he gave a slight smile. "Better?"

The girl gazed at him, and her eyes grew wide. Her hands flew immediately to her mouth.

He swung his chin over his shoulder and gripped the pistol tight in his hands. "What's wrong?" He returned his attention to her.

With an index finger, she made a circle around her own face.

At first, he wasn't sure what she meant by her action. Then he realized that, seen clearly, his face was a mess of cuts and bruises. He touched his nose and winced. "I ran into a wall." Then, he remembered the picture in his pocket. He pulled out the photo and shared with her his most valuable possession.

At first, she hesitated but, at Cole's repeated invitation, she examined the photo.

"This is me and my family."

"This man is you?" She gasped.

He noticed the increased strength of her voice then pointed to each person. "That's me and my wife and our son, Max."

The girl glanced back and forth between the photo and him. She eventually settled on his face. Her mouth hung open. "You're Cole Haufner."

He jerked, not sure of a proper response. He took a moment to collect himself. "How do you know?"

"You're the famous American fighter." Her eyes opened wide. "You used to live here!"

He thought she resembled nothing more than a teenage girl meeting her favorite pop star. "Well, I—"

She rose and threw her arms around his neck in a tight squeeze. "I can't believe you are here."

Cole was accustomed to this sort of reaction in the States but expected no such treatment this far from home. Who was this young woman? Did the corporate data center in the back bedroom belong to her? "Yes, yes." Reassuringly, he patted her back.

She released her chokehold. "I'm Lilly. I'm so glad you're okay."

"I'll be fine. You?" *What in the world is going on here?*

She slumped back on the bed. "Yes. I will be okay. But, I must find my father."

He took both her hands in his. "I swear, I will protect you. And your father, too, if he needs my help. No one will hurt you as long as I live."

Tears formed in her eyes and spilled onto her cheeks. Her lips trembled.

Cole bridged the distance between them, enveloping her in a reassuring hug. He heard a knock at the door.

"Everything okay?" Hammer asked.

Pulling back, he smiled at her and motioned toward the big Texan. "He's my friend. We need your help, Lilly. The whole world needs your help."

For a brief moment, Lilly regarded both men. "I know everything," she said in English.

Cole remained unsure if her comment was a positive or a negative sign. If she spoke the truth, she held news of Butch. "Start from the beginning."

Chapter 53

Cole's first opinion of Lilly was someone shy and awkward around other people. Now, sitting in her computer chair in front of monitors and keyboard, she presented a commanding figure completely in her element. The transformation was swift and certain. He remained convinced she spent a majority of her waking hours in this room. He made little of the data streams racing across multiple open windows, but listening to her describe each one created the impression that, for her, sophisticated cyber-research was child's play. Cole listened with rapt attention as she eagerly shared what she knew.

Speaking fluent English, Lilly described her attacker as a North Korean Special Forces operator named Park who, along with his subordinate, desperately searched for a device the size of a suitcase. She claimed the two men, with a small team, entered from the neighboring country illegally after a boat malfunction. Further, she knew of the battle between Park's group and the Americans who now possessed the case.

She explained the North Koreans pressed her into service, using her expertise as a freelance computer specialist with entree into the PLA's digital warfare group. She demonstrated her methods of infiltration inside the city's various departments, including police and military, as well as the CCTV video feeds throughout *Dandong*.

"Lilly, have you seen anything on the cameras we should know?" Hammer asked.

"We've seen almost everything since your team landed on the docks," she responded.

Hammer's eyes grew wide. "What?"

"We watched the battle between the Americans and the North Koreans. I saw two men, and I'm assuming you and another one of your American teammates, escape from the shipping yard. One carried the suitcase."

"You said, 'we'." Cole worried too many others knew of Butch's illegal presence in China. "Who else saw this video?"

"My father."

Cole narrowed his eyes as he recalled the scene from the library. "I don't suppose he's older-looking with thin, gray hair."

"Yes, that's him!" she exclaimed. "He was born in America."

Cole's mouth dropped open. "Your father is a Westerner?"

Hammer shot a glance at Cole before turning his attention to Lilly. "Is his last name Jennings?"

"Yes, Barrett Jennings. Do you know him?"

"He was with you, at the library?" Cole interjected.

"Yes. The North Korean agents demanded we accompany them. My father held no voice in the decision. These men are very dangerous people."

Cole nearly exploded with urgency surrounding his next question but held his tongue when Hammer silenced him with a quick shake of the head. He focused on a spot on the wall and employed his breathing techniques for calming his nerves. *Please be him.*

"The other man at the library—the monk—describe him," Hammer said.

Her gaze drifted to one side. "He is much larger than other monks. He had really big muscles. He displayed many scars and old wounds. The story he repeated many times included him using the computer for communication with a woman he loved. The North Koreans didn't believe him. Park's subordinate hurt him."

Cole trembled with anger. The thought of these monsters violently interrogating his brother sent shock waves through his body. Against rising visuals of Butch's torment, he closed his swollen eyes.

"Why did Park take you to the library?" Hammer asked.

"My father did not let on. I deduced Park doesn't trust him. The men needed me for computer expertise. The monk's email recipient led me to a dead-end address. I found no further evidence."

Cole noticed Hammer's shoulders relax. *She missed a clue?* Willing the thoughts of his brother's disappearance from his mind, he turned his attention to the man whose name held a familiar ring. "How is your dad tied to Park? How do they know each other?"

"He never talks about those men." Lilly chewed on her lip. "I do know he once worked for the American CIA—before I was born. He worked here in *Dandong*, and something happened causing his termination. The North Koreans somehow played a part. Their agents always expect my father's assistance. He cannot refuse their demands. Leverage, I think, is the correct word. My father promised me an escape from China that we might live quietly in another country. Somewhere safe where Park can't find us."

"This incident—would you say this event happened more than twenty years ago?" Something kept nagging at Cole's mind.

"I'm nineteen so, yes, the timing seems reasonable."

Hammer leaned closer. "Lilly, do you know where they took the monk?"

She shook her head. "My father made me hide down in the front seat. I didn't see anything until we arrived at a small workshop along a dirt road."

"What about the city cameras?" Renewed energy flowed through his body. "Can you pull up the footage?"

Lilly shook her head. "We traveled outside camera range. My research shows the car driving northbound when we exited the security systems. I have no way of determining the location."

"If you were at this shop with the North Koreans and the monk, how did you end up back in the apartment?" Hammer queried.

"Commander Park blindfolded me and drove me here. He used my computer and connected with a sympathizer, here in *Dandong*, who owns a boat for crossing the *Yalu* River."

"Then what?" Hammer asked.

"Once I established a link between the two, that's when he—" Moisture formed in her eyes. She took off her glasses and rubbed away fresh tears.

Hammer motioned for Cole to follow him. The two

walked into the living room. "We need the coordinates of the meet-up between Park and this boat owner."

"No." Anger gave vehemence to Cole's reply. "We need Butch. He's the only person who knows the location of the case."

Hammer jabbed a finger in the air. "Dammit, Cole, for all we know, the Koreans already have the objective. That device cannot cross the river. Get on board, or get out of my way."

Choice words sat at the edge of his lips. Before he replied, he heard Lilly call out from the computer room.

"Cole?"

Her tone drew him back into the room. On the center monitor, he saw a red box flashing an emergency alert.

Lilly pointed to the scrolling code. "Authorities responded to a suspicious fire. I discovered cell-tower records indicating a call from a known criminal's phone, at that location, to your number…and my father's."

Hammer's chin dropped to his chest. "How bad?"

"With many dead bodies yet identified, I'm afraid the city police responders alerted the PLA internal security."

Oh, no. Cole realized his desire for revenge might have cost him everything.

Chapter 54

"Oh, shit," Cole muttered. *Dammit, I'm an idiot.* In his literally murderous rage, he forgot the accuracy and permanence of a cyber-trail. Given enough time, the Chinese might connect the killings to his cell phone. Along with the discovery of the three SAD members, seven dead bodies held one thing in common—him.

"Lilly, stall the PLA technical division," Hammer demanded. "Use everything you have."

Her fingers flew, and lines of computer code scrolled across the screen. "I don't know how long I can hold them. They are the best in the world at digital warfare."

Cole pulled at his blood-crusted hair. "I'm sorry. I don't know why I set that fire."

"Let's hope your DNA disappeared in the flames." Hammer withdrew Gold Tooth's phone from his tactical vest pocket.

"Don't use that." Lilly opened a desk drawer, reached deep into the cavity, and produced a headset with attached mic. She connected the device to a USB cable extending from a CPU tower then opened a new window tab. "I have a secure voice-over-internet-protocol line. If you must contact someone, use this setup."

"So much for procedure," Hammer said. "I hope you're as good with operational security as you are at everything else." With two fingers, he tapped out a string of numbers and letters on a keyboard. "Nest, this is Two, confirming voice print."

Cole barely heard the exchange. He fretted over his actions placing his brother, and the mission, in jeopardy. He blew out a lungful of air and turned full attention to the other two and their efforts in thwarting the police.

"Roger, Nest." Hammer launched into a summary of the latest events, which included Lilly and her capabilities, as well as additional information on Barrett Jennings and the PLA's heightened awareness and pursuit of Cole.

Lilly continued tracking police reports. She also hacked into a PLA program keying on her father's license plate number.

As his limited skills didn't offer additional aid to his new teammates, he felt helpless. While Hammer continued with his report, Cole leaned close to Lilly. "Can you contact your dad?"

She stopped typing and gazed upward. "Park took my cell phone. I could link into my father's phone through my computer." Her eyebrows furrowed. "You won't hurt him, will you?"

"Not at all. He might still help us." *He's involved with Butch's capture. I want to pull him apart limb by limb.*

"Shouldn't I wait until your friend is finished with his call?"

He knew Lilly spoke logically, but he remained irrational with the fear of losing his brother. Hammer had all but told him only a few minutes ago he would, if necessary, sacrifice Butch in exchange for the case.

Now was the time for bold action. "You're right. We *could* wait for Hammer's instructions. But from what you've told me, your father is in grave danger. I can tell you with absolute certainty, the moment he is no longer useful, the North Koreans will kill him. You and I should work together. The American government won't risk extracting your father if that means failing their mission."

Lilly glanced at her computer screen for several seconds then turned her attention back to Cole. "What is their mission?"

"The same as the North Koreans—obtaining the suitcase. Only the monk knows the location of the device. We save the monk and your father—you and I." *Sorry, Hammer, but Butch won't survive without my help.*

"What do I do?" Lilly whispered.

Cole thought for a moment. "Tell your dad the North Korean is on his way to kill him and the American. Also, the U.S. government placed five million dollars in an offshore account for the return of the monk. The Americans offer safe passage for you both to any location of your choosing, including any country without an extradition treaty."

Her eyebrows furrowed. "But he might not believe me. How would the U.S. government contact me?"

Cole thought for a moment. "Make up something about being tracked down through your computers."

Lilly's hands lay still on the keyboard. Then a grin settled on her lips. "The satellite. I always told him the orbital spy craft was our biggest weakness against the Americans."

Lost in conversation with Lilly, Cole hadn't heard

Hammer sign off with JSOC.

"What about the satellite?" the Delta man asked.

At the Texan's booming voice, Cole held up a hand. "We're talking about the city cameras tracking individual cars. Something I said reminded her of a weakness in a satellite."

"What weakness?"

Lilly's gaze flitted between the two men. She settled on Hammer. "I have a blocking program running inside one of your satellites positioned over this region. The computer code disrupts ground imaging of certain coordinates."

Hammer's eyes turned to slits. "Let me guess— downtown *Dandong*? You're just now remembering this? What else have you not disclosed?"

Lilly recoiled in her chair.

Cole saw the Texan's jaw clench. He stepped between the two. "Hey, I just untied her a few minutes ago. Give her a break." He turned to Lilly. "Can you remove the program?"

"Yes. I need a few minutes."

"We'll be in the living room." Cole jerked his chin for Hammer to follow.

Back in the main living area, Hammer grabbed Cole's arm. "Look. We have no idea if us finding Lilly is a setup. She could be playing us. For all we know, some team is outside the door ready to take us down."

Cole pulled away then walked over to the window and peered out between two blinds. "We have just over two hours before this city lights up. With Butch out there somewhere getting God knows what done to him, what choice do we have? Anyway, I trust her."

Hammer glared. "When I go back in there, she *will*

disclose the North Korean meet location. She's smart. I'll bet she knows the coordinates. I expect zero interference."

You're letting my brother die for that damned case. "Translation—Butch dies." His accusation hung in the air. He saw Hammer's eyelids clench tight.

Hammer opened his eyes and stood straight. "I have my orders."

Cole turned and faced him. "I know Butch means more to you than orders."

"Because of what he means to me…" Hammer joined Cole at the window. "That's the exact reason for going after the case instead of your brother." The Texan's shoulders sagged. "Interdicting the North Koreans is precisely what Butch would want me to do. Any action less than recovering the device discredit his beliefs."

You're right. I wish I didn't believe you, but I do. He knew this special breed of men, particularly those in his brother's unit, were closer than any group of alpha males in the world. On multiple occasions, Butch told him they viewed one another as true brothers. They risked everything, including their lives, for each other, no matter the need. Cole wondered if Butch felt closer with his teammates than he did with him. He couldn't imagine playing second string to a non-relative but, if true, then Hammer's decision must be the toughest call for any man forced to make. He understood, but only to a point. "Tell me. What's so important you'd sacrifice my brother's life?"

Hammer exhaled. "Imagine a device that turns North Korea into the world's strongest nation—overnight. Think of what China might do with a weapon so potent, for that matter. Three of my teammates, your brother's too, died less than twenty-four hours ago in the hope of preventing such a catastrophe."

Cole couldn't have imagined Hammer's revelation. Still, his instinct called for protecting his brother. "Butch is the only one who knows where the case is hidden."

The big Texan pursed his lips. "You already know the North Koreans will make him talk. No one holds out forever. Because of that eventuality, I have to find the meet site—if Lilly isn't some decoy designed to throw us off the trail. If I fail, the imbalance in power will tear apart this planet. Butch's legacy is tied to this mission."

Cole regretted questioning the depths of loyalty and love his brother shared with his teammates. Their bond transcended anything Cole and Butch ever shared. He shut his eyes and lowered his head.

Hammer clasped a strong grip on Cole's shoulder. "I promise you. If we don't find him, we will have our revenge. Butch Haufner's name will live forever."

He couldn't speak, not even in agreement. Though Hammer's impassioned speech hit home, the Delta operator failed to extinguish Cole's hope for his brother's survival. *I have another mission that doesn't include him dying.*

"Come quick." Lilly shouted.

Both men sprinted into the computer room and skidded to a halt behind her chair.

She pointed several times at one of the monitors. "There."

A blown-up, photographic image showed the faces

of two men in the front seat of a car. The man driving showed pale skin, thinning hair, and pudgy cheeks. The other was a bald, Chinese man wearing soiled, torn robes. The passenger displayed significant facial trauma.

"My father." she gleefully announced. "The other is your monk."

Out of an abundance of excitement, Cole smacked Hammer's arm. "Where are they?"

Lilly quickly pulled up a map showing the vehicle traveling southwest along a four-lane road. "They are on *Shanshang* Street coming from the north. The outer-ring cameras in that section of the city identified his license plate."

"Where are they headed?" Hammer asked.

She turned her gaze toward both men. "I swear I do not know."

The flash of an idea jumped into Cole's awareness. The road passed near an important location. *Why didn't I think of this sooner?* He straightened to his full height. For him, the answer appeared obvious. "I do. We'd better hurry."

Chapter 55

Metal workshop
Ten minutes earlier

Butch feared few things in life—death not being one. He resigned to the probability, in his line of work, he might die alone and a long way from home. He'd come to terms with that likelihood in the belief the vital missions he performed were worth the sacrifice. Everyone in his unit shared similar thoughts. What he *did* fear most was betraying his teammates. That event had now come to pass. The knowledge proved too much for him to bear.

He raised his head and gazed directly into the North Korean's face. "Kill me," Butch said in Mandarin.

The North Korean glanced toward the Anglo male, who stood off to one side against the far wall. He shouted something in Korean.

"You got what you want. Kill me," Butch forcefully spoke in English. Curiously, the white male's gaze never left the screen of his cell phone.

The North Korean strode across the room and snatched the phone out of the other's hands.

"What the hell?" The white man bellowed in Mandarin.

The North Korean yelled something Butch couldn't

translate. With his eyesight clouded by lack of sleep and physical abuse, he couldn't clearly interpret the interplay between the pair. The relationship, obviously, was contentious. Beyond that, he could not determine the balance of power.

The North Korean commando peered down at the cell phone's screen. His eyes bulged, and his mouth hung open.

Butch expected the North Korean's resumption of his tirade. But the yelling didn't happen. Instead, he saw a flash of movement followed by a loud *crack.*

The back of the North Korean's neck exploded outward in a shower of flesh and blood, and he dropped to the ground in a heap.

Over the course of his twelve-year military career, Butch witnessed more than a few men die, most by his own hand, but he fell stunned by the turn of events.

The older man stood motionless, staring at his victim, a small handgun clutched in his right hand. Robotically, he glanced at Butch and, after a moment, drew closer.

Butch wasn't sure whether the shooting of the North Korean was accidental or planned. *Am I next?*

"You okay?" the man asked in English.

"You're kidding, right?" Butch made a point of gazing at the handgun in the man's grasp. He noted the shooter's demeanor appeared trancelike in quality.

Beads of sweat flashed across the man's forehead. "My first time...shooting a person. I don't know what I should feel."

"You're an American?" Butch asked. *Am I dreaming? Did they drug me?*

The gunman slowly nodded.

"You gonna shoot me, too?"

The American stuffed the pistol into his front pocket. "No, no. I'm with the CIA. We need to get you and the device out of here."

Butch shook his head. "I'm on a reality TV show, right? *Good Cop, Bad Cop, Extreme Edition.*"

"What? No…I'm just an analyst. I've never been in the field."

"I believe you." *Is any of this situation real?* He searched his mind for any recall of receiving an injection.

The older American surveyed the room before settling his gaze on the dead North Korean. He walked to the corpse and retrieved his cell phone. Next, he searched the dead man's pockets and found the keys to the heavy padlock securing Butch to the boiler. He returned and released the chains.

Feeling the slack, Butch tensed, hoping he wouldn't smack his head on the floor. The toll to his body left him without the necessary strength, and he fought a losing battle against gravity.

"Gotcha." The proclaimed CIA analyst caught him.

"What do I call you?" He knew many lies lay ahead—the man's name being the first.

"I'm Ted. I'll give you the full info dump once we get clear."

Careful what you say. Shooting the North Korean might be a fake. "You could have stopped all this a long time ago, *Ted.*"

"I'm sorry. Guess I'm not cut out for this sort of work."

No shit? Butch still wondered if he existed in the grasp of some psychedelic drug. He fought for control of his mind and continued his mental indexing of the treatment he received since the library. The change in dynamics of his situation gave him pause for revealing any more information to Ted. *Am I still under interrogation?*

With significant energy expended, the pair finally reached Ted's car. The men sped away into the darkness of the early morning hours.

Slumped in the passenger seat, Butch ruminated. His betrayal of his mission, of his teammates, ate at his soul. Of all the physical torture he'd endured, no other pain compared to his mental anguish. Revealing details of the fusion device ground the very essence of his being into a fine dust. The fact the man next to him put a bullet into the base of the North Korean's brain—saving Butch's life and possibly salvaging the mission—did not remove the emotional impact of his own failure.

A pothole in the road jarred Butch from his thoughts. Glancing out the window, he noted the roads were empty and the sky black. He'd lost all sense of time. *What day is it?* Though self-aware, his critical thinking lacked as if he awoke from anesthesia. The fine details of the past few hours, few days even, remained hazy.

Ted drove at a breakneck pace, which didn't distract him from launching into an elaborate explanation. He—a local CIA desk jockey tasked with monitoring the Chinese side of the border—fell into North Korean hands earlier in the day.

Butch thought the man said all the right things, giving him at least superficial credibility. But, the Delta man remained guarded. He realized Ted needed no further driving directions. The CIA man knew where the secreted case lay. In between episodes of simulated drowning, Butch revealed the general location. In his panic for survival, he failed at describing the *exact* spot at the Temple.

"We'll be there in five minutes. Tell me exactly where you hid the case. We can arrive at the Shenyang embassy by sunup," Ted said.

Butch thought of cross-checking his bona fides. "Why not just meet with the SAD team? Aren't they waiting for us?"

Ted glanced to his right. "You didn't hear, did you? Someone interdicted them. We lost them."

So, he knows. "Isn't the bus terminal a risky place for a massacre? Even for the North Koreans, that's kind of ballsy."

Ted returned his gaze to the road. "The ambush occurred in the alley behind the Crowne Plaza Hotel."

He's tied in for sure. But, which side? Butch stared out the side window. "Where's the other North Korean? The man in charge?"

"He's setting up his exit strategy. He'll discover his dead comrade any minute. We need to move fast."

"Just get me to the Temple. Stay with the car. I'll take care of the rest," Butch said. *And once I lay hands on the device, I'll be long gone before you realize I screwed you.*

Chapter 56

Mituo Temple
0406 hours

Nearing the *Mituo* Temple, Butch performed a mental inventory of his physical status. His upper extremities functioned well, but his legs might pose a significant challenge. At the workshop, he found his ambulatory status lacking and remained dubious the time spent in the car insufficient for recovery. Weak from the torture, he called on his military training and mental toughness. Could he walk? Once they stopped, he needed to test his balance.

Ted negotiated the right turn onto *Yujia* Road then a quick left left onto the *Mituo* Temple side street.

Seeing the large Buddha statue made Butch's heart thump against his chest. He welcomed the surge of adrenaline. He required every advantage for securing the fusion device—without Ted's assistance.

The car slid to a stop at the edge of the pavement. With a flip of a switch, the headlights winked off. The low hum of the idling engine filtered into the cabin. Neither man moved.

On the surface, Butch played along with the highly-questionable claim Ted worked for the CIA. In return, he allowed Ted the notion he accepted his role in the Butch-Ted alliance. Surviving the next hour took precedence. Truth's exposure awaited the winner of the battle for possession of the case.

Butch wiggled his toes then slowly flexed his legs. His knees barely budged. *Walking is gonna suck.* He gazed left at Ted. "Get on the horn with the embassy and tell them we're two minutes out from moving with a critical extract." He reached for the door handle.

"Wait." Ted grabbed Butch's arm. "I know you're the field man. I'm not convinced staying in the car as lookout and getaway driver is the smartest move. Shape you're in, you shouldn't risk going alone."

Butch fixed his hard stare on the man. "Holy shit, Ted. We've been over this. I need you here for a quick exit. That's the plan. Do as you're told."

Ted's eyes went wide, and he withdrew his grasp.

As Butch predicted, Ted didn't offer any more objections. This guy was no torturer. He stood aside as the North Koreans took Butch to the edge of sanity, and he wouldn't get his own white-collar hands dirty. Butch knew his type—a coward.

Ted turned his gaze straight ahead. He busied himself with his phone.

In disgust, Butch grunted. With the hope none of his lower vertebrae fractured during his ordeal, he swung his legs onto the pavement. He took two deep breaths then pulled himself upright. A couple of seconds passed before his right leg registered sensation. Satisfied his inner ear produced the necessary balance, he released his grip on the door. *One step at a time. Don't let anything stop you.* As he'd learned during grueling Delta Force selection and training, he focused on his immediate goal and blocked everything else from his mind. Butch took several successful steps, compartmentalizing the terrible sensations crying out from his body. Lumbering, he made for the small residence off to the right.

Butch assumed Shen slept inside the cottage. He counted on his cousin's help—whether through persuasion or force, he planned on cutting Ted from the equation.

Upon arrival outside the darkened home, Butch didn't bother knocking and instead grabbed the doorknob and let himself inside. He knew Shen never used the lock. The interior was dark but, thankfully, Butch remembered the layout, and his night vision remained intact. He pulled himself gingerly over the threshold, shut the door, and crept toward his cousin's sleeping cot. "Shen?" Butch called out in a whisper. "Shen. Wake up."

He heard no movement. *Curious.* He recalled his cousin as a light sleeper. Stepping closer to the bed, he noticed the empty cot. His senses revving up, he saw a blanket balled up in the corner of the small room. The air carried a different odor, some new incense fragrance not present the last time he visited. *I remember that smell at the Temple.* His gut tightened. Something wasn't right.

"Shen? Are you home? It's Butch," he said louder. He scanned the area one last time but saw nothing else disturbed.

He shuffled toward the top of the short staircase leading to the lower area. Hanging onto the doorframe for support, he gingerly lowered himself onto the first step. Moving at a painfully slow pace, he safely reached flat ground. He found the small chain attached to the single light hanging from the ceiling rafter. Closing one eye, thus preserving his night vision, he pulled the cord, and light filled the cavern. He saw no sign of his cousin.

Butch headed toward the small closet where he stowed his gear. Scanning the hide location, he froze. He didn't see his equipment. *Where's my stuff?* Panic threatened his thoughts. Did someone capture Shen?

Fighting pain, Butch leaned into the small alcove and ran his hand above the wooden, cross-member, arch support half-buried inside the rough stone. He pressed a release button, and the rear wall clicked open. Stepping inside, he pushed the hidden door wide. *Thank God.* Relief flooded his system. Whoever took his gear didn't know the existence of the device—or at least the location. The objective hadn't moved.

Butch struggled lifting the twenty-five-pound object. Determined, he half-carried, half-dragged the box from the hiding spot. The transport took far more time than he expected with the stairs proving the most difficult portion. Once he reached the front door, he needed a moment of rest.

With Shen missing, his hope faded for a distraction of Ted. Butch couldn't risk getting back in the car. As much as he desired believing Ted's story, he couldn't bring himself to trust the man. With no obvious other option, he planned on turning the corner to the right and fade into the trees at best speed. *Let's get this done.* He took a deep breath and cracked open the door.

The car remained idling in the same spot.

Good. He grabbed the case's handle, pushed open the door, and slipped outside.

"Took you long enough," a voice called out from behind.

Butch froze. *The bastard was inside the whole time? How did I miss him?* He slowly turned and faced Ted. "You piece of shit."

Ted stepped out of the doorway Butch just passed through. He waved his pistol, the same weapon used against the North Korean. "Did you really think I'd trust a portable fusion device to anyone's hands but my own?"

Butch closed his eyes and shook his head. *I should have killed him in the car.* He lowered the case to the ground. "Who do you work for?"

Ted raised his eyebrows. "As of twenty minutes ago, myself. Now, all profits come to me."

You idiot. "You *do* realize the risks? Those you crossed won't be kind with their payback. All the money in the world won't save you."

Ted shook his head. "The CIA came for me once before and failed. I like my chances."

"The CIA will be the least of your worries once interested nation-states decide you screwed them. Let's put this genie back in the bottle. There's still time."

Ted grinned. "Clean, unlimited power...a truly momentous discovery for mankind—and my bank account."

Butch chuckled. "Do you really think that's all the device offers? Uncontrolled energy release is on par with a two-kilo nuclear blast. Without the radiation, there's no fallout. No need for plutonium. A completely undetectable bomb. You can't be stupid enough to think the DPRK won't hold the world hostage."

Ted rolled his eyes. "Spare me the science lesson. While the superpowers squabble over the scraps, I'll sip margaritas on my own island."

Butch pointed at his own face. "You saw what those two did to me. You won't find a safe place on this planet."

"Nice try." Ted pointed the pistol at Butch's chest.

He took a step toward Ted. "You don't believe in this thing's military application? I know the inventor." His gaze hardened. "So do you."

Ted took a step backward, his eyes bulged. He waved the gun at Butch. "You're one of the Haufner boys! I should have known. First, your brother and now you."

Cole? His hands balled into fists. "What about my brother—"

The racing engine of an approaching car cut off the sentence.

Ted directed his attention toward the noise.

Butch leaped for Ted. Inches from his intended target, he heard the report of a gunshot, and a massive blow slammed against the right side of his chest. He spiraled into the doorframe. He tried rising to his feet, but his legs wouldn't respond. Intense, shooting pain enveloped his torso. Butch could only lie motionless in the dewy grass, listening to his own ragged breathing as one car departed and another arrived.

Chapter 57

0418 hours

With Hammer in the passenger seat, and Lilly providing course corrections from the back, Cole raced along the city streets driving Gold Tooth's sedan. His instincts proved correct—Butch and Jennings headed for the Temple. He blew through two red lights along the deserted city roads in pursuit of his brother and the former CIA operative. After absorbing Lilly's description of the events at the workshop, Cole couldn't understand why his brother traveled with her father. He caught Lilly's image in the rearview mirror. "How could they escape the North Korean?"

"I don't have a clue." Her gaze remained fixated on her laptop screen. "I don't believe the North Korean knowingly allowed such a thing."

Cole stole a glance at Hammer in the front passenger seat.

The Delta man gave a quick shrug.

With no answer forthcoming, he refocused on the road. The Temple was near. Cognizant of the police substation, Cole slowed and turned off *Shanshang* Street then made a quick left onto *Yujia* Road. The Temple grounds sat to their right. Taillights up ahead caught his attention. They disappeared onto *Xinhua* Street. "Police car?"

"Or the other two leaving the scene," Hammer added.

I hope you're wrong. Cole brought the sedan to a stop and gazed over his right shoulder. The brightly lit Buddha statue commanded his attention. Cole wasn't sure of Hammer's plan, but he expected instructions as soon as the soldier surveyed the surroundings.

"Oh no!" Lilly exclaimed.

"What?" Hammer hissed.

"Is that someone lying on the ground next to the front door of the house?" she cried.

Cole scanned farther over his shoulder. A robed man lay crumpled on the lawn. Panic enveloped him. He leaped from the car, bridging the distance between him and the figure. "Butch?" He skidded to a halt and dropped to his knees. He gently rolled the bald-headed figure onto his back. Despite the man's swollen and battered face, he recognized his flesh and blood. His heart pounded against his chest. "No, no, no…"

"Cole?" Butch rasped. "Am I dreaming?"

Kneeling next to his brother, he heard an alarming wheezing coming from a location other than Butch's mouth. "Yeah, it's me." He held his brother's shoulders in a reassuring grip. "You're safe now."

A rattling cough erupted from Butch's throat. "What are you doing here?"

"Long story, brother. I'll fill you in after I get you to the hospital."

Hammer arrived and assessed his team leader. The Texan ran his hands over Butch's body. In seconds, he pinpointed the bullet wound to the chest. "You know of any good Chinese restaurants around here?"

Aghast, Cole glared at the soldier.

Butch grinned, showing blood-streaked teeth. "Asshole."

"Let's get him to the hospital," Cole said to Hammer.

"No time, Cole." Butch grabbed his arm. "Get the guy that just left here. He took the case." Another cough started, this time producing flecks of blood.

Hammer ignored both men as he deftly patched Butch's chest wound with an oiled gauze pad.

"You need a chest tube, ASAP," he confirmed to his team leader. "I don't have the correct medical kit."

With sudden strength, Butch grabbed Hammer by his combat vest and yanked him close. "The guy in the car that just left...he has the case!" He caught his breath. "An American. Says he's CIA—called himself Ted."

Son of a bitch. "Balding, pudgy guy?" Cole asked.

Butch nodded.

Hammer swung his gaze from Cole to Butch. "His name is Barrett Jennings. Ex-CIA working with the North Koreans in *Dandong*."

"I can't believe..." Butch groaned.

"You know him?" Cole asked.

Butch stared at something in the distance. "He recognized my name. He's the one responsible for Dad's disappearance. Back when we were kids."

Gut tight, Cole sat back on his heels. Barrett Jennings—*that* explained the nagging memory. Two decades ago, when Cole was six years old, he met the man escorting his father in *Dandong*. The meeting occurred when the family brought back his mom's remains for burial. The memory of shaking Barrett's hand flashed in his mind. Now, twenty years later, the former CIA man shot Butch. Was he intent on killing them all? "Why did they take Dad?"

Butch launched into a coughing fit. Drops of blood sprayed from his lips.

"He needs a chest tube, *now*." Hammer reslung his pack and prepared to move.

Butch grimaced and grabbed Hammer's battle harness. "Get...the case. That's an order." Except for the wheezing, he fell silent.

"I'm on it, Boss." Thompson summoned Cole out of Butch's earshot. "We take him to a hospital, and the PLA will snatch him. Is there anyone you know who can care for him...quietly?"

Butch's breathing grew shallow and rapid.

Cole drew a blank. Then a thought occurred. He sprinted back toward the car. Inside his bag was something that might prove invaluable—if the authorities believed what they saw.

Chapter 58

"What are you doing?" Hammer called out.

Cole slapped his hand against the car's exterior. "Lilly, release the trunk!"

Still sitting inside, she leaned across the armrest between the front seats.

A few seconds later, he heard the latch release. He lifted the rear deck and yanked out his duffel bag. Rummaging through the contents, he found his small, blue booklet then ran back to the group.

"What did you find?" Hammer asked.

"My passport." Cole grinned. "We can drop Butch at the hospital using my ID. If anyone questions him, he'll have the answers. He knows everything about me."

Hammer pursed his lips. Then, a grin slowly crept across his face. "Dude, that's brilliant. But, what about you?"

Cole waved off his question. "Let's worry about that later."

Hammer explained the plan to Butch, whose breathing grew increasingly labored.

Butch nodded to his teammate. He grabbed hold of Cole's hand. "The case...Father invented...a fusion device. Jennings...stole Dad's...invention."

"He what?" Cole's hands trembled, and his mind went blank.

311

Butch's arm dropped to the ground, and his head lolled to one side.

"We're leaving." Hammer rolled Butch into a firefighter's carry and jogged toward the car.

Clutching her beefy laptop, Lilly, wide-eyed and speechless, opened the rear door and moved to the front passenger seat.

Cole scrambled past the Delta men and dove into the rear of the car. He prayed Butch didn't feel the jostling pain atop his teammate's broad shoulders. He helped load his brother into the back seat. Butch's head lay across his lap.

Hammer jumped into the driver's seat and fired the engine. He stomped the gas pedal, leaving a trail of exhaust behind.

Lilly frequently glanced up from her laptop screen and called out directions to the nearest hospital, just a mile away.

Gazing between the front-seat armrests, Cole caught glimpses of her computer monitor. He watched Lilly resizing an earlier photo of Butch then place the image inside an official-looking document. *Is she reporting us to the authorities?*

Over her left shoulder, she caught Cole's gaze. "I'm creating a patient profile for the hospital. I grabbed the monk's, I mean your brother's, picture from one of my programs and placed the visual ID into his virtual chart. Not my best work but should buy some time."

"An Internet search will blow his cover," Cole said. "We don't look enough alike."

"I'm really sorry. I don't have the horsepower for accessing the State Department database where they store the passport photos."

"The shaved head and facial injuries helps muddy the water," Hammer said. "Good work, Lilly."

Cole turned his attention to his brother. Butch's skin coloring took on a grey hue. The painful memory of Claire and Max rose to the forefront of his thoughts. The same feelings of rage and despair rushed to the surface. *I can't lose you, too. I won't let that happen.*

"The hospital is coming up on the left," Lilly said.

Hammer slowed and maneuvered onto the U-shaped front entrance.

Following Butch inside was Cole's greatest desire. He needed visual proof the hospital staff performed flawlessly in saving his brother's life. Logically, he knew that plan only compromised the identity switch. To save him, Cole must abandon him. He stroked Butch's forehead. "We're here, brother."

Hammer pulled up to the ER entrance.

"Cole...I love you. Find Jennings...kill him," Butch whispered.

Cole quickly glanced at Lilly. He saw no indication she heard his brother's wish. He leaned close to Butch's ear. "I promise. Hang tough. Remember the plan— you're using my passport. You're me." He kissed his brother's forehead.

The car door flew open, and two orderlies pushed a wheeled stretcher next to the vehicle.

As planned, Cole and Hammer remained inside the car in the hope of keeping their faces from prying cameras.

The two staff members extracted Butch and placed him on the bed.

Lilly exited the car, handed the passport to one of

the transporters, and briefly spoke.

The hospital worker gave a quick nod then grasped the side rail of the gurney and pushed toward the entrance.

Cole watched helplessly as the ER doors closed behind his brother. Butch was gone.

Was this the right call? Will I ever see you again? The intensity of Cole's despair matched his deep resolve for completing his brother's last wish. Just as Hammer honored his teammate by finishing the mission at all cost, so too was Cole's promise. *Payback time.*

With Lilly back inside the vehicle, Hammer circled onto *Shanshang* Street heading south.

Cole lay slumped in the back, conscious of little except Lilly's furious keyboard clacking. He didn't bother asking Hammer where they headed. Dawn neared, but Cole's thoughts remained dark. Butch's disappearance after Claire's and Max's deaths caused him significant mental trauma. Now, equally excruciating was his suffering at not knowing in which direction his brother's life headed.

He shifted in the vinyl seat and felt sticky blood. Remnants of Butch clung to Cole's hands and clothes. He smelled the dusky iron released from the ruptured red blood cells. Half asleep, Cole refocused on his personal mission.

Barrett Jennings—an American expatriate. A former CIA employee. Now, he worked with the North Koreans. Had he grabbed the suitcase for himself or for the DPRK assassins? The fusion device—invented by his own father? He stopped for a moment and considered Butch's claim.

What was the relationship between his father and

Jennings? To what extent was Jennings involved when his father disappeared? *My God, Lilly's dad is a prime suspect in the Haufner kidnapping.* His promise to her of protection for her father occurred before his newfound knowledge. He needed no further justification for putting a bullet into the man's head.

"Damn!" Lilly exclaimed.

The expletive shocked Cole fully awake. His impression of her didn't include her using foul language. "What?"

She stabbed at the keyboard for several seconds before answering, "Sorry, I don't mean your brother. I erased all the city camera footage associated with him. The authorities have no video records for their investigation."

"And?" Hammer shot a glance in her direction.

"The PLA. They're tracking my dad's car. They're looking for him."

"We must find him first." Cole ground his teeth. *No one interferes with my mission.*

Chapter 59

0500 hours

The road angled southwest, away from the dense inner city. The northern edge of the vast farmlands ahead pushed against the urban city lights. Thompson overheard Butch's whispered desire for revenge against Barrett Jennings. He hoped Lilly, following her father's car on her laptop, didn't hear the words. His mission hinged on her successful tracking of the man with the fusion device. Farther ahead, on this route, several camera hits on Barrett's license plate gave Hammer notice of his correct steerage.

As they left the urban core, they crossed feeder rivers emptying into the larger *Yalu* waterway. Up ahead, *Shengli* Street connected with the 201 National Road. Thompson worried that, once on the highway, the Chinese authorities gained an advantage for tracking him and Jennings. To succeed, he had little choice but to follow his quarry wherever the road took him.

Thompson happily obliged Lilly's belief the plan included saving her father, though he suspected her goal held no chance of success. He and she worked at cross purposes. He could not help but admire her determination even as he co-opted her skills for his own aims.

"So, a fusion device? What's so special about that suitcase?" Cole asked from the backseat.

Thompson considered the implications for divulging the answer. *I'm damned either way.* "When you were a kid, your dad invented a miniature fusion machine, or at least he figured out the engineering for one. One of the biggest concerns was the energy release if weaponized. The government hid his technology but not before spies caught wind of his discovery. Recently, we shared news of the invention with a key ally. The North Koreans stole the only working unit from a conference in Nagasaki. My unit specializes in this type of recovery mission."

"So, you're worried North Korea will blow up a city?"

Thompson glanced over his shoulder at Cole. "No…an entire country. Possibly others."

"Is that why J—" Cole started.

Thompson loudly cleared his throat, cutting off the rest of the sentence. He needed Lilly focused on the immediate task. If she understood Barret shot Butch or played a role in the Haufners' father's disappearance, she might find the distraction too great a burden.

"Wouldn't America retaliate with their bombs? North Korea stands no chance against their might," Lilly added.

"If verified, yes," Thompson noted.

"My father wouldn't build a bomb." Cole paused for a moment. "I'm sure of it." He tapped his hands against both head rests. "What if his goal involved saving the world?"

"How?" Hammer asked.

"Free energy." Cole pushed his upper body

317

between the gap in the front seats. "No more wars over oil fields, no more babies dying from poverty and lack of clean water, and no more corporations ruling our lives. My father wanted people living equal and free."

Thompson followed his logic. He also knew the souls of men. He'd hunted them his entire career. The man from Texas saw what greed and power did to people. "And like all good intentions, this one has a dark side."

Cole pushed back into his seat. "You're right. So is Lilly."

She glanced up from her computer. "I am?"

"North Korea knows if they use the invention as a bomb, the U.S. will wipe them out."

Thompson wasn't privy to all the intelligence discussions gathered over the past two decades. He found Cole's train of thought compelling. "What are you saying?"

"I bet the DPRK plan is what our government fears most—economic destruction. With a single announcement, they'll collapse the largest sector of every major country's GDP. North Korea will own the world's energy supply."

Lilly's computer chirped as a CCTV monitor pinged Barrett's car up ahead. The discussion halted.

"Lilly, the highway coming up—where does the road lead?" Thompson asked.

"A north-south byway along the inner coastline passing close to the Port of *Dandong*."

Right back where we started. "Sounds like—"

"Yes, the same place where you landed," she interjected.

"Any other significant landmarks along the route?

Does your father know people in the area?"

Lilly rubbed her forehead then pushed her glasses up her nose. "He has some ties to the port authorities." She bit her lip. "I don't know how much he trusts them. Would they help him?"

Thompson shrugged. "Don't know, but the port makes a likely exit point for someone running from danger. If he gets on a boat, he'll have a good shot at a clean getaway."

"Dad wouldn't leave me." She shook her head.

He'll do what he must for survival. He assumed Barrett knew the value of the device in his possession. He'd found the opportunity worth shooting Butch. Either the ex-CIA agent still worked with the North Koreans, or he made a play for the case on his own. Finding a buyer was a complex matter, but the vast sum of money, billions, provided extraordinary motivation.

Thompson committed to the four-lane highway route, convinced the coastline was Barrett's objective. Continuing south into the rural terrain, he watched the streetlights disappear. The landscape turned decidedly darker.

After a few minutes of silence, Cole spoke from the back. "Why is the PLA looking for your dad?"

Lilly glanced up from her work. "The PLA has ties into everything. They likely received an alert the city police sought a foreigner. My guess is the cyber team tagged his car, from city video feeds, somewhere close to your last known location."

"Plus, as an American, he's scrutinized more than the average Chinese citizen," Thompson added.

She nodded. "Literally dozens of computer specialists like me monitor nearly every aspect of day-to-day life. Right after I erased the videos of your brother, I lost access to some of their systems—but not before I read an alert. The PLA ordered law enforcement to detain my dad. I'm blocking the license-plate detection program from feeding back to their cyber team. I'm not sure if I've succeeded."

"Could the city cameras record you at the library?" Thompson asked. "I used Cole's cell phone near the building around that timeframe."

"That event is very possible."

Thompson drummed his fingers on the steering wheel. "The PLA—they know you well. If they issued an alert for your father, wouldn't they add you to their search? Perhaps that's why they blocked your access."

Lilly swallowed. "If you are correct—if they are looking, they will find me. The government does not fail in such matters."

Thompson thought the situation couldn't get any direr. If the PLA pinpointed Lilly and her computer, they might add airpower to the search. Miranda Rights and Due Process didn't exist in this part of the world. An air-to-ground missile provided a quick and efficient solution.

All three fell silent. Only the sound of the keyboard clicking filled the void inside the car. The tires hummed along the pavement.

"No, no, no, no." Lilly repeated.

"What happened?" Thompson didn't like her tone.

"The cyber team is shutting me out!" She smacked the keys. "They haven't found me, not yet, but they blocked me from the cameras."

Thompson fought the rising panic in his chest. "What are the options?"

"We're blind. I can't track Dad!"

"The docks." Cole leaned forward and patted Lilly's shoulder. "Can you get into their system?"

Lilly typed rapidly. She grinned. "Thank you for the reminder, Cole. I'm in!"

Thank you, Jesus. "How?" Thompson was puzzled.

"I have an old account I created a long time ago. My dad used their system for keeping tabs on his contact. As long as I have a satellite connection, I can hide from the Cyber Teams inside their closed network."

"How long do you think you have before they shut you down?" Thompson asked.

"I'm actually siphoning a signal from the American satellite. As long as the PLA doesn't find me inside, I'll stay live."

Thompson moved to the next logical step. Tracking Jennings meant she required continuous access to the overflight. *Farther down the rabbit hole we go.* "Lilly, can you patch me to my command?"

Her eyebrows rose. "You sure? I cannot guarantee a secure connection."

"We have little choice." Having made the decision, Thompson gave Lilly the communication links with JSOC. Within thirty seconds, she connected him with the ISA operations group via the digital system. He hated delaying further pursuit of Jennings, but he needed off the road. He pulled onto the shoulder and killed the headlights. He balanced Lilly's computer in his lap. "Nest, this is Two for voice identity."

After a ten-second delay, a heavily digitized voice replied, "Two, this is Nest. Confirmed. What's your status? Over."

"I'm at one hundred percent. Have two passengers with me, and we are in pursuit of objective. Our status is under heavy national scrutiny. We are at critical phase. Over."

"Standby, Two."

Thompson turned to Lilly. He kept his tone gentle, belying the harshness of his words.

"You are involved with one of the most secret military units in the world. I will not hesitate eliminating either you or Cole if I believe for one second one of you is compromising the integrity of this mission or the identity of this group. Am I clear?"

"Y-yes," Lilly stammered.

He glanced toward Cole for acknowledgement and received a middle finger in reply. On some level, Thompson enjoyed the second answer more than the first.

"Two, this is Papa Bear," the general's gravelly voice came through the laptop's tiny speaker. "Son, I understand things are a little tight there. What's your sitrep?"

The Delta operator spent the next couple of minutes relaying pertinent data. He spared no detail of Butch's precarious medical condition, and he explained the identity switch. Thompson finished with the PLA's Cyber Warfare unit's thwarting efforts against Lilly tracking her father. "Sir, we need those cameras tracking the package."

"Two, I will do everything in my power for your team leader. Focus on completing this mission. Do you have any threads left to pursue?"

"One left, Papa. Our computer tech believes our target might attempt a rendezvous with a contact near our original insertion site. We have electronic eyes into the location. We need the overhead satellite operational. That's our ticket inside. How copy?"

"ISA will throw full weight at the satellite. I've also redirected a below surface asset for a southerly extraction. Do you copy my meaning?"

Thompson knew exactly what the general insinuated—once they recovered the case, a waterborne rescue awaited the tiny band of warriors "Roger, Nest. I understand and concur. Over."

"I'm proud of all of you. Let's finish this and get out of Indian country."

"Good copy. Two is out." Thompson ended the link. He handed back the laptop to Lilly.

"What do we do now?" she asked.

Thompson started the car and pulled onto the road. "We find your father's contact."

Chapter 60

Two miles from the Yalu River
0540 hours

White-knuckled, Barrett negotiated the left turn off the 201 National Road and onto *Tuda* Line, heading east toward the canal running along the *Dandong* port's inner coastline. In thirty minutes, he expected the first hints of the morning sun. By sun up, he'd mix with the rest of the fleet of fishing vessels chasing their quarry— his final destination yet determined.

Given a choice, Barrett preferred returning to his apartment and retrieving Lilly. *I'm sure she's safe.* He brushed aside thoughts of Park's secondary motives for taking her back to their home. He refused considering the meaning of his abandonment of the young lady he raised as his own daughter. *Leaving you behind isn't my fault. I'll come back for you.*

Barrett's port contact, unhappy with the early wake-up hour, nevertheless sprang into speedy service at the promise of fifty grand in U.S. currency. The old fishing trawler the sailor offered perfectly fit his needs. One last task remained before his escape—along with the object worth billions.

Immediately after shooting Haufner and escaping with the case, he contacted Park and relayed a concocted story of treachery by the 14K organization.

Because of the North Korean sniper's bravery and ultimate sacrifice, Barrett escaped with the device. The prisoner died in the crossfire. He determined his final escape hinged on Park believing both the possibility of the event and the agent's steadfast loyalty to his Dear Leader's mission. Barrett couldn't truly remain free so long as Park lived. They agreed on a meeting location.

One hand on the steering wheel, Barrett grabbed his cell phone with the other and thumbed the *redial* icon. A single ring sounded.

"Yes?" Commander Park answered.

"Boat confirmed. I arrive within five minutes," he told Park.

"If you plan a double cross, you will not live long."

"I do not benefit from lying." Barrett hoped his voice reflected a steely calm he did not feel. "Your comrade died nobly at the hands of the 14K gang. He refused the money they offered for the prisoner. I could not foresee their treachery."

"Your failure is obvious," the man hissed.

Stay calm. "By surviving, I located the fusion device based on the monk's disclosures."

"Curious the gang let you live."

"I killed two of them. I don't believe they intended I survive their assault." Barrett allowed a nervous chuckle to escape his lips. "At great risk, I have your comrade's body with me so you may see the evidence for yourself." Barrett hoped Park interpreted the quaver in his voice as fear of the commander's wrath. "I just want to live in peace." That much was true.

"Your daughter…"

Finding Park's mention of her almost unbearable, Barrett shook his head. *You sick bastard!* He increased his grip on the steering wheel.

"At the moment, she is tied and gagged. If I discover betrayal, I will send someone to your dwelling and exact my price."

"I will have everything ready when you arrive." News of Lilly left alive in the apartment buoyed his emotions.

"No more disappointments," Park warned.

Barrett opened his mouth, but the call disconnected. He dropped the cell phone onto the passenger seat. Mere minutes remained for review of his plan. In every scenario running through his mind, eliminating his greatest threat—Park—remained the most essential component. The unfortunate aspect regarding the North Korean was his skill as a professional operator. Barrett required more than a little luck.

His route took him toward the *Yalu* River. Veering southwest, he turned onto *Wanghai* Road where, at the bend, he entered the small town supporting the port. Warehouses, small family-owned shops, and ramshackle housing dotted the enclave. Like most portside neighborhoods, the scenery reflected a lower-income, working-class population. The locals managed the seaport's day-to-day operations.

Barrett turned left onto *Binhai* Highway, a crumbling blacktop littered with water-filled potholes. He headed for a boatyard repair station on the banks of a fingerling of water feeding into the larger section of the *Yalu*. Park couldn't resist the location. The main advantage of this spot was China shared this water section with North Korea. The border between the two countries ran down the middle of the muddy inner river, and a North Korean-owned island sat less than three hundred yards from the Chinese side. He counted on Park's knowledge of these facts.

Barrett drove the last quarter mile and pulled up to a dirty warehouse building. On the edge of the bank stood a towering, yellow crane. A dry-docked, rusted ship sat directly underneath. Even with the car windows closed, he smelled the combination of rotting vegetation and sea salt. This patch of soil represented his last moments in China—in life or death.

He took a deep breath, opened his door, and stepped onto the tightly packed dirt. The sky showed the faintest hint of light. For a moment, he stood scanning the area. He noted diesel fuel vapors and the stench of fish. Not seeing his sailor contact, he walked to the river's edge and found the moorings.

Gently rocking in the slow-moving water, a sea-battered, thirty-two-foot fishing trawler occupied one of the slips. A quick check of the hull markings confirmed this boat as his purchase. The side riggers sagged like the boughs of a weeping willow tree. A tangled fishing net lay in a heap in the open aft. On closer inspection, he noted the knotted nylon partially obscuring a dozen or so short barrels of fuel. He requested enough gas for travel into international waters and, hopefully, to a South Korean port. That was, if this piece of junk didn't sink in the first hundred yards.

Barrett climbed onto the open deck. In the small, forward wheelhouse, the engine's ignition key lay on the wooden dash. He tested the battery. Despite the boat's pre-World War II appearance, all gauges immediately lit up. Avoiding unwanted attention, Barrett decided against firing the engine and instead turned off the electronics and pocketed the key.

He headed back to the car, where he'd left the fusion device, and the body of the North Korean sniper. He wondered if Park's inspection of his dead comrade might offer enough of a distraction for a needed advantage. Within the hour, the moniker of billionaire or dead man awaited Barrett.

Chapter 61

One mile behind Jennings
0550 hours

Cole struggled to keep his emotions in check. The man responsible for so much destruction in his life still breathed. At the moment, all that kept him going was the desire for his pound of flesh from Jennings for what the man inflicted on Butch and the agent's role in his father's kidnapping. Raised as a practicing Buddhist, honest to a fault, he no longer recognized his promise to Lilly. He wasn't that person anymore. Circumstances changed him.

"Hit!" Lilly shouted from the front seat. "He turned left about one kilometer ahead."

Cole gazed over her left shoulder and saw an arrow pointing east on the map overlay. A blinking cursor showed the turnoff. He leaned closer for recognition of any names or landmarks suggesting Barrett's destination.

"Are we inside the port area?" Hammer asked.

"I believe so," Lilly replied. "I don't have any access other than the Port cameras."

A tiny voice in the back of Cole's mind hinted at something amiss. Warning bells sounded in his thoughts. He recalled a time when he was a young boy. Master Li brought him to this southern area. Further scrutiny of the map gave him a worrisome insight. "Unless I'm wrong, I don't think the turnoff is considered part of the inner port."

"What difference does that fact make?" Thompson asked.

Cole leaned forward. For Lilly's sake, he pointed to a small section of backwater off the *Yalu* on the computer screen. "You see where the road ends at the water's edge? Just off the bank is a tiny island controlled by the North Koreans. Because of the close proximity of foreign soil, the PLA likely monitors this section of the border. That means this road is controlled by the military and *not* the port authority."

Lilly brought up a map overlay whose blinking blue pixels showed CCTV locations owned by the PLA.

Cole noticed the port-controlled cameras showed in green—the nearest one a full two miles farther ahead from where Barrett turned left. The crossroad was, indeed, outside the official port control. He sank back into the rear seat. *We're screwed.* "Someone restored Lilly's access to her locator program."

"Shit." Hammer's expletive was a loud whisper.

Lilly's hands hovered inches above the keyboard. "The Cyber Team...they're tracking me. They know where I am!"

"If true, the PLA is already on their way." Cole also assumed the Cyber Team suspected Lilly of helping her father avoid the authorities with the use of her technical access and expertise. The implication of her as a co-conspirator, in whatever the Chinese suspected of her father, appeared complete.

"We don't have much time. Where does that turnoff lead?" Hammer asked.

Lilly remained frozen in her seat. "To a ship repair yard at the end of the road."

I bet I know what Barrett has planned. "You think a boat's waiting?" Cole asked Hammer.

Lilly tapped a hand against the dash. "We have to hurry. My dad."

Cole exchanged glances with Hammer in the rearview mirror. *He's not coming back.* Lilly's youth and gullibility blinded her from the truth about her father.

But was North Korea the intended destination? If Park *was* with Jennings, then the two men need only cross a narrow strip of water. Jennings, if alone, required a destination farther away—and that meant he'd lined up help from someone other than the North Korean.

Suddenly, the car engine's whine dissipated, and the vehicle dropped speed.

Cole directed his attention through the front windshield. Approaching blue-and-white flashing lights filled his vision. He tensed. *Oh no, they found us.*

"Local or federal?" Hammer applied the brakes and coasted to a stop.

Lilly stammered and did not provide an answer.

The official-appearing vehicle halted at the T-intersection and blocked both roads.

Cole squinted against the painful illumination of the strobe-like pulses. The blinding lights prevented him from identifying the car's occupants. *We don't have time for any delay.*

"Don't panic," Hammer said. "Whatever alerted them might not involve us."

"What if they're not cops?" Cole couldn't explain

why, but something in the tableau aroused his suspicions.

"See if you can get my command back online," Hammer murmured.

Lilly tapped on the keyboard.

No, something isn't right. We can't wait. Cole took advantage of the front-seat distraction. He retrieved Butch's pack from the foot well and removed the helmet and night-vision gear. He flipped the power switch then donned the Kevlar. Staying low in the seat, he grabbed the rifle and confirmed the red dot glowing in the combat scope. He didn't stop and consider if the equipment worked against the powerful police lights. Waiting for orders from some general thousands of miles away only delayed the mission. He recalled Butch's final request. *Out of my way.* He opened the rear door and sprang to his feet.

"What in the hell are you doin'?" Hammer's muffled voice called from inside the vehicle.

He didn't reply. Rifle to his shoulder, Cole peered through the red-dot aperture and searched for movement inside the cop car. Through the flashes of light, dimmed by the night-vision electronics, he counted two figures in the front seats. While aiming at the driver's chest, Cole quickly shuffled toward the vehicle. He saw a flurry of motion erupt inside the car.

The passenger threw up his hands.

The driver drew a sidearm and brought the weapon into a firing position.

Cole squeezed the trigger in three rapid successions, which caused a trio of smacking noises as bullets connected with the windshield. Puffs of pulverized glass scattered with each impact. He lowered the rifle and sprinted the twenty-five yards separating the two parties. Approaching within ten feet of the official vehicle, he returned the rifle to firing position and surveyed the car's interior. He no longer saw a weapon pointed in his direction.

Both passengers waved their raised hands.

Cole assumed their intent on surrender. Pulling open the driver's door, he heard two male voices babbling incoherently. He roughly grabbed the driver, who showed no signs of a gunshot wound, and pulled him out of the car with a single yank. The man landed hard on the cement, and Cole stomped down on the uniformed back of a port security guard.

Hammer, armed with his rifle, ran onto the scene.

"Got you covered! One male in passenger seat," Cole shouted to the Delta operator. He turned his weapon toward the second man, who continued crying out and waving his hands.

Hammer ran to the opposite side of the car, pulled open the door, and dumped the second port security guard onto the ground.

Presuming the threat neutralized, Cole lowered his weapon and took in several deep breaths. He noticed a set of handcuffs on the guard's leather belt and quickly applied the restraints.

The Texan dragged his prisoner around to the front of the car and hoisted the terrified young man by the throat onto the hood. The aluminum buckled as the weight of the guard formed a dent.

Cole leaned into the front seat, found the overhead light switch, and turned off the strobe. The return of darkness provided a presumed sense of security. Standing, he walked around front and joined Hammer.

Through his night-vision gear, he noticed a huge grin on the bearded Delta man's face.

"Damned if you don't remind me of your brother." Hammer pinned the security guard with his beefy left hand. "How did you know not to shoot the guy?"

"I didn't." Cole examined the windshield and surveyed the three, tightly-grouped holes. *Lucky bastard.* He flipped up his NVGs and leaned close to the face of the frightened guard. "And if he doesn't tell me what I want to know, I won't miss a second time."

Chapter 62

Road intersection one-quarter mile from shipyard
0605 hours

Thompson had performed his fair share of field interrogations. He'd seen some bloody sights. The way Cole approached his subject reminded him of the toughest CIA Black Site specialists. Because Cole spoke the language, he stood back and allowed Haufner free rein. The approaching daylight spelled doom for the group. Seconds counted.

Cole withdrew the rifle suppressor from the guard's left eye socket, wiped a layer of sweat from his forehead with his sleeve, and turned to Thompson. "Says they got an urgent call from the area precinct. Their orders include halting all vehicle traffic. He doesn't know why. My guess is the PLA are on their way." He pointed the weapon's barrel toward the turnoff road. "He also says this road ends at a repair yard at the inner canal of the *Yalu* River. Normally, the road veers off and continues back north along the inlet, but that section is closed for repairs. Barrett is down there somewhere. No way out except back this way."

"Good work. We gotta hustle. If I were in charge, I'd send helicopters." Thompson scanned the sky. The faintest hint of light bounced off a passing cloud.

Cole jabbed his rifle at the two prisoners. "How do

335

we handle these guys?"

"Hold off, Cole." This time wasn't the first Thompson witnessed good men with strong moral compasses become mentally lost in the field. Robot-like, they acted as if driven by pure, sometimes cruel logic. "We're not executing anyone."

With Cole's help, he loaded the bound guards into the trunk of the port authority car. Once stashed, Thompson checked on Lilly. She appeared no worse for the wear. In fact, when asked of her status, she merely shrugged. *Was she growing as callous as Cole?*

"I still have full access." Lilly gave an update on the government network. "Very suspicious. And your command is standing by."

"Put them through," Hammer ordered.

"You're on."

"Nest, this is Two. How copy?" he transmitted.

"Clear, Two. Status?"

"We have a strong indicator our location is compromised. Objective is nearby. Making our way there now for interdiction. Request water exfil near origination site. Over."

The computer speaker remained silent. A spinning hourglass, mid-screen, signaled something wrong.

Lilly gasped and pounded on the keys.

Oh shit. "What happened?"

"The connection…we've lost the satellite."

"Everything?" *Just when I didn't think the situation could get worse.*

Slowly, she shut the laptop's lid and closed her eyes.

Did JSOC receive my last transmission? Does the PLA know the plan? His throat tightened at the thought of inbound government troops. "We're moving," he told Lilly. Hammer leaned out the window and shouted to Cole, "Get the other car. Follow me."

Cole dashed toward the port authority vehicle. Once inside, he flashed the headlights.

Thompson flashed once in return. He led the way down the side road leading to the river.

"How far to the shipyard?" he asked Lilly.

"Under half a mile," Lilly answered. "After a small rise in the road, the yard is on the right at the water's edge."

Thompson pressed ahead, wondering if he possessed the time for a quick reconnaissance at the bump in the road. The last thing he wanted was to lead Cole and Lilly into an ambush. What else might cause mission failure? His mind raced with possibilities.

He drove past thin stands of trees and small groups of waist-high, scrub brush. The cracked pavement rattled the rifle in his lap. A few moments later, a crest in the road appeared in the headlight glow. The morning sky showed enough illumination for his needs, and he switched off the headlights. *I better check ahead*. For all he knew, an armored brigade awaited his arrival.

Behind him, Cole slowed his car and shut down his lights. Both vehicles coasted to a stop. Parked near the peak in the road, Thompson switched off the interior dome light. "Stay here. I'm checking out the shipyard." He carefully opened his door and, with rifle in hand, slunk outside.

Hunched low, Cole sidled up to Hammer.

The two men edged their way to the ridgeline. Thompson tilted his head to the right, rendering his outline as small as possible to anyone who might scan their direction from down the hill. With his left eye, he spotted a yellow crane. He inched ahead until he saw the roofline of a large building. He slowly tilted his head upright. The dark shape of a single vehicle stood parked in a large dirt lot. He shouldered the rifle and peered into the low-power scope.

A man stood near the trunk of the vehicle.

Thompson handed Cole the rifle. "Look familiar?"

Haufner raised the scope to his eyes. "Yep, that's Jennings. I'd recognize that asshole anywhere." He scowled while passing the weapon. "Can you make a kill shot from here?"

"At this distance, we're at max range for this weapon. I'm not confident."

"You—" Cole started.

Thompson caught movement left of Barrett, and he smacked a hand against Cole's chest for quiet. He watched a lone figure emerge from a hedge some fifty yards away from the ex-CIA man. Judging from Barrett's relaxed body language, the incoming man was his partner, or at least a trusted contact.

Thompson brought up his rifle a second time, working a solution on the second subject. The male figure walked with confidence and seeming power. Something was slung over his shoulder—he thought likely a rifle. He again shared the scope with Cole.

Cole gazed through the aperture then froze. He pulled his gaze away from the weapon and turned to Thompson. "That guy doesn't look Chinese. He looks more like a North Korean."

"You're sure?"

Cole handed back the rifle. "I'm fairly certain." He

then pointed toward something farther in the distance. "See that stretch of island just across the river inlet? *That* is North Korea."

Shit. Any moment, he expected the PLA's arrival, and he knew these two assholes stood closer to North Korean territory than he to them. Despite his sniper training, he understood a confident shot with his weapon meant less than two hundred yards to target. Presently, he stood outside the highly modified rifle's effective range. "I gotta close the distance."

Chapter 63

0612 hours

Cole's downhill view showed little effective cover for a stealthy approach on foot. Scattered scrub bushes and a few thin trees dotted an otherwise open terrain. As he regarded Barrett and the man he thought likely a North Korean, his mind raced for a solution. An idea surfaced. *Hope the distraction works.* "Gonna check on Lilly," he whispered.

"Yep." Hammer continued scanning the area.

Cole's real destination was the port authority car, but he didn't want the Delta man knowing his intention. Reaching the guard vehicle, he slowly opened the door and slid behind the wheel. He reached for the ignition key when Lilly startled him from the passenger seat.

"I need to know." She narrowed her gaze.

His heart thumped against his chest. Cole swallowed the lump in his throat. "What are you doing?" he rasped.

She never broke eye contact. "I'm coming with you."

Cole noted a resolute look on her face. "Stay with the big guy. You'll be safe."

Lilly shook her head. "Is my father a bad man?"

He pursed his lips. At least a dozen potential answers, all of them lies, ran through his mind. She didn't deserve anything other than the truth. "Yes."

"Did he hurt your brother?" Her eyes watered.

Surprising even himself, Cole nodded. He couldn't lie to Lilly—not anymore. He felt an emotional alliance with her. She lost her biological parents. She suffered through her own torture. Now, she stood a strong chance of losing her only father figure. For all her abandonment and devastation, she deserved the truth. We can't choose our parents." He kept his voice soft. "You're a good person, Lilly. I promised I'd protect you. That's why I want you to stay here."

She sniffed. "No. I *must* go."

"If you go, you'll die. Almost certainly."

"You don't intend to die, do you?"

"I'm not on a suicide mission, no. But the odds are…" His voice trailed off.

Unblinking, she regarded him. "Part of me already died. I need closure. I'm sure you understand."

I know exactly how you feel. Cole understood her entire world occupied a meeting at the end of the road. She yearned for the truth in her father's eyes—not the stories force-fed over the past nineteen years. He'd experienced the same longing since arriving in China— the homeland of his childhood—less than two days ago. He, too, discovered the truth on many levels and, despite the pain some of the revelations caused, he remained grateful for the experience. "Okay."

Lilly smiled. "What about the guys in the trunk?"

He looked to lighten the mood. "They wouldn't miss the show for anything."

Her hands flew up, and she stifled a giggle.

Cole synched tight his seatbelt. He noticed Lilly following his example. As his sense of danger receded, he recognized the void replaced with excitement. He wondered if Lilly truly realized the level of risk. Perhaps, at this point in her life, she no longer cared the final result. He gazed out the windshield and saw the morning's first light. *Let's get this party started.* "Stay down so they don't see you."

Lilly scrunched low in her seat and braced both hands on the dash.

He started the car and stomped on the gas pedal. He caught a glimpse of Hammer's shocked face as the Delta operator turned and waved his arms. *Sorry.* The car leaped over the top of the rise and hurtled down the broken pavement toward the shipyard.

Cole bore down on the two men, closing the distance in seconds. Shadows from the flashing roof lights danced across the landscape. He hoped the shock-and-awe of intruding law enforcement might paralyze Jennings. He watched the unidentified man take cover behind the parked car.

Jennings stood transfixed on the approaching vehicle.

The ex-CIA man held his position even as the port authority vehicle came to a screeching stop just fifty feet away.

Cole desired nothing more than snuffing the life from Barrett's eyes. In addition to Butch's gear, the cruiser offered him an arsenal of additional tools. He pulled the handheld mic from its dashboard holder and pressed the speaker button. "Aren't you forgetting something?" His question, in Mandarin, blared at a high-decibel level from the engine-bay-mounted speaker.

The second man's head poked up from behind the

other car's front end.

Jennings stared directly at Cole.

Cole read confusion in Barrett's expression. He doubted Jennings identified him through the windshield. He reached his right arm over to Lilly and pushed her below the dash.

Jennings half turned and said something to his contact. He redirected his attention back to Cole and motioned with his hand.

I'm not leaving the car. Your partner will shoot me. Cole knew better than obeying Jennings. He didn't have a plan, but he wasn't keen on ending his life this soon. At this distance, he and Lilly sat overexposed, even inside the car. Again, Cole pressed the button. "You forgot your daughter. Isn't she going with you?"

Jennings' eyes bugged out. "No one else is here. Did Shao send you? Why isn't he here?"

"Shao. That's his contact," Lilly whispered.

"Shao will be here any minute," Cole's distorted voice came over the external speaker a second time. "He mentioned two men and a girl. Where is she?"

"The woman is not your concern!" Barrett shouted. "My colleague and I are ready for departure. Show yourself, immediately!"

Cole paused. He thought he maintained the upper hand but didn't have a plan moving forward. *What should I do?* Suddenly, the passenger door handle ticked, and he saw a flash of movement. Before he could react, he witnessed Lilly exit the vehicle.

She stood just outside the car, the open door acting as a shield. Tears streamed down her face.

"Lilly?" Barrett's jaw hung open.

Cole interpreted the man's expression as a mixture

of shame, affection, relief, and horror. He sat frozen behind the wheel—Lilly exposed herself to two men, one of whom willing and capable of killing her on the spot.

"Why, Father?" Lilly sobbed. She latched onto the door frame with her right hand. "You are leaving me? Why?"

Barrett's face turned red.

With no answer forthcoming, Lilly's wailing intensified.

Barrett held out his hands with palms up. "I couldn't tell you the plan for your own good. I was coming back for you. Comrade Park forbade me from saying anything!" He pointed an accusatory finger toward the man partially hidden behind his car.

Park. Cole finally received confirmation of his suspicions. Jennings partnered with the enemy state. This man shared responsibility for his father's disappearance and Butch's injuries. His hands shook from the rage building inside his mind.

Park yelled something at Jennings.

The ex-CIA officer closed his eyes and dropped his chin to his chest. "Lilly, get back in the car. Please, I beg you."

Her hands covered her face as a quiet wail escaped from her throat.

The standoff had turned ugly. Tension filled the air. Cole's skin tingled, and he gripped the steering wheel. Everyone remained still. Then, a faint thumping wafted in from the distance. *Helicopters.*

Chapter 64

For the first time since the North Korean took cover behind Barrett's car, Cole clearly saw Park's face—skin stretched tight across angular bony structures. The man's appearance projected sinister determination. He assumed the commando never allowed witnesses.

Jennings stood transfixed on Lilly.

At the pounding of aircraft rotors from the east, Park's eyes narrowed. He raised a rifle into firing position.

Sucking in a breath, Cole dove across the front seat. The concussive noise of the rounds jarred his senses. As bullets connected with the car's exterior, pieces of glass and aluminum showered him. He latched onto Lilly's leg and, with all his strength, pulled her into the front seat.

The pounding of supersonic projectiles nearly drowned out her screams. She pressed her hands against her ears.

Cole, acting as a human shield, pushed Lilly flat on the seat and lay on top of her. Muffled shrieks from the two men in the trunk rose to his ears. The three-round bursts came in perfect tempo.

Fight back. He pawed into the backseat, groping for his rifle. He caught the end of the barrel and muscled the weapon into the front seat. With little finesse, he brought the gun into firing position and poked his head just above the dash. He caught sight of Jennings partially hidden behind the rear bumper of his own vehicle. He didn't see Park. *Shit. Where did you go?*

The ringing in his ears caused mild disorientation. Cole rose, seeking the North Korean through his electronic sight. Movement caught his attention.

Park dashed right in a flanking maneuver.

Cole flipped off the safety with his thumb and fired a barrage of rounds through the broken windshield. He saw dirt kick up in front of the running target, and he tracked his adversary's return course to Barrett's car. Seeing Park dive behind cover, Cole swung the barrel toward Barrett's position. Neither man remained visible.

Whimpering loudly, Lilly lay with both arms covering her head. Multiple scratches and scrapes showed on her forearms.

Cole brushed away the larger pieces of material scattered across her back. Thankfully, he saw no obvious signs of a gunshot wound. "You okay?"

Lilly didn't respond. Her sobs came in long bursts.

Time to root out Jennings. "You'd kill your own daughter?" Cole shouted the question in English. "You'd sell out your own flesh and blood helping the piece of shit next to you?"

"Is that you, Haufner?" Jennings asked from his hiding spot.

"Yeah, the one that got away." Cole's bellow required no amplification. His anger grew even as the approaching helicopter's rotors pounded a louder note. "I'm gonna kill you for what you've done to my family."

A heated exchange in Korean erupted between the two men hiding behind the other car.

Cole eased upward and sighted further above the window frame. He wouldn't let Park escape his vision a second time. *Dammit, Hammer. Where are you?*

"Listen, Cole," Jennings spoke in English. "Park and I are leaving. Keep down, and he won't shoot you. Understand?"

His grip tightened on the rifle. "If you think Park will let us live, you're an even bigger idiot than I thought! He'll kill Lilly."

"Sweetie?" Jennings shouted. "Stay down. I'll come get you as soon as I finish this one last job. Okay? I'll return in less than an hour."

"Just stop!" she screamed. "I don't believe you."

"No, honey, I promise. I'll be right back."

Lilly squirmed against Cole.

Fearing his weight hurt her, he shifted in the seat.

She popped up, again exposing herself to the two men outside.

Cole saw Park rise from behind the hood of the car with the butt stock of his rifle against his shoulder. "Get down!" Without aim, he brought his weapon to bear and squeezed the trigger. The mechanism didn't budge. The open bolt position signaled an empty magazine. He dropped the rifle and threw his body in front of hers.

A loud *crack* erupted from behind the other car.

Park's head snapped to the right, a splash of blood jetting out the side of his skull. The commando disappeared from view, his rifle falling against the hood.

Barrett's left arm hung suspended in the air. A thin

smoke trail spiraled upward from the end of his pistol's barrel. "Lilly! Are you okay?" he shouted into the eerie silence.

Cole turned his shoulders and frantically searched the backseat area for his pistol. For several seconds, he scoured under the seats and the foot wells to no avail. His gut clenched. He'd left the handgun in Gold Tooth's car. He possessed no means of defending Lilly.

While the still-distant helicopter drew closer, he thought of his brother back at the hospital. Was Butch alive? Had the hospital staff discovered his true identity? Cole's mind turned to Claire and Max and even his father. His entire family deserved justice—so did Lilly. Cole couldn't bring back his family, but *could* he save the young woman seated next to him?

Cole turned and gazed at the motionless young woman. "Stay here. You'll be safe." Resolute with his choice of confrontation, he exited the bullet-riddled car and stood on the clay-packed ground. At that moment, a sliver of sun crested the horizon, casting a brilliant light on his face. Warmth covered his exposed skin. Even through swollen eyes, he clearly noted the details of his surroundings. His body ached. Pain and exhaustion threatened his consciousness.

"Lilly?" Jennings shouted from behind his vehicle.

He squared his shoulders toward the voice. "She's okay. Physically, anyway. No thanks to you."

"Don't come closer." Jennings warned.

"PLA will be here any minute." Cole glanced toward the sky. "They tracked us through your daughter's laptop. I'd say your plan for stealing the case is screwed."

Jennings peered over his car.

Cole held up his empty hands, confirming he stood unarmed.

His pistol trained on Cole, Jennings rose. He slowly rounded the trunk and approached, stopping ten feet away.

"You gonna kill me in front of Lilly—in cold blood?" *Do you have one shred of concern for her?* He jabbed a finger at Barrett. "How do you feel knowing your daughter finally understands the truth about you?"

"The truth?" Jennings spat. "My definition is quite different than yours. There's survival, and there's death. I did what I must to remain alive. She'll understand one day."

"Oh, she already discovered the real meaning behind all the bullshit you fed her all these years—like you allowing my father's kidnapping by the North Koreans. Shooting my brother, and I'm sure you had a hand in Master Li's death. Let's not forget your friends who worked me over." Cole pointed a finger toward Lilly. "She knows everything!"

Barrett's lips flattened, and his eyes narrowed. "Your father was an accident. I was just a kid. If I could, I would go back and change the outcome." His voice rose to a shout. "You have no idea what it's like being hunted by your own government."

Cole glanced in the direction of the beating rotors growing louder. "I don't?"

Jennings followed his gaze. "You should have stayed home."

He clenched his jaw. "You should have kept your allegiances straight."

Barrett's skin reddened. "You don't know how long I've blamed your father for my shitty life."

"Blamed my father?" Cole hissed. The mention of his dad sent a jolt of adrenaline through his body. He craved ripping the flesh from the traitor's bones. But he realized his action robbed Lilly of her sought-after truth. So, in a sudden fit of clarity, Cole chose another course of action. The outcome promised one hundred percent certainty.

Cole gazed over his right shoulder toward Lilly. "You're nothing like him. He's a thief, a coward, and a selfish prick." He turned back to Jennings. "Sound about right?"

"You forgot filthy rich." Jennings sighted down the barrel of his pistol.

At least Lilly now knows. He stared directly into Barrett's eyes. Cole hoped Jennings pictured his face every time he lay in bed. "Go ahead, you gutless coward." He released the air in his lungs and thought of his family. *Be right there, sweetheart.*

"I'm finally rid of the name Haufner." A crooked grin rose to his lips.

Crack!

Barrett's head snapped backward. A dark hole appeared in the middle of his forehead. The ex-CIA man's legs instantly buckled, and his body dropped to the ground. Every time his dying heart contracted, a pulsing fountain of blood squirted through the gunshot wound.

Cole spun toward Lilly. Seeing she sat in the front seat with her eyes closed, he let out a sigh of relief. *Thank God, you didn't see anything.*

Farther behind the bullet-riddled car, Hammer ran toward them, half-dragging a small, disheveled Chinese man with his left hand. The Texan struggled keeping his much-older captive moving forward.

"Took your time, didn't you?" Cole deadpanned.

"Coulda' been sooner. You kept gettin' in my line of fire," Hammer huffed.

Cole nodded to the Chinese man. "Who's your new friend?"

"No idea. Right after you ran off, he came up behind me sayin' 'Shao'."

Cole walked to the newcomer and slapped the Chinese man's back. He grinned at the Delta man. "Well, how about that? He's Barrett's port contact."

Hammer's eyes shot wide. "No shit?"

Cole glanced at Barrett's corpse. "Not anymore." *Mission accomplished. Rot in hell.* Concerned Lilly might catch a glimpse of the body, he walked to her and helped her from the destroyed vehicle. Luckily, she followed his instructions and hid her gaze from the results of the gun fight.

The sun was fully ablaze in the eastern sky. A slight gust of wind rustled Cole's hair. Judging by the loud *thump-thump,* he thought the helicopter might dip from the sky at any moment. *No time left on the clock.*

Hammer shoved his prisoner at Cole and jogged to Barrett's car. The Delta operator popped the trunk then peered into the cavity. He lifted the case and planted a kiss on the shock-resistant polyurethane.

Cole chuckled. His father's invention appeared intact. *Wish you were here, Butch. I know you'd be so proud.*

Chapter 65

An old fishing trawler chugged while marking a steady pace. The diesel engine spewed cloudy exhaust from a single, rusted pipe rising above the deck. The vessel's wheelhouse roof line stood barely six feet in height. An opening in the rear allowed fishermen unrestricted movement between the steering mechanism and back deck as they plied their ocean trade. At the helm of the thirty-two-foot vessel, Barrett Jennings' port contact, Shao, piloted the craft.

From the steps leading down into the lower cargo hold, Hammer stood watch over the Chinese man's movements.

As he'd likely done many thousands of times over the decades, the old fisherman waved to nearby craft. His presence here at the mouth of the *Yalu* River, as it emptied into the East China Sea, likely appeared familiar to anyone seeing him—including the authorities. A gun aimed at his chest and a promise of a better life in America provided necessary motivation.

Below deck, the body of Barrett Jennings lay wrapped in an old tarp.

Hammer obtained hair samples from Park's body for DNA mapping, snapped a few pictures, and left the North Korean's body where he'd fallen. He'd done the same with the sniper's corpse, stowed in the trunk of Barrett's car. Two dead North Korean operatives, along with two terrified but alive Chinese security guards locked inside the trunk of the stolen car, hamstrung the PLA long enough for the fishing boat's timely departure.

Shrouded in a hat and rain jacket, Cole sat hunched in the co-pilot's chair next to Shao. He kept a careful eye on the man at the wheel, watching for any physical signs of an impending shouted warning to passing vessels. Thus far, the old fisherman seemed eager leaving behind this part of the world.

Reflecting on the final battle, Cole thought of his last moment facing Jennings. *Why did I give up so easily?* Though he told himself his action was for Lilly's sake, he knew his reasoning didn't align with the truth. Exhaustion prevented clear thought surrounding his death wish. He glanced toward the young woman.

Lilly sat on the floor next to Cole, legs drawn up and arms wrapped around her knees. She spoke not a word. Her only possessions included her clothes and her laptop.

Despite Hammer's vehement warnings, Cole retrieved the computer prior to their escape, knowing the piece of hardware represented Lilly's lone connection to her life in China. Cole drew painful comparisons between his prior feelings of loss and abandonment to her own.

"Anything?" Hammer asked from his partially hidden position.

Cole scanned through the dirty starboard window and saw the ends of the docks of *Dandong* falling behind at a safe distance. Shipping cranes lifted cargo containers onto an ocean transporter. "So far, okay. We're clearing the port area. I don't see anything overhead, either."

Hammer simply nodded.

Seeing the site where his brother landed, Cole thought of the Delta soldiers who perished along the shoreline. "Is that where your teammates…" he could not bring himself to finish his question.

Hammer dropped his gaze then turned his head and hid his face from Cole.

"The authorities won't find your men," Lilly said.

A jolt raced through Cole's body. "Huh?"

Shrugging, she glanced at him then Hammer. "I moved them."

"You what?" Hammer's eyes bulged.

At the Texan's voice, she flinched. "Before we left the apartment…"

Cole leaned forward and patted her shoulder. "Go on."

"After the battle, Park ordered the American remains hidden in one of the containers. I used my computer and issued shipping instructions for the box's delivery to San Diego, California. They will all arrive within the next ten days." She gazed at Hammer. "I hope that's okay?"

Hammer's shoulders sagged. "I don't have the words for how much your effort means. Thank you."

She nodded at the big man. "When I re-establish an Internet connection, I'll help you identify the container." Lilly gazed up at Cole.

He smiled and noted a sparkle to her eyes. *You must be the smartest and nicest person on the planet.*

Lilly grinned then dropped her chin to her chest.

Cole returned his attention to the shoreline. *How could anyone hurt you?*

The vessel continued south toward the open ocean. Shao described a location he knew about one-hundred kilometers away where large commercial ships fished when the currents and weather proved favorable. The old boat being in that region would not raise any particular alarms. This tack allowed them safe distance from the mainland, away from prying eyes, before making a heading change.

The mild sea brought calm to the boat occupants. Sunny skies and the drone of the engine lulled Cole into complete relaxation, and he released his worry, even his concerns for Butch. When he woke with a start, he saw from the clock on the dash he'd slept for almost five hours. Next to him, Lilly snored softly, curled up under a blanket someone placed over her. Fearing he'd let down his friends in the surveillance department, he glanced toward Hammer. Keeping tabs on Shao through heavy-lidded, bloodshot eyes, the Texan hadn't moved from the steps. Cole stood and joined the Delta man. "Sorry. Didn't realize I passed out. Can I take over?"

Hammer waved him off. "I got it."

With Lilly sleeping and Shao preoccupied with navigating the boat, Cole took up a position next to the Texan. "Did my father *really* invent the fusion device?"

For several seconds, Hammer stared. "Yeah. But that's not how Butch made the team. A few years ago, when this specific unit formed, Command chose the very best operators. This mission was near the top of Washington's needs for a dedicated group—one covering the Pacific region and one on the Atlantic side—ready for the highest of priority missions." His eyebrows furled. "I already told you too much."

Cole nodded. He thought of his dad. A German

immigrant who—if the scenario held true—solved one of the most complicated and important engineering questions in modern history. Though he remembered little of his father, Cole couldn't be prouder. His throat tightened. "Is he…is he still alive?"

Hammer shrugged. "Don't know. Some of the best we got been lookin' for him for a long time. Butch is convinced he's still alive somewhere in North Korea."

Butch? Convinced their father lived? His big brother never breathed a word of his suspicion. The possibility threw Cole into an emotional blender. "What do you think?"

"Knowing Butch, and now you, my gut says the Haufner men are a tough bunch of hombres. I haven't seen any proof-of-life confirmation, but something tells me your old man is still around."

Cole tempered the rising excitement at the prospect. He knew hope was all he had but, for now, an inkling was enough. "I know you live with a code of silence on intel. I appreciate your honesty."

Hammer nodded. "You earned it."

The old Chinese seaman knocked on the wooden dashboard and pointed ahead.

The two men joined him at the wheel and gazed in the direction of what captivated Shao's attention. Something lay floating in the water.

"Tell him I want that junk on the port side." Hammer walked onto the open rear deck.

Cole translated the Texan's order then joined the man aft.

As the debris edged against the hull, Hammer leaned low over the left rail and grabbed at the object. With his free hand, he motioned for Shao to idle the engine. The Texan loosened his handhold on the black material. Frowning, he stood and gazed in multiple directions.

After a moment, Cole thought he saw a slight smile on Hammer's face. *What's so funny?*

"Cut the engine," the Delta man barked.

Still confused, Cole glanced over his shoulder and relayed the order in Mandarin.

Shao's eyebrows rose. He turned the ignition key to the left, and the diesel motor stopped with a metallic *clank*.

"What's the fascination with floating garbage?" Cole asked.

Hammer threw a sideways grin at him. "Let me introduce you to some friends of mine."

Cole looked over the ocean but saw only water stretching to the horizon in every direction. "Dude, you need some sleep."

Hammer's answering laugh came from somewhere deep in his chest. "All right, you assholes. Come on up!"

Six human heads sprang above the surface. The figures wore scuba masks and black neoprene suits. The divers pointed short-barreled weapons directly at the occupants of the boat.

Cole jumped then retreated several steps. His heart pounded against his chest.

One of the swimmers popped out his mouth regulator. "Challenge phrase?"

"Your mother is a helluva pole dancer," the Delta operator answered.

A second swimmer removed his breathing apparatus. "You must be Hammer."

Cole placed his hands on his knees and sighed. *I'm coming home, Claire. I'm coming home.*

****

Once aboard the USS *California*—the nuclear attack submarine loitering just outside the internationally recognized territorial waters of China and North Korea—Hammer escorted the fusion device elsewhere with a contingent of nuclear specialists in tow. Before walking off, he shook Cole's hand. "You're as brave a man as I've ever known. You honor your father's name."

Cole's throat tightened. He understood the men in Butch's unit rarely issued complements. The fighter simply nodded his reply.

After arriving in the medical ward, Cole received a detailed physical exam from the onboard physician. Despite the massive beating, he escaped with moderate injuries—the worst being a small fracture of his left cheekbone.

The doctor mentioned his top physical conditioning likely saved his life.

After the suturing of his scalp laceration, he showered and shared a meal with several of the SEALs. He enjoyed the attention from such hardened warriors. To a man, the frogmen insisted he speak with their commanding officer regarding an appointment for BUDs training. Deeply honored, Cole experienced an emerging brotherhood with the seasoned operators. He understood the draw of kinship with other men who shared similar stories. The contemplation of becoming a SEAL appealed to a hidden voice buried deep in his psyche, whispering his need for a new family.

Lilly also showered and changed into fresh

clothing. Forgoing food, she opted for a private room where she dropped fast asleep.

Shao transferred aft with a Marine escort. His new life began with an orange jumpsuit and a long list of questions prepared by a team of military intelligence officers.

With a full belly and wearing clean clothes, Cole followed a ship steward to Captain Bill Morris's well-appointed stateroom. The sub commander displayed short, gray hair and a tall, trim build. His tan slacks and short-sleeve shirt sported razor-sharp creases, and the left side of his chest displayed well-earned service ribbons—a career's worth of major accomplishments.

"Captain." Cole shook the man's outstretched hand with what he hoped was an equally firm handshake.

Morris motioned Cole into a leather chair at a small coffee table then took his own on the opposite side. "How's my staff treating you?"

"Like royalty, sir." He meant every word.

"Good. I'm sure you understand, once you arrive at a safe location, you'll undergo a thorough evaluation of everything you experienced. And, of course, you'll have a few questions regarding next steps."

Cole nodded. "I'm worried about Lilly. She experienced some rough treatment. I don't know the details, but I have some guesses. I hope the government knows how much she's done for the mission."

"Above my pay grade. But, let's say I heard a story about a similar situation a few years back. Completely fictional, right?" A smirk crossed the captain's face.

Cole understood the unspoken hint about a likely, top-secret encounter. "Just a wild guess, of course."

"Precisely." Morris nodded. "Anyway, as you'd

imagine, this person received a debrief then accepted a new identity and started work in a chosen field. My guess is your friend falls under a similar circumstance. If I were in your shoes, I'd feel confident Lilly has a bright future ahead."

I hope he's right. She deserves much more than anyone can imagine. Cole straightened in his chair. "I'm counting on people doing the right thing."

A rap on the door interrupted the conversation.

Standing in the doorway, a hulking figure wearing jeans and a faded concert T-shirt occupied the entry. The man's biceps strained the seams of the shirtsleeves. "Permission to enter?"

Captain Morris grinned. "They'll let anyone on board my vessel. Get your ass in here."

Hammer chuckled and casually stepped inside.

Morris stood, and the two shared handshakes and a quick hug.

Unsure of protocol, Cole sprang to his feet.

Hammer answered his unspoken question by pulling him into a huge bear hug.

The acceptance by one of Butch's teammates, easily one of the best military operators in the world, felt like winning the lottery. He now *knew* why these men thought of each other as more than brothers. A twinge of guilt rose in his mind for questioning Hammer's love or loyalty for Butch. "Hey, about some of the things I said at the apartment—"

"Stop," Hammer interrupted. "We don't go whining or apologizing on the teams. We despise weakness."

Cole's mouth hung open. "But, I'm not—"

"You are." Hammer poked a finger into Cole's

chest. "If anyone says otherwise, they'll be on the wrong end of me and the rest of the boys."

"You two done jerking off each other?" Morris walked to his office desk. "We don't serve alcohol on this boat. But, the SEALs swear they found something floating on the surface." From a desk drawer, Morris produced a bottle of Johnnie Walker Blue and three crystal tumblers. "In this case, I won't question their unofficial intelligence report."

Hammer grinned and rubbed his big paws together. "Fuckin' SEALs."

The captain made three healthy pours and handed one to each man. "No one on this vessel has clearance for whatever you two accomplished on dry land. Cole, please hold all discussions regarding the mission until we arrive home. To a sailor on this vessel, you both have our undying admiration. *Skol*."

All three tapped the heavy crystals together.

Cole took a sip, then—seeing Hammer's empty glass—gulped the remaining golden liquid. He welcomed the warm burn running down his throat.

The big Texan nodded. "*That's* how teammates drink."

Morris refilled their glasses then motioned for the men toward the chairs.

"Captain, you appear familiar with this ugly gorilla." Cole tilted his head toward Hammer.

"That detail is a fact. My younger brother played football with Ron at Texas. Before I left for the navy, I saw all their home games."

"Ron, huh? I took him for a jazz dancer," Cole said with veiled seriousness.

"Jazz dance your ass into the ground," Hammer

growled.

The captain set his tumbler on the coffee table. "Twenty minutes ago, JSOC forwarded a grainy video. Though the source is unknown, they addressed the message directly to Cole."

"Me?" Dread grabbed his gut. If the news involved Butch, he feared what might show on the clip. His brother, after all, remained in enemy territory and—making the situation worse—under false pretense and identity.

With a remote, Morris turned on a wall-mounted TV. The screen came alive, and a video cued-up on the screen. "I'll pretend I never saw the footage."

As if recorded by someone running with a camera, the video showed a jumble of indiscernible images. The audio sounded as if something rubbed against the microphone. After a few seconds, the picture stabilized. A male speaking Mandarin entered the center of the frame—early sixties, gray hair, and glasses. He wore a long, white lab coat, and a stethoscope draped around his neck. By all appearances, he was a doctor.

As the camera panned left, a younger woman—a uniformed nurse—took notes inside a metal chart.

Cole sensed whoever filmed the event did so without the knowledge of the subjects.

"What's he sayin'?" Hammer whispered.

As he translated, Cole's pulse quickened. "You are very fortunate. I do not anticipate any long-term issues."

The video shifted quickly to a hospital bed. With a white sheet covering his lower extremities, Butch came into focus. A chest tube in his right side dropped over the side railing, and an IV hung above his left arm. His brother gazed at the older man. "Buddha's blessings upon you."

Cole gripped the chair arms—Butch was alive! Further, his brother possessed necessary clarity, staying in character as a monk, bestowing traditional blessings onto the staff. *You are truly the toughest man I've ever known.*

Clumsily, the video zoomed on Butch. The false monk glanced at the person recording then, returning his gaze to the doctor, discreetly stuck out a middle finger without lifting his hand from the bed.

"You dirty asshole," Cole muttered. His brother performed the same action during morning prayers when they lived at the Temple.

More than once, Master Li rebuked the younger Haufner for his reaction to the hidden insult.

Sporting a placid facial expression, Butch winked.

The video abruptly ended. Though the footage lasted only seconds, for Cole, the evidence of his brother's survival provided a lifetime's worth of emotional impact. Jumping from his chair, he gave a war cry. He fell silent and stared at the final frame, still frozen on the monitor. The relief of knowing his brother was alive flooded him with pure joy.

Hammer stood and saluted the image of his teammate with his glass.

Cole elbowed the big Texan. "Look at that asshole just lying there, getting sponge baths from the nurses. He must think he's on vacation."

Hammer clapped a strong hand on Cole's shoulder. "Now you're talkin' like a teammate, son."

He turned and hugged the big guy. "I'm feeling like one."

Epilogue

Bunkers Memory Garden Cemetery, Las Vegas,
Nevada
Two weeks later

The heavy, dark-colored clay at the burial site from three weeks earlier displayed a grayish-brown hue. The dried, crumbling soil blended into the surrounding desert landscape. Green grass bordering the rectangular shape of dirt below the headstone remained alive by the daily watering from ground sprinklers. Things changed quickly in the desert—none more so than Cole. The events of the past twenty days molded him into an entirely different man.

From a short distance, he watched Kip, seemingly unaware of his presence, obsessively polish the family headstone with a well-used rag in one hand and a bottle of bluish solution in the other. Kip's long-arm cast appeared soiled, his T-shirt threadbare, and gray stubble covered his once-handsome face. To Cole, his friend and his son's godfather looked ten years older. He imagined the hell Kip experienced since the car accident.

Providing security, Zeus sat on his haunches next to the grave marker.

Cole patted his thigh and watched the eighty-pound missile bound toward him. Within seconds, he roughhoused with the Sheppard who ran tight circles around his legs. "I missed you too, big guy."

At the sound of a voice, Kip jerked upright and gazed at Cole. "When did you get back?"

He stood and watched Zeus jog back to his master. "This morning. Guess the Pentagon figured I didn't have anything left inside my brain." Two weeks of intensive debriefing followed his return to the States. The doctors, psychologists, and military intelligence apparatus pulled out every last ounce of information. Cole felt completely drained of emotion.

"Someone is doing a shitty job of taking care of the marble. No pride in work." Kip wiped the chest-high monument.

"They wouldn't let me talk to anybody," Cole confessed. "I wanted to call you, but I couldn't." He approached his friend.

"I...um...I just figured you didn't because of this..." Kip waved a hand at Claire's grave marker.

"No, man." *None of this mess is your fault.* Cole rocked on his heels. "Not even close."

Kip twisted the rag in his hands. "Butch's commander told me you were alive. He wouldn't say any more."

Cole studied his friend's face, looking for any more recognition of Kip's thinking. The person he knew as a boisterous and fun-loving guy now presented as a grief-stricken shell of a man. *We've both changed.* He pointed at the bottle in Kip's right hand. "I appreciate the help."

Kip nodded. "Melody is here in Vegas. She wonders when she'll see you."

Cole thought of the black-haired British woman

he'd saved from the 14K gang back in *Dandong*. The DoD investigators relayed how she navigated her way to America. His promise of returning home, alive, provided the catalyst for her trust in him. *She's a tough cookie. She reminds me of Claire.* "Tell her I'm okay. I'll see her soon."

Kip pursed his lips. "Yeah, okay."

Cole heard no judgment in his friend's tone. Quiet moments passed, and he became lost in his thoughts.

Kip cleared his throat. "I know you can't say anything—"

Holding up a hand, he stopped his friend from finishing the sentence. *He deserves the truth. Screw the government's threats of prison.* "You should know...I found Butch. Hopefully, he comes home soon. That information is worth thirty years in the federal pen."

Kip bent over at the waist then rested his healthy left arm on his knee. He let out a loud sigh. "Thank God."

No, not God. Not this time. For Cole, great conflict raged inside him regarding his religious beliefs and the Buddhist teachings of his uncle, Master Li. Over the past two weeks, with little time for reflection, he found no footing for where he stood with his spiritual self. Of one aspect he remained certain—the sacrifices made by his uncle and his cousin would never tarnish, and he would forever cherish the memories of his Chinese family. "I need a favor. Promise me you won't ask anything else."

Cole wondered if his friend saw the physical pain he endured at the hands of his torturers. Surely, Kip knew the facial bruising and cuts hadn't come from the Saturday night fight. Didn't he?

Kip's eyes teared. "You're my brother. I love you with all my heart. I swear I won't ever say a thing."

His friend's words bit deep. Suppressed emotion welled to the surface. His lower lip trembled. "You're my brother too." He stepped closer and embraced his wounded friend. Relief, joy, and sorrow flowed through him. His ears rang from Kip's sobs. The release of emotion was palpable.

Eventually, the two men pulled back from each other.

Kip cleared his throat. "What you said at the house—that you saw Claire and Max when you look at me. Do you still?"

He saw the sad, pleading look in Kip's bloodshot eyes. "Yeah, but not in the way you think. I remember how happy you made them. I always loved how you protected them." Cole ran his hand down his face. "I never meant those words. I'm sorry I hurt you."

"It's all my fault. I miss them so much. I don't think I can take the pain anymore." Kip dropped to his knees. A guttural cry escaped his throat.

A sudden clarity enveloping his thoughts, Cole knelt next to him. He couldn't sit idle, witnessing the two of them wallowing away in despair.

Four weeks ago, meditation provided peace to troubled thoughts.

Not now. He required action, not reflection. "We're fighters. We don't ever give up. You and I owe them everything we've got."

Kip nodded and threw his left arm around Cole's waist. "I won't quit."

Determination swelled inside him. Blinking against burning eyes, Cole stared at the names of his beloved family carved into the marble. He rolled back his shoulders. *I'll make a difference in this world. I'll make you all proud.*

A word about the author...

After a career in medicine, Mike succumbed to the call to hang up his stethoscope and pursue his other passion as a writer of fast-paced thrillers.

A rabid fan of authors such as Clancy, Brad Taylor, Vince Flynn, and Brad Thor, Mike loves series writing with strong characters, fast pacing, and international locations, all of which explode into action in his debut novel, a 2017 Zebulon Award winner.

When not at the keyboard, he can be found on the firing range, coaching youth sports, or trying out the latest dry-fly pattern on a Gold Medal trout stream.

He lives with his wife and two young sons at the foothills of the Rocky Mountains just west of Denver, Colorado.

Thank you for purchasing
this publication of The Wild Rose Press, Inc.

For questions or more information
contact us at
info@thewildrosepress.com.

The Wild Rose Press, Inc.
www.thewildrosepress.com

To visit with authors of
The Wild Rose Press, Inc.
join our yahoo loop at
http://groups.yahoo.com/group/thewildrosepress/

CPSIA information can be obtained
at www.ICGtesting.com
Printed in the USA
LVHW011211080920
665327LV00001B/61